Finistère

LITTLE SISTER'S CLASSICS

Finistère

FRITZ PETERS

ARSENAL PULP PRESS
Vancouver

FINISTÈRE

Copyright © 1951 by Arthur A. Peters
Preface and introduction copyright © 2006 by the authors
First Arsenal Pulp Press edition: 2006

ARSENAL PULP PRESS
341 Water Street, Suite 200
Vancouver, BC
Canada V6B 1B8
arsenalpulp.com

Little Sister's Classics series editor: Mark Macdonald
Editors for the press: Robert Ballantyne and Brian Lam
Text and cover design: Shyla Seller
Front cover illustration from the Signet Edition, 1952
Little Sister's Classics logo design: Hermant Gohil

Printed and bound in Canada

Library and Archives Canada Cataloguing in Publication:

Peters, Fritz, 1913-1979
    Finistère / Fritz Peters.

(Little Sister's classics)
First published: New York : Farrar Straus, 1951.
ISBN 1-55152-211-X

    I. Title. II. Series.

PS3531.E8F55 2006   813'.54   C2006-903309-9

ISBN-13: 978-1-55152-211-1

Contents

Preface

In the canon of gay male literature, _Finistère_ has always held a unique place. By any standard, this novel's contribution to the development of self-awareness was key for a generation of homosexual readers. How can we even relate today to the appearance of a book – in 1951 – that dealt so intimately with the emotions of the gay soul? Neither a dime-store pulp nor a moralistic condemnation of "perversion," _Finistère_ attempted to expose youthful passions and torments with honesty, but also with conviction.

Passions and torments were subjects that author Fritz Peters knew all too well. The details of Peters' life reveal a man almost embracing conflict in his own sexuality. Were his works largely autobiographical? Without direct contact with the author, this question may never be adequately answered. However, this new edition of _Finistère_ boasts a wealth of biographical information, almost entirely supplied by the poet Edward Field, to whom we are eternally grateful.

The text of this novel has been carefully transcribed from the 1952 Signet edition, complete with numerous anachronisms in editorial style: for example, cigarettes are "lighted" in this book, not lit. In the spirit of authenticity, we chose to remain faithful to the original text.

And, for the second time, Little Sister's Classics is complemented with an introduction by gay literary scholar Michael Bronski, whose ongoing enthusiasm for the project adds ever more fuel to our fire. In one email exchange as we prepared this edition for print, Bronski wrote, "I was racing through, and rewriting, so much material yesterday – my office is covered with old paperbacks, notes, books on Gurdjieff, copies of reviews of Peters' books – that I was a bit over-whelmed." This is an image we shall cherish!

Finally, we would like to extend our thanks and appreciation to Kate Peters, who has handled her father's literary estate with patience and good humor. Without the involvement and understanding of family members, many of these books would become unavailable for entire generations of readers.

With great pride, we present the Little Sister's Classics edition of *Finistère*.

– *Mark Macdonald, 2006*

[*A word of caution:* Elements of the plot of *Finistère* are discussed at length in this introduction, including the book's ending. Some readers may prefer to enjoy the introduction after they have read the novel.]

Introduction

FINISTÈRE – THE END OF THE EARTH, THE BEGINNING OF GAY FICTION
MICHAEL BRONSKI

The title itself is mysterious, almost mythical: *Finistère*. It has a foreign – French – look and sound to it that made it "not American," yet emblematic of America's 1950s popular culture enthrallment with the gallic. For gay men who were out in the 1950s, *Finistère*, published in 1951, was immediately recognizable – along with James Barr's *Quatrefoil* and Gore Vidal's *The City and the Pillar* – as one of the most important and widely read novels with a gay male theme. But in the imagination of the common gay reader, *Finistère* stood apart from the other two novels. This was, in part, because it did not have a military theme that was so common in post-war American fiction (including gay-themed fiction) but, more importantly, because it ends in the tragic, self-inflicted death of a young man, indeed, a sixteen-year-old boy who has recently awakened to his first deep love for another man. This fictional suicide – as renowned in gay letters as Violetta's death in *La Traviata* is in grand opera – defined Peters' novel as allegoric of gay male life in the pre-Stonewall 1950s and 1960s.

In a curious but important literary evolution, *Finistère* became a completely different novel in the years after Stonewall and the birth of Gay Liberation. And given the changes over the thirty-five-plus years since the 1969 riots, *Finistère* is a very different novel for readers today. While it is not surprising that a text will be read differently over a long period of time – this is as true for *Hamlet* or *Middlemarch* – the difference here is that the evolving readings of *Finistère* reflect the enormous, and very distinct, social and psychological changes that have occurred in the gay male community over the relatively short span of fifty years. Furthermore, it is a tribute to Peters' artistic vision and imagination that this novel, written more than half a century ago, not only speaks to readers today, but does so with a new voice and new meaning.

Enjoying and appreciating *Finistère* today is easy – it is a complex, multi-layered novel with vital themes and compelling characters – but one of the challenges for today's gay reader is to understand both *Finistère*'s changing reputations in specific historical context as well as its enormous importance to the history of gay male literature.

The most important key to understanding what *Finistère* meant to gay readers in the 1950s is to view it not so much as a "gay novel"– a genre that did not come into clearly defined existence until after the birth of the Gay Liberation Movement in 1969 – but rather as an American postwar novel. In the years following World War II, the American novel blossomed. New literary writers – including Norman Mailer, Truman Capote, James Jones, Ralph Ellison, Sloan Wilson, Hamilton Basso, Ross Lockridge, James Michener, Allen Drury, Edwin O'Connor, and William Brinkley – found eager readers across the country. Many of these books were bestsellers, but the low cost of a newly published cloth novel (never more than $4.50 and in the early 1950s, often as low as $3.00), the popularity and prevalence of lending libraries, and the explosion of inexpensive mass market paperback publishing (popular fiction cost never more than fifty cents during this time) ensured that literary fiction could find an expansive and eager readership.

But it was not simply easy accessibility that made these novels popular. They also spoke directly to the social issues that deeply concerned Americans in the late 1940s and 1950s. The war profoundly altered many aspects of US culture. Ideas about race, class, work, children, money, ethnicity, politics, crime, and cultural power – especially concerning sex and gender – that had been relatively stable for at least a decade were now effectively turned upside down. There are many reasons for this. The vast deployment of troops overseas, the urgency of war, and the constant proximity of death jangled people's expectations of family life, marriage, and sexual behavior. The need for women to enter the home-front workforce during the war radically altered gender expectations. And the close homosocial environments of the armed forces also forged new – erotic and non-erotic – relationships between both men and women in the military. When the war ended, the US economy shifted from production-based to service- and consumer-based, which reflected the emergence of a strong middle class with buying power. These ever-shifting changes produced enormous anxiety and a need for public discussion. One of the primary roles of the postwar novel, then, was as a facilitator, or a clearing house, of the vigorous public debate that was happening on all these issues.

We can see – and viscerally feel as we read these novels – how these enormous postwar social changes were being discussed. Novels such as Sloan Wilson's *The Man in the Gray Flannel Suit* (1955) highlighted the effect of the postwar economy on male identity and the family. Edwin O'Connor's *The Last Hurrah* (1956) and Allen Drury's *Advise and Consent* (1959) were meditations on the tremendous changes that were happening in American politics. Ross Lockridge's historical novel *Raintree County* (1948) and Ralph Ellison's *Invisible Man* (1952) grappled with issues of racism in US history and contemporary culture. The prominence and critical acclaim of Jewish writers discussing overtly Jewish themes – Bernard Malamud, Saul Bellow, J.D. Salinger, Herman Wouk, Leon Uris – marked a new stage in the public discussion not only of cultural Judaism, but broader issues including immigration, ethnicity, religion, and what it meant to be an "American."

It is no surprise that along with sexuality and gender, issues of homosexuality and same-sex desire would also come to the fore. As Allan Berube beautifully details in his 1990 book *Coming Out Under Fire: The History of Gay Men and Women in World War Two*, the postwar years in the US saw the beginnings of what we now know as contemporary gay and lesbian communities. After men and women came out during the war, they returned to the United States, not to their hometowns, but to large cities where they could both find community with other gay people and personal safety in urban anonymity. Not only did gay neighborhoods flourish in New York, San Francisco, Los Angeles, Chicago, and other cities, but some brave men and women began to form political organizations – the Mattachine Society and Daughters of Bilitis – that were the beginning of our contemporary gay rights movement. While homosexuality was still illegal, often seen as an illness, and generally considered wrong, it was also gaining an enormous place in the public imagination. Alfred Kinsey's 1948 *Sexual Behavior in the Human Male* told the public what they already suspected – that male homosexual activity was far, far more prevalent in the US than people were willing to admit. If Kinsey's work opened the floodgates of discussion and debate, mainstream media was not far behind. This animated – and not always negative – public discussion took place in a number of venues. Sociologists and psychiatrists published scholarly articles in professional journals, social commentators lectured on the topic, and articles about homosexuality appeared with extraordinary frequency in magazines and newspapers. Perhaps most surprisingly, established publishing houses – from the early 1940s onward – were releasing novels with openly homosexual characters and themes.

Published in 1951, *Finistère* was solidly in the flow of homosexual-themed novels being published and read by men and women interested in new literary fiction. Some of these novels continue to be read today – Carson McCullers' *Reflections in a Golden Eye* (1941), Charles Jackson's *The Lost Weekend* (1944), Truman Capote's *Other Voices, Other Rooms* (1948), Patricia Highsmith's *The Talented Mr. Ri-*

pley (1955), James Baldwin's *Another Country* (1961) – but far more have been abandoned to used book shelves and tables at church rummage sales. The plots of many of the homosexual-themed novels of this period were, not surprisingly, concerned with men in the armed forces. Novels such as Richard Brooks' *The Brick Foxhole* (1945), John Horne Burns' *The Gallery* (1947), Gore Vidal's *The City and the Pillar* (1948), James Barr's *Quatrefoil* (1950), Loren Wahl's *The Invisible Glass* (1950), Lonnie Coleman's *Ship's Company* (1955), and Dennis Murphy's *The Sergeant* (1958) dealt directly with how the military and the experience of fighting World War II shaped ideas about sex, masculinity, and homosexuality. While all of these novels have since been classified as "gay novels," they are also – indeed, by some measure, primarily – World War II novels. All postwar fiction – especially if it concerned men relating to one another – was written in the looming shadow of the war.

While *Finistère* is set during the 1920s, not the mid-1940s of World War II, it shares many of the same themes that are found in homosexual-themed postwar novels. It is, to varying degrees, a coming of age novel, a social problem novel, a story of divorce and family, and a Jamesian exploration of the clash between American and European sensibilities, but it is principally a novel about masculinity and the question of what it means to be a man. However, while many other homosexual-themed novels of the period explored this topic by examining a sexual relationship between two adult men, Fritz Peters takes a bolder tack and explores a series of relationships between grown men and a teenaged boy. *Finistère* gives us a kaleidoscope of problematic – sometimes loving, sometimes exploitative, sometimes just confusing – eroticized, intergenerational male/male relationships. *Finistère* is a great novel, and a classic of gay male literature, but it is not a comforting book. Peters' view of humans' ability to love one another – emotionally and sexually – is profoundly pessimistic. This pessimism is, to some degree, balanced by Peters' clear understanding of the enormous potential of homoerotic love to be psychologically redemptive. It is, in many ways, not only a product of its time, but also a visionary template for the future.

It is impossible to discuss how *Finistère* reads differently across generations without giving a brief summery of its plot and characters. The novel begins in 1927 on an ocean liner that is taking young Matthew Cameron to Paris. He is traveling with his mother Catherine, who is divorcing his father and preoccupied with her own life, and will solely be in her custody until he turns sixteen. In Paris, Matthew has few intimates except for Scott, a close family friend in his late twenties, on whom he has a crush. Scott understands this and treats Matthew's feelings with restraint and respect. Catherine arranges for Matthew to go to a boarding school where he meets André, who is a year older but more sophisticated, and they become boyfriends. Within the year, the now divorced Catherine marries Paul, alienating Matthew, whose feelings for Scott become more intense and complicated. The core of the novel concerns the events later that year when Matthew – who is just turning fifteen – begins an affair with Michel Garnier, his school's athletic director who is actively homosexual and in his early thirties. Matthew and Michel fall passionately in love, but need to keep their relationship secret from everyone, especially Catherine, Paul, and Scott – as well as Matthew's father and his new wife – which becomes increasingly difficult when they spend the summer together. As the season unfolds, the tensions between all of the characters intensifies until the novel reaches its inevitable climax.

This quick outline of *Finistère*'s plot gives only a limited indication of why gay male readers of the 1950s were drawn to it. Gay literary mythology states that *Finistère* was a popular novel then because the severe oppression of homosexuals at the time created social and political atmospheres that allowed gay male readers to relate easily to a narrative in which homosexual love is doomed. But this is, I believe, a facile reading. While Matthew's suicide at the end of *Finistère* is devastating – now, as well as for readers fifty years ago – Peters makes it clear that Matthew's death is a result of personal betrayal and homophobia, not an innate predisposition for homosexuals to kill themselves. But it is not simply a re-reading of the novel's ending that makes *Finistère* a complicated, totally homophilic work. Throughout the novel Fritz Peters repeatedly, and quite thrillingly, illuminates for us the excitement of new-found gay male sexuality. More than other writers of homosexual-themed novels of the 1950s, Peters is never afraid to explore how sex feels and what it means to his characters. *Finistère* is the most explicitly embodied of the postwar homosexual novels. At the end of Chapter Four, Matthew and André wake early in the morning and, from their separate beds, gaze longingly into each other's eyes:

> As he watched his friend, he saw him suddenly throw
> down the covers to expose his body, lying naked on
> the bed. André glanced down at his own nakedness
> and Matthew's eyes followed until he had seen again
> what he had already seen at once. If André had looked
> at him or spoken, he would have had to turn his head
> or close his eyes, shut his ears, but the other boy said
> nothing: Matthew had only to watch and watch and
> watch, his own body twisting under the covers at what
> he saw.

Later in the novel, when Matthew and Michel are summering with the former's parents, they spend the morning together:

> The first two weeks passed quickly, in a daze of hap-
> piness for them both. Matthew and Michel were up
> early, to walk along the muddy roads or to make for the
> beach where they would lie, stripped and open to the
> sun (no other people ever came to the beach and Cath-
> erine did not swim before lunch), their bodies turning
> from white to bright red-brown. Even Michel, as if his

wish had been granted at last, no longer held back the
feeling of happiness of which he had been so afraid.
The days lost their separateness, blending into each
other in an unchanging, almost monotonous, round of
comfortable pleasure. Their legs and arms grew sleek
and hard and strong, and they began to fill out from
the air and the solid country food they ate every day.
Matthew's hair became streaked with gold and stiff
with salt. Once a week they would drive to Le Conquet
for baths, supplies, and mail.

In these two passages – 120 pages apart – we see Matthew maturing,
from a boy into an adult, a man, and a self-identified homosexual.
Making grand statements, or concrete connections, between a novel
and the culture in which it was written usually results in easy, often
lousy, literary criticism. But I think a case can be made – a speculative
case, at any rate – that gay male readers in the 1950s were strongly
attracted to *Finistère* not only because it was self-affirming about homoeroticism, as well as sexy, but also because they saw in it, in some
way, the growth and maturation of their own homosexual culture and
community. The gay men and lesbians who had returned from the
war in 1946 had been actively, and quickly, building life-sustaining
communities in cities across the United States. Despite repressive
legal, social, and political pressures these communities flourished and
gave birth to a fully realized and organized political movement – labeled, quite boldly for the time, "homophile" – when in November
of 1950, Harry Hay and other men began the Mattachine Society in
Los Angeles.

Contemporary readers today might think that if this hypothesis
were true, the gay male reader of half a century ago might have been
attracted to a more simple narrative, one that was purely celebra-
tory and, at the very least, ended on an upbeat note. As Oscar Wilde
noted in *The Importance of Being Ernest*, "The good [end] happily, the

bad unhappily. That is what fiction means." But surprisingly, none of the important homosexual-themed novels of the late 1940s and early 1950s – Willard Motley's *Knock on Any Door* (1947), Calder Willingham's *End as a Man* (1947), Thomas Hal Phillips' *The Bitterweed Path* (1949), Ward Thomas' *Stranger in the Land* (1949), Frederick Buechner's *A Long Day's Dying* (1950), Douglas Sanderson's *Dark Passions Subdue* (1952) – reflect such a view. Historically, critics, gay and straight, have labeled these novels as self-hating, even homophobic, because they often lack a traditional "they lived happily ever after" ending, or described relationships that were blandly uncomplicated. But read carefully, none of these novels – especially, *Finistère* – fit that description. It is also condescending for post-Stonewall readers to presume that 1950s gay readers could not make sensible distinctions between life and fiction. In *Sam*, Lonnie Coleman's terrific 1959 novel, two gay men discuss contemporary homosexual novels. The title character, a publisher, complains "The only [novels with homosexual characters] are trashy or sentimental. A dream world of television drama, with the sexes changed a little. They all end in suicide or a murder. How many of us do you know who've killed ourselves, or each other?" While Sam is wrong about the postwar homosexual novel being just trashy, he is completely correct in understanding that there is a difference between reader's material and imaginative lives. The 1950s were a tough but very exciting time for gay men and lesbians. In spite of severe political repression, there was a wealth of self-affirmation, community building, and political organizing. It may sound like a truism, but turbulent times are going to produce turbulent fiction, and *Finistère* presents us with a wealth of turbulence and complications.

If there is any one aspect of Fritz Peters' novel that is going to strike the reader today as surprising, edgy, or even troubling, it is that Matthew is a young adolescent. In today's political climate, few novelists would dare write a book in which an explicitly sexual affair between a fifteen-year-old boy and a thirty-something man would be anything other then frowned upon. Young adult novels today with gay male themes – Brent Hartinger's *Geography Club* (2003), James Howe's *Totally Joe* (2005) – often deal with sexual relationships between young males of similar ages, but a novel that deals, in a non-prejudicial manner, with an affair between a fifteen-year-old and a man twice his age would certainly be a lightning rod for criticism from both the right wing and even many voices within the gay community.

Obviously, the world in which Fritz Peters wrote *Finistère* was radically different – and, as many readers today might feel, unenlightened – than the culture we live in today, which would quickly label a sexual relationship with such age disparity abusive, or, at the very least, in all probability coercive. But what is even more surprising is that intergenerational affairs between boys and men were not that unusual in postwar homosexual novels. While novels such as John Horne Burns's *Lucifer With a Book* (1949) and William Goyen's *House of Breath* (1950) contain a free floating eroticism that often connects the worlds of their older and younger male characters, there are also novels and stories that – like *Finistère* – deal explicitly with sexual relationships between grown men and adolescent boys. "Spur Piece," a story in James Barr's 1951 collection *Derricks*, is explicit in its delineation of a deepening relationship between Tom, newly discharged from the Navy, and Chris, who is thirteen and working on the family farm. The irony of the story, which is set in 1946, is that Tom spends most of his time and energy suppressing his feelings for Chris because he feels that they are inappropriate, while the younger man is doing his best to pursue the relationship. After four years, when Chris is about to be drafted, Tom finally lets his himself out of his "four-year prison of frustrated desires" and opens himself to the possibility of a physical relationship. Barr's massage here is not that Tom is morally mature to wait for Chris to grow older, but that he had deprived them both of a nurturing relationship.

This theme is also the core of Gerald Tesch's *Never the Same Again* (1956), which tells the story of thirteen-year-old Johnny Parish who becomes involved with Roy Davies, a man in his late twenties. While Roy is sometimes conflicted about the relationship, Johnny is not, and the crisis of the novel occurs when their love affair is made public by the evil, closeted leader of a local youth group who desires Johnny himself and is determined to force Roy out of the town. Like *Finistère*, *Never the Same Again* views the intergenerational relationship at its core as a moral and healthy one. As implausible as it may seem, there is almost no record of the reading public or critics in the 1950s having strongly negative reactions to these relationships. While some critics claim that the theme of *Finistère* is the betrayal of innocence, they are referring to the emotional betrayals Matthew experiences from family, friends, and lovers, not his sexual relationship with Michel. The 1958 paper edition of *Never the Same Again* features a front cover that asks "Was their relationship too intimate? What would you decide?" And the copy on the back cover reads "An unconventional intimacy – A seething scandal – One man's decision could destroy their lives – What would you decide?" At a time when paperback covers had no problem being very directive – the word "shocking" appears routinely on the cover of any novel with a hint of sexual content – the open-ended "What would you decide?" seems, well, shockingly non-judgmental.

So, why was *Finistère* (as well as *Never the Same Again*) allowed to present essentially positive sexual relationships between men and young adolescents in a decade that was ripe with fear about the innocence of children? The myth of the homosexual child molester was very strong in the 1950s. Beginning in the late 1940s, many states passed "sexual psychopath" laws to protect children from "predators," and conservative religious and political forces in the United States railed against comic books, rock and roll, and tight pants as leading to the corruption of youth. Objectively, the lax attitude of these novels to relationships between men and young teenage boys should have rendered them completely unpalatable for the average reader – both books were widely and well-reviewed in the mainstream press – and certainly would have put many homosexuals on the defensive.

For the general reader, the implicit acceptance of these relationships maintained the delicate cultural dichotomy in the 1950s that viewed children as completely innocent as well as potentially sexual. The decade's cultural mythology of the child encompassed both the hyper-innocence of TV sitcom children on shows such as *Father Knows Best* and *Lassie* as well its flip-side: the flirty evil of Rhoda in *The Bad Seed*, or the extreme sexuality of Vladimir Nabokov's *Lolita*. But for gay readers, these books may have had a much different resonance. Told repeatedly that homoerotic love and expression were morally and socially wrong, they welcomed stories that featured – or explicitly flirted with – the idea that young men, really almost children, could contain and express homosexual desires. Who better than the innocent child, or pre-adult, to metaphorically symbolize the naturalness and the ingenuousness of homosexual desire.

If the homosexual reader of the 1950s was drawn to *Finistère* because, even with its tragic ending, it reinforced so many positive emotional images of homoeroticism, the next generation of gay readers – those who viewed the book with a post-Stonewall sensibility – had the completely opposite reaction. These readers were born in the late 1940s and were in their infancy when *Finistère* was published. They "came out" in the late 1960s and were shaped not by World War II but by rock and roll, the drug culture, the women's movement, the civil rights movement, and the gay liberation movement. They were of a brave new world, with little patience for gay culture of the past. Indeed, gay liberation was a decisive break from the homophile movements of the 1950s and 1960s and younger gay men not only rejected the Mattachine Society and other reform-minded political groups, but also much of the pre-Stonewall culture as well. This included, for many people, elements of drag and camp that had defined gay male culture in the 1950s and 1960s as well as popular literature, particularly iconic classics such as *The City and the Pillar*, *Quatrefoil*, and *Finistère*.

This rejection was wholehearted and decisive. These were self-hating novels in which the major characters were usually closeted, gay love was troubled, and the protagonists usually died in the last chapter. Gay liberationists felt no need for these works – and had little understanding of the conditions under which they emerged. The reading practices of these new gay readers were also fairly limited. Any close, sympathetic reading of *Quatrefoil* and *Finistère* would certainly have contradicted the widespread impression that these were profoundly homophobic works. They were, at the very least, novels that accurately and often devastatingly portrayed the effects of homophobia on their characters. But liberation was an exciting and urgent business and often there was never time, energy, or patience for reading closely or cherishing literary nuances. Also, the new gay reader of the 1970s may have been misled by the cover art and jacket copy of the paperback editions of these books. Almost all of them featured dour, unhappy-looking images of gay men often sitting alone or set apart from other characters. And the copy on the front cover of these editions would hardly encourage a positive interpretation. The Signet paperback edition of *Finistère* called it a "Powerful Novel of a Tragic Love." The first Signet edition of *The City and the Pillar* called it "A Masterful Story of Personal Tragedy" which transmogrified into "A Masterful Story of a Lonely Search" on an edition two years later. Indeed, words like "lonely," "twisted," "tragedy," "anguished," "pain," "alone" – all of which were "compelling" – appear on nearly all of the homosexual novels of the period and were used almost interchangeably. Interestingly, even the cover art was sometimes interchangeable. The lonely-looking young man in the foreground cover of the 1951 Signet edition of *Finistère* – which is reproduced on this Arsenal Pulp Press edition – was lifted and used as the sole cover art image on the 1955 edition of *The City and the Pillar*.

While it is understandable that gay readers of the 1970s would reject these earlier novels in favor of a new wealth of literature that was being published by both mainstream and alternative publishing houses post-Stonewall, the rejection incurred emotional costs as well. Not admitting these novels into a growing canon of gay and lesbian literature meant that the gay reader of the 1970s did not allow himself access to the world view – and more importantly, the emotions and the psychological mind-set of homosexuals who had come before him. The interpretations of *Finistère* and *Quatrefoil* were so radically different – moving quickly from life-affirming to self-hating in less than a decade – that it is easy to see how the new gay liberation and gay rights movements had alienated the older generations of gay people. These new gay cultural norms were so set that they did not allow gay liberationists to take the time to understand the people or the cultures of the recent past. This lack of historical empathy created a generational divide that was difficult for people on both sides.

The rejection of this past is also deeply unfortunate for another reason as well. What post-Stonewall generations lost was not simply the pleasure of reading these novels but also a point of entry to an enormous trove of gay and lesbian history. A quick look at the life of Fritz Peters – whose biography deserves far more space than can be offered here – illustrates this beautifully.

Born Arthur A. Peters in 1913 in Madison, Wisconsin, his single mother suffered a nervous breakdown and gave him and his slightly older brother Tom to be raised by his aunt, the noted lesbian editor and writer Margaret Anderson, who was the founder of the influential journal *The Little Review*, and her lover Jane Heap. Peters and his brother were formally adopted by Anderson and Heap in 1919 or 1920, and sometime in 1924 they all moved to Paris to live at the Institute for the Harmonious Development of Man or Château du Prieuré, founded and run by George Gurdjieff in Fontainebleau. Peters and his brother spent four years here studying Gurdjieff's mystical philosophy and living communally with his following. He returned to America, and his mother and a new stepfather, in 1929 at the age of sixteen. This arrangement did not work out, however, and he struck out on his own. For the next two decades, Peters' life is only a historical sketch since he was a private person and left very few writings about it. In the 1930s, Peters lived in various major American cities and worked at a series of low-paying jobs. He also maintained a distantly casual but complicated relationship with Gurdjieff and his disciples. By 1942, he was in the US Army, 29th Infantry Division. After a horrific experience in the Battle of the Bulge from late December 1944 to nearly the end of January 1945, he visited Gurdjieff in Paris to recover from emotional and physical exhaustion. Back in the US after the war, he entered into a short marriage to Mary Louise Aswell, a prominent New York magazine editor.

Much of Peters' life in the postwar US is shrouded in mystery. He published his first novel *The World Next Door* – about a man recovering from shell shock – in 1949 to excellent reviews. *The Book of the Year*, a short children's book, followed the year later, and in 1951 he published *Finistère*, again to generally excellent reviews. *The Descent*, a novel reminiscent of Thornton Wilder's 1927 novel *The Bridge of San Luis Rey*, in which the lives of a group of strangers converge during an accident, was published in 1952. It is also during this time that Peters is married again, to a woman named Joan with whom he has two children, Katherine and Fritz. In 1953, his editor Roger W. Straus rejected a new novel, *The Brothers*, telling Peters in a letter that "… we honestly don't believe this is a novel we should publish or you should publish."

A decade later Straus rejected *The General*, another novel. (The Special Collections at Boston University's Munger Library has a manuscript copy of it, with an alternative title *Spring in Brittany*.) This same year, Peters seems to be working on two novels – *The Winter Moon* and *The Seven Sisters* – which he mentions in letters to Straus, but there is no record of them being submitted or rejected by the publisher. Peters' next publication, a memoir, is more than a decade later – *Boyhood with Gurdjieff* in 1964, and then *Gurdjieff Remembered* a year later in 1965. In 1966, *Blind Flight*, which revisits some of the themes of mental illness that are present in *The World*

Next Door, is published in England but not America. In 1971, *The Record of a Journey* – possibly a novel, or perhaps another memoir of Gurdjieff – was rejected by Roger W. Straus Jr., Straus also rejected *A Certain Melancholy*, a novel set in a psychiatric home and dealing with a sexualized relationship between two brothers, in 1974. (A copy of this novel is in the Munger Library as well.) *Balanced Man: A Look at Gurdjieff Fifty Years Later* was published in 1978, a year before Peters' death.

I give this biographical sketch in part simply to show how much work can still be done on excavating Peters' life and work. But this is not only biographical work, although that would be fascinating since his life was intertwined with some of the most interesting times, places, and people in the 20th century – but his literary output as well. Each of Peters' novels – aside from *Finistère* – have informative content about sexuality and human relations. While it is tempting to read them as strictly autobiographical, examining them – and his life – would also give us great insights into the creative process. Peters' books on Gurdjieff are filled with intriguing thoughts about the connections between sexuality and spirituality, which give us an interesting look at the connections between pre-Stonewall lives and popular spirituality. From all accounts, Peters was a very private person – although he certainly gives many intimate, revealing insights into himself in his books about Gurdjieff – but it is curious, even alarming, that no openly gay newspaper or writer conducted an interview with Peters in the last decade of his life. No doubt his sense of privacy was at play here, but what writer doesn't like, on some level, to be asked about his work? I believe that it was the post-Stonewall culture's rejection of, or at least its complete disinterest in, *Finistère* that is also to blame here.

If *Finistère* had very different meanings for readers in the 1950s and 1960s than for readers in the two decades that followed, what might it say to readers today? Surely Peters' dissection of familial homophobia is not simply as pertinent today as it was half a century ago, but his insights and distillation of what Freud calls "the family romance" are more accurate and incisive than much of what has been recently published on the topic. It is his radical understanding of young gay male sexuality and intimate relationships that makes *Finistère* so potent, so topical today. While we – as gay readers and a gay community – have come a very long way in the last half century, it is still difficult to engage in public discourse on the sexuality of children, especially when their sexual desires concern older men. What *Finistère* does so beautifully is to delineate, and explore with great sensitivity and depth, the real, visceral complications of male sexual longing and desire in a variety of forms – both loving and selfish, giving and taking – that are part of being human. What exact meaning *Finistère* will have for gay readers in the twenty-first century we will see in the future, but in many ways those readers will just be catching up to the work that Fritz Peters published more than fifty years ago.

Finistère

the end of innocence

This is a love story – but a love story in a very special sense. Brilliantly and poignantly, it portrays a tortured young man's search for love – the strains and wonders of that search, its sexual upheavals and its eventual descent into a world of corruption.

The bitter ironies of homosexual life have never been so sensitively revealed – and you will never forget Matthew....

Chapter One

Matthew Cameron stood by his mother, peering down into water; down, down, down over the little humps of rivetheads, the brass-rimmed portholes, down, down to the red line circling the hull of the ship, to the rich, restless water, oil-surfaced, slapping the steel of the ship and the wooden pier with old grapefruit and orange rinds, wood, paper and miscellaneous, unidentifiable objects. He took a last look at the faces among the group on the dock, waving and shouting, some of them almost looking at him, but even the faces he knew – the faces of his mother's friends – were not looking at him but at his mother as she stood, towering and distant by his side. She seemed parted from him, unavailable, as if she herself were with her friends on the pier, and out of reach.

We are going to France, she had said to him, and then added: *Paris, France*, looking at him to see what effect this would have, as if something in her eyes would carry him across the open atlas she held in her lap to the green blotch on the map which was France, *a country where*, her voice had gone on, *they speak only French*. To encourage him (for his answering look had been blank and uncomprehending), she had said it was where Napoleon and the Three Musketeers lived, *you know, dear*, but of course they were dead now. He had looked at the map, half expecting it to come to life but it brought nothing to his mind except the phrases from his eighth-grade geography: *France is bordered on the north by Belgium*, or a caption beneath the photograph: *Shepherds in the picturesque Basque region of the South*. To please her, he had taken the atlas and stared at it, shaking his head until his eyes had fastened on the word *Atlantic*, and the wide blue space leaped into reality. "You mean where Lindy flew to? Across the *Atlantic*!" He had barely heard the answering "yes." His mind was filled again with the wonderful impossibility of that moment, only a few weeks before. "LINDBERGH FLIES ATLANTIC" – he could still see the headlines, the pictures, the excitement on people's faces. For a long time he had sat there rigid, the atlas in his hands transformed into the controls of that plane, the sound of the motor roaring in his ears, the sudden appearance of the wild, grey windswept ocean beneath him....

He moved slowly away from his mother's side, away from her unawareness of him. He murmured the name of this ship, and even the thought of Lindbergh was pushed out of his mind by the actuality of the deck beneath his feet. To be on a boat, a fifty-thousand ton boat, was already too much. He kept as close as possible to the railing, walking around the legs and hips and backs and arms, avoiding the uniformed stewards and the passengers rushing here and there. He was small for his twelve years (almost thirteen, he would have admitted) and nowhere was this handicap borne in on him so surely as in a crowd. Because he was also precocious and ahead of his age in school, he seemed always to have lived at a lower level than his classmates. He had spent his life looking up, like an intelligent dwarf. Here, in this crowd on the deck, he felt himself at the mercy of the treacherous limbs of people whose chests he faced and whose heads towered above him. When he passed a small boy – the only child he had yet seen on the ship – he drew himself up, pausing momentarily, and glowered down at him. The little boy stared back, wide-eyed. It helped a little.

He made his way along the long deck to the rear of the ship, informing himself that he was going *aft*, towards the *stern*, knowing that below him under the water he might perhaps see the propellers, or as the Cunard Line booklet said, the *screws*. He wondered briefly whether he was on the starboard or port side of the ship, and glanced at his hands as if they might reveal the secret of seaborne right or left, but there was no answer in them. He went down the companionway to the deck below and stopped when he came to the very end of the ship. He pressed his head against the iron bars under the wooden railing and looked down but he could not see anything except water. The screws were invisible, hidden under the stern that projected, like a great porch with a round bottom, out from the hull. He turned around and looked up, his head against the high wooden rail, up to the top of the steel mast with the flag flying. Although there were rope ladders leading up to nothing near the top of the mast he knew they were fakes, he had read the booklet thoroughly. The masts, at least the forward mast, were of hollow steel, with an inside ladder.

He looked up at the funnels, all three of them, leaning towards him. They were big enough for a train to pass through. His fingers gathered themselves into small fists and he pressed his hands against his chest. It was really true, he knew now; he was really on this boat, he was going to stay on it, he was going to Europe – although that didn't matter so much, it was the boat. If only it could have been the *Mauretania*! Well at least this *Berengaria* was bigger and it was named for some queen, too. The *Mauretania*, though, had four smokestacks and it was the fastest ocean liner in the world. The Greyhound of the Seas; the holder of the Blue Ribbon of the Atlantic. The sister ship of the *Lusitania* that the Germans had sunk during the war. Maybe they'd come back on the *Mauretania*.

He turned again and looked under the rail down at the water. Perhaps if he climbed up and leaned over he could see them. He gripped the wide wooden railing with both hands, it was too wide to hold easily, and pulled himself up on the iron bars, climbing them as if they had been the rungs of a ladder. By leaning over as far as he could, he looked down under the projecting stern, past the great letters reading *Berengaria, Liverpool*, and down to the rudder. Through the murky, greasy water something was moving, caught for an instant in the bright June sunlight. The screws – one on the left and another on the right – turned slowly, cutting through the water, gradually increasing in speed.

He looked up and around, no one was watching him, although there was a man standing about ten feet away, leaning on the rail, looking at the Jersey shore. He looked back into the water. They were moving faster now, catching the sun, flickering and shining up at him. But he could only see two of them. The other two projected at the sides, he knew, where the hull of the ship slanted and curved inward.

Suddenly, without any warning, his body was filled with a violent blast of sound, so enormous that every nerve in him became rigid and trembled with it, forcing him over the railing, pushing him from behind, down and down, his hands reaching frantically for the wide gutter, his eyes fastened on the brown cigarette butt and the rust, the crinkling of once-white paint. As if his eyes were travelling of their own accord, rushing ahead of his body, he could see himself being caught up in the tons of yellow metal whirling below him, being sucked in and cut relentlessly to pieces ... he closed his eyes and screamed but the sound stayed inside him, obliterated by the deafening roar of the whistle.

When he opened his eyes, he was shocked to find himself on the deck, held tightly in the hands of the man who had been standing near him at the rail. The man looked and looked at him, into and through him, before he spoke. Then he smiled and said: "That was close, son," and the smile grew bigger on his face. He relaxed his grip. "Where are your parents? Where's your father?"

Something pounded back into Matthew, he could feel it in his chest, but it was difficult for him to speak and when he did the words came out of their own accord: "My father's divorced," he said, and then his face reddened. For some reason he knew he shouldn't have said that. For some reason ... but he did not quite know why. What he did know was that it was not really true, that the reason he was going to Paris with his mother was so that she could get a divorce from his father. He had looked away from the man in his confusion and now he looked back squarely into his face, the inadvertent lie form-ing on a small, hard pain in his chest. "Not really," he said quickly, his eyes flickering at the man, "my mother's going to Paris to get a divorce from my father."

The man looked at him without saying anything and the steady, unblinking eyes embarrassed Matthew. He straightened his shoul-ders and forced himself to smile. "Thank you very much," he said with dignity. "You saved my life." He shook the man's hand formally and started away from him, adding over his shoulder: "My mother's right up there."

The man continued to watch him and Matthew turned to look back. The man waved his hand at him and turned again to the rail, the water, and the Jersey shore.

When he found his mother, she had left her place by the railing and was walking agitatedly down the deck away from him. He caught the sleeve of her coat and tugged on it sharply.

"Matthew!" she exclaimed breathlessly, a frightened look in her eyes. "Darling! Thank heaven! Where have you been? You mustn't run away like that!"

She knelt beside him on the deck, her arms around his waist, oblivious of the passengers, a few of whom had turned to watch them. In that moment, the alarm which was in their faces for different rea-sons made them look very much alike, but the likeness was an illu-sion of expression. Although Matthew's hair had been very light as a young child, it was already turning darker, and the shape of his head, bulging out at the back, with a high smooth forehead, was very differ-ent from hers. Whatever differences there were between them, they were undeniably mother and son, but it was the look in their eyes that proclaimed it. Catherine kissed him on the cheek. The attention em-barrassed him and yet he could not pull himself away, wishing only that she would let him go. Her distress seemed out of place, almost false; she was too well-dressed, too expensively put together for any strong emotion. The insecurity in her face was incongruous with the flowers on the jacket of her suit, the high polish of her fingernails.

A couple standing nearby was watching them. He hugged her tightly and warmly, and then kissed her, looking back proudly at the man and the woman. The fear disappeared from Catherine's face, leaving only the beauty and the polish, and she stood up and took his hand in hers. She did not hold it, but grasped and regrasped its smallness with her soft fingers, twisting it gently, making sure that it was his. They walked along the deck together and she smiled down at him. It was as if nothing had happened. Then he remembered.

"What exactly is a divorce, mother?"

They turned into the narrow hallway of the deck, stepping over the high metal projection – the doors were built that way, he knew, to keep the water out – and his mother's step faltered. She did not answer him right away, but only smiled – a little sadly he thought. It was not until they were in their cabin and she had taken off her hat and seated herself on the edge of one of the two beds, taking his hand once more in hers, that she spoke to him. She had been through all this before, but children were fantastic creatures, utterly incomprehensible. Probably all her explanations had been in vain, she patted the bed beside her. "Sit here, darling," she said. "I'll try to explain."

He waited patiently next to her, wanting to give her time, sorry to have asked the question. He toyed with the idea of telling her about the man who had saved his life, how he had almost fallen into the water, into the churning propellers, and then decided against it. She would only exclaim and hug him and kiss him again.

"When people get married," she began slowly, "they go to a minister or an official and they sign a paper," she looked down at him, hesitating, "a kind of a contract ... an agreement. They ... they love each other, they want to live together, to ... to have children."

"I know about marriage," he said.

She nodded. "Of course you do, darling."

"But what about...?"

"Yes. I'll try to explain." She looked away but her hand gripped his more tightly. "A divorce is just the opposite of marriage. It's when you agree not to live together any more. You find that you don't feel the same way about each other, you..."

"What?"

He watched the conflict in her eyes and she patted his hand. "I wasn't going to tell you this," she said, "but you'll learn it someday and I suppose it is best that you hear it from me. Your father wants to marry someone else," she continued, "another woman. It isn't just that we don't love each other any more, it's that he loves someone else."

"You mean he doesn't love you any more?"

"That's right, dear. He can't help it. Things like that happen."

"Do you love him?"

"Well...." her shoulders stiffened and she looked away again. "Under the circumstances, I suppose I don't."

He looked down at his shoes and swung his feet back and forth. "Does he love me?" he asked suddenly.

"Of course he does!"

"But he's not going to see me any more, is he?"

She hesitated. "Not for a while, Matthew. Of course, if you want to see him...."

He shook his head firmly. "If he doesn't love you, I don't ever want to see him again. I hate him!"

"You mustn't say that! You mustn't even think it! He's your father!"

He was surprised. He had not expected her answer, but it was all right when he looked at her. He could tell that she was pleased, even if she didn't say so, even if she did tell him he mustn't say it or think it, because she was looking away from him at her own reflection in the mirror, and at the image of himself beside her and there was a smile on her face. Matthew felt as if the look they exchanged in the glass was a secret between them, that they could not have looked at each other directly in just that way.

Her reflection changed from pleasure to concern. "You aren't going to miss America, are you dear?"

Miss it? Up to now he had thought only of going, his feelings and his mind had gone ahead of the boat at the dock, out on the sea, aiming towards France. It had not occurred to him that he was departing from anything.

"No," he said slowly, wondering if he would or not.

"Remember that Scott is in Paris. Won't it be fun seeing Scott again?"

He had forgotten Scott Fletcher and now he tried to form a picture of him in his mind. He smiled. "Oh, yes," he said, and put his arm around her. "And we'll be together," he said, "won't we?"

"Of course, darling."

"I'll never stop loving you, mother," he said firmly. "I promise I won't. We'll be together always, and when I'm grown up, I'll take care of you. Really I will."

Her eyes lingered on the mirror and then moved slightly to fix themselves on his reflection. "Darling…" she began, but even as she spoke, he pulled himself away from her and ran to the window to stand on tiptoe. "We're moving!" he called, without turning to his mother, and she stood up, her lips still parted. He faced her, turning quickly: "Let's go out on deck … we're moving!"

Chapter Two

The last few miles of the trip had been driven in silence, and as he slowed down and took the turn through the gates, past the sign reading "St. Croix, École de Garçons," Scott Fletcher took one hand from the wheel of the car, coughed and lighted a cigarette. He glanced quickly at Catherine sitting beside him, in the mirror at Matthew in the back seat and then looked up the gravelled driveway to the building ahead of them. The last time they had come here the grounds had been empty, the building shuttered, with only M. de St. Croix to greet them and take them through the empty classrooms, opening the doors with the large bunch of keys that had jangled in his hand as he walked ahead of them. But today the athletic field was crowded with boys playing some unrecognizable game involving a great deal of running and shouting and a bat and ball. However it might resemble American baseball, even at a glance Scott knew that it was not, if only from the occasional shouts of "*Pas moitié!*" that shook the air.

The building could have been built at almost any time during the late eighteenth or early nineteenth centuries. It was the kind of country house that was automatically called a château. Three storeys of stucco with an elaborate and irregular border of stones around the windows and doors. Now, all the shutters were fastened back against the outside walls and many of the windows were open. There was another car nosed in towards the building near the main door and Scott headed in next to it and stopped the car. At first, none of them moved or spoke; all three seemed to be waiting for some signal to set them in motion. Meanwhile they looked at the building, the field … listening to the boys rather than watching them. They were all momentarily immobilized by the realization of the moment that had descended upon them. They had arrived, and both Scott and Catherine knew that their next actions would lead to their separation from Matthew and their return to Paris, leaving him behind. The silence hung upon them in different ways and the only thing they all shared was a desire not to break it by any sudden action.

Scott felt, very strongly, what he had felt to a much lesser degree ever since he had first met Catherine and Matthew at the station in Paris in June: that he was an outsider, someone who was about to witness something that was, or should be, a private experience. However much he had tried to accustom himself to the circumstance, he was unable to accept Catherine's separation from John. Because of his friendship for both of them, because of his sense of responsibility towards them, he had felt it his duty to help Catherine in every way possible. But even in the discharge of that responsibility, he was not comfortable. Their first visit to the school was a good example: M. de St. Croix, naturally enough, had mistaken him for Matthew's father. Natural or not, the mistake had been embarrassing to Scott. He was at least fifteen years younger than Catherine, and certainly looked ten. He had seen the old man's eyes measuring them, calculating and then taking it upon himself to say, before Catherine could introduce him or explain: "And this is Monsieur Cameron?" Still, it had been a question: Perhaps he had not really thought....

Sitting beside him in the car, Catherine had also thought of this first visit and of her explanation to M. de St. Croix: "No, this is Mr. Fletcher, a friend of mine who has been kind enough to drive me here from Paris. You see, my husband and I..." she could not remember the rest of her sentence. She remembered only the feeling she always had when it was necessary to explain to someone that she was no longer married, that she was getting a divorce, that this man was only "a friend." She had wondered then just what M. de Croix had thought, or what other people thought. She had searched his face, looking for something in his eyes to indicate that he assumed Scott was not just a friend. Now, she looked at Scott, almost angrily. Why did it have to be like this? Why did people have to assume that any man you were seen with was likely to be your lover? She was sure it was not her imagination. She had seen the thought too often in the eyes of other people, unimportant people like this school man, or the concierge at her apartment building, strangers, ticket sellers, gas station attendants. Something in her cried out that it was unfair and all wrong, not only the assumption, but the kind of assumption. It was no discredit to a man to be some woman's lover whether the fact was accurate or not, but to a woman … she had always hated the word "mistress," too. Well, whatever M. de St. Croix had thought, he had accepted her son as a student, and her money for his tuition.

She heard a movement in the back seat and turned to look at Matthew. His head was turned away from her, he was looking at the boys on the playing field, and the shape of his head at that moment was painfully like John's. He seemed withdrawn and somehow smaller, sitting there alone in the back seat. She felt a quick surge of shame at the realization that she had been sitting in front, away from him, not even thinking about him when he was on the threshold of an important and probably difficult experience. This was his first time away from home at a boarding school.

Matthew was aware of his mother's eyes upon him, but he gave no sign. He did not turn his head or speak or smile or move his body. He held his breath until he felt his eyes leave him, as if his immobility would prevent any immediate action from either his mother or Scott. It was not that he was gripped by any great regret at leaving Paris or coming to this school. When they had left Paris that morning, he had been glad that they were going and that he would not be spending the winter with his mother. Catherine's Paris had bored him: museums, monuments, excursions, restaurants, art galleries, *beauty*. Not that he had not liked some of these things individually. But all his time in Paris since their arrival was overlaid with the feeling of strained thoughtfulness he had felt flowing continuously from his mother. She had spent her time with him as she spent money. No matter what they did – the two of them – she seemed to allot him time. Although it had never been said aloud, he could read it in his eyes. What shall I do with Matthew? Where shall I take him today? How much he had longed to be older, to be independent of her, to be just old enough so that she would not have felt she had to be doing things with him. In his mind he defended her against these accusations: she had been careful never to voice such thoughts, and she had always protested that whatever she did was because she wanted to do it, not because of him. If only she had protested less!

And Scott. Matthew looked at the back of his head, and he was suddenly twisted by self-pity. He wished that he had a tangible link to Scott. Unlike his mother, there was no guarantee that Scott would always be around. There was nothing safe or secure in their relation to each other. For no other reason, or so it seemed, except that Scott had been there ever since Matthew had been born, Scott had taken him on when they had come to Paris. It had become routine for them to meet almost every Saturday afternoon: to play chess, which Scott had taught him, or tennis, or to go swimming or riding. He had wondered why Scott spent so much time with him, and when he had protested, once only, that it must be boring for a man to be going around with a boy, Scott had been genuinely hurt. Even if there was no absolute assurance that Scott would always be available, Matthew knew – at least – that Scott's affection for him was genuine and that his time with him had not been a sacrifice because he was sorry for him, or because he felt responsible.

Still staring at the back of his head, Matthew would have liked, more than anything, to be like him. The blue eyes, dark hair, firm jaw – to Matthew it was the kind of face he had seen in advertisements in American magazines. Scott was the man who walked a mile for a Camel, wore an Arrow collar, drove a Packard. Absolutely handsome, completely desirable. If Matthew could have chosen to be like anyone, in looks, manners, ability – in every way – it would have been like Scott. He clenched his fists together and looked away from that head. He was going to miss Scott here, and he only knew it now when it was irrevocable. He thought of his mother with anger, for it was she who had done this. Scott had agreed, yes, what else could he do? But it was she who had decided, firmly, that this was the place for Matthew.

And what was this place? This isolated building and all these black-aproned boys. In Paris, the school had had the glamour of a refuge, but now he saw it for what it was: a leap into the void in the company of strangers. He knew only a little French, he could not understand any of the cries of these boys from the playing field, recognizing them only as joy, or anger, or encouragements, as one recognizes the sounds of animals and attempts to interpret their meaning. What was he to do when he was left alone with them? How would he communicate with any of them – and who here, beyond M. de St. Croix and the English teacher, could speak English? And when would he see M. de St. Croix, and if he did what could he say to him? An old man, erect and forbidding, who peered at you through steel-rimmed glasses and said in a ghastly accent: "How old are you?" The English teacher he had not even met, he only knew there was one. And would he, an American boy, even be in his class? Why should he learn to speak English?

He looked at his watch, a present from his father sent from America for his birthday, and was startled to see that they had been sitting there for less than two minutes. It seemed, already, an eternity that he had been here, behind the two backs in the front seat of the car, with the building and the boys pressing down into him. The loneliness caught fire inside him and rushed through his veins, so that he wanted to reach out to them and beg them not to leave him here, to start the car now and drive him back to Paris. But he did not move. He was thirteen, as the watch had reminded him. Thirteen and responsible; it was up to him to go through with whatever plan they had made for him, to be sure there were no tears, to behave like a man. A man. Perhaps it would have been different if his father were here … but his father! Except for his letters and occasional presents – he looked again at the watch – his father did not exist; and these things did not bring him closer, they only underlined the distance between them.

The door of the front seat opened and Scott got out of the car. Automatically, as if she had been waiting only for this moment, Catherine opened her door and stepped to the ground. Although she was not often acutely conscious of the motivation behind her own actions, at that moment something had become piercingly clear to her. She felt as if she had discovered what her separation from John really was. Divorce was not simply a question of separating two people, it meant a readjustment of one's self, a making-over of each individual, and it must also be like this – in opposite ways – for John. She had waited until Scott had opened the door of the car for a reason, because for fifteen years her instincts, her whole pattern of living had been geared to following and not to initiating action. As she stood upon the gravel, feeling it pressing into the thin soles of her shoes, she left John completely for the first time. Even away from him in Paris (and this also she had not known before) the letters from his lawyer to her lawyer, or the letters from John to Matthew, and particularly the occasional letters he had written directly to her had been the only things to which she had reacted genuinely and directly. It was still his action that set her into motion – or in some things, Scott's. Scott agreeing to some plan of hers had in reality been Scott making the decision for her. Scott helping her to find an apartment had been Scott telling her to live in an apartment, as John would have told her or as her father would have told her before him. Even Matthew sometimes, but not often. For Matthew, mostly, sensed her indecision, her inability to take action for herself, and held back, non-committal, saying that he didn't know, or didn't care, or that it was all right with him.

She would have said something to Scott then, so strong was the sense of explanation and discovery inside her, except for Matthew who chose that moment to open the back door of the car and step out beside her. As he did so, she was redirected towards him, once more with the flush of shame that told her she was not thinking of him when she should be. "Here we are!" she exclaimed, and the signal they had been waiting for had come. They each seized a piece of luggage, each closed a car door firmly, and started quickly for the door of the school and M. de St. Croix's office.

After another quick tour, a visit to Matthew's room, bare and stern, too light, sparsely furnished and with the work-table placed squarely in front of the window, demanding attention, they returned to the office. M. de St. Croix, the glasses sliding down his bony nose, held Matthew's shoulder with one hand, as if he had taken possession of a hostage. There could be no question of a sentimental farewell in this man's presence. Scott shook hands with him, and then with Matthew, looking the boy firmly in the eye and patting him roughly on the upper arm. Matthew looked up at him quickly and his eyes filled with tears. Then it was Catherine's turn. She extended her hand to M. de St. Croix who took it only tentatively, saying at the same time that he would come to the car with her, and with a gesture almost of introduction, presented her with her son. She became, sensing that it was already too late, all mother at that moment. She seemed to soften so that she was inextricably joined with the warmth of the fur around her shoulders; the angles and contours of her tall, slim body disappeared into one large curve as she bent over him, hiding his face against the warmth of her breast. Then she drew back a little, kissed his cheek and then his mouth. There were things to say now, things that would never be said, and perhaps would not even be felt by him. "My darling one," she said and pulled away from him, holding his two hands in hers, unable to let him go now that the time had come when she must.

It was Matthew who pulled his hands away from her and moved back under the protecting arm of the old Frenchman. His hand still on Matthew's shoulder, M. de St. Croix smiled, showing the stained brownish-white teeth, exuding the faint smell of rust and wine that seems to be common to all Frenchmen. "So," he said definitely and clearly. "It is best not to prolong the goodbye. Matthew will wait here while I take you to the car."

He left the door open behind him after he had bowed Scott and Catherine out of his office and through the front door, and gave Matthew one sharp glance over his shoulder, seeming to say that any continuation of this farewell was in Matthew's hands and not his. As Matthew made no move, he turned back to the two people ahead of him and followed them to the car, opening and closing the door for Catherine. He smiled again. "It is much better that you go quickly," he said. "He will be lonely for a little while, only." He shook their hands again, one quick shake each, and then stood back from the car as if to get out of its path, urging it to leave. Scott, looking first at Catherine and then quickly back into the black hole left by the open door, started the car and backed it around. With a wave at M. de St. Croix, still smiling and bowing faintly towards them, he turned and started down the driveway. Matthew had not appeared in the doorway at all, and in both their minds there was a picture of him, small in the dim room – small, erect and defiant. Impulsively, Scott put his hand on Catherine's: "He'll be all right, Catherine. Don't worry about him."

But there was no response from her hand. "Yes, I know," she said quickly, forcing herself to smile. It was as if the shadow of Matthew was sitting between them in the seat, something over which they could not cross or meet.

෮

There is an element of risk in any major decision. An unknown factor, an area of chance and of unforeseeable consequence. However the mind may calculate, reason and justify in advance, at some indefinite point in the future, when the decision has already been made and acted upon, the moment will come when doubt will enter and when one will question the assurance and confidence which made the decision possible. The first warning of the appearance of doubt may manifest itself in various ways: a sudden loss – for apparently illogical, of self-justification or some action calculated to strengthen whatever unforeseen weaknesses may have appeared to question and undermine the rightness of the decision.

Driving away from the school and back to Paris with Scott, Catherine was haunted by the memory of Matthew in the École de St. Croix. In her mind the large empty rooms transformed themselves into dining rooms, classrooms, libraries, study halls, filled with strangers speaking a strange language, and in the midst of them Matthew, young, inexperienced and frightened. Driven to it by some force that was stronger than she was, she identified herself with Matthew, placing her spirit inside him. He had become an extension of herself, cut off from her, unprotected and threatened by the life of the school. Simultaneously, she was besieged by what had seemed all the logical and proper reasons for choosing this particular school. It had been recommended by Matthew's headmaster in America, it had an excellent scholastic rating, he would be forced to speak French at all times, he would be away from his mother – which Catherine knew was necessary – and he would be with his contemporaries. This last was a particularly important reason, he had been too much with older people; he did not make friends easily, he was already too attached to herself and to Scott.

As they drove in silence, Scott obeying a warning instinct not to talk to Catherine or to attempt to console her, she argued with herself, but without success. However good her reasons had seemed one month before, she now found herself facing a self-accusation which she was unable to answer. She felt that she had abandoned Matthew, even as she agreed vehemently that the school was an excellent place for him. There was another element in this feeling of fear and guilt compounded inside her, that she did not understand.

When she was alone in her apartment, having left Scott peremptorily, anxious to be alone, her sense of guilt began to clarify itself in her mind. Matthew's absence – and therefore the sense of him, alone and away from her – filled the apartment. She felt his presence in the hall as she entered, and her first act, even before she took off her coat and hat, was to cross the living room and open the windows wide. She stood in the open window of the room, looking down on the Quai, at the river at the Tuileries directly across from her, the Louvre and the Île de la Cité to her right and the Place de la Concorde to her left. She loved this view of the river, it had enchanted her when she had first seen the apartment.

Standing in the window, she took off her hat, patted her hair automatically and then took off her coat which she let fall on the chair behind her. Slowly, she turned from the window, facing the room again. She felt that there was a clue to her troubled mind here, something she had to discover in the apartment. Without any conscious aim she crossed the living room and walked down the hall towards Matthew's room at the end. She was pulled along by a current that originated in that room. When she opened the door, she held her breath momentarily, half expecting a shock from the room that she knew must be empty. She let the door swing wide but did not enter. Here she could smell Matthew. It was not an emanation, nor was it her imagination, it was the peculiar combination of odors which join together and produce the sensation and picture of a boy. Something that is not quite male, no longer child; it is not a definite, frank smell – but tentative, uncertain – sweet, sour dirty and clean at once.

It was not the smell alone that made Catherine pause in the doorway. The fresh, unaccustomed order in the room seemed calculated to erase any traces of its past occupant. The books were stacked neatly on the shelves, there were no stray objects lying about. Everything had been hidden from sight or placed in symmetrical and absolute order. The room, with the aura of Matthew still in it, was nevertheless cold and unfriendly, so much so that without entering, Catherine reached for the door knob and closed the door, darkening the hall. As she walked back to the living room, a slowly increasing sadness mingled with the doubt and the loss of confidence already in her mind. She began to feel that it was not only today that she had committed some offence against her son; at some point in the past, the action had been taken. Leaving him at the school was like one more figure in the predetermined pattern.

It was not only of Matthew that she was thinking, however. She realized that this was the first time she had been really alone in her apartment. Through the curtains of her thoughts, she looked absently at the furnishings in the room, seeing them not as her own things but as the belongings of a stranger. Inanimate, almost hostile, the chairs, tables, lamps, books, rug, pictures stared back at her as objects with which she could not identify herself. No longer could she look at them as things that she had bought to furnish the new life she had planned for herself and her son. She could not recapture the feeling with which she had purchased them, remembering only that she had insisted on *buying*, where Scott had suggested that she rent for the time being. They seemed now to have been bought with determination rather than taste, as symbols and not as articles destined for use. They lacked personality and they did not express anything more than an attempt to fill an otherwise empty room. Watching them, she felt a chill pass through her body. She was afraid of them, afraid of what they represented.

Once Catherine had decided to divorce John, she had accepted the point of view and the frame of mind of an injured person. She did not express it in just that way to herself, but the decision had been based upon that premise. She had ample legal grounds for divorce. Her husband, the father of her child, had committed – and admitted

– adultery. He had placed no blame on her. He had not even attempted to justify his action. She had not suspected him, and she had not examined their relationship in any thoughtful or introspective way. She had known, instinctively, when she first married John, that it was not a special or unusual marriage. They had known each other for a long time and their engagement had seemed a natural culmination. She had assumed that she was in love with him, and without any experience by which to measure her own or his love, the assumption was as good as fact. They had been entirely happy (as she thought this, fifteen years later in Paris, she modified it to "quite happy") those first years through Matthew's birth and until John enlisted in the Army. Perhaps his enlistment should have been a warning to her, an indication that they were not as successfully married as she had thought. For he had not had to enlist. He was married and a father. At the time it had seemed patriotic, noble – a handsome gesture, one that any full-blooded man should have made. And she, too, had fulfilled her duty. She could still see herself, earnestly occupied with the Red Cross, rolling bandages, driving cars, buying and selling Liberty Bonds. She saw it now as a kind of deluded dream, a false element introduced to interrupt and distort their relationship. Their very roles in the war had made something unreal of them; they had become the exemplary couple, giving their all: time, money, and risking at least John's life.

The war over, with John safely back in business, they were stripped of everything but the example. Their friends had been unable to forget their sacrifice, their unselfishness, the fact that they only thought of their country and not of themselves. Even Scott. He would not be in the foreign service now if it had not been for John. Scott, too young for the army, had had to do his part, too. He had decided, after long and serious consultation with John, that there was a great deal still to be done. One honorable way of making up for the handicap of his youth, his inability to serve his country actively, was to devote himself to that country for the rest of his life. How serious, how idealistic he had been … and still was.

Suddenly impatient with the flood of recollections passing through her mind, Catherine stood up from the chair where she had been sitting. Propelled by the force of the feeling inside her, a feeling that was blind and angry, she began to pace up and down the room. She stopped at the mantelpiece to light a cigarette and glanced sharply at the mirror over it. Her face was flushed and the reflection pleased her. The face she saw in the mirror now seemed to have some relation to her *self*, to a kind of reality that she had not known for months. She was stripped as she stared at herself of the role of injured wife and noble mother. She knew then what she hated about the room, the furniture, everything. It was false and contrived, put together by hands that were not really hers, fabricated in a dream world that had no relation to reality. For the first time – at that moment, looking into her own bright and angry eyes – she thought of herself, John and Matthew as real people, involved in a dilemma that was not and never would be solved. Fifteen years – however unreal they might seem now – cannot be wiped away and leave no trace. She and John had been inextricably involved, interanimating and exchanging each others' lives, during all that time. It did not matter who was to blame or why, it was of no use to measure and weigh and consider; it did not matter that theirs had not been a world-shattering romance. What was important was the weight of those fifteen years.

She started to pace the room again, despising its confines and the objects within them. The books: sets of books bought for Matthew's good, books that *should* be read. And the pictures. New enough to be smart, good enough so that she would be thought, if not a connoisseur, then astute. Marie Laurençin and Foujita at opposite ends of the room – originals, of course. It was the same with everything. There was nothing in this room that had any real meaning for her. She had not acquired any of these things for the only good reason that exists, because she had to have them, but for a thousand other reasons: they were safe, they were in good, if not impeccable, taste.

They were decorative, or instructive, or worthy, or proper, and, she remembered, they were insured. She had had them insured in the way that you insure a fur coat, or any replaceable object, and in the absolutely certain knowledge that in case of fire or theft or act of God, they would be replaced by something of equal if not greater value: their equivalent in money.

It seemed to her that her whole life was like that now, and it was immediately unbearable to her. Everything she had done was right, proper, suitable for the eyes of the world, and that was all. Far from having achieved a substitute for her fifteen years with John, she had built a meaningless structure around herself that she had foolishly intended to replace the life from which she, by her own act, (for it was finally *her* decision, not John's) had cut herself off. Even if she had hated John it would have been impossible to replace all those years of his comings and goings in and out of the house. The years of breakfasts, laundry, cigarette ashes, the sounds of doors and windows closing and opening, the smell that is the permanently mingled odor of two people. She did not, even at this moment, personally regret the lack of John, but only the lack of a presence. His betrayal of her – that was the word she used – had offended her too deeply to allow her to regret him, but she could not forgive him for taking away, inevitably, a part of herself that had linked itself inextricably with him.

They had been able to divide their possessions: property, books, furniture, bank accounts, gifts – and even their friends. The Wilsons were his friends, the Martins hers. The Stracheys were friends of her mother, the Allens were involved in John's business. Scott had been the only indivisible friend and he had presented no real problem because he was in France and therefore temporarily ceded to Catherine.

But what about themselves? It was right enough, logical enough, and certainly proper to seek a divorce under the circumstances. But what did you do with the marriage? Divorce, like the executioner's knife, could be used to sever them quickly and almost painlessly, and then it could be wiped and stored away. But the marriage lay there, a great, dead body waiting for burial. What she had attempted to do with her life since she had left John was like an attempted concealment of that body – and it remained to plague her constantly.

As if carried back to her on the very air of the room, the presence of Matthew infiltrated her again. What about him? She had asked herself that, of course. She had discussed it interminably: with John, with the lawyers, with Scott, in her dreams, and even with Matthew himself. Again, she had done the legal, the proper, the right, the usual thing. Not that she could or would have acted otherwise. She could not have *not* divorced John but what did happen to Matthew in the process? If she found it impossible, in reality, to separate herself from John's presence, what was Matthew doing? How was he managing to adjust to the abnormality of the situation, and what was he building to replace his father, his home, his parents? He had a mother, yes, but a mother is not parents; a mother is not that particular intermixture of two people who are jointly responsible for the third person they have introduced into the world. In what small, blind way was Matthew attempting to build for himself what had been taken away from him?

Chapter Three

Stiff, silent and unseen from the darkness of the small office, Matthew had watched Catherine and Scott leaving. Apart from one quick impulse to run after them which he had stifled immediately, Matthew did not feel much of anything. He was overawed and chilled by the large house, the strange boys on the playing field, M. de St. Croix, and the sensation of complete unfamiliarity with anything or any person around him. As he waited for M. de St. Croix to return, he began to dread the moment when those boys would invade the house and see him. He could already feel himself under the scrutiny of an enormous number of unfriendly and calculating eyes. For the average boy, there is little that is more dreadful than the anticipation of the moment when he will be under the examining eyes of a large number of his contemporaries who are strangers to him. Such an examination is invariably direct, frank, open and usually hostile.

When M. de St. Croix did return, chattering to him about how much he would like the school, what fine boys there were, what excellent professors, what good food, what comfortable beds … Matthew barely listened to him. And finally came the moment for which he had been waiting: his dismissal. He was told to look around for himself, to go and make friends with the boys outside, as if it was something that required no effort. There was no further resisting, there was nothing he could do except comply. He made his way slowly through the door into the hall and then out of the building. He heard the door to the little office closing behind him and he could picture the old Frenchman thankful to be rid of him at last.

He walked along the wall of the building until he saw a large tree at some distance from the playing field. He made for the tree and sat down on the ground under it. It was hot outside and he was glad of the shade. Also, from here he could watch the other boys almost unnoticed, or so he hoped. He had only to wait until the bell rang for lunch: twenty minutes of grace.

It was not as bad as he had expected. When the bell rang, the boys ran in from the field, shouting and knocking their way down the stairs to the washroom. Matthew followed them into the house, the very last, just in time to meet the first few of them coming up the stairs, their hair combed, their faces quieter and cleaner, their hands washed. He looked quickly at his own hands and followed the first boys into the dining room. He was met at the door by a young man who shook his hand, introduced himself as Professeur Colbert, checked his name off a list and told him to go to table number 12.

There were perhaps fifteen tables in the dining room, set with four places on the sides and one place at one end. Matthew watched the other boys who had preceded him into the room and following their example stood by the side of table 12 as the dining room continued to fill up. When all the tables were filled, eight boys and one man at each, they sat down. The man at the end of the table was also one of the teachers and after introducing himself, he presented the other boys to Matthew in turn. André *something* was opposite him and was the only name he could remember for sure. Two of the other boys were named Georges and Marcel, but Matthew did not know which two they were, and he could not even remember the teacher's name.

They ate for the most part in silence. Aside from the occasional glances at him, no one seemed to take any special interest in Matthew and as the meal wore on, he felt himself becoming absorbed in the group, the frightening strangeness disappeared and he felt less conspicuous. When they had finished eating, they remained seated while M. de St. Croix stood in the middle of the dining room and told them the plan for the afternoon. He spoke so loudly and distinctly that even Matthew could follow him. They were to go to their rooms immediately after lunch and wait until someone came to supervise their unpacking and check over the equipment they had brought with them. Later they would meet in the salon opposite the dining room where certain general rules would be explained to them and when they would be assigned to their classrooms. Then they would have their *goûter* and after that they would be free to do what they wished until supper.

The day passed slowly. By the time he had had supper, Matthew could find his way around without difficulty from room to room; he knew a few of the boys by sight, even if he could not remember their names, and was able to smile at them. To his great relief he found that he could at least understand most of what was said to him even if he could not bring himself to speak French to anyone. Most of the teachers who had addressed him had spoken to him in very slow and distinct French, and one or two of them had even addressed him in English.

After supper, he sat in the corner of the library at the end of the hall opposite the entrance with an open book in his lap. He had taken it quickly from the shelf and opened it at random. It was a protection, a buffer between him and the other boys standing and sitting in the room, talking together. He knew that they were watching him, as they had watched him all day. In one more hour it would be time to go to bed. Some of the boys had already gone to their rooms, and if it had not been that he had misinterpreted a sign in the hall, he would have been there himself. But now he could not bring himself to walk across the room from the distant corner, under the eyes of all these boys.

Although he did not move his head, he saw the boy who had sat opposite him at the table, the boy named André, come to the door of the room. He, particularly, had been watching Matthew all day, and now again his eyes stopped when they came to Matthew's corner, and

Matthew could feel him looking at him. He had heard the other boys speak his name in that particular tone of respect and envy that is reserved for the natural leaders, the boys who are confident and at ease because of their superior size or knowledge or for some similar reason. Matthew had spotted that about him at once – there was always someone like that in every school. He hoped urgently that this boy would leave him alone. He knew that if any one of them was going to make a move in his direction, it would have to be this boy first. The others would not act without him.

André put his hands in his pockets, looked around the room airily, and then entered slowly. From the way he walked, not looking in any particular direction, it was impossible to tell what he was going to do, or just where he was going. The other boys continued to talk, but their voices were hushed and their attention was fixed on André. He walked to the center of the room, nodded in the direction of a group of boys who nodded back quickly, and then turned in Matthew's direction. Another moment had come, as Matthew had feared.

He remained motionless and rigid until he felt the boy's presence behind him, his hand on the back of the chair, just barely touching Matthew's shoulder. He lifted his head to look into the boy's eyes. He did not smile, he merely looked. André, however, smiled. Superior, friendly and menacing. His hand moved from the back of the chair to Matthew's shoulder. At last, after what seemed an age of silence, he said, in English: "You're an American, aren't you?"

Matthew nodded and smiled faintly. "Yes."

"How old are you?"

"Thirteen."

"How long have you been in France?"

Matthew calculated quickly, never questioning the boy's right to ask all these questions. "About four months."

"Do you like it?"

"Yes."

"You don't speak very good French, do you?"

Matthew shook his head. "No, I don't."

"Do your father and mother live here?"

"My mother does."

"And your father?"

Matthew hesitated. "He's ... he's in America."

"Then why are you here?"

Matthew's voice dropped to a whisper. "My ... my mother's getting a divorce," he said quickly, hoping that the other boys wouldn't hear him. Perhaps they didn't speak English.

"Who was that man you came with today?"

"A friend."

"Of your mother's?"

Matthew nodded again, and then added: "And my father's, too."

"I thought maybe he was your father."

Matthew shook his head.

The boy laughed and then the smile on his face warmed. "You're all right," he said unexpectedly.

Matthew breathed a sigh of relief and smiled openly at him now. He did not know what he had expected, but nothing would have surprised him; he might even have been struck by this boy who seemed, as he stood by the chair, almost a giant. "Thanks," he said.

André looked around the room, the other boys looked quickly away and he laughed. "You aren't reading that book, are you?" he asked Matthew.

"No." His face colored as he said it.

"Do you want to come up to my room?"

"Sure." He stood up, put the book on the shelf and turned to face the room. He felt embarrassed, shy, proud and relieved all at once. The ice that had held him rigid all day long had been broken. He had the approbation of André, and he knew instinctively that the other boys would accept him because of it. He looked at the big boy, surprised that he seemed much less enormous as they stood side by side, and he was grateful. Then he followed him across the room obediently, conscious of the looks that the other boys were giving him. Looks that were charged with envy, approval and curiosity. He was relieved when they went out of the door and he hurried up the steps after his new friend. At the top of the stairs, past his own room, they turned down the hallway. André's room was at the very end and when he had opened the door, he switched on the light, and walked in ahead of Matthew. "Come on in," he said.

In contrast to the bare neatness of Matthew's room, this room was disordered, friendly and much larger. There were two beds, two tables, two armchairs, two straight chairs in front of the tables, two chests of drawers and an enormous *armoire*. Books, magazines and clothes were lying on the chairs and on one of the beds; there was an open box of candy on a table, and pictures – mostly photographs of André – were tacked to the walls. Matthew looked at him: André on a bicycle; André in a bathing suit; André with a tennis racquet; André with a girl; and finally just André, a large and handsome head, photographed so that he looked almost like a movie star, self-possessed and glamorous. Matthew sighed to himself, envying both the boy and the room at the same time. He felt insignificant and small compared to him, but his regret was lessened by the fact that it was he, Matthew Cameron, who had been selected to come up here. A sudden doubt pierced him: perhaps it was just because André felt superior to him, or for some other reason that he had not yet revealed.

"Do you have this room all to yourself?" he asked.

André nodded. "I insisted on it," he said. "I didn't like any of the other rooms. I don't like the school much, but I guess it's as good as any other. They aren't so hard to get along with."

"Who?"

"The professors, of course. Old St. Croix is all right after you get used to him."

Matthew stared at him in admiration. *I insisted on it. They aren't so hard to get along with. Old St. Croix is all right....* He wondered if he would ever be able to speak in this offhand, adult way of anything so important as the school or the teachers. And as for insisting on anything!

"How long have you been here?" he asked reverently.

"Just last year. I went to school in Paris for a while before that but I got tired of living at home. You know how it is with a family."

Matthew nodded. "Yes, of course," he said, not knowing at all. He tried to imagine what it would be like with André's family, and his mind conjured up a picture of a small family, intimidated and cowering in the presence of this handsome, blond giant who insisted on this and that, who chose to be rid of his family at will. But why choose this?

"How did you learn to speak such good English?" Matthew asked him.

André smiled scornfully. "I was at school in England for almost three years, but I didn't like it. I don't like the English much. No sense of humor, you know."

"Of course," Matthew said quickly. He was not absolutely certain what was meant by a sense of humor.

Gesturing to one of the armchairs, André said: "Might as well sit down," while he himself threw a pair of pants from the other armchair onto the floor, sat down in it with a deep sigh, and took a package of cigarettes from his pocket. Watching Matthew closely, he put one between his lips, lighted it and puffed smoke into the air. He looked at the cigarette with half-closed eyes and with real contempt and then offered the open package to Matthew. "They're no good," he said, "but you can have one if you like."

Matthew was even more stunned. He was proud to know this boy and was also frightened of him. "I've never smoked one," he said quickly. "You aren't supposed to smoke, are you?"

André laughed and waved his hand in the smoke. "They won't find me out!" His eyes narrowed again. "Go on, try one. It can't hurt you."

Matthew shook his head again. "I'd better not," he said. He was tempted, but he was sure that he would make a fool of himself. He could never throw back his head and blow out the smoke, or flick the ashes into the wastebasket in that lordly way.

"Oh come on. What's the matter, are you afraid?"

"No." He could not afford to seem to be a coward. He reached out quickly and pulled a cigarette from the package.

"That's better! Well, put it in your mouth. Here, you can light it from mine."

Matthew puffed on the cigarette until it was lighted and then blew out the smoke, blinking and waving his hand in front of his eyes. The taste in his mouth was extremely unpleasant. "Very good," he said, smiling.

André shook his head, and took a long pull on his cigarette. "Rotten brand," he said, "but better than nothing." Then he leaned across the open space between them. "You have to inhale, you know."

Matthew held the cigarette away from him. "I do?"

André nodded. "Sure. Here, watch me." With Matthew's eyes fixed on him, he took another long pull on the cigarette, making the end of it glow brightly, and then he opened his mouth and Matthew saw the smoke curling down into his throat. The very sight of it made him a little sick. Then the smoke poured out of André all at once, coming from some unseen depths inside him.

Matthew shook his head. "I could never do that. I'd be sick."

André smiled at him. "Sure you can. It's easy. Come on, try it."

It was more than urging. Matthew felt that something depended on this moment. He put the cigarette gently to his lips, breathed in and tried to swallow the smoke, but he only coughed furiously and the tears came to his eyes. André laughed at him and patted him on the shoulder. "It's always like that the first time, but you'll get used to it. Try it again."

Matthew shook his head hard. He knew he couldn't do that again. He was already feeling sick at his stomach. But his friend insisted and in spite of his queasiness, Matthew could not hold out. He tried again with the same results, and this time it was as if his stomach had turned upside down. He put his hand to his belly, and held the cigarette out at a distance, gasping for breath. "I hadn't better smoke any more," he said, pleadingly.

Whatever André wanted, he apparently didn't want Matthew to get sick, for he took the cigarette from him and tamped it out on the edge of the wastebasket. He continued to smoke his own and when he had finished, he put it out the same way. Then he spread a newspaper on the floor, dumped the contents of the wastebasket into the newspaper and rolled it up and threw it in the fireplace. He lighted it carefully and watched it burn. "See?" he said, satisfied with himself.

Matthew leaned back in his chair. His stomach was still churning inside him and his head was spinning. The window was open behind him and he stretched his head back, breathing in the air in great gulps. "Maybe I'd better go back to my own room," he said weakly. "I don't feel very well."

André did not take this seriously. "You'll be all right in a minute," he said. "It's always like that at first. Besides, I've got something to show you."

Matthew watched him, his head not moving from where it lay on the back of the chair. André took a wallet out of his hip pocket, opened a small compartment in it and drew out some photographs. He looked at them one by one, smiling to himself, and then pulled his chair a little closer to Matthew's. He held one of the pictures under Matthew's eyes and smiled at him. "Pretty good, eh?"

Matthew started in his chair, and the color rushed to his cheeks. It was the picture of a naked woman, leering at him. He stared at it, attracted and repelled at the same time; he could not take his eyes away from it. Then it was snatched from his view and replaced by another and then another and still another. He had never seen anything like these pictures before: men and women, always naked. His stomach churning and his head on fire, he stood up quickly, supporting himself on the chair. "I think I'm going to be sick," he said urgently and started for the door.

André did not move. He only laughed, but not unkindly, and watched Matthew open the door. As he was about to close it behind him, André called: "Good night. See you in the morning," and Matthew heard his voice echoing behind him as he ran down the hall to his own room.

He was not sick. But he lay on his bed, his eyes wide open, staring into the night at a picture that seemed to be pasted on the ceiling above his head. His body was burning.

Chapter Four

André Marat was born with a worldliness, an instinctive knowledge of things and people, that he never had cause to doubt. He did not acquire knowledge as he went along, other than the facts, dates and statistics that were necessary for his school work; the knowledge he had was born with him, and he had no interest in learning. His life was devoted to the development and use of his native talents, and by the time he was fourteen he rarely made mistakes. His assets were his uncanny awareness of his own limitations and an unbounded self-confidence which took the place of charm, poise, manners or intelligence. He did not attempt to compete with anyone of equal or greater strength than himself, and he dealt with people – even at fourteen – on his level and never on theirs. Reason, right or wrong, judgment and conscience were only meaningless terms in his vocabulary. He knew by instinct how far he could go, what he could get away with, when it was necessary to stop or hold back. He could not have explained why he had selected, out of a group of almost one hundred boys, Matthew Cameron. He would have said that it was because he liked him, and he would have meant that Matthew was weaker and could be possessed.

He was not alarmed when, after that first evening, Matthew avoided him. Given time, Matthew would come back of his own accord; he only needed to get over the original shock that André knew he had given him that night. Curiosity, wonder and lack of knowledge would do the rest. They always did.

As usual, André was right. In less than a week, during which time

Matthew had only smiled quickly when he saw him – or averted his eyes in an effort not to see him at all – it was Matthew himself who made the opening move in their reconciliation. They had sat opposite each other at breakfast, dinner and supper every day and never spoken or looked at each other. Finally, during dinner, almost one week after that first day, Matthew did not hide his eyes and when they left the dining room, he spoke to him casually in the hall. André immediately asked him to play some table-tennis in the gymnasium.

It was not wisdom on André's part that made him choose that particular game, but it was a good choice. It was sufficiently competitive and active so that Matthew, who played fairly well, could spill out some of the resentment and anger which had been boiling inside him against André. By the time they had played two sets, Matthew winning both, they were friends again, and once more Matthew was invited to the room, and once more he accepted. This time, when they were again seated in the armchairs facing each other, there were no cigarettes and no photographs. André produced an album of stamps, handed it to Matthew, and seated himself on the arm of Matthew's chair to explain his collection to him.

That week had been more than a matter of waiting for Matthew. Before he had begun to recover from the original shock he had received that night, he found himself filling up with horror and resentment and fear against this boy. He felt that he was powerful and evil and not to be trusted, and he hated himself for the loneliness and isolation that made him prey of such a creature. Only gradually, with his mind in continual torment, did his resentment begin to turn upon himself rather than André. It was his own innocence and ignorance that he hated, and the knowledge that André must think him stupid and weak. And finally the admission that André's friendship – which represented areas of experience and knowledge that he himself did not possess – was something he wanted. Also, as André had foreseen, he had been bitten that first time; now he wanted to know more. But more than anything, it was his loneliness that drove him back to

André. The sudden estrangement from the world that he felt when he was left in the school had not been replaced by any other element. He was alone and unhappy here, too proud to make advances to any other boys, and too rigid to accept the tentative gestures they made in his direction. With André it was different. There was nothing half-hearted about his approach. And, after all, Matthew reasoned, what had André done that was so terrible? It was all his own fault. It was he who was ignorant, unworldly and stupid. By the time that he finally built up sufficient courage to speak to André, he felt he owed him an apology.

Once again, André knew he could afford to wait. Not only was he pleased that he had outwaited Matthew and not pursued him, he was conscious that Matthew belonged to him now, that there was no hurry. He was not interested in stamps. His mother had given him the stamp collection and by pretending great enthusiasm for it he had extracted money from his father, who had a collection of his own of which he was very proud, to buy rare stamps. In addition, he was a shrewd trader and an expert liar. Within a few months, thanks to his father's interest in stamps and his own obsession with trickery and bargaining, he had acquired a great many stamps, had impressed his family with his active interest in them, and had become bored with the whole thing. The album only served as a demonstration of his knowledge and capability to someone like Matthew, who was duly impressed.

When every page had been carefully gone over, André took the stamp album from his friend, put it back on the table and rested his hand on Matthew's shoulder. The gesture was both genuine and generous. He liked Matthew in the way that a solitary man likes his dog. Magnanimously, knowing that he could well afford it, he said: "I guess I owe you an apology for the other night. I'm sorry, old man."

Even though the last words sounded slightly ludicrous when pronounced in André's distinctly French accent, there was something intimate, so all-accepting in the sound of them, that Matthew was greatly flattered and pleased. He blushed, thinking of the way he had behaved with André before. "Not at all," he said. "How would you know that I was so stupid?"

"Hadn't you ever seen anything like that before?" André asked.

Matthew shook his head. He did not want to talk about it, but he was still curious.

André smiled. "I guess I was just lucky. I've been around a lot for my age."

Matthew looked at him dumbly. "I guess you have."

André nodded, but he did not seem to want to continue the discussion of his exploits. "How about a game of cards before you have to go to bed?"

Once again Matthew had to admit his ignorance. "I've never played much," he said, worried.

But André expected this, too. "That doesn't matter. I know lots of games I could teach you."

He walked around the table near Matthew's chair, pulled out the drawer from which he took a pack of cards and began to shuffle them, dividing the pack, flipping them together expertly. Matthew watched him admiringly. It seemed there was nothing he couldn't do well. Of course he wasn't very good in his studies, Matthew had seen his marks posted in the office, but that didn't mean anything. He passed, even if he didn't get very good marks, and anyone could be good in class. André knew other things; things that mattered. Besides, everybody seemed to like him, including the teachers.

With a sigh of regret, André laid the cards on the table between them. "It's almost nine o'clock," he said, "hardly worth starting anything now." He looked at Matthew and there was a big smile on his face. "You know," he said, "I like you. It's too bad we aren't in the same room together."

The idea of sharing a room with someone like André had never occurred to Matthew. Now it presented itself as a wonderful scheme. Not only would he have a friend, he could tell André everything about his own life, André could advise him, answer his questions, and André could tell him so much … he thought of those pictures again. He knew he'd never have the courage to ask him to let him look at them, but if he were living with him it would undoubtedly happen of itself. And there were probably so many other things….

Matthew looked up into André's smiling face. "Gee," he said, "that would be wonderful, wouldn't it?"

André was delighted with his reaction. "Why don't you move in here then?"

Matthew looked at him amazed. "Do you think they'd let me?" He had not believed that it was even remotely possible. Even as he asked the question, he had a sudden warm and intimate glimpse of them living together in the same room: waking up in the mornings, going to bed at night and talking until they went to sleep.

"Why not? We'll see about it in the morning. I wanted somebody in here with me from the start, but I like to pick my own friends, not just anyone."

André did not need to say anything more. Once again Matthew saw himself, reflected in André's eyes, as someone chosen: a good guy, a friend, a friend André had selected for himself. The pride that had held him rigid and alone now fastened itself onto the fact that it was he, Matthew Cameron, who had been chosen as a companion by this boy. Even if André didn't manage to get him into this room, they were friends; he could spend his evenings here with him, they could do things together. His life had suddenly acquired importance and meaning; he could hardly believe in his good fortune.

André did it all. M. de St. Croix was not only not displeased but seemed, on the contrary, quite happy about the projected move. To Matthew, he said simply that he was pleased that he had found a friend in André, and then with a wink suggested that since he was such a good student, he could perhaps set an example for André, who was, after all, a year behind and only just passing. Personally, he was relieved that Matthew, who had seemed so distant and almost unfriendly, had found himself a companion. He was not entirely deluded about André, nor did he feel that he would be the best example for Matthew in everything, but André seemed to him on the whole a good boy. A liar, surely, and lazy in his work perhaps, but not a bad influence and probably a healthy one for someone as introspective as this young American.

Quickly decided and quickly achieved. The very next day, Matthew moved into André's room. André helped him transport his clothes and books, and together they rearranged the room, André insisting that Matthew have the best light and the bed nearest the window. When it was all done and they were contemplating the new arrangement with satisfaction, they exchanged a look of real companionship and affection. Whatever exterior motives, whatever small meannesses, desires or curiosities had brought them together, there was something else of which they were both aware then. Matthew, less mature and closer to the reality of himself than André, was the first to recognize it and to acknowledge what it was that passed between them. André only felt it and did not understand it, but he too, with all his superiority, his conniving and his animal logic, was lonely. The sudden warmth that was created in the room by the arranging of their clothes side by side in the closet, the pairs of shoes under each bed, the sets of books on each table, communicated itself to both of them unmistakably. The room acquired a balance and an air of comfort that it had not had before. If they had been girls, they might have kissed each other. As it was, they looked directly into each other's eyes and were embarrassed. Finally André reached over and punched his friend's arm. *"On est bien, hein?"* It was the first time that he had spoken to Matthew in French and Matthew knew that he would be eternally grateful for the gesture and the words.

For the first few days it was all that Matthew had dreamed it would be. The act of friendship that had taken them unawares had stripped them of their competitive shells, opening them up – in different ways – to their individual selves. Used to the admiration and envy of all boys in all schools, André was not accustomed to the kind of friendship he had from Matthew. In his own way, he felt admiration and affection for this boy who had everything he did not have. He felt that Matthew was honest and direct and not mean. He talked to him in the evenings, not of his experience and his prowess, but slowly and with effort of his parents, of all the different schools he had been in, and finally of his loneliness. With Matthew there beside him, he began to work harder at his studies, accepting Matthew's help easily because he felt safe with him – safe from any ridicule or scorn. Matthew did not seem surprised that André had difficulty with mathematics or history or that he could not remember dates, he was only embarrassed that something that was so hard for André should be so easy for him. He was flattered that he was able to do something for his new friend; it seemed an ideal arrangement in every way.

After several days of this shared happiness, Matthew awakened suddenly early in the morning. He had been dreaming and his mind was still trapped between the dream and the early morning light coming through the window. It took him several minutes to come to himself and to the reality of the room around him. But even as he came slowly to full wakefulness, he felt a subtle alteration in the atmosphere of the room. He turned his head to look at the bed across from him and met André's eyes. They stared at each other searchingly, looking deep into each other's eyes, and it was André who broke the silence by saying huskily: "How do you feel?"

As if visited by some extra perception, Matthew understood dimly what he was saying. The atmosphere in the room, as tangible as a smell, *had* changed. It had changed back in time to that first night he had been here and again he was fascinated and frightened, but this time not repelled or sickened. As he watched his friend, he saw him suddenly throw down the covers to expose his body, lying naked on the bed. André glanced down at his own nakedness and Matthew's eyes followed until he had seen again what he had already seen at once. If André had looked at him or spoken, he would have had to turn his head or close his eyes, shut his ears, but the other boy said nothing; Matthew had only to watch and watch and watch, his own body twisting under the covers at what he saw.

Chapter Five

From the windows of his mother's apartment, Matthew looked at the river and the bridges, the buildings across from him. Everything was softened and blurred by the winter mist and fine rain, and he felt a quiet sadness reaching into him through the joints of the windows, through the glass itself. He was unhappy and ill-at-ease here after his months in school, and he was glad it was a short vacation. He would be back there soon, in a familiar routine, in his own life. When he had left school, he had been glad to get away. Now, after a few days, he did not feel that he belonged in Paris any more.

The little room in the back of the apartment was no longer his. It was a storehouse of his past, containing only things from which he had grown away. Even the clothes he had left there were a little too small for him; he had had a sudden spurt of physical growth along with all the other changes that had taken place inside him. At the school, his association with André, the fact that he carried in his wallet two of the pictures André had given him, had made him feel important and self-confident. Here, they only served to remind him of his secret life, a life that caused him shame and regret when transported to these rooms, this furniture – as if he had brought something disreputable into the apartment.

He watched a string of barges, moving silently along the river, displacing the mists like ghosts pulled along by some unseen force, and he felt that he was, himself, caught by forces greater than he, pushed and pulled by incomprehensible currents. Although he blamed himself, he knew that his relationship with his mother, for instance, had changed. She talked a great deal about the divorce now; the proceedings were well under way, she would probably have her decree in September, perhaps even in August – only seven months away. She had reminded him, more than once already, that his father would be getting married again, that he would have a stepmother.

Preoccupied as she was with her own life, she made a point of asking him if he was enjoying himself. She seemed concerned about what kind of time he was having at school and whether or not he was really happy, but when he talked to her about it, she listened almost indifferently as if she were thinking about something else. Her whole manner of life had changed since he had last been here. She had acquired, as if by magic, a large number of acquaintances and a much more active life. Her time was filled with engagements and people, and whereas in September she had seemed to have no friends other than Scott, she now had too many to fit them all in. With one exception. There was one person for whom his mother always had time: a man named Paul Dumesnil. Paul was there at some time every day. He took Catherine to lunch, to dinner, to the theatre, to parties. Many times Matthew had lain in the dark before going to sleep listening to the sound of their voices – Catherine's and Paul's – in the living room. When Catherine gave one of her little parties (he hated the way she said the words "little party") and Matthew had to be there to be introduced as "my son" and addressed as "my darling" every few minutes, to pass the canapés or light the ladies' cigarettes, he was always aware of Paul's voice and Paul's presence until it seemed as much his party as Catherine's. His mother did not mind at all, in fact she enjoyed it, and she would thank Paul afterwards for his help. He would kiss the old ladies' hands, or whisper compliments to them, and when they had left, he would make sly remarks to Catherine about their hats, or the way they talked.… Whatever he did, Catherine loved it all.

She was secretive about Paul, too. When Matthew had asked who he was, she had said quickly that he was just a very good friend, a terribly nice man and she was sure Matthew would love him. What did he do? He didn't *do* anything, she said. He had an income. In France, it was not like America – men didn't have to be in their offices all the time.

Because of his own feelings of guilt and because he felt that he was not, somehow, worthy of his mother any more, Matthew tried to like Paul. Although instinctively suspicious of him (where had she met him? why were they together so much? how did he come to be such a "good friend"?), he felt that he had no logical reason for his suspicions, and his feelings of shame increased.

He turned from the window at the sound of a step in the outer hall, and his breath came suddenly fast. For no reason, except that he did not want to see anyone, Matthew dropped the curtain and made his way quickly and silently across the living room and down the hall to his own room, leaving the door ajar. He sat on the bed, breathing hard and listening intently. He heard his mother go to the door, heard her voice greeting Paul and then Paul's voice. *How good of you to come, how nice to see you, wasn't yesterday pleasant? isn't it a lovely day? How is Matthew…?*

The voices lowered and became more relaxed. He could no longer hear the words, but he pictured them sitting together in the living room, smiling, nodding, gesturing, smoking and talking. He wondered just what it was about Paul … Paul who was attentive and thoughtful with him. Paul, who had brought him a book as a present the day before, who was careful to include him in his conversations with Catherine when the three of them were together, who made an effort to think up things that Matthew might like to do while he was in Paris. If Matthew had not felt a lack of spontaneity in these gestures, he would have been pleased. As it was, he knew, somehow, that Paul liked him less than he pretended. He guessed that he would be glad to see him go back to school and he felt that he had intruded upon his mother and Paul by coming to Paris.

He looked at his watch with relief. It was almost time for him to meet Scott.

When he had met him at the train, Scott had said: "I wanted to be here to welcome you back," and Matthew felt again the flush of happiness that had come over him in spite of that other feeling that made him feel so inferior. If Scott should find out about André, for instance! In a rush of feeling that wiped away the past months, he was filled with tenderness for Scott. If he could only tell him everything that had happened, everything he had done, and beg his forgiveness. Scott would understand....

Matthew shook his head wearily. However much Scott would understand him, Scott would never have done anything like that; would never have moved into a room with a boy like André – or even wanted to. If only he was like Scott, or as Scott must have been like at his age!

He walked down the hall, put on his coat, and then went into the living room. Catherine and Paul looked up at him as if they were surprised and pleased to see him. After he had shaken hands with Paul and they were settled in their chairs again, he explained that he was going to meet Scott.

"What are you going to do, darling?" his mother asked.

Matthew shrugged his shoulders. "I don't know. Play chess or something."

Catherine looked proudly at Paul. "Did I tell you that Matthew plays chess? He's really very good at it. Aren't you, Matthew?"

He looked away from them both. "Oh, fair," he said.

"Well, you don't want to be late. You'd better run along."

Was she anxious to have him go? Or was it just that she wanted to continue her talk with Paul? He shook Paul's hand again, kissed his mother, and went out the door. When he closed it, he stood silently behind it, listening. They began to talk, almost at once.

"Then you think you will get your decree in September definitely?" That was Paul's voice.

"Yes!" His mother sounded excited. "Perhaps even in August, but that's not likely. Still, it's possible...."

He walked away from the door and down the stairs. What had

changed his mother? Whenever she talked about the divorce now, and she talked about it a great deal, her tone was excited. Before, she used to speak solemnly and almost sadly. Now, she seemed to look forward to it. Divorce, marriage, love…. He shoved his hands into his pockets and hurried down the stairs onto the sidewalk.

☙

Matthew looked at Scott, sitting across from him over the chessboard. He saw a man not quite old enough to be his father, too old to be his brother – a face that was changing from youth into maturity – an expression that was sometimes wide, sometimes enthusiastic; simultaneously soft and solid. He looked away to ponder his next move on the chessboard, and was again reminded that there was no security in his relationship with Scott. Scott and his father had been great friends, their friendship had something to do with his present association with Scott, beyond that…? But why had they been friends and why did Scott spend his time with him now? For his father's sake? Scott was an adult man, and all adults led a mysterious life in which children did not participate. He apparently decided to make room for Matthew in his life, but what held them together? *Why* did Scott like him? Was he sorry for him because his mother and father were separated? What was it?

"Your move, Matthew." Matthew was startled by the sound of Scott's voice. He looked up, his face flushed, and then looked back at the chessboard and made a quick move.

"Are you sure you want to do that?"

Matthew looked back at the board. "I think so, why?"

Scott leaned back in his seat, lighted a cigarette and did not look at the board. "You don't seem very interested today, Matthew. Anything wrong?"

Matthew drew in his breath and let it out slowly. "Nothing special, I guess."

Scott raised his eyebrows and waited. What was wrong? It occurred to him that he and Matthew had never talked very intimately. There was something about Matthew that made you forget he was a boy. Looking at him, he realized with a pang that Matthew had, in a way, forced this forgetfulness on him because of his desire to please and retain his interest. He remembered having thought this before – that it was unnatural for a boy Matthew's age to be interested in the interminable masterpieces of the Louvre, in learning to play chess, in visiting public buildings and palaces. Now the look on his face made Scott feel that Matthew had never been interested in those things at all; that he had feigned an interest because he felt it was expected of him, to pay for the attention he received. What stared at him from Matthew's eyes was loneliness.

"Maybe it's not special, Matthew, but it's something, isn't it? Anything you want to talk about?"

Matthew looked away from him. "You wouldn't be interested."

"Oh, I might," Scott said carefully. "Does it have anything to do with your mother, for instance?" He wondered how Catherine's divorce was getting along. There might be some connection....

"Are you going to get married, Scott?"

He was taken unawares by the unexpected, personal question. Where had that idea come from? He shook his head slowly. "I suppose I will someday," he said, "but I'm not planning to now. Why? Did something make you think I was?"

Matthew shook his head. "No. But if you did, I suppose I wouldn't see you any more, would I?"

"Of course you would! I'll always be a friend of yours, Matthew, you know that. What makes you think such nonsense?"

Matthew stared at him silently. He did not know why he had asked the question. "I guess it's the divorce," he said. "I don't understand why people get divorced. I mean, what makes them get divorced?"

"That's a hard question, Matthew. I don't know that anyone

knows the real answer. Marriage isn't always easy, you know. I suppose people get tired of each other, or they like someone else better. I don't know."

"Don't you think that if people have children they ought to stay together?"

Matthew stopped and his voice hung on the air, then he went on quickly. "I suppose I shouldn't say that, since my dad and mother are getting a divorce, but…" he looked up to Scott as if expecting him to finish the sentence.

"It's a perfectly good question, Matthew. You'd probably have to ask it sometime. The only trouble is that I don't know how to answer it. I know it doesn't mean that your parents don't love you, though."

Matthew looked away again, fingering one of the chessmen. "I suppose not," he said. "I shouldn't have said it."

"That's where you're wrong," Scott said quickly. "If you thought it, you should certainly ask it. Tell me, did you ask your mother that?"

Matthew's voice was weary. "No, I couldn't. She'd think I blamed her, or that I didn't love her."

"Do you blame her, Matthew?" Scott reached across the table to him, touching his sleeve. "You have to be honest with yourself about it. Even if your mother wouldn't like it, you have to know how you really feel."

Matthew smiled. "I guess I do," he said, "but how can you blame somebody you love? I can't help how I feel, so I guess they couldn't help how they felt when they decided to get a divorce, could they?"

"No, I suppose not."

Then, as if he had won an unexpected point in the chess game, or made a brilliant move without foreseeing it, Matthew said: "If they can't help how they feel, how can anybody get married? How can anybody pretend that they can love somebody all their life?"

"Nobody does, Matthew. Not really. At least I think not. Marriage isn't just a question of love, it's a lot more than that. It's a kind of mutual responsibility that people take on. Of course they can't always guarantee...."

Matthew laughed. "Responsibility?" he echoed. "It's not really responsibility if you can get out of it, is it?"

Scott tightened his hand on Matthew's arm. "It isn't so simple, Matthew. You can't blame people that way. Nobody is perfect, nobody is absolutely reliable. If your mother and father found out they were wrong about each other, that they couldn't go on with their marriage, you can't just blame them and dismiss it at that. You said yourself that you can't help how you feel about things."

"I know." The loneliness was in his face again. "Scott," he asked, "how can you be sure of *anything* then?"

"If you're sure of yourself."

"But how can you be?"

"I don't know how *you* can be, Matthew, but I know how I can be sure."

"How?"

"Because I believe what I feel, because I trust myself. For instance, you asked me if I'd stop seeing you if I got married. I know I won't. I know how I feel about you. I know that nothing – not marriage or anything else – will change that. It's true because I believe it, that's all. Because I never question it."

"Maybe you will someday."

Scott shook his head. "No, Matthew, I won't."

"Yes, but how can you say you *know*?"

It was Scott's turn to hesitate, to search for something to eradicate the doubt in Matthew. "How do you know the sun is going to come up tomorrow?

Matthew smiled, twisting his lips, and pushed the chessman away from his side of the board. "That's just it," he said. "I don't *know* it will."

Chapter Six

"I have to get up," Scott said, having waited, watching her, for almost ten minutes before he said it. In spite of the warmth of the air from the open window, there was already a feeling of fall in the atmosphere. It was the beginning of the end of a wonderful summer; wonderful, he decided soberly, because of Françoise. It was extraordinary to have made the inner shift from a courteous, manufactured reluctance to this: he simply did not want to leave her now.

It was not especially astonishing that a man should not wish to leave the bed of his mistress, except that it was, for Scott, new. He had experienced reluctance at other times and with other women, American women, but it had always been overruled and cancelled by whatever obligation lay ahead of him. As he watched her now, he would have liked to tell her this, to tell her that because of her and for no other reason, he did not want to go; to tell her that the thing she called his "American conscience" was defeated. He did not because he was absorbed in a question that had never sprung to his mind before, a question as to the nature of love, the special chemistry – or was it not just a matter of chemistry alone? – that made him desire this particular woman. He was startled to find that he not only wanted her, loved her, but that he liked her – liked being in love with her.

Why this woman, of all women? Her hair looked as if it had been dyed, she wore to much make-up and the morning traces of it on her face were not very attractive; her fingernails were too long, her nose was not quite straight, her body, compared to the American girls Scott had known, seemed almost misshapen: she was long-waisted, her legs were not only not good, they were almost bad – there was something wrong with their length, actually. Not that her physical looks had anything to do with their affair, but surely they counted for something....

She smiled up at him, leaning above her on his elbow: *"Commes tu es grave ce matin,"* she said.

He was surprised at the sound of her voice. "I'd better get up," he said, and then, boldly, he kissed her. "I love you," he added, embarrassed.

The smile was still fixed on her face. "I know," she said in English, and then, turning her head from him: "You will always have something to do."

"Everyone has something to do, darling; even you have things to do. You can't spend your life in bed."

She shook her head. *"Tu ne comprends pas,"* she said, "what I have to do can always wait. With you it's different, not only do you have something to do, but you do it. It is always something that cannot be put off, cannot be postponed, cannot wait. What is it today? Today is Sunday."

He leaned over and kissed her again, on the forehead this time. "I promised to call Matthew."

She looked at him in silence. "Such a pure kiss," she said slowly, and took his head in her hands. "When you go away," she said, "you kiss me like this…" and when she had released him, she added: "until you met me you knew nothing about love, nothing."

He laughed. "You speak very good English. Except for your accent. Without your accent, you could be an American."

She pushed him towards the side of the bed. "Get up," she said. "Get up and stand there for a minute to let me look at you."

He did not move. "Why?"

She smiled at him. "Because when you stand before me you are still embarrassed like a boy. You think I want to see your body, you think French women like to look at men's bodies, but it is at your eyes that I like to look. You look so innocent."

He got out of the bed and stood before her. What she said was true and he could feel it. Feel the shyness creeping into his face as the hairs on his arms stood on end in the fresh breeze from the window. "Everyone passing on the street can see me from here," he said and turned away from her.

She laughed at him. "So you turn around? But they can still see you, darling, only not all of you." Then she waved her hand at him. "Go ahead. I can tell from your back that you are thinking about Matthew and not me. Are you afraid that he will be angry at you if you don't call him?"

"Angry with you," he said, "not at you."

She made a face at him. "Mad at you," she said.

"Yes," he said seriously, "that's all right."

"Well, will he be? Does it matter?"

He sat on the edge of the bed. "You don't understand. It isn't that. It's just that I'm worried. I feel a responsibility...."

She looked at him seriously. "I know. I know. You always say that. But why? Is he your brother, your son? Why are you responsible for him? You are a friend, you want to help him, but you are not responsible. It makes you sound guilty."

He shook his head at her. "Maybe it does. But it's partly for John's sake. I owe a lot to John and I know he wants me to see Matthew as much as I can."

Françoise looked out of the window, withdrawing herself. "What about his mother? It is her place to worry about him, not yours. That is a responsibility." She waited for him to say something and when he remained silent, she added: "Well, telephone him."

He stood up and looked at the floor. "I will. I'll be right back."

She listened to his voice on the telephone from the next room. He had closed the door and she could not hear the words he was saying, only the sound. She felt a mild resentment towards Matthew and Catherine; Scott had been thinking about them ever since he had awakened. He had brought them to bed with him the night before. The voice stopped, the door opened and Scott came quickly across the room and slid into the bed beside her. His body was cold. "I guess he's all right," he said.

She put her arms around him, holding herself close to him, warming him. "Do you have to see him?" she asked.

"No," he said. "Not today. Catherine wants to keep him at home, she's ... it's just as I thought...." he turned to face her. "I'm not so sure everything is going to be all right. Her divorce will be final any day now and she's going to marry Paul Dumesnil – at least he's asked her to marry him, and she wants to tell Matthew today."

"*Marry* him?"

"That's what she said. Besides, what do you mean '*marry* him?' What do you expect her to do?"

"Well ... why does she have to marry him? She could take him as a lover ... but...."

Scott looked shocked. "Catherine would never take a lover!"

"Why not?"

"She wouldn't, that's all. What if Matthew found out?"

"Why should be? He's always in school, isn't he?"

"Yes, but anyway she wouldn't take a lover. She's not that kind of woman."

Françoise laughed. "Oh? Only special kinds of women have lovers? Like me?"

He smiled at her. "Oh, you know what I mean. You know Catherine."

"Yes. And I hope she does marry him."

"I wish I agreed with you. I'm not so sure about Paul."

"What do you mean? Don't you like him?"

He frowned at her. "I mean I don't know. Catherine seems to like him well enough, certainly. The only part of it that concerns me is whether Matthew is going to like him. I hope he does, I think he needs a man. Catherine babies him too much."

She raised her eyebrows. "Paul is making a good marriage," she said. "He is marrying a fortune."

Then he laughed. "You're the one who doesn't like Paul, aren't you?"

"Like him? I know his type. He's a smart French country boy who came to Paris to get married to a woman with money. Now he does it. It's simple. And tell me, Scott, does she really have a lot of money?"

"Yes," he said, "a lot. Her family is very rich."

"You see," she said, "Paul is smart. Very rich even. Not just a little rich. Darling, tell me something."

"Yes, what?"

"Why do you like Matthew so much?"

"Don't you like him?"

She nodded her head into his back. "Yes, but I asked you why you like him so much."

"I guess I feel sorry for him." He turned around in the bed to face her. "The divorce and everything. It isn't easy for him. And now this."

"It is never easy to be a child," she said. "And then he loves you, doesn't he?"

"I suppose so. I keep wondering what goes on in his head, what it feels like to be alone now. I wonder if Catherine should have sent him away to school."

"Scott, tell me: why doesn't his father come to see him?"

Scott made a wry face. "Catherine got custody in the separation agreement."

"You mean he can never see his father?"

"No. He can decide for himself later on. When he's sixteen, I think."

"But maybe he wants to see him now...."

"You don't understand much about the law, do you?"

She shook her head. "The law! If he wants to see him, what of the law? He's his father. Why did he let him go to the law?"

"He had no choice. Catherine could have gotten complete custody if he'd tried to fight her. She could have sued John for adultery in New York."

"Was he living with another woman?"

Scott nodded.

"The law!" she exclaimed again. "And this custody business! If your Madame is a good mother she will let him see his father when he wants. What has the law got to do with it?"

He shrugged his shoulders. "Actually, she's been very generous. She didn't demand complete custody. Only until he's finished high school."

"Generous! How can you be generous with your own son?"

"It's all beyond me, darling. Anyway, Catherine thinks she is being generous. What if Matthew should decide to go back to his father when he's through school?"

"What if he does?"

"Don't you think children should be with their mothers?"

"Don't you think children should grow up, too?" She moved her head towards him and kissed his cheek. "Your kind of kiss," she said. "Also, I don't think children should necessarily be with their mothers. She will be better off married to Paul, then you can stop being Matthew's stepfather."

He laughed at her. "I think you're jealous of Matthew."

"Only a little," she said. "I can do some things that Matthew cannot. I can make you forget Matthew."

He drew her head down to his and kissed her. "I could forget him right now," he said.

"Yes?"

He nodded and kissed her again.

Chapter Seven

Tears, at fourteen, are not what they were at nine or ten; not even what they were last year. Then, while they might have come furiously, painful and choking, there was a simple reason for them: physical pain, violence, anger, injustice. When they ended and the face was washed, they were forgotten and filed away with other common experiences, relegated to the past.

Tears at fourteen are incomprehensible and baffling; if you are a boy they are also shameful. You do not cry at fourteen if you cut your finger, or if your mother is angry with you, or if you are struck unexpectedly. At these things you bite your lip, feel the tears coming, and hold them back, returning anger for anger, violence for violence, injustice for injustice, but you do not cry. When you do, you cry because you have been attacked out of all proportion to any justice. The attack is more than unjust, it is monstrous and enormous in its weight, because you do not know how heavy it is, and yet you cannot support the weight you feel. It is always, in some sense, you yourself who have caused them.

Matthew had waited all day for some word from Scott. He had said he would see him today, but he hadn't even telephoned. Angry, confused and uncertain about his mother and Paul, Matthew had stayed in his room most of the morning, and had only seen his mother for long enough to suggest that he might telephone to Scott. "He told me he was going to call today," he had said and Catherine had looked at him, frowning as if she were making a decision. "You'd better wait, darling. You must consider Scott, you know. I'm sure he'll call you when he can."

So he hadn't called him then, not after what she had said, and he couldn't call him now. Too many hours had passed, too many tears … the day was over. At no time, in words, had Matthew expressed to Scott what he meant to him, how he really felt about him, how important his presence had come to be, and yet he knew that Scott knew all of this, he had seen it in his face. He had known it from the way Scott would answer a question that he had not asked aloud, or suggest something that Matthew would have been afraid to suggest himself. Yet with all that knowledge and understanding, he had let this happen, he had not stopped it….

Desperately, as he had already done again and again that day, he went over last night's telephone conversation. *I will see you tomorrow for sure.* The sentence burned itself into his brain. Scott knew this would be his last Sunday in Paris all summer. He had known it for months; he had even written to him when he had known Matthew was going to spend the summer at Le Touquet and would not be in Paris until just before school. *Too bad about the summer, but we'll certainly have some time together before you go back to school.* Matthew had memorized those words, too. He had a flash of hatred against his mother then, it was she who had kept him away from Paris all summer, brushing aside his suggestion that Scott might come to see them for a weekend. Paul came often enough, but not Scott. It was as if she didn't want him to see Scott any more.

He pictured his mother and Paul in the living room now, talking and talking, probing into each other with little exclamations of delight, and between them sat the telephone, black and silent. Wasn't there some mistake? Had Scott misunderstood him? Did he expect him to call? He shook his head dumbly. He could not telephone with them in there, and there was no mistake. Scott knew. The tears, which had almost stopped, filled his eyes again and he cried silently, his head buried in the pillow to drown out the sound of his sobbing.

Finally it ceased of itself, and only the stains on his face and the occasional sniffle, the look of pain, remained to give him away. He sat up on his bed and listened to the murmur of their voices. He would have hated discovery at this moment, but more than that he hated the complete disregard. He had been here for hours and no one had come to the door, no one had called to him, no one had mentioned his name. He could as well have disappeared for all it mattered to them.

Whatever the reasons, wherever the blame, Matthew knew with the knowledge that is uneasily visited upon all adolescents, that his friendship with Scott was essentially over; and yet he also knew that it would go on and on, dishonestly and awkwardly, for a long time yet. He knew that the next time he saw him he would have to stifle the reproaches, the anger he would feel; that he would continue, helplessly trapped in his own feelings, in the same dumb love and admiration for him, waiting to receive the blows that he could foresee and fear. There was nothing he could do about it. Nothing except hope that somehow his heart would close up and make him immune and invulnerable. For it was not Scott who had attacked him so much, not nearly so much, as what he felt himself; and in what way could he punish himself for that? For loving in a place where he had no right to love?

The sound of voices in the living room ceased, and he stood up. He took his handkerchief from his pocket and licked a corner of it, then wiped it over his face. He combed his hair and blew his nose and looked at himself in the mirror. His eyes were still red and the lids were swollen. If only they would give him a few minutes! There was no cold water in here, and he would not risk going to the bathroom and reminding them of his presence.

Mercilessness has a way of persisting, and they gave him no time. His hair was barely straight before he heard quick footsteps and his mother had opened the door and was smiling at him. Her face was flushed. "What on earth have you been doing, darling?" she cried out to him. "You've been gone for hours! Paul's here and I have something wonderful to tell you!"

It was only after she had spoken that she looked at his face. She took a step toward him and took his hand in hers. When she spoke again her voice had softened. "Come into the living room, Matthew. Perhaps you'd like to celebrate and have an *apéritif* with us. And then we'll tell you the news."

He followed her into the living room, and there was Paul, seated by the window as if he had lived there all his life. He did not – and Matthew was particularly aware of this – he did not even get up, at least not until it was too late to be anything but an afterthought, an awkward gesture. He got up to pour himself and Catherine a drink from the bottle of Cinzano which stood on the little table between two chairs. "Pour one for Matthew, too," Catherine said, handing him another glass.

Matthew looked at his mother, lifting the glass in his hand.

"What are we celebrating?"

Catherine hesitated, glanced at Paul, and then back to Matthew. "Have your drink first, darling."

He looked at her stiffly and tasted his drink. As she watched him, the happiness inside her seemed to flatten and dissipate itself. What was the matter with him? He was really impossible the way he would not enter into things. She brightened her smile and looked at him imploringly: "How did you like your first *apéritif*, darling?"

Matthew was unable to resist the temptation to deflate this moment for both Catherine and Paul. He picked up the little glass, drank the rest of its contents, and then turned it around in his hand. "It's not my first," he said.

Her smile disappeared and she smoothed her dress absently before she spoke again. "Oh," she said, "Scott, I suppose. Was it Scott who bought you your first *apéritif*, Matthew?" She exchanged another glance with Paul.

Matthew nodded, pleased with himself. "Yes," he said, and then: "Well, I've had it, what did you want to tell me?"

She turned in her chair, looking away from both of them.

"Perhaps I shouldn't tell you now, Matthew. It doesn't matter. It can wait."

Her voice was sad and disappointed, and Matthew's triumph faded quickly. He was sorry for his attitude, for telling them about the drink. "I'm sorry, mother," he said quickly, embarrassed because of Paul's presence. "Please tell me what it is."

Catherine turned slowly to look at Paul and it was as if some sign had passed between them. He got to his feet immediately: "If you'll excuse me for a minute, please?" and he walked between them and down the hall.

When Paul was out of the room, Matthew walked quickly to his mother's side and took her hand in his. "I'm sorry, mother, really. Please tell me."

She faced him, a melancholy smile on her face. "That's all right, darling. I know you didn't mean it."

He knelt on the floor beside her. He felt closer to her in that moment than he had felt all summer. With her hand in his, she looked at him quietly and then said: "Will you tell me something honestly, Matthew?"

"Yes." He nodded quickly, trying to reassure her.

"Do you like Paul?"

Because of his guiltiness about what he had done, and his desire to retract, to make her feel all right again, he said: "Sure. Of course I do."

She looked at him for a long time before she said anything. "I hope you mean that, darling. Do you?"

He could only nod vigorously again. "You know I do, mother. Why?"

"Because..." she paused and started again. "My divorce will probably be final this month, Matthew."

"Yes?"

She looked away from him again. "Well," her hand tightened on his, "Paul has asked me to marry him."

Matthew's body went suddenly rigid and cold. He felt the tight grasp of her hand, and his position, kneeling on the floor next to her, seemed ridiculous and awkward. "When?" he asked.

She turned her face back to him. "As soon as the divorce decree is granted."

His face did not tell her anything. "What did you tell him, mother?"

"I haven't said anything yet, Matthew. I wanted to talk to you first."

With a sudden flash of intuition, Matthew knew that this was not true. He remembered the way she had looked when she had come to his room, the "wonderful" news she was going to tell him. He knew that it had been decided already, and that it was only the way he had behaved when he had come into the living room that had made her change so that she had become suddenly unhappy. He knew also that he was the only obstacle, the only problem. He forced himself to smile at her – a smile that had to be genuine. "Tell him yes, mother," he said, and then he stood up.

Paul was standing in the entrance to the living room, neither of them had heard him come back down the hall, and as Matthew rose from the floor, they looked into each other's eyes. It was the strangest, deepest look that Matthew had ever exchanged with anyone in his life. He felt that he and Paul understood everything about each other forever. With one accord, they advanced in each other's directions a few steps and automatically shook hands. It was not congratulatory nor thankful nor happy, but it was a declaration of peace. Matthew did not hate nor fear Paul at that moment, he accepted him inevitably, not knowing why, and he felt almost nothing.

Chapter Eight

Matthew lay back in the tub and pushed the rubber sponge away from him. He looked up at the ceiling and sighed. He hoped that Paul was waiting to come in; let him wait. The apartment wasn't really big enough for the three of them anyway. What were they going to do after they got married and he was here all the time? He grabbed the sponge and gave it another push – as if Paul wasn't already here almost all the time! And then that announcement last night. "Tell him yes, mother." What else could he say? Tell him no? They'd been planning it for months, all the time that he had been away at school and then all during the summer. Did Scott know? He had a sudden pang at the thought of Scott, but now he was suspicious about that. Scott would certainly have come to see him or he would have called, there *must* be something he didn't know....

He pulled himself up in the tub when he heard the knock on the door.

"Yes?"

"May I come in, please?" It was Paul.

Matthew got out of the tub, dripping water, walked to the door and turned the lock. The door opened and Paul came in. "You don't mind, do you Matthew?" He gave him a searching look as Matthew let himself down into the water again.

"No." It really was as if they were already married!

Paul laughed. "I'm sorry if I disturbed you, but you know how it is."

Matthew looked at him. The blue suit, the tiny flower in the buttonhole, the striped shirt, gold cufflinks, dark-blue tie; the trousers were a little too short and showed blue stockings, and the black shoes were too pointed for Matthew's taste. Then looking up again, the white handkerchief in the breast pocket of the coat, the slightly overpadded shoulders, the smooth-shaven face, faintly blue; the full underlip and small nose and the naked space between the nose and lips. Paul looked as if he had had or should have a moustache. Above his nose, the sharp, dark eyes, the heavy eyebrows, and then the black hair, shining and perfectly combed.

Paul had unbuttoned his coat and was standing over the toilet. He might have at least used Catherine's toilet with Matthew taking a bath ... but no, Catherine couldn't have anyone using her bathroom, no one *ever* used it except Catherine herself. Matthew saw and then heard the stream into the toilet and he turned away. He always aimed for the side so that you couldn't hear him. Paul didn't seem to care who heard him. He sighed and came to stand next to the tub, buttoning his fly, looking frankly at Matthew, examining him slowly over the roar of the flushing toilet. "You're getting to be quite big," he said. "Almost a man already." His English was as good as his suit.

Matthew felt his face getting warm. "I'll be fifteen next year," he said, still not looking directly at Paul's face, wishing that he would stop staring and go away.

"Quite a big boy," Paul continued, and then he laughed – it wasn't really laughter, although it had some of the sound – and his teeth showed, not very white. "You'll be very popular with the girls," he went on. "Handsome, too."

Matthew looked into his face. "I don't like girls much," he said sullenly.

"Don't worry," Paul said, "you will." Then he turned from Matthew and walked out the door, closing it behind him. Matthew noted contemptuously that he hadn't even rinsed his hands. If his mother knew that! She was very particular about that kind of thing.

When Paul had left, Matthew stood up in the bathtub and looked at himself in the mirror. He had changed a lot since he had come to France. Paul was right, he was growing up. It was almost as if his arrival here had acted upon his glands, particularly in the last few months; he felt as if he had grown several inches. And that wasn't all. Hair had appeared mysteriously on his body, like a miracle. One day his skin had been smooth and hairless, and then the very next day a tiny dark hair had appeared, sprouting from under his skin. He felt his face and leaned over to peer at it in the mirror; nothing there yet, but as André had told him, that was always the last place hair grew.

He looked at his body again, fingering the three hairs on his chest and looking in the mirror at the little growths like shadows under his arms and on his groin. Not only had he grown, he had learned things since he had been here – almost all of them from André. André was different from any boy Matthew had ever known. He talked about anything openly and easily; he was almost grown up. Conversations that Matthew had heard whispered in the school lavatories at home were things that André laughed about; even the other boys at school didn't seem to be embarrassed by them; even he, himself, was not so embarrassed any more. Except with someone like Paul. Paul was like the boys at school in that way, but it was different because they were boys and he was a man. He looked as if he knew something more than any of the boys had learned yet. And he had a way of looking through you at times … a look that was very like a certain look in André's face, a look that meant all that André said and a great deal more.

Matthew looked at the door and got out of the tub, pulled the plug, and then stepped to the door and turned the lock. Paul could stay out this time. He looked at himself again, wondering what it would be like to be a woman. Of course, he knew all about the differences between men and women and why they were built the way they were, in fact he knew quite a lot about sex. He knew, for instance, that there was a lot more to it than just having babies.

Still watching his reflection he remembered as he very often remembered these days, the first time André had given him a demonstration. How he had watched him, excited, breathless and frightened, torn between his desire to watch and a formless, violent need to experiment for himself. He could not, particularly at André's urging, bring himself to any experimentation then and there, and André had laughed at him and then later questioned him unceasingly until he had learned that Matthew, too, was one of the initiated, as he called them.

The first time it had been terrifying, and what was worse, painful. But even with the pain there had been some compulsion that had forced him on and on. Gradually the pain had disappeared – the physical pain, at any rate. But it had been replaced by something else, something that formed inside him, between his ribs, and hurt almost as much. It was always afterwards that he felt it, hating himself, making promises and vows for the future. But then the next time, he would be beaten again, trapped by himself, unable to resist. That was one thing he had never mentioned to anyone, not even to André, although their conversation was otherwise detailed, leaving nothing to the imagination.

He was startled by his mother's voice at the door. It was a good thing he had thought to lock it again!

"Hurry up, darling," she said. "You're keeping us waiting!"

"I'll be right out," he answered quickly and seized the towel from the rack behind the door. He dried himself and then tore into his clothes. His haste was not because he had delayed them, but because he had been caught – almost – and his rush to dress himself seemed to make up for his sense of shame. When he had dressed, he combed his hair very quickly, took one look at his face in the mirror, and unbolted the door.

As he walked into the living room, Catherine looked up: "Well, there you are at last! We're going to the Fontainebleau for lunch."

Matthew hesitated awkwardly. "I'm going to call Scott," he said after a moment. "There must have been some mistake yesterday."

"But he's at his office, dear!"

Matthew looked at her coldly. "He has a telephone in his office.

I've called him there before."

Catherine's smile was stiff when she spoke again. "But we're all ready to go, darling!"

"It will only take a minute."

Catherine exchanged a look with Paul, and then said slowly: "We think there is something you should think about, Matthew. Don't we, Paul?"

Paul inclined his head slowly in agreement.

"What?"

"Well," she smiled more broadly and reached out her hand towards him, forcing him to take it. "We think that you should consider Scott more than you do. After all, he can't spend all his free time with you. He has things he wants to do, and then there's Françoise to consider … and, well, now that Paul is practically a member of the family, you and Paul should begin to do things together. Paul is a wonderful tennis player, for instance. Aren't you, Paul?"

Paul lifted his shoulders and spread his hands. "Not wonderful, no."

"Well, awfully good. I know," Catherine said emphatically.

Matthew looked at her. "You mean I'm not supposed to play tennis with Scott any more because Paul can play tennis?"

"Matthew!" Catherine exclaimed. "I didn't say any such thing. Of course you can play tennis with Scott, or whatever you want to do, but just not so often. It isn't fair to Scott, as I said, and…" she paused and Matthew looked at Paul, then heard his mother's voice again: "You shouldn't talk that way to Paul, Matthew."

Paul spoke up quickly, making a self-deprecating gesture with his hand. "That doesn't matter," he said amiably. "But your mother is right. We could play tomorrow afternoon if you like."

Matthew smiled at him briefly. "Fine." Then he eyed the telephone. "I'd still like to know what happened to Scott," he said. He started for the phone and his mother stood up. "I talked to Scott yesterday, Matthew."

"You what?"

"I talked to Scott. I told him that you'd be going to dinner with us. Besides, I happen to know that Scott was planning to go to the country with Françoise yesterday."

He looked at his mother incredulously. "He didn't say anything about that when I talked to him."

Catherine smiled at Paul and then looked at Matthew again.

"Did he ask you, Matthew, or did you ask him?"

"I asked him. Why?"

"Well, Matthew, that's exactly what I mean. You didn't ask him if he had any plans of his own, did you?"

"No, but...."

Catherine moved towards the door and Paul stood up, too. "I'm sorry, Matthew, if you're disappointed," she said in a level, serious voice, "but you must be more considerate of Scott in the future. Since I knew that Scott often spends his Sundays in the country with Françoise, I felt it was up to me to...."

Matthew did not even hear the end of her sentence. She hadn't even asked him! He bit his lip furiously, holding back the tears that were threatening to begin all over again. What about Scott! Didn't Scott care? Why hadn't Scott asked to talk to him? Why hadn't she at least let him call?

"What did Scott say?"

"He said that was fine and that he hoped he'd see you soon."

"Didn't he ask to talk to me?"

Catherine took his hand again and squeezed it firmly. "Why, darling? I arranged it all."

Matthew looked at her angrily and pulled his hand away. "Well, I wish you hadn't!"

"Matthew!"

Chapter Nine

Scott ran down the steps, stopped on the sidewalk and turned to face the open doorway through which he had just come. He opened his camera, sighted through it briefly, and then looked up. They were coming out. He held up his hand to them and Catherine and Paul Dumesnil stopped at the head of the steps leading out of the Mairie, while the small procession behind them came to an obedient halt. Paul's mother, dressed in black, looking severely at the ground, stood between and behind them. Her air and her costume seemed intended for a funeral rather than a wedding, and the same was true of the other people – all, except Matthew, Paul's relatives – they exuded a kind of predetermined gloom behind the smiles that occasionally flickered over their faces.

Catherine looked well. Well-dressed, handsome, poised, decently happy, and just a little older than Paul. She was not older than Paul and she had worried about his appearance. As she had once said to Scott: "The only thing wrong with Paul is that he *looks* so young. We're exactly the same age, you know." Then she had smiled and added: "Did you know that we were born under the same sign, Scott?"

When he had taken three or four pictures, he released the group with a gesture, closed the camera, and waited for them. All through the ceremony, he had been unable to forget Catherine's first marriage in New York. It was only the second time he had ever seen her. He wondered if Matthew, at fourteen, felt as he had at sixteen, when John and Catherine had been married. It was as if someone had come along and taken John away from him. John who had lived next door to the Fletchers ever since Scott was old enough to remember; John who had taken him camping in the summer; John who had taught him practically everything he knew; John who had been the older brother that Scott had never had; John who had betrayed him by marrying this interloping, cool woman. How he had hated her when she had kissed him lightly and purred: "Scott. How nice to see Scott again." Even as he had looked furiously at her, she had lowered her voice: "We'll be great friends, you and I," she had said.

To his surprise, they had almost become great friends. By the time he was in college, it had seemed only natural that he would visit them, spend the night with them in New York. After Matthew was born, and John was in the Army, Scott had slipped naturally into the role of uncle or brother or something like that to Matthew. Curious how the pattern had insisted upon repeating itself. He had done all the same things with Matthew that John had done with him, particularly since Catherine had come to Paris. It occurred to him that it was his turn to have a baby now, a boy to be Matthew's nephew. Maybe that was what Matthew was going to need. Like a counter-theme to his memories of the past, the thought of Matthew, baffling and difficult, kept beating its way into his consciousness. Something had happened to him; he had changed: he was silent and taciturn, rude and unfriendly, and, above all, lonely. He would have to talk to him, and he was glad that Matthew would be spending the night at his apartment after Catherine and Paul left. He could talk to him then, or perhaps when he drove him back to school the next day.

He looked at the group, dismissing Matthew from his mind for the moment, going back again to that first wedding. It had been nothing like this. It had been one of those big affairs, and John had given him a glass of champagne at the reception and told him secretly that nothing had really changed between them – that Catherine wouldn't make any difference.

His own position now was a curious one. He was the only person, the one friend, that they still shared. Because of that fact, he felt a little less friendly with both of them. Of course, when Catherine had come to Paris she had assumed that he was her friend. Not to the extent of criticizing John, at least not any more than by veiled references to "that woman" or to "poor Matthew," but in the way that she took him for granted. Yet what had really happened was that he had become primarily Matthew's friend, as if he had been allotted to Matthew by vote, though even that had not worked out very well – at least not recently.

Why had John and Catherine really divorced? Were they just bored with each other? What is the impulse that makes people divorce after fifteen years of marriage? He could not believe that John had fallen irresistibly in love after all this time. He believed rather that it was some mutual lack, something that did not really burn between them. Their marriage had never seemed to him complete, or absolutely essential. But, until he had first heard about the divorce, it had been a marriage, and it was less their separation than the idea of divorce that shocked him. Fifteen years was a long time to be married. How much had they thought about divorce before they actually decided upon it? Had they always thought of it as a possibility? Did they really want to begin all over again at that point? Whatever it was, they had begun all over again. Now they were both married, and now Matthew had four parents instead of two.

He looked at Matthew, standing motionless on the fringe of the group, remembering the few times that Matthew had spoken of the divorce to him, seeing in his eyes what he had expected to see there: the knowledge that four is a great deal less than two under some circumstances. The totality of Matthew's feeling about this, the questions, fears, resentments, the sum of his feelings for his parents and step-parents, Scott did not pretend to know. Matthew might have good reason to be withdrawn and hostile; the divorce, the remarriages were reason enough. His feeling of responsibility – a feeling that had wavered inside him ever since Matthew had come to France

– possessed him again. He felt that he had failed Matthew in some way, though perhaps it was not he, but just his father's marriage, and now this…. Whatever it was, Matthew's position was that of one more piece of common property to be disposed of, part of the spoils of the battle.

Scott's worry stayed with him through the reception, where he sat in a corner of the room with Françoise. It was going on too long, there had been too much food, too much champagne, people were staying too long. The few times he had spoken to Catherine or exchanged a look with her, he had felt uneasy. He was not openly enthusiastic about this marriage, and she knew it. He was worried about Matthew and he could not bring himself to like Paul. As if he had, by feeling as he did and not being able to hide it, committed some inexcusable error of taste, Catherine criticized him silently, not forgiving him, he knew. Perhaps that was the clue to Catherine. Things had to be *so*; more than that: things *were* a certain way in Catherine's mind; she did not accept variations easily. His inability to carry out successfully the role which she had, in her mind, assigned to him – the role of her best friend – was not something for which she could forgive him. It was as if he had been late, or had not come at all, or had failed to give her the proper present. More than ever, at this moment, he was conscious of a rigidity in Catherine, and it occurred to him that it was that particular quality which had been the fundamental difference between herself and John. He thought back to that earlier reception, and even then he had sensed that something was missing between them. Something that didn't give somewhere; even then he had felt that, whatever it was, it had come from Catherine and not from John. He could still hear her voice saying: "But John, darling, you said…" "You promised…" "We told the Wilsons…" "What do you mean *why* do we have to…" "But mother *expects* us!" And the way she had felt about children, too. John had told him that once: John, looking at Matthew, aged six, shaking his head and smiling. Catherine had said, he told Scott, that they had to wait a decent interval before their first child. The interval had turned out to be over two years. And why only one child?

Scott looked at them, Paul and Catherine. This was better. It was a more likely combination than John and Catherine had been. Here neither of them gave anything completely, you could feel it. He could imagine them, never protesting, firmly agreeing. In fact he had heard them already: "Paul thinks we should," and then her head would turn to Paul and she would say, "Don't you, darling?" Or Paul: "Catherine and I feel that so and so is best, *n'est-ce-pas, chérie?*" Even before they had decided to be married, it was as if they had signed an agreement to agree under all circumstances, at the expense of feeling if necessary. When they had decided not to be married in a church, it was agreed that it was the right thing. After all, she had been married before. Besides, Paul was not a practicing Catholic, so what did it matter?

They were better for each other physically, Scott decided. Except for the slight look of age difference (and that really did not exist, so it was of no importance) they looked alike, they had exteriors that were noticeable in the sense that they differed from their interiors. Not so with John. John was what he was, whatever that happened to be. John became his circumstances so that when he was in a canoe he looked as if he had always been in a canoe. Catherine and Paul would always look as they did now. If they ever got into a canoe it would look like an unimportant error in judgment. They did not adapt with their bodies, but they agreed to adapt to everything. As Paul had agreed, apparently, to adapt himself to the circumstance of Matthew. It was impossible to associate him with Matthew, to imagine that they would ever have selected each other as friends, let alone stepson and stepfather. Still, there was no war between them; Matthew had agreed to accept Paul, too. Perhaps it was the best that could be expected under such conditions. If only it was not going to mean a still deeper withdrawal on Matthew's part.

❧

Françoise left them after dinner, and Scott and Matthew walked back to Scott's apartment. Matthew, even more silent than usual, had contributed nothing to their conversation at dinner. Ever since they had stood together and watched Catherine and Paul drive away, he seemed to have retreated entirely from them. He had spoken only when he was spoken to, and because of his silence and his manner of observing them, he had cast a cloud over Scott and Françoise. It was he who had been in their thoughts all during dinner. More than ever, Scott determined to talk to him that evening. He knew that a real gulf existed between Matthew and himself now and that he must do something to bridge it. The hope of any successful relationship between Matthew and Paul had almost vanished from his mind. When they had spoken of Paul at dinner, Matthew had only smiled to himself scornfully, as if expressing his real thoughts about his stepfather for the first time that day.

When Matthew was addressed it was quite different. He was elaborately civil with both of them, he had smiled and replied as briefly and politely as possible. There was no doubt that he was changed. As they reached the door of the apartment, Scott looked at his watch. It was only eight-thirty, there was still time. The thought of putting it off until tomorrow passed through his mind but he rejected it, he could not let this silence continue any longer. In the apartment, he took Matthew to his room, waited until Matthew was seated on the bed, and then sat down beside him. He felt awkward and out of contact with him; even a little irritated. He did not know how to begin to talk to him. After a thick silence in which they did not even glance at each other, Scott said, his voice a little too loud, a little overjovial: "It's been quite a day, hasn't it? Are you tired?"

Matthew smiled at him non-committally. "No, not at all."

"I thought we might have a little talk," Scott began again slowly. "I haven't seen you for ages."

Matthew looked away from him. "I know." He paused before adding: "I guess you're pretty busy."

Scott shrugged his shoulders. "Yes, I have been. How was your summer?"

"All right."

"I haven't really seen you," Scott said, "for months. It's longer than I realized."

Matthew looked at him directly for a moment; the look was deliberate and almost insolent. "Do you have a cigarette?" he asked finally.

"Well ... yes," Scott said slowly. He took a package of cigarettes from his pocket and offered them to Matthew. "Since when have you taken up smoking?"

Matthew laughed. "Mother thought it was charming for me to have a cigarette with her once in a while," he said. "Now I'm an addict. It makes me so grown-up, you know."

Scott lighted Matthew's cigarette and then lighted one for himself. He looked at the carpet, as if studying the design on it, and said: "Matthew, what's happened? I know it's something. If it's my fault, I wish you'd tell me. Is it something I've done? Or is it just because we haven't been able to see more of each other...?"

"What are you talking about?"

"About you ... and me."

Matthew stared at him and puffed on his cigarette. "You and me?" he echoed. "I don't think anything's happened, Scott. After all I'm only fourteen and you're ... how old are you, anyway?"

"Thirty-two."

Matthew made a gesture with his hands. "That's quite a difference," he said. "Our interests could hardly be identical."

"Are they so different? We used to have a good time together, Matthew, didn't we?"

"I guess so. People change, though."

"What do you mean … 'people change'?"

"Don't they?"

"Are you thinking of anyone in particular?"

"No. Just everyone in general. You change. Mother has changed. I change. You know how it is: growing up or something like that."

"They don't necessarily cut themselves off from everyone when they change, do they, Matthew?"

Matthew looked at him hard. "Some people do, I think."

"You, for instance?"

Matthew sat up on the bed. His cigarette had burnt down to almost nothing and he threw it out of the open window. "Yes," he said, "me for instance."

"Is there any good reason why you should have changed towards me, Matthew? Is it because of anything I've done?"

"If you don't know, why should I tell you? If you don't even know if anything happened, then nothing did as far as you're concerned. If anything happened, it happened to me and not to you, so it's my problem."

"Then it was something I did…."

"It was nothing you did, Scott," Matthew said, shortly. "What time do we have to leave tomorrow, by the way? Maybe I ought to go to bed."

Scott looked at his watch. "It's not so late, it's only just after nine o'clock. We don't have to leave until noon."

"Well, I might as well go to bed anyway. I am kind of tired."

Scott stood up. "In other words, you don't want to talk to me about it, whatever it is?"

"You can put it that way, if you want to. I'd say there was nothing to talk about." He stood up next to Scott, and Scott was aware for the first time that evening how much Matthew had grown. He was quite tall for his age now, and yet he did not seem to have grown awkwardly. He was becoming extremely handsome; even the bitterness in his face suited him, suited his thinness, the hollowness of his cheeks.

"I'd like to think we were still good friends, Matthew. We've known each other for a long time, you know."

Matthew's lips trembled and he blinked his eyes rapidly. The wall, which had seemed so impenetrable, dropped completely from his eyes as he looked at Scott again. "Yes," he said. "Oh, Scott, I..." and then he turned away from him and sat down on the bed again.

Scott dropped to the bed beside him and took his shoulders in his hands. "What is it, Matthew? What's the matter?"

Matthew's shoulders moved in his grasp, but he did not turn. "I don't know," he said. "I hate it here. I'll be glad to be back in school again. I..." he pulled himself away from Scott's hold on his shoulders and looked at him. "It's not your fault, Scott. I'm sorry. But everything's so different now. I guess you didn't mean anything..." and then his voice faded away.

Scott racked his memory. There was something. He had done something, he knew it from the way Matthew had spoken. It began to dawn on him slowly, his mind went back ... "It wasn't ... it wasn't anything to do with last September, was it, Matthew? I wrote you about that." His memory was suddenly clear. "I wrote you and you never answered the letter. Was that it?"

Matthew nodded slowly. The tears had come to his eyes. Was it the letter? How could he ask that? *Sorry we missed each other while you were in Paris, but I'll see you in November.* That's all he had written. No explanation, nothing.

"I'm terribly sorry, Matthew. If I'd realized..."

Matthew interrupted him. "It wasn't your fault, I guess, but you had said you'd see me that day and when you didn't ... besides, that was the day mother told me she was going to marry Paul, and she said she'd talked to you. I know it was silly, but I thought when I got your letter that you'd explain..." his voice hesitated and his eyes accused Scott again. "Even when you wrote you just said you were sorry we missed each other, you didn't...."

Matthew did not finish the sentence and Scott, with Matthew's eyes on him, did not know how to answer him. He was suddenly angry with Catherine, wondering what she had said to Matthew, trying to remember his conversation with her that day. *I've explained everything to Matthew*, or something like that....

"There's some misunderstanding, Matthew. When I called, your mother told me about Paul, and then she said that she hadn't told you yet but that she wanted to tell you that night. I'm sure she didn't mean...."

Matthew laughed. "Then it *was* all her fault," he said. "She doesn't want me to see you any more. She just wants me to see Paul! Except when it's convenient, like now."

"I'm sure she doesn't feel that way, Matthew. After all, under the circumstances..."

Matthew stood up, smiling. "It doesn't matter, Scott. Really it doesn't. It was only that I thought that you..." he blushed. "Oh, you know."

Scott did not protest further. What could he say without blaming Catherine? Apparently, it was her fault, but he did not want to say anything against her. "I hope it really is cleared up, Matthew. You know I'd never let you down, don't you? Why..." he stumbled, and his face reddened. "Why ... you're like my own son, or my brother." He put his arm around Matthew's shoulder clumsily, and Matthew smiled at him. They were both embarrassed, but Scott could see that Matthew was happy. "It's all right, Scott," he said.

Chapter Ten

M. de St. Croix had been standing in the window of his office for perhaps ten minutes when he heard the car. He watched it enviously as it made a wide circle in front of the building and then came to a stop just a few feet from the window. Such a big car, and only last year Madame Cameron – he checked himself, she was Madame Dumesnil now, he must remember to address her correctly – had had a perfectly good car, quite new. But one could not judge Americans by ordinary standards. They wanted a new car, something bigger or more powerful, so they bought one and that was that.

As he moved from the window to the door, he adjusted his glasses, brushing the lapels of his coat. The car made him feel faintly inferior, and he opened the door but kept himself from going out to meet them. He would wait for them here. As they entered the main door of the building, he made a little bow from the waist, shook their hands, and motioned them into his office. When they were seated, he stood for a moment behind them and then said, clearing his throat, "Shall I send for Matthew at once … or did you wish to talk to me, perhaps?"

They did not wish to talk to him, they said, thanking him. They would like to see Matthew right away. He closed the door behind him. He was irritated with himself for having said "send for Matthew" – there was no one to send. He straightened his shoulders and walked quickly down the hall.

Sitting next to Catherine in one of the two chairs in front of M. de St. Croix's desk, Paul fingered the leather on the arm of the chair and looked around the room. "How did you happen to choose this school, darling?" he asked.

"Matthew's headmaster in America recommended it," Catherine said. "Why?"

"It seems a little…" Paul hesitated, "simple, perhaps?"

Catherine smiled. "I think that's all to the good," she said, "and it has an excellent scholastic rating."

Paul nodded. "Yes, and Matthew likes it, doesn't he?"

"Very much. He's been here two years now and I think it has turned out very well for him."

They were interrupted by the door opening behind them and Matthew stood before them, red in the face and out of breath. Before Catherine could stand up, he had his arms around her and his face against hers, kissing her hard. Then he looked at Paul for an instant before shaking his hand cordially and formally. "They only just told me you were here," he said excitedly. "How are you?"

Catherine stood up, smiling at him, and put her arm around his shoulder, holding him close to her. "We're fine, darling, and it's so wonderful to see you!" She looked quickly at Paul, "…And what do you think, Matthew?"

"What?"

"We have a real surprise for you!"

"What is it?"

"Tell him, *chéri*," she said to Paul.

The smile grew on Paul's face and he looked at Matthew tantalizingly. "We have a new car!"

"Where?"

"Outside."

Matthew hesitated, looking first at Catherine and then at Paul, and then ran to the door and out of the building. They stood, facing the door, and Catherine reached for Paul's hand. She was suddenly very happy.

❦

The summer began well. Matthew was delighted with the trip they had planned: Biarritz, the Basque Country, the Pyrenees, Carcassonne, Nîmes, Avignon, Arles, then Marseille and the Riviera for swimming, and finally the Alps. He loved the car and soon learned everything about it. Gas consumption, horsepower, number of cylinders, maximum speed, size of tires. He would have wished for a Packard or a Lincoln, but consoled himself with the fact that the Delage was a champion hill climber and had won races in France for years. He sat behind his mother and Paul, leaning over the back of the front seat so that he could watch the speedometer, urging Paul to go as fast as he could and then watching the needle climb to 120, 130 kilometers – sometimes even higher. He complimented Paul on being such a good driver and Paul, to his delight, promised to give him driving lessons sometime during the summer.

In the first week of the trip Catherine began to feel that she had been mistaken ever to have worried about Matthew. He spoke of the school with evident satisfaction and he made enormous progress with Paul. Although he was primarily interested in the car, and not in Paul, he seemed happy, and the days went by without any of this stubborn silences and without arguments or bad temper.

It was in Biarritz that the first cloud was cast over the summer. Catherine came down on their second morning to find them standing beside the car. She sensed at once that something had gone wrong. Paul was leaning against the car, smoking a cigarette, with Matthew at some distance from him, his back turned to Paul. They both looked at her as she approached and each of them greeted her perfunctorily as if they had something far more important on their minds.

She smiled at them, and when Matthew only looked sourly in Paul's direction, she said: "What's the matter with you two?"

"Paul said he'd teach me how to drive and now he won't!"

Catherine put her hand on Matthew's head, rubbing his hair gently with her fingers, and glanced questioningly at Paul. He shrugged his shoulders and sighed. "I told him not here. This is a city, there are too many cars. I said we'd have to wait until we were in some small place, where there'd be no traffic. But it's now or never with him. He wants to drive the car now."

Catherine turned to Matthew. "That sounds reasonable to me, Matthew. If Paul said he'd teach you how to drive, he will. But he's quite right that this isn't the place for it. Can't you understand that?"

Matthew edged away from her and stared straight ahead of him without replying.

"Maybe you'd better let me talk to him alone, Paul," Catherine said quietly, sensing that there was something Matthew would not reveal while Paul was there.

"Certainly." Paul's tone was firm and cold, and he snapped the cigarette from his fingers as he walked away from them into the hotel.

Catherine took Matthew's head in both her hands and looked at him directly. "Now, Matthew, what is this all about?"

He pulled his head away from her again. "Oh, nothing. You're always on Paul's side anyway!"

"Matthew! How can you say that? You know it isn't true!" She opened the door of the car and took him by the hand. "Now sit down here and tell me what happened."

He walked past her sulkily and sat in the seat of the car with his feet on the running board. Then he looked up at her. "Well, I came down and Paul had just driven up in the car." He looked up and down the street for a moment. "It was just like it is now," he went on, "there was nobody driving a car here. See?"

She looked down the street. "Yes. Go on."

"So I said couldn't I drive the car now ... I mean, couldn't he give me a lesson here?"

"Yes. And then?"

"He just looked at me and said 'no'."

Catherine shook her head. "But, darling, you heard him just now. Didn't he explain to you...."

"But there wasn't anybody on the street. There isn't anybody here now!"

"I know, Matthew," Catherine said patiently, "but there are regulations about where you can teach people to drive. The police don't allow you to drive everywhere. Paul would know about that. Now was that all that happened?"

"No."

"What else?"

"Well ... I asked him why not and he said all that about it being a city and everything, and then I said there weren't any cars and what difference did it make and then he ... he...."

"He what, Matthew?"

"He got mad at me. He said that he'd teach me when he got ready to, and that I should do what people told me to do and that I acted like a spoiled brat and wanted everything my own way."

Catherine sighed. "I'm sure Paul didn't mean it just the way you thought, Matthew, and he is *partly* right, you know. You do have to trust what Paul tells you about a thing like that."

"I knew you'd be on his side!" Matthew glared at her.

"Matthew! It's not a question of being on Paul's side. Paul happened to be right, and I doubt very much that he actually called you a spoiled brat. If he did, I think he was wrong in that and we'll talk about it later." She took his hand in hers again. "But Matthew, listen to me. You're not a little boy any more. You must listen to reason about things like this and not get angry. Paul will teach you how to drive later on, I'll see that he does. In the meantime, I think you should apologize to him and clear things up. After all, we want to have a nice day, don't we? It's been such a good week and you've been so happy until today."

"Apologize?" Matthew stared at her incredulously.

"Of course, darling."

"Never. Never! And you just say he'll teach me to drive. But I know him. I know he won't. He thinks it's *his* car."

"Matthew! Stop it."

"Well, he does!"

"Does what?"

"Think it's his car."

"And whose car do you think it is?"

"Yours. You paid for it, I bet."

Catherine stood quite still for a moment, and then she looked at Matthew for a long time before she spoke again. "Just what do you mean by that, Matthew?"

"Well, you did pay for it, didn't you?"

"As it happens, I did. Yes."

"All right then."

"And ... Matthew, I'm married to Paul. The car is *ours*." He got out of the car and stood by it, digging his toe into the grass at the edge of the curb.

"Will you apologize to Paul now?"

He looked at her furiously, kicked the side of the runningboard with his foot and ran into the hotel.

Matthew watched Paul pouring the brandy and was relieved when he saw Scott put his hand over his glass. "I don't think I'll have any, thanks," he said, glancing at Matthew, "if we're going to play tennis, we'd better get ready." Matthew breathed a sigh of relief and smiled gratefully at him. "I'll go and change my clothes," he said. "I won't be a minute."

When he had left the room, Catherine looked at Scott and Françoise with mixed emotions. Scott had changed a great deal since she had first known him. It seemed incredible to her that the gawky American boy who had been such a pet of John's should now be sitting here in her apartment, quite at home in France, obviously living with a French girl, and apparently untroubled about it. She envied him; she had never felt at ease until she and Paul had been married. Of course, it was different when you had a child to consider. She thought bitterly of Matthew. The summer had gone so badly after that stupid quarrel he had had with Paul in Biarritz, and then he had been so perversely delighted when he learned they were going to cut the trip short and come back to Paris. He could see Scott again! She checked herself. After all, she wasn't jealous of Matthew's affection for Scott, and she did have to admit that Paul was not the ideal companion for a young boy. She checked herself again. Paul was mature, while Scott was, and would always be, a kind of overgrown boy. It seemed so complicated, she spent half her time justifying Matthew or Paul to herself. If only they could have liked each other more! She wondered what Matthew had told Scott about the summer. She would have liked to talk to him, but with Paul and Françoise here … and then he'd be leaving in a few minutes. She looked up at the sound of Matthew's footsteps coming down the hall. He stopped in the doorway of the living room, and he too was quite different from the unpleasant boy she had known all summer. He looked very handsome in his white shirt and shorts, his tennis racquet under his arm, and the bright smile on his face. "Are you ready?" he asked Scott.

Before the door had closed behind them, Scott called: "I'll see you at six, Françoise," and then they were gone.

It was only as Scott left and they sat down again that both Catherine and Paul realized that Françoise was almost a stranger. This was the first time they had ever been alone with her; Scott had taken easiness and familiarity away with him when he left. Catherine lifted her glass to her lips, sipped a little of her brandy, and smiled at Françoise. "Have you had a good summer, Françoise?"

Françoise shrugged her shoulders. "We were in the country for weekends," she said, "but the rest of the time we were right here in Paris. You know Paris in the summer. But what about you? How was your trip?"

"Oh, it was wonderful," Catherine began breathlessly. "It must seem incredible to you, but you know I've never been to the Basque Country or the Riviera or the mountains before." She glanced at Paul, hesitated, and then went on: "Of course, Matthew..." and then she stopped.

"Matthew did not have such a good time?" Françoise asked, finishing the sentence for her.

Catherine shook her head. She offered a cigarette to Françoise, took one herself, and Paul lighted them. He did not smoke, but settled back in his chair. By his silence and his posture he excluded himself from the conversation as if he were only a spectator.

"I don't know why I should tell you about all this," Catherine began hesitantly, and then more firmly, "except that I suppose you've heard a great deal about all of us from Scott."

"Yes," Françoise said. "I certainly have!" She laughed easily and the direct way in which she had spoken broke the strangeness between them, giving Catherine confidence.

Again she looked at Paul before she spoke and this time he gave her an encouraging smile. She took a long pull on her cigarette and turned to Françoise. "I had wanted to talk to Scott about Matthew," she said, "but perhaps it would be even better to talk to you. You are more on the outside than any of us, if you know what I mean."

"Yes," Françoise said. "I know exactly what you mean. But, if I may say so, I don't think you should worry too much about Matthew's summer. A motor trip is not so very exciting for a young boy."

Catherine shook her head again quickly. "Oh, it wasn't that! It's just that Matthew..." for the third time she glanced at Paul. This time he leaned forward abruptly in his chair. "What Catherine is trying to say is that Matthew and I do not get along very well together," he said. "I, too, am worried about that but I do not think it is as serious as Catherine does. I believe it is natural for boys to … to hate…" he smiled briefly to himself, "their stepfathers. At least for a while. I imagine Matthew will get over it in the course of time."

"Darling!" Catherine exclaimed. "Matthew doesn't *hate* you! I know he behaved very badly this summer. But he doesn't *hate* you."

Paul smiled at her. "Perhaps that is too strong, but whatever it is, I don't think it is so very serious. In the course of time…."

"In the course of time! But Paul, we've been married for nine months."

"Is that so long?" Catherine was surprised at the flatness of the question, and still further surprised that it had come from Françoise. She had almost forgotten her. She stared at her. "Well it seems a long time to me," she said defensively.

"How did Matthew like Paul in the beginning?" Françoise continued. For all the world, Catherine thought, as if Paul wasn't even in the room.

"Well…" Catherine began, still looking from time to time in Paul's direction. "He seemed to like him quite well. Didn't he, darling? The trouble is, he's always been so fond of Scott…."

"Which is no fault of Scott's," Françoise interposed quickly.

Catherine stiffened in her chair. She had never really been drawn to this girl. "I wasn't suggesting that it was," she said coldly.

Françoise smiled at her. "Forgive me," she said quite calmly. "It seemed to me that you were."

Paul looked at them both. "I don't think you should be angry with Françoise, *chérie*," he said to Catherine. "I'm sure she didn't mean anything, any more than you did. Also, perhaps it would be easier if I left you alone?"

Françoise looked at him. "It is I who should go," she said. "As Catherine herself said, this is not my business."

Catherine put her hand out quickly and touched Françoise's arm. "No, please. I'm sorry. I wasn't … angry … I think I'm just being stuffy. It's only because I'm worried about Matthew."

Françoise sat back in her chair. "Well, I am perfectly willing to tell you what I think," she said, "but I think Paul should stay, too. After all," she smiled at them both, "it is his problem, too? *N'est-ce-pas?*"

"Yes, of course it is," Catherine said quickly, "and he has been very worried about it, whatever he says. Now do tell us what you think, Françoise, please."

Françoise crushed the butt of her cigarette in the ashtray on the table next to her chair. "Well, I think you have a very difficult problem, but it seems to me…"

"What?" Catherine asked eagerly, anxious not to offend Françoise in any way.

"Aren't you going at it … *de travers* … backwards, would you say?"

"Backwards? I don't know what you mean."

Françoise stared at Paul for a moment. "I think you know what I mean," she said to him. "You knew all this before you were married, didn't you?"

Paul nodded. "And you think we should have worried about it then?"

"Perhaps. Or at least that you should not be surprised now. I feel that *you*," she inclined her head in Catherine's direction, "are surprised that Matthew does not like your husband."

"But I told you that Matthew seemed to like him perfectly well at first!"

"What else could Matthew do? *You* like him. Matthew is a boy. He does not see things the way we do. You wanted to marry Paul so he had to like him, if he could. Now he can't. And Paul, as Matthew sees him, has taken you away from him."

"But that's not true!" Catherine exclaimed. "Surely Matthew knows that I love him just as much as ever, that I…"

Françoise raised her hand and sighed. "I really don't think we can talk about this. It is a mistake to try."

"But why, Françoise?"

"Because you are too involved with it. You should look at this situation like a mathematical problem. But you feel too much. You take everything as criticism of you, personally."

"I'm very sorry," Catherine said. "I didn't mean to…"

Françoise interrupted her again. "But *that* is what I mean. First you are upset because I say something, and then you are sorry that you are upset." She shook her head. "That is like Scott. He always talks from his feelings and not from his mind. Perhaps all Americans are like that. I'm sure that Paul and I could talk about all this quite calmly. Couldn't we, Paul?"

"Perhaps," Paul said quietly.

Catherine looked at them both, flashing her eyes from one to the other. "You can talk to me, Françoise, really you can. You're perfectly right. I mustn't be upset or hurt by what you say. Now do go on."

"*Si vous voulez.*" Françoise swallowed the cognac in her glass and lighted another cigarette. "From Matthew's point of view," she said emphatically, "Paul has taken you away from him. Matthew does not know anything. Matthew only feels. You say that it does not make any difference, that it is not true, but it does make a difference to him. Paul is here all the time! It doesn't matter that it is *Paul* … it could be anyone. Before it was just you and Matthew, now it is you and Matthew and Paul. Paul has to be considered. It is not important for Matthew to know, from you, that you feel the same way about him. What is important is that he has to share you with Paul now. Your *time* is not his."

"But neither is Scott's time his!"

Françoise shook her head. "Not all of it, no. But there is no other person, in Matthew's mind, who comes ahead of him."

"What about you?"

"Me? But I'm not married to Scott. I am not with Scott and Matthew when they are together. It's quite different. Matthew hardly knows that I exist."

"But I'm sure Matthew likes you," Catherine said quickly.

Françoise laughed. "Why do you say that? Matthew and I understand each other very well. If I am anything in Matthew's life, I am a threat. But since Scott and I are not married, I am only a threat, nothing more. When Matthew has time for Scott, Scott arranges to be with him. He comes first."

"You aren't suggesting that Scott's affection for Matthew..." Catherine began.

Françoise shook her head. "No, in Matthew's *mind*. You must think of this as Matthew sees it. Scott plays tennis with Matthew, Scott swims with Matthew, Scott plays chess with Matthew. Not Scott and myself. Can't you see the difference?"

Catherine reached for the cigarette box and lighted a cigarette nervously. Her first one was still smoking in the ashtray beside her. "But Paul has done all those things with Matthew, too!"

"Matthew doesn't want to do those things with Paul!" Françoise said sharply, and then added: "Forgive me, I didn't mean to..."

Catherine interrupted her. "No, don't apologize. I see what you mean. But are you suggesting that Paul and I should never have been married?"

"I am not suggesting anything, Catherine," Françoise said flatly. "Let's be honest with each other. You wanted to marry Paul and you did. I might have done the same thing in your place. I don't know. Whatever I might have done, I would have had to consider Matthew, as you have had to; and I don't see what else you expected to happen."

"You mean, then, that I shouldn't have divorced John?"

Françoise shook her head wearily. "No. I simply said that your problem with Matthew is a natural consequence of your divorce and your remarriage."

Catherine looked at her angrily. "Well, is it too much to expect that Matthew might have liked Paul ... might like him still?"

"I would say that it was expecting a great deal," Françoise replied coolly.

"But if you think that," Catherine cried out, "then what do you think I should do about him?"

"Isn't it a little late to be asking that question?"

"Well … really!"

Françoise put out her cigarette and stood up. "You see, now I have offended you. As I told you this is none of my business. We should not have talked about it."

There was complete silence in the room, and neither Catherine nor Paul looked at Françoise until she spoke again suddenly. Her voice was harder now. "That is not quite honest," she said. "It is my business. What is going to happen to Matthew when Scott tells him that he is going to marry me? And who besides me has thought about that?"

Paul and Catherine were taken aback by the seriousness of her voice. "You see," she continued, looking at Catherine, "our positions are not so very different, after all."

"But I didn't realize that you were going to get married so…" she looked up at Françoise and gestured to the chair. "Do sit down again," and when Françoise was seated, she continued: "I mean when *are* you going to get married?"

"Nothing has been decided … except that we *are*."

"I think that's very exciting!" Catherine smiled across at Françoise. "It's a little as if you were going to become my daughter-in-law. I've known Scott for such a long time." She turned to Paul. "Isn't it exciting, darling?"

Paul stirred in his chair. "Yes, it certainly is. We both…"

Françoise cut him short. "Thank you, I know … but we were talking about Matthew. Who is going to tell him, and when, and how is he going to feel about it?"

Paul smiled. "Of course," he said, "Scott must tell him."

Catherine laughed. "Well, Françoise! It isn't as if Matthew was … I mean, Matthew can't stand in the way of you two getting married."

"No, he can't," Françoise said positively. "But, I assure you, he will feel that he has lost his last friend in the whole world."

"Françoise! You exaggerate. I know how good a friend Scott is to

Matthew. But he's not his only friend. He has friends at school and whatever he feels about Paul now, he has me, and I'm sure he knows that. It isn't as if he didn't have *anyone* else."

"Isn't it? First he loses his father, then he loses his mother, now he loses Scott. As for his friends at school … did your school friends replace your parents? Did you love them the way Matthew loves Scott?"

"No, of course not, but you talk as if Matthew would never see Scott again after you two are married. Surely you…"

"Matthew can see Scott as often as he wishes. I am talking about how Matthew is going to feel. It is not a question of what he will actually lose, it is, simply that no one and nothing will be Matthew's. His alone."

"Well, we can't just stop living because of Matthew," Catherine said briskly. "He's going to have to adjust himself to these things, that's all."

"Yes," Françoise said. "So there is no point in worrying about him, is there?"

"Well, I don't say that, but I mean that…"

Françoise stood up again. "What you mean is perfectly clear," she said. "I agree absolutely that you must stop worrying about Matthew, but I also think you are going to have to help him adjust himself, as you put it."

Catherine stood up and faced her. "But that's just it. How?"

"Yes," Françoise said slowly. "How? I am glad that it is not my responsibility."

"Of course it isn't."

"No. But it is yours."

Catherine watched her silently. There had been something ominous in the way she had said those last words. Things certainly couldn't be as bad as this girl tried to paint them. It was probably just spite on her part … she'd practically admitted she was jealous of Matthew.

Paul watched them for a moment and then got up from his chair. "I'll take you home," he said to Françoise, "or wherever you'd like to go. The car is downstairs."

"Thank you. If you could take me to Scott's apartment, I would appreciate it very much."

Catherine raised her eyebrows. How cool this girl was. "Take me to Scott's apartment" – as if they were already married. She didn't even try to make a secret of it.

Françoise shook her hand and looked into her eyes. "Thank you for lunch," she said, "and I hope you have not misunderstood me. Matthew does, somehow, make us a family … even if we do not entirely like it."

Catherine smiled at her. "I *did* behave badly, didn't I? And I don't think I misunderstand you, Françoise. Thank you for what you've told me."

Paul took Françoise to the door, then returned quickly to kiss his wife. "I'll only be a little while," he said.

Catherine watched the door close behind them. Strange girl. What was it that Scott saw in her?

Chapter Eleven

When they were in the car, Paul glanced at Françoise and asked: "Scott's apartment, you said?" It was a relief to talk in French.

Françoise looked at him as if she was about to ask him a question and then said: "If you don't mind, I'd rather you took me to the Place de la Madeleine."

"*D'accord*," Paul answered and leaned out of the window to look down the street. He made a U-turn and started down the Quai. "So you are going to marry Scott Fletcher," he said.

"Does that surprise you?"

Paul shook his head. "No. But I think it surprises my wife."

"Why?"

Paul's hands left the wheel as he made a gesture signifying that he did not know the answer. "I think she thinks of him as part of her own family."

"*Sans doute*," Françoise said. "I sometimes wish Scott's connection with Catherine and Matthew was a little less..." she hesitated and then added, "*familiale*."

They drove across the Pont du Carrousel in silence. When Paul stopped the car at a sign from a gendarme, he turned to look at Françoise again. "I am surprised that you seem to take the question of Matthew so seriously," he said.

"So? You mean that you do not?"

Paul shrugged. "I don't think we take children quite so seriously in France."

"Not French children," Françoise said quietly as the car moved again. "But I think American children are different."

"In what way?"

"I think they are brought up to think of themselves as very important. If Matthew's importance is exaggerated, it is because he has been made to feel that his problems are important."

"Then you think, *au fond*, that it is not so serious?"

Françoise shook her head firmly. "On the contrary, because he is what he is I think it is perhaps very serious."

Paul laughed quietly, almost to himself. "Well," he said, "I am perhaps not the perfect playmate for Matthew. On the other hand, I did not marry Matthew."

"No," Françoise replied slowly, as if choosing her words with great care, "but you became his stepfather, and you knew that when you married his mother."

"Yes," Paul agreed. "And when you marry Scott we will be, as you said, very much *en famille*."

Françoise studied the side of his face a moment. "Perhaps," she said, "but I assure you that I have no intention – as you said – of marrying Matthew, although I like him."

Paul looked at her surprised. "Ah? You think it is as serious as that with Scott?"

"He is very conscientious, he worries about Matthew, but because of me, Scott will also find it difficult."

"But why?"

"Because of his conscience. I am sure he will feel that he has failed Matthew or wronged him."

Paul shook his head. "I don't understand that at all, why should he?"

"*Why?* He is fond of him … I don't know. What is important is that he will feel that way. And if I marry him…."

"*If* you marry him?"

Françoise blushed. "Well, yes. *If.* I have told Scott I will marry him; I want to marry him but … I wonder if he really wants to get married. He hesitates to tell Matthew, he postpones it … I don't know."

"But when you spoke to Catherine … I thought it was all settled."

"I know. I decided to tell Catherine today just to force the issue a little – and now I wonder if I was right. If Scott does not tell Matthew today, Catherine will. It was perhaps very stupid of me."

Paul stopped the car on the rue Royale, near the Madeleine. "Are you in a hurry?" he asked.

"No."

"Then I would like to know, really … I don't understand why you are so concerned about this question of Matthew. What has it to do with you?"

She looked at him almost angrily. "*Et bien!* What has it to do with any of us? Matthew has changed a great deal since you married his mother, and probably since she divorced his father, too. He has suffered."

"Oh … suffered! After all, he is still a child."

Françoise raised her eyebrows. "And children do not suffer?"

"They get over it."

"Not so easily as all that."

"Well, perhaps you are right, but you still have not answered my question. Why should *you* be so concerned?"

"Because I am concerned!" Françoise said sharply. "Because the situation exists … and because someone has to be concerned!"

"Oh, I see." Paul's voice was cooler now. "You think that no one else is."

"I think," Françoise said, "that a great deal of concern has been expressed."

Paul looked at her silently, lighted a cigarette without offering one to her and then said: "It seems to me that you are suggesting that my marriage was a mistake."

Françoise smiled. "Not for you … not for Catherine. But I think that for Matthew…" she paused and Paul finished for her: "For Matthew it was a mistake, yes?"

She nodded.

"And what do you think we should do now?"

Françoise gestured widely with her hands. "It seems to me that you could be more of a father to Matthew than you are. With your help he *could* like you."

Paul smiled. "Are you looking for a replacement for Scott?"

"It's a good idea, don't you think?"

"For you and for Matthew it is probably splendid," he said.

"You don't really like Matthew, do you?"

"I think I would like him better if I were not married to his mother."

Françoise was amused. "*Tiens!* I thought only Matthew was jealous."

Paul smiled again. "Jealous … I don't think so. But when we talk about Matthew, Matthew, Matthew…."

"You are married to a mother, my friend," Françoise said.

"What do you mean by that?"

"Just that! Catherine is not just a woman, she is a mother. And you … you are not just a husband, you are a ready-made father."

"Yes." He sighed. "Perhaps we did not consider all this enough before we were married."

Françoise's eyes narrowed. "You are not regretting your marriage, are you?"

"No," he said simply, "but it is true that I am not much as a father."

Françoise looked at him with a sudden feeling of sympathy; he was not joking, she knew. "It is not so easy for you, is it?" she said.

Paul shrugged his shoulders. "I don't understand children very well," he said. "They don't interest me. I try to do things with Matthew, but his attitude…" he paused, turning to look at her, "he can be very difficult, you know, and then ... well, I lose my temper. He irritates me."

"*Oui*. We talk a great deal about Matthew, but it is not easy for anyone. It must also be very difficult for Catherine, all this."

Paul nodded his head sharply. "It is not agreeable for her, certainly. Sometimes I think it might be better for Matthew to be with his father for a while."

"Perhaps." Françoise opened the door of the car. "I think I had better go," she said. "Thank you for driving me over here."

Paul shook her hand and smiled at her. "*Pas de quoi*," he said. "Thank you for..."

Françoise got out of the car. "We talk a great deal but I don't think we come to any conclusion," she said. "I hope things will work out, somehow. For all of us."

"Yes," Paul said gently. "And good luck to you"

"Thank you ... you, too."

They smiled at each other once more, she closed the car door and walked directly away from him without turning back. He started the car again, and then sat back and watched her walking down the street. There was something about her ... it was easy enough to understand why Scott wanted to marry her. He would have been a fool not to. Paul shook his head quickly. After all, he did not have, as he had told Françoise, any regrets.

Chapter Twelve

Scott pulled up alongside the curb in front of his apartment and stopped the car. Matthew had been watching him admiringly, he drove so well. With his hand on the door, he said: "You're a wonderful driver, aren't you?"

"I like to drive," Scott said, smiling at him. They got out of the car and he added: "Paul's a good driver, too, isn't he?"

Matthew made a face. "Not as good as you are."

In the apartment, Scott went into the bedroom, taking off his jacket and throwing it on a chair as he went. "Sure you don't want to take a shower here?" he asked.

Matthew shook his head. "I'll have to change when I get home anyway."

"Make yourself at home, then," Scott said over his shoulder. "I won't be long."

Matthew put the tennis racquets on the couch, walked over to the chair where Scott had thrown his jacket and picked it up. He brushed it gently with his hand and then walked to the closet, opened it, took out a hanger and draped the coat over it. Before he put it away, he smoothed it out again and then hung it carefully in the closet. After listening to the sound of the shower with his head cocked on one side, he walked to the table in the window, flipped the pages of a magazine, looked out of the window, and then walked over to the radio which he turned on. He waited in front of it until it had warmed up and then twisted the dial until he heard some music. He began to hum with the music as he continued to walk around the room, examining it. What fun it would be to live here with Scott! If Catherine and Paul would only go away … if Paul had a business, for instance, that would take him to India or someplace, then Matthew could spend his vacations here with Scott. He would even keep the place clean for him, make the beds, and whatever else you had to do … sweep.

The sound of the shower ceased as he stopped in front of the mantelpiece. He rubbed his hand across it, looked at his fingertips, grey with a film of dust, and looked at himself in the mirror and smiled, showing his teeth. He did a kind of pirouette to the music and then stopped, facing the mantel and the mirror again. He could hear Scott in the next room. He checked an impulse to go in, and looked at the mantel again. There was a cigarette box just below the mirror and he opened it. He picked up one of the cigarettes and was surprised to see that it was an English one. He raised his eyebrows, closed the top of the box without putting the cigarette back and walked over to the door of the bedroom. "Since when do you smoke English cigarettes?" he asked in a voice loud enough to be heard over the music.

Scott was buttoning his pants and he looked up at Matthew in the doorway.

"I don't," he said. "What made you ask that?"

Without looking at him, Matthew held up the cigarette in his hand and said: "Then why do you have English cigarettes here?"

Scott's face reddened for a moment. "I keep them here for Françoise," he said. "She likes them better than American or French ones."

"Does she come here very often?" Matthew asked.

"Oh…" Scott hesitated. "Quite a bit, why?"

Matthew began to hum to the music again. "Nothing," he said. "I just wondered." He walked back to the mantelpiece, still doing a kind of dance step; replaced the cigarette in the box and then returned in Scott's direction. "I wish I could live here with you," he said.

Scott smiled at him. "Yes," he said absently. "Well, I guess we can go now."

Matthew looked at him and laughed. "Aren't you going to wear any shoes?"

Scott blushed. "I must be getting old," he said. Matthew watched him for a moment and then snapped off the radio. He walked over to the bookcase, picked up a book that was lying on the top shelf and opened it. On the flyleaf he read the name *Françoise Lauret* and he frowned slightly before closing the book and replacing it on the shelf. "*Les Fleurs du Mal,*" he read on the cover. As he turned from the bookcase, Scott entered the room. "Françoise does come here quite a lot," Matthew said, "doesn't she?"

Scott looked at him puzzled.

Matthew pointed to the bookcase. "Her book," he said.

"Oh, yes. She lent it to me. I'd never read Baudelaire."

"Do you like it?"

Scott picked up Matthew's tennis racquet. "I'm not much for poetry," he said.

"Are you in love with Françoise, Scott?" Matthew asked the question suddenly and they were both surprised. They stared at each other for a minute and then Scott said awkwardly: "Yes, I guess so."

Matthew looked away from him. "Oh," he said.

"Are you surprised?"

Matthew shook his head. "No, I guess not," but when he looked at Scott again, the light had gone out of his eyes. "I suppose we'd better go, hadn't we?"

"Yes." Scott started for the door and then paused. "You don't … you like Françoise, don't you?"

Matthew nodded, looking at the floor. "Oh sure," he said. "I like her fine."

Scott sighed and put the tennis racquet down, leaning it against the wall. "I think we'd better have a talk," he said.

Matthew looked up at him quickly. "What about?" He looked

at his watch. "It's almost five o'clock," he said. "Mother's probably waiting."

"I know. But I still think … look, Matthew. I want you to know this from me and not from anyone else."

"What?"

Scott hesitated. "Well, you know that I went down to meet Françoise's parents this summer, didn't you?"

Matthew shook his head and stared blankly at Scott. "You did?"

"Yes. You see, Françoise and I … well, I do want you to hear it from me … we're going to get married, Matthew."

"Oh." Even in the solitary word, Matthew's voice seemed to have gone back inside him.

Scott put his hand on Matthew's shoulder. "Look at me, Matthew. Françoise is very fond of you, you know."

"Yes, I know."

Scott's hand gripped him harder. "This isn't going to make any difference." Even as he said the words, he remembered John saying the identical thing to him so many years before. Why had he had to tell him *now*?

He was relieved when Matthew looked at him directly and openly. "I know," he said quietly. "It isn't that. I was surprised, that's all."

"You're sure?"

Matthew nodded. "Yes." And then he looked away again. "Everybody is getting married, aren't they?"

Scott felt vaguely uncomfortable. Matthew was taking it almost too well. "Yes, I guess it does seem like that to you."

"When are you…?"

"Pretty soon, I hope. We haven't decided on the day yet. You're the first person I've told."

"Haven't you even told mother and Paul?"

Scott shook his head. "I wasn't going to say anything until we'd set a date, but I wanted you to know before you went back to school. I wanted to tell you myself while you were here."

"Thanks, Scott. I'm glad you did." He looked at his watch again. "I think we ought…" he glanced at Scott without finishing the sentence; his voice sounded tired.

"Yes, it is getting late, isn't it?" All the ease and happiness Scott had felt when they had come into the room together seemed to have disappeared now. He took a step towards the door and then punched Matthew's arm affectionately. "You're sure it's all right, Matthew?"

"Sure." He picked up the tennis racquet and waited as Scott opened the door. They walked down the stairs in silence, and it was not until they reached the car that Matthew spoke again. He smiled at Scott, a look of embarrassment on his face. "I forgot to congratulate you, Scott. I think it's swell."

"Gee, thanks!"

He got into the car and Matthew climbed in after him, threw his racquet on the back seat and slammed the door. Before he started the car, Scott patted Matthew's leg and Matthew smiled at him. Then he started the car and pulled away from the curb. Matthew looked out of the window, humming the same tune that he had been humming in the apartment, and Scott sighed. He shook his head. You could never tell with Matthew. Everything was all right after all.

Chapter Thirteen

Between Le Havre and Rouen, the Seine is very wide, narrowing imperceptibly as you travel inland, against the current of the river. It is wide and deep enough for ocean-going freighters and the swimming is excellent.

In the two years that he had been here, Matthew had come to know the Seine and the country around it very well; he knew it especially well now because he encountered it in a mist of personal gloom, and his state of mind, the inner world in which he lived, received the impressions of the country, the names of the villages, deeply, marking them with his melancholy. Across this countryside, the vision of which was hung in the back of his mind like the scenery for a play, all the events of the last two years shuttled in and out of his imagination. His first coming here: his early meetings with Paul; the ups and downs in his relationship with Scott; the announcement of the divorce and his father's marriage; his mother's marriage and her honeymoon; his first Christmas with his new stepfather, and then their first summer together, just ended. Even the places they had visited did not blot out this landscape, which seemed more permanent and durable than any other single thing in his life. More than two years in France. Two years and three and a half months, actually. And in that time he had acquired a second self: a Matthew who spoke French like a native, whose parents were named Dumesnil while his own name, Cameron, still clung to him like a remnant of something he had brought with him in 1927.

Matthew dwelt on these things as one might become absorbed

in watching a play from the wings, waiting for some expected cue to appear on the scene. His own life had disconnected itself from his mother and Paul as it had once been disconnected from his father. It, too, was a play, another unreality of his mind in which he did not quite believe. There had been André during those first two years, and real as that relationship had been at the time, now that he was no longer at the school it was as if it had never existed. André had not returned this year, having gone on to some other school or some other country in much the same way that he had come here from England or from wherever he had been before.

The school, in which his active, outer life was lived, had changed only a little. There were more boys now, and a few new teachers. The recess periods had become formal and organized, and M. de St. Croix had hired an athletic director, a M. Garnier. But this everyday world was neither real nor exciting to Matthew. He studied, played and ate his way through his days; it was at night that his life acquired reality. At night, when he closed his eyes and began on the recurring dream that finally ended in sleep; a dream that he was sure would someday become reality. It was not always the same dream, but the basis of it never changed. It was the playing over and over again of some situation in which he was the central figure, affecting the lives of all the people he knew; it was he, in these fantasies, who had power and wealth, charm and importance. In the beginning – then he had been King Arthur or Sir Lancelot or Sir Galahad or Richard the Lion-Hearted: conquering, loving, defeating – it had been pure fantasy; he had never really believed that he was any of those people. But, gradually, the central figure had become Matthew Cameron himself. Handsome, kind, generous, understanding, he dreamt of himself as gentle, tender, and noble, telling his mother – as he comforted her for Paul's death – why she should not have married him and how much he had (willingly, of course) suffered because of that marriage. Or telling her why she should have stayed married to his father. There were no such scenes with his father. The picture of John that stuck in

Matthew's mind was the picture of him as he had last seen him, when they had said goodbye in America. He, too, was married again; but in Matthew's mind he was married out of sadness, or because Catherine had left him unworthily. It did not occur to Matthew that it could have been, even partially, John's fault – the divorce. He was sure, somehow, that his father embodied the elements of nobility and generosity, kindness and virtue, that he pictured in himself. He wanted to be like him. It was the others, all the others, who were wrong.

These daydreams, although separate from his daily life, penetrated his actions sufficiently to increase still further the distance between him and his fellow schoolmates and teachers. He felt in himself a virtue and a wisdom which they could not achieve and which they would certainly not understand if they were aware of it. He was not literally cut off from the boys around him, but he was separated from them in his heart and in his mind by the gap of his purity – the purity of his dreams.

It was the beginning of his third year in the École de St. Croix, and they had come down to the river to swim. The weather was unseasonably warm though the water was already becoming cold, a little too cold for comfortable swimming. It would probably be the last time this year. Matthew had wandered away from the group of boys to sit down near the water's edge; he could hear the sound of their voices mingling with the rustling of the leaves on the trees, the occasional ripple of the water at the river's edge. He closed his eyes and thought of the countryside: Lillebonne and the other towns he had visited, or where his mother had taken him to lunch on weekends when she came to see him: Rouen, Caudebe-en-Caux, Château Galliard, Les Andelys. He remembered Scott and Catherine driving away from the school that first time, and with that memory came the feeling that he had been sent here so that his mother could be rid of him. She had probably known Paul even before that, and thought that to have her son around would make things difficult. He remembered all her conversation about the school, how *charming* it was, how progressive, how he would absorb something really French here, something that was not available in Paris. And from that it had become something else again: now he was kept here – sent off every year – so that Paul would not have a stepson around. Well, that was all right with Matthew. He was as sick of Paul as Paul could possibly be of him. Paul and his manners, Paul and his conversations, Paul and his "*ma chérie*" … Paul, Paul, Paul. There was nothing in Matthew's life that Paul did not plan when Matthew was with him. He planned his summers, his clothes, his amusements. Every bit of it. He had not only married Matthew's mother, but he had become in every outward way Matthew's father. The only difficulty was that he was not and never could be a satisfactory father. As for Catherine herself, she seemed to love it. It was so good for Matthew, having a man around the house; Paul was so interested in him, doing all those things for him, thinking of Matthew first … thinking of him first! Making the gesture, saying the right thing, but never, never was anything other than an empty hollow pretence….

Matthew was disturbed in this not unpleasant, angry reverie about his stepfather and his mother by a voice at his side, and he looked up from where he was sitting. "*Alors, tu ne vas pas dans l'eau, Mathieu?*" It was Monsieur Garnier, who always called him *Mathieu* with a special inflection in his voice. He had laughed when he had first pronounced his name, saying that he had never known anyone named *Mathieu* before, and that it always made him think of Saint Matthew.

Matthew did not answer at once. He was troubled by the intrusion, he would have liked to be left alone today. He looked at the water, stretching away from him to the opposite bank which rose suddenly green from the water's edge. He could never see this without surprise and pleasure, he was so accustomed to beaches and sand. He stood up and smiled. "*Oui*," he said, and started away form the man. In the water he could be by himself.

He stopped short of the river's edge, to stand first on one foot and then on the other, to take off his shoes and then his shorts. He felt vaguely embarrassed in the very brief swimming trunks which all the French boys wore, and as he dropped his shorts on top of the shoes, he turned to look back. Michel Garnier, to his further embarrassment, was looking at him steadily, and when their eyes met there was no flicker of recognition, only a continuing stare. Matthew could not, although he wanted to, remove his eyes form Michel at once – something gripped him inside, holding their eyes together. It was Monsieur Garnier who removed his eyes deliberately from Matthew, shifting them to a point directly beside him on the ground. There was a distance of perhaps twenty feet between them and as Matthew continued to watch him, he saw, quite clearly despite the distance, the man's hand move to pick up a large insect – a beetle? – between his fingers. He could not see any expression on Michel Garnier's face, it was impassive and quiet. The fingers themselves, holding the beetle, seemed to be watching the futile struggle of its legs beating against the air, and then in a sharp, decisive and impersonal thrust, the fingers came together with a click, severing the body.

Matthew caught his breath and stepped back. As he did so, Monsieur Garnier, wiping his fingers on the grass, looked up at him and smiled. The smile was open and very friendly, enough so that Matthew, unable to smile back at once, waved his hand and then turned quickly towards the water. He did not feel anything but shock from what he had seen. He did now *know* what he had seen, even.

He moved towards the water again, across the lumpy green grass which had been under water once, when the Seine – years before – had been twice its present width. The greenness of the overgrown river bank, the transition to reeds near the water's edge, the irritated movement of the water against the muddy shoreline – all these things fixed themselves indelibly in his mind, and with them the image of Monsieur Garnier. He could not look back at him again, but the seated figure superimposed itself on what he actually saw. He had never noticed it before, but there was a sloppy, casual competence about this man when he brought them to the Seine, that was quite unlike the figure of Monsieur Garnier at the dinner table; the Monsieur Garnier whose hair was carefully combed and whose tie was knotted perfectly. Here, by the water, he seemed a kind of overgrown boy; pants that were certainly unpressed, shirt open at the neck with a rumpled collar, old tennis shoes. Matthew shook Monsieur Garnier out of his mind and walked into the river.

The water was cold ... cold enough to startle him, and as his blood recoiled from its touch, he wished that he was a really good swimmer, that he could swim across the river and back without any difficulty. As it was, he had never managed anything more than breast stroke and side stroke (and a curious ability to swim underwater with his eyes open), and his wind was not very good. The other boys would swim from one bank to the other, even here where the river was so wide, sometimes supporting something on their heads to show what good swimmers they were. He was just not destined to be a really good athlete.

He let his body down into the water quickly and ducked his head under, wetting his hair, and started to swim. He swam as quickly as he could to get over the shallow part where the reeds waved up through the water, catching your legs if you were not careful and winding themselves about you like slippery serpents. He hated those reeds. When he was safely over them, he relaxed and swam slowly, oblivious of everything except the sunlight, the fresh bite of the water on his body, the movement of it around his head, the way his arms cut into it, and the eddying wake he left on its surface.

The world seemed to come to a stop as he swam, as if he were the only object in motion in an otherwise still landscape. He closed his eyes to deepen the sense of quiet, the stoppage of time. When he opened them again, he was in the middle of the river, further than he had ever been before. In his surprise, he opened his mouth, swallowing a little of the dark-green water, losing his breath momentarily and coughing. Like the tick of a very faint clock, he felt a sensation of alarm inside himself, not so much fear as a reminder that he should be afraid, that he had perhaps overreached himself.

He made a wide circle, heading back towards the shore where he could see the figures of Monsieur Garnier and the boys. He was the only one in the water now, and they seemed incredibly small to him. The river was wider than he had imagined – distances, he remembered, are difficult to judge over water – he would have to concentrate on getting back. Back. Even as he swam he was overcome by and caught between two equally strong impulses, so much so that he slowed down automatically. The pleasure, the sheer physical delight, of his body in the water possessed him to such an extent that he wanted to stay in it forever; against this, like a warning hammer, came the feeling of danger – a quiet danger lurking in the water, threatening to pull him under and envelop him, drag him to the muddy bottom. As if the direction had been taken from him, and in an effort to get it back, he made a forward lunge, a response to the sensation of peril, and was immediately overtaken by laziness, the desire to rest here; it was like a struggle against sleep, or the beginning of a dream.

He was not sure how far he had progressed towards the shore (he seemed to be making no headway) when he felt the undercurrent of the river pulling him down relentlessly. His body was dulled and leaden, and his arms and legs thrashed uselessly to keep it up. The feeling of alarm heightened inside him but did not bring with it any strength. He had no force with which to combat the overpowering opiate of the water itself; quite gently his head vanished under the water and the world turned from sunlight to a murky green. It occurred to him, and the color of the idea forming in his mind was red – spreading through him as blood through a bandage – that he was drowning. He made a great upward surge, a surge that was not enough, even though it brought his head above water and filled his open mouth with it again. He *knew* that he was dying – remembering, as if his memory had betrayed him and had taken his energy away, that drowning was something he had always feared – remembering an earlier picture of falling into water this same color, and the image of the propellers waiting for him far below.

He was experiencing the moment he had dreaded all his life; the moment that we all look forward to in secret, whatever we may feel about it. It was not painful – although he had heard that drowning was torture – perhaps that was still to come. Neither was it terrifying. Since it was – as experience – completely novel, there were no words for it. No one had lived to invent the words, to combine language in such a way that would approximate this. He had read of people who had narrowly escaped death, and yet it was not of death that they had written or talked later, but of life; not of the death that had been escaped, however miraculously, but of the life that had not been lost.

As his mouth filled with water again, he looked and looked for the last time, but his eyes could find no one, the figures had disappeared from the shore as if to leave him to die alone. It was not for help or rescue that he was looking – he knew that it was already too late for that – but for a spectator, an onlooker. Someone who would see and understand this in a way that he, himself, could not. For while he did not understand the acceptance in him which was making this possible, he understood that it was acceptance, as if he had always known that this would be his end. Although he saw no one, the command to understand, a visual directive to any possible spectator, glared forth from his eyes; the last remnant of life itself was concentrated in the beam of that look.

He had not looked long or far enough, because he had not had time to see the movement, the figure pointed towards him like a human torpedo, slashing its way through the water. Michel Garnier had watched him and as surely as if Matthew had called out to him, he had sensed what was happening. The boys were already changing their clothes, and he ripped off his pants and ran to the water. Even as he swam, his forehead was wrinkled and his mind troubled. This was more than drowning; it seemed very close – in his mind – to an act of suicide.

꙳

When he opened his eyes, the first thing Matthew saw was the furrowed brow of Michel Garnier, crimson and wet with sweat. He moved his head slowly from side to side, feeling the water dribbling from his mouth, and the face above him broke into a smile. "Do not talk," the man cautioned him in English. "One of the boys has gone for the car." He wiped his face with the back of his hand. "*Grâce à dieu!*" he said. "You are all right."

They carried him, four of them, up the winding path to the road and Matthew watched the silent serious faces of the boys reflecting the brush of death that had, through him, touched them. Over their heads, the branches of the trees were spread against the sky, like a giant spider web. None of them spoke to him, not even when they laid him carefully in the back seat of the open car. They retreated, averting their grave, unsmiling eyes. When the car stopped in front of the school building, Matthew raised himself up on one elbow and then fell back against the leather seat, and Monsieur Garnier gave him a warning angry look and put his finger to his lips. Once more he was carried, through the hall and up the stairs to his room, to be laid on his bed.

Michel Garnier had sent someone for the doctor. As they waited, he stood beside Matthew's bed, baffled, wondering. When the doctor arrived – one more face, serious, elderly – he looked at Matthew and then bent over his chest and listened to his heart. Matthew remembered, with the greying head almost touching his chin, the ear against his bare chest, the hand on his forehead, that his mother had been particularly impressed because there was a resident doctor at the school, something that was very modern, almost unheard of in France. He was neither sorry nor glad to be alive; only surprised. At first he had not been sure, even the faces of the boys and the teacher had not convinced him. But the car, the building, the bed, the doctor … he was alive, all right.

The doctor listened to his heart with a stethoscope, looked down his throat, pulled his eyelids up to look into his eyes, shook his head and gave Matthew a pill. He whispered something to Monsieur Garnier and they both stared briefly at Matthew once again. Then they left and he stared at the high blank ceiling above him. Gradually his body descended into a restless sleep in which he could still taste the river water, feel the slippery touch of the reeds reaching up to him from the black mud.

࿇

He awakened suddenly, his body dripping with sweat. Michel Garnier sat on a chair by his bed, indistinct and shadowy in the semi-darkness. He must have slept through the afternoon.

"*Alors, tu vas mieux maintenant?*"

Matthew nodded to him and cleared his throat. "Yes, thank you. If it wasn't for you...."

"That was nothing," the man said, interrupting him, "but tell me, why did you go so far, why didn't you call for help?"

Matthew looked away from him. He asked himself the same question but he could not find an answer. It was as if the instinct for self-preservation had died in him while he was in the water. "I don't know," he said. "It was as if I couldn't ... but I don't know why."

Monsieur Garnier did not reply, but continued to sit beside him silently. Matthew stared at him and then closed his eyes again, shutting the lids tightly and frowning to himself. His mind went back over the scene, and he could remember nothing between his last long look over the water at the empty landscape, and then this man's face, red and sweating. He did not know how he had actually been rescued. He wondered, idly, if he had perhaps really died – at least for a moment – and then been brought miraculously back to life. Something was no longer the same – that moment of death, for it *was* death, had changed him. Now he could feel his breath, the air penetrating into his body and then coming out again, and his body was no longer the same. He was conscious of it in a way that he had never been before, he seemed to have acquired a reality he had never possessed; a door inside him had been opened, or perhaps the water had released a spring and broken through that melancholy dreamlike existence of his, bringing him back to a life that he had never known. Even with his eyes closed, he was fully aware of the bed, the room, the window, the man sitting beside him. He felt his surroundings – and Michel Garnier's presence – sharply, almost painfully, not needing his eyes. He was suddenly aware that Monsieur Garnier was going to speak to him, as if the effort required for speech in the man's body had communicated itself through his own pores. He tightened his ears as if frightened of the sound, afraid that it would hit him too loudly.

"How do you feel now?" he heard. "Would you like something to eat? Some food has been saved for you."

Matthew shook his head from side to side on the pillow, his eyes still closed. He was not hungry for food and he was reluctant to break into the current of awareness that he felt between the two of them. Yet there was a disturbing emptiness in his stomach, requesting – not demanding – fulfillment. "I'm not hungry," he said. "Don't go.

"Are you sure?"

Matthew nodded, opening his eyes, and then put his hand out tentatively, until it rested weightless on the knee of Michel Garnier. It would have been very easy for him to call him Michel now.

"All right," he heard him say. "I'll stay."

Even as he heard the words, even as he did not respond other than with his own inner sensation of relief, he had a recollection of this man sitting near the shore of the river with the beetle in his fingers. He could not believe that this was the same man who was sitting beside him now, and he raised his head a little from the pillow as if the movement would enable him to see further into Michel, to fathom the difference between this man and the man who had killed … well, only an insect after all! He dropped his head back on the pillow and closed his eyes. He was glad that Michel was not going to leave right away, and his mouth formed the first name: Michel, Michel, Michel.

୬

The young hand still lay quietly on his knee and Michel's eyes stared at it. He felt a wave of affection spreading through him for this unhappy young boy, whose last words to him had been: "Don't go." That voice had come from deep inside him, begging him to stay, and at the same time touching something in Michel that had been buried for years. It was the cry of a puzzled and tormented human being, tormented into a kind of stupid acceptance, driven to what was – at least unconsciously – a deliberate self-drowning.

Michel sat rigidly in his chair, as if the straightening of his backbone might, mysteriously, silence his brain. Keep him from thinking. He felt naked and young sitting here next to this boy, and filled with pity, compassion, and a kind of love. He covered Matthew's hand with his, feeling the long fingers, the bony structure, holding it without pressure, and the hand responded, the fingers digging into his knee, the knuckles rising against the palm of his hand. Perhaps it was at that moment – for there is an exact moment when things begin – that his stomach seemed to turn upon itself, converting the sympathy and tenderness inside him into a harder and firmer core, a wad of feeling and sensation that he recognized as desire. As often as he had felt it before in his life, it had never been like this; it bubbled in his blood, filling him and drying our his mouth, sharpened and twisted by his feelings.

"I must go," he whispered to Matthew, feeling the tightened hand still on his leg. But his breath was harder now and he was rooted to the chair, he could not go. First his back seemed to stiffen even further, as if his body was withdrawing itself, shrinking away from the bed without actually moving, and then it was pulled forward by a kind of gnawing loneliness that filtered through the actual desire he felt. Uncontrollably his body moved towards Matthew with a strength and direction of its own, until his head was close to Matthew's, until, finally, his lips touched the boy's cheek, and his hands rested on Matthew's shoulders, clenching and unclenching. From some distant place, his mind shouted at him to go, but it was already too late. Matthew's hand had left his knee and now both of the boy's hands caught Michel's head between them and brought it closer, so close that his lips found Michel's and his arms circled his shoulders as he kissed him.

The loneliness, all the lack of love that Michel had felt with all the men and women he had known, poured out of him, blinding his will, shattering his resolutions. Whatever mental struggle was taking place in him, the real strength of his will was now showing itself in its ability to outwit him, to justify the actions which it must allow. His body overpowered him, working with the skill and competence which he had learned, not through love, but rather in the mercilessness of parks, alleys, and darkened bedrooms – with strangers. "You're a nice boy," he said.

Chapter Fourteen

*"You're a nice boy," the whispering voice said, "what have
you to fear? I don't know your name, you don't ever have to
see me again if you don't want to. No one knows you're here,
no one need ever know. And I know you like me a little. I
can feel it."*

*Michel held his breath, making no reply. He could not
stop him now ... and what the man said was true. He didn't
even know his name, no one knew that he was here, what
difference could it make? He felt the hardness of the man's
body against him, his hands, his mouth ... he didn't want
him to go.*

Faintly embarrassed by his uniform, which seemed conspicuous in
the Paris of 1922, Michel had noticed the man looking at him as
soon as he had entered the car at the Étoile Metro station. They
stood about ten feet apart, and as the train pulled out of the station,
the man gave him a long, hard look. Michel turned away, becoming
absorbed in reading the notices to the passengers, studying the map.
When he looked back, finally, in the man's direction, the eyes were
still on him. At the Place de la Concorde, Michel was the first to get
out of the train, and without a moment's hesitation, the man followed
him.

Walking through the long tunnel of the *correspondance*, Michel
could feel the man behind him, as if some special faculty was able
to select that particular presence from among all the people walking

hurriedly in each direction. When he reached the other platform, they waited, apparently oblivious of each other's presence, for the train, and when it came to a stop they got into the same car. Corporal Garnier, on his final leave in Paris before his discharge, was not disturbed or alarmed. He was certain that the man was following him deliberately, and he knew that it could be for one of several reasons. There were still men who wanted to talk about the Army and the war, but more often than not, soldiers were followed by small-time procurers, offering anything from cheap women to filthy postcards. He took another quick glance at the man; he could not quite place him. He was too well dressed, just a little too elegant. And yet he bore the mark somehow: the hands in the pockets, the hat a shade too low over the brow, the covert glance. When he got out at the rue du Bac station, the man followed him again.

On the Boulevard St. Germain, Michel Garnier was startled at the voice behind him; he had barely crossed the boulevard when he heard it, "*Bonsoir, chéri,*" at his elbow. He turned to look into the veiled face of the woman who had spoken, and looked at her long enough to smell the cheap perfume. He shook his head and walked away from her. He was sick of the bare rooms, the dim lights, the old, used, fat bodies, the mechanical endearments, and most of all the smell. He wanted something, someone, but not that. At the first corner, he stopped to look at the signs on the kiosk: concerts, movies, plays, lectures. He studied them automatically and without interest, and as he did so, he felt the man coming to a stop beside him. He did not turn his head and they waited together, reading. He could feel the man's eyes glancing at him from time to time, and finally – as he had known he would – he spoke:

"On leave?"

Michel nodded.

"How about a drink?"

He hesitated for a moment. He looked at the man and shrugged his shoulders. What difference did it make? "All right," he said.

They started to walk, side by side and not quite touching, down the boulevard towards the lights of St. Germain des Prés. They were within a block of a café when the man paused. "Why not come up to my place?" he suggested. "I've got plenty to drink, it's warm there. What do you say?"

Michel looked at him again, trying to find some clue. He'd known men who were queer, but this man didn't look the part. "Sure," he said suddenly, "why not?"

They turned off the boulevard, into a dark, narrow street leading towards the river. When they had walked about a block, the man took his arm and turned into one of the open archways leading into a courtyard, crossed the courtyard, still leading Michel. They went through a doorway and the man said, in a low voice: "Top floor" and pushed Michel in front of him. He did not turn on the light. In a state of faint alarm, excitement, and curiosity, Michel started up the stairs with the man following close behind him. He did not know what he was getting into, but he wanted to know what there was on the top floor. Mechanically, he checked off what he could possibly lose if the worst should happen: he had nothing on him but his papers and a few francs. He was somehow sure that there was no personal danger involved in any of this. When they reached the top floor, he waited while the man stepped past him, opened a door, switched on the light, and gestured him in, holding the door open for him. He entered into a hall and directly to his left was a small room, lighted by two lamps and comfortably furnished. There was a couch on one side of the room, several chairs, a desk between the two shuttered windows at one end, a fireplace, two or three paintings, a mirror above the fireplace, and on the wall over the couch a large number of photographs.

"Take off your coat," the man said to him, already taking off his own coat and hat. He was dressed in a grey suit, clean white shirt, red tie, black shoes. His hair was tinged with grey and thinning; he was taller than Michel and had once been goodlooking. He walked away from Michel, took some matches from the mantelpiece and bent over to light a fire that was already prepared. Michel watched particularly for any effeminacy in his movements, gestures, or voice. There did not seem to be anything other than an attitude of excessive courtesy that seemed slightly affected. When he had lighted the fire and watched it to be sure that it would catch, he stood up again, smiled, and gestured towards it. "Sit down here," he said, "and I'll get us something to drink. What would you like? I have everything, I think. Pernod, cognac, whiskey...." He hesitated and then added with a little laugh, "Beer?"

Michel raised his shoulders and hands. "I don't care. Whatever you're drinking."

The man did not insist. He waited until Michel was standing beside the fire and then walked past him out of the room and down the hall. When he was out of sight, Michel walked over to the couch and looked at the pictures. All photographs, and all of men. Some of them had obviously been cut out of physical culture magazines, others were snapshots, mostly of men in bathing suits, in one or two cases entirely nude. He was still looking at them when the man came back in, carrying a tray on which there were two glasses, a bottle of whiskey, and a siphon. He set the tray on a table near the fire.

Michel sat down and when the man handed him a glass, he took it, raised it slightly, and then drank from it. It was good whiskey, warming and smooth. He put his glass down and extended his open hands in front of the fire. "That's a good drink," he said.

"Thank you."

They sat in silence for some time and finally the man said, quickly, "Are you hungry, by any change?"

"No." Michel shook his head. "I had dinner just a little while ago."

"You're sure? I have food here."

"No, thanks."

The man took a drink from his glass. "Where are you stationed?"

"I was in Germany. I'm on my way home. I have four days in Paris before my discharge."

"You're not a regular, then?"

"No. I did my military service at the end of the war and then volunteered for another two years."

"Why?"

Michel shrugged his shoulders. "Why not? Patriotism or something. Somebody had to stay on."

"Where is your home?"

"Rouen."

"What are you going to do when you're discharged?"

"I'm not sure yet. Take a rest first."

"Of course."

They continued to talk this way, more or less impersonally, through three more drinks. Michel waited, on the alert for some gesture. There was no suggestion of anything but polite interest and pleasant companionship in anything the man said. He talked about his own war service, poured the drinks as soon as his own or Michel's glass was empty, reached over to stir the fire or put on another log; and gradually Michel relaxed. He felt a certain sympathy with this man, and yet he could not entirely dismiss the impression he had had of him when they were on the Metro and in the street. Now with his hat and coat off, he seemed friendly and innocuous.

It was only after his fourth drink, when he was feeling warm, relaxed, and a little tight, that Michel leaned over and looked at him, straight in the eyes. "Why did you ask me to come up here with you?"

The man looked at him, seeming almost puzzled. "I don't know," he said. "No particular reason. You looked lonely."

Michel laughed and glanced significantly at the photographs on the wall above the couch. "What about those photographs?"

The man looked at them and smiled. "What do you mean? What about them?"

"Who are all those men?"

"Friends of mine. Why?"

Michel looked at the pictures again. "They're all men. Don't you have a girl?"

"No."

Michel's glass was full again and he took a long swallow from it. "Then you're…" he said slowly.

The man looked at him questioningly. "I'm what, *mon ami*?"

"You're one of those, aren't you?" His voice had a fierce edge as he said it. "You like men, don't you? That's why you asked me up here."

The man laughed and picked up his glass. "You came up," he said in a very level voice. "Why?"

"I was curious. I've never had anything to do with your kind."

"I'm surprised."

The coolness of the man's voice and the self-assurance of his attitude startled Michel. He lurched to his feet and supported himself on the mantelpiece. He was feeling the whiskey more than he realized. "What do you mean by that?"

The man stood up, facing him, and laid his had on Michel's arm. "Look, my friend, you have no reason to be angry with me. What have I done? I asked you to come up and you came up. If you wish to go, I will not stop you." His hand had tightened on Michel's arm as he spoke. "I like you. But that's all. You can do what you wish." Then he released Michel's arm and moved away from him. "The cigarettes are there," he indicated the table, "and the whiskey. Or take a nap if you wish, or … go."

"What are you going to do?"

"I'm going to take a bath." And then a look of surprise came over his face. "Pardon me. I should have thought of it before. Perhaps you would like a bath yourself?"

Michel shook his head and fell back heavily into his chair, staring at the fire. The man watched him a moment and then walked out of the room again, and Michel heard the water running in the bathtub.

&

When he opened his eyes, he was still sitting in front of the fire, fully dressed, and the first thing that met his eyes was the figure of the stranger, seated opposite him in the chair, smoking. He was wearing pajamas and a dark blue bathrobe and, as Michel looked at him, he smiled pleasantly. "You've been sleeping very hard," he said. "It's quite late."

Michel looked away from him, yawning. "What time is it?"

"Half-past two. You've been asleep for almost four hours."

Michel looked at him angrily. "Why didn't you wake me up? I have to go."

"I couldn't wake up anyone sleeping so soundly. Besides, you can stay here. Where can you go now?"

"Oh no!" Michel's voice was firm. Everything was coming back to him. "I'll find some place."

Once again the man laughed at him. "But why? I am not going to do anything to you. You can have my bedroom, or you can sleep here. You are perfectly safe from me." He looked into the fire for a moment and then back at Michel. "I won't deny anything. What you thought about me is true enough. But I assure you that I will not go against any wishes of yours. Take a hot bath, go to sleep here, and in the morning you can leave, just as you came."

Michel looked at him doubtfully. "What I can't understand is why you asked me to come up here with you if it wasn't for…"

"But I didn't say it wasn't for a reason. Since you insist that I am mistaken about you, what can I do? I cannot force myself upon you. I liked you when I first saw you. You are young and handsome, you came with me readily enough. I see that I was wrong, but you cannot blame me for thinking what I did. I hoped…" and then he stopped.

Michel shook his head, uncomprehending. All things being

equal, he liked this man well enough. It was true that he had nowhere to go at this hour. Even the Metro was no longer running. What was more, he believed him. He was perfectly safe here. "All right," he said without looking up. "I'll stay."

"*Et bien, enfin!* Now you are being sensible. I will run you a bath and fix your bed while you're bathing."

Michel shook his head. "That isn't necessary. I'll just sleep on the couch. I can put a blanket over me…"

But the man insisted. "You're just out of the Army! You might as well be comfortable when you can."

Once again the bath water was running. Michel, still suspicious, kept his uniform on until the stranger told him his bath was ready. In the bathroom, he found a pair of pajamas and a bathrobe. He locked the door, undressed, and got into the tub. It did feel good to him. As he washed, he began to feel ashamed of his suspicions and his outburst. Who was he to be so scornful of this man? He had been treated well, the man was honest and open with him and had not tried any tricks. By the time he was out of the tub and dressing in the pajamas and robe, he began to feel that he owed him an apology. He found him still sitting before the fire. He stood up as Michel came in and held out a glass to him. "Here's a nightcap," he said, "and I have fixed this bed for you, I think you'll be comfortable in here." He glanced at Michel's bare feet and then at the clothes he was carrying on his arm. "I'm sorry I had no slippers for you," he said, "and if you'll give me your clothes, I'll hang them up."

Michel did not resist this time either, and watched him hang his uniform on a hanger and then put the hanger on the hook on the back of the front door. He sat down again in front of the fire, warming his bare feet, and sipped his drink. When the man had come to sit opposite him again, he looked up at him and smiled. "I guess I owe you an apology," he said. "You have been very nice to me. Thank you."

"It's nothing. Please. I'm sorry if I offended you." He tilted his glass and then stood up. "I know you must be tired now. When you finish your drink, you can get into bed and I'll turn out the lights."

Michel finished his drink quickly and left the fire reluctantly. He had slept enough so that he was no longer tired, but he walked over to the bed, and with one more glance at the pictures, took off his bathrobe and then got in between the sheets. He sighed with comfort and pleasure and lay back on the bed. The lights went off suddenly, leaving the room in the faint, flickering light of the fire.

"Are you comfortable?"

"Yes, very."

"Then I'll say good night."

But he did not go. Instead he came over to the bed and sat on the edge of it, his hand on Michel's shoulder, the fingers touching his neck. Suddenly he rubbed his cheek against Michel's. "I'm sorry you don't like me," he whispered, and kissed him gently on the cheek and then lay against him, not moving. Michel did not move but lay rigid, feeling the weight of the man's chest, the warmth of his breath down his neck, the pressure of his fingers on his throat. He could even feel the beat of his heart. They remained that way silently until he felt the man's other hand on his chest and his face moved, the lips kissing him gently again and again and finally meeting his own lips. "You're a nice boy...."

Chapter Fifteen

After a few days at home, Michel returned to Paris and a world that was different from anything he had ever known. Under the crust of the normal world of the city he found a special and unique civilization. A small world with its own special cafés, restaurants, nightclubs; a world of every kind of man of every race. Here he found men from the Army, boxers, businessmen, movie stars, weightlifters; married men and single men, old men and boys. Some of them were permanent inhabitants of this particular world and others were only transients or novices. It was a world without limits or rules, a world of share and share alike. Friends – for they could not be called lovers – were exchanged at will and for any, or no, reason.

He learned the universal language of the milieu: the language of indirection, gesture, and the significant glance. Honesty and dishonesty existed in such completely equal measure that it was impossible to distinguish between them. The lack of truth in most of the sharp, witty, and fantastic exchanges that passed for conversation was so obvious and so enormous that it was no longer untruth. There was no way of separating fact from fiction, nor was there any reason to do so. Under the guise of endearments or highly civilized verbal cruelties existed an elaborate, formalized, and continuous chase. Everyone was hunting, hunted, searching and searched, wanting and wanted. The aim was constant and unchanging: conquest. Not one conquest, but continuous conquest, from one victory to another, for it was the conquest alone that was important and never the prize.

Like many of the others, Michel worked in gymnasiums in the

winter, swimming pools in the summer. In winter, he helped with the preliminary training of young athletes, supervised the regimes of older men who wanted to reduce, rubbed thousands of bodies with alcohol and hammered at their hips and arms and shoulders. In the summertime he held other bodies up in the water, coaxing and urging feet to kick this way, arms to move that way. His body became wrinkled and bloated from the water, temporarily unrecognizable at the end of a day.

Finding his own way through this world of intrigue and subterfuge, Michel moved from friend to friend, learning to avoid the young boys who might be underage, from the older men whose virility was weakening and who had to have recourse to innumerable experimental obscenities in order to gratify their failing powers. It was they who astonished and shocked him, not so much by what they did as by the extraordinary ingenuity of their imaginations. A group of them had even organized a special sort of house, honeycombed with dark corridors specially fitted with peepholes, from which they could spy upon their own hirelings and the customers whose perverted tastes they set out to satisfy. When they had found a friend whom they could persuade to come with them, they would bring him to this establishment, roam through the dark halls, pausing here and there to watch until, stimulated and rejuvenated, they would retire quickly to some previously prepared cubicle. Even these cubicles were often exposed to the halls, for the additional stimulation of knowing that they, too, were observed and were in turn stimulating others. A few such visits were enough for Michel.

He also learned to avoid the alcoholics and the dope fiends, the procurers and the ones who began by offering money. The extraneous element: money, alcohol, dope or whatever it might be, involved an extra degradation that he could not stomach. He did not attempt to deny his own perversion, he could do nothing about it; it existed, definitely and irresistibly, but he had not come to the point where he could do business with it.

When he met Tom Rogers, a young Englishman who had fled from his native land and his family for some of the same reasons that had brought Michel to Paris, he escaped with him into the outer edges of the perverted world. They moved into an apartment together, cooked, did their laundry and cleaned the little rooms, washed the dishes, bought the groceries for all the world like any young married couple. They interchanged each other's languages, avoided their former friends and hurried home to each other in the evenings as if afraid that something might have happened during the day to break the little bubble of their intoxication with each other. Their first months together were happy enough; they slept in the same bed, had little anniversaries commemorating their first meeting, and congratulated themselves on having found each other.

As in a marriage, but for different underlying reasons, this first happiness began to fade slowly. Although they argued that it was only natural, their preoccupation with each other lost its intensity; they forgot just when it was they had met, moved into separate rooms, came home less quickly in the evenings. But, because it was important to preserve the dream, they continued to live together. After almost four years, they could no longer delude themselves – living together was not enough. They began on a series of infidelities which it was finally impossible to conceal; they were pulled apart by fantastic jealousies and then pushed together again, protesting their love and need for each other, making promises and vows for the future, clinging to their relationship as the only stable element in their individual lives. It came to an end, finally, when Tom brought a young boy home with him; a boy young and inexperienced enough to be dangerous. In the summer of 1929, Michel had left Paris angry and disgusted with the entire relationship; his father, by some miraculous chance, had heard of a job for an athletic director in a school near Rouen.

❧

They took the train on a Sunday morning early, and when they arrived at the Lillebonne station, something began to happen inside Michel. They hired the carriage they had found waiting at the station and began the trip of a few kilometers to the school. He seemed to see the land, the greenness of the trees and grass, the firm, stable lines of the hills and the roads, the fences and hedgerows, as if for the first time. Like an echo of his childhood calling him back to life, some impulse rose up in him connecting him to the richness of the earth. He breathed the air deeply into his lungs, tasting its freshness, and exhaling the year's stale smoke and debauchery. In those few miles of sunlight, green, and clear air; behind the old driver and the sweating horse, next to this father in the carriage, he became a young man again. He smiled at his father, deeply and openly for the first time in years, and the smile was returned. They did not say anything, but they both sensed what had happened, and even the driver and the horse seemed to have felt some hint of what was passing between them for their pace quickened and the driver flicked his horse joyfully with the whip, urging him forward.

It was only when they arrived at the school and drove through the gate that Michel became suddenly frightened. What if his secret should be discovered? What if it should communicate itself to the man he was about to meet? Sensing the fear in his son, his father turned to him quickly, gripping his arm, reassuring him with his eyes, and when they left the carriage waiting in the school yard, Michel walked ahead – as confidently as he could – to meet M. de St. Croix. There had been no reason for him to be afraid; his father had already paved the way, and M. de St. Croix not only suspected nothing but was eminently pleased with him. His work in Paris at the gymnasium had kept him in good trim; he was strong and healthy, alert and goodnatured, and at that moment, filled with self assurance. The possibility of a final escape had given him a poise that he thought he had lost. He was accepted.

It was on the way back to Lillebonne, his future safe in the school, that Michel allowed himself to look honestly at his past. He had seen, or so it seemed to him, more aspects of human vice than most people see in a lifetime. He began making silent promises to himself for the future, vows of chastity, purity, reform. He would make up to his parents and to himself for all this wasted time ... to his mother especially. He was filled with courage, and with gratitude to his father, the schoolmaster, even the horse and the driver. He was severed from his old life. He could forget Paris, and Tom, and the innumerable others who were known to him by their first names: Jacques, André, Pierre, Georges, Louis, François, or by no name at all. He returned to Paris that night and within twenty-four hours was once again on the train to Rouen ... his life beginning over again.

Chapter Sixteen

Love, Matthew *knew*, is not something that happens twice. With a singleness not of purpose but of inevitability, he knew at fifteen what he himself might forget at twenty, that love is – he invented the phrase himself – a passport to immortality. Because he did not know or recognize the possibility that love is in any sense mortal, that it can die or fade; because his love for Michel had made him come to life and not buried, whatever doubts Matthew had had about himself and the world around him had been erased.

No longer did he dream or fill his mind with fantasies. There were no debates, no questions, no internal arguments. The sense of guilt that had formed questions inside him, pointing an angry finger at him because of what he had learned with André, not only did not reappear, but vanished. What had happened to him, for it was not that he had *done* anything – he would have been powerless to direct or prevent any of it and had only followed the current in himself and in Michel – was an answer, an end to all fear. He was in love, there was nothing in him that was not open and free to the person he loved, and his separate parts, individual segments of his self which had warred inexplicably against each other, were fused into one whole vital unit. There was no question of good or bad, right or wrong, normal or abnormal. It was as useless for him to pretend that he could make any moral judgment of himself as it would have been to pretend that a volcano had no right to erupt. He had exploded into life, a process that defied judgment. It was not a question of approval or disapproval, acceptance or rejection; he could not have been more dominated by what he felt if he had lost the power of reason entirely.

More and more he regarded that day – "the day I died" he some-times said to himself – as a miracle. He could remember it only as the day when, in every sense, Michel had brought him back to life. He knew for certain that now, for the first time, something had taken place inside him that was absolutely right. Through whatever tortu-ous paths and for whatever reasons he had come to this, none of that was of any moment or concern to him any more. All that mattered was that he had arrived at the only place where he had ever really belonged. He had known it at once, and in the deepest recesses of himself he was happy and quiet. "I love you, I love you, I love you," he had said to Michel, asking no response, demanding no assurance. The assurance was in his blood, in his heart, in his mind. He had found his place in the world.

For Michel, older, aware of his responsibility, hammered by the self-doubt he had bred into himself, it was not so simple nor so easy. His face had gone white with fear when, after that first fatal step had been taken, Matthew had appeared in the gymnasium, flashing him with a look so full of his own feelings, so replete with a love he could not possibly have hidden, that Michel was certain everyone in the room saw and understood it. Curiously, they did not – not in the sense that Michel feared and expected they would. That they saw it was undeniable, but it was so open, so exposed, it carried with it its own immunity. Because of Matthew's complete lack of guilt, doubt, or uneasiness, the effect of his obvious adoration of Michel was com-pletely opposite to what Michel had anticipated. There was a marked change in the boy, as if he had acquired something that every human being desired and which, at the same time, no one envied. His soli-tude, the wall he had presented to the other boys, had disappeared overnight. He seemed to have leaped into his own dreams, becoming the legendary hero, full of wisdom and kindness, that he had imag-ined himself to be.

In everything he did, a sure confident touch asserted itself.

When he played tennis now, he no longer played with caution, fear, and reserve; where before he had calculated with his mind, he now played with his instincts, and from a good player he emerged into an unexpected and brilliant opponent. He surpassed himself. He played with his life. The agony of classroom recitation was replaced by a joy and ease which were incomprehensible and delightful to himself and to others. When he made an error in recitation, instead of feeling incompetent and ashamed, the very error seemed to please him and with a word, a look or a gesture, he would turn it into a joke. He acquired a sense of the ridiculous and this, combined with his happiness, communicated itself not only to his classmates and teachers, but reached into the corners of the school itself, almost as if he had brought light into the building.

What was most remarkable and also most troubling to Michel, was the confidence and understanding that he felt in Matthew. Matthew was neither possessive nor jealous, emotions that Michel had always linked to love, and he made no demands on Michel's time. The time, and there was not much of it, that they could spend together was enough for him. He had no romantic illusions or even wishes; he did not question the demands of Michel's position which kept them apart. He seemed to understand, without ever speaking of it, that a certain distance must be maintained between them, that he must not betray his intimacy with his teacher. When Michel had, uneasily apprehensive and wanting to warn Matthew, apologized for having to lead this double life with him, Matthew had looked at him astonished. "We have our whole life ahead of us," he had said.

When they were together – Michel would sneak into his room at night – they rarely talked. Michel was silent for practical reasons which he urged upon Matthew: they might be overheard, someone might investigate. But Matthew did not seem to want to talk to him. It was he, gradually, who assumed the active role in their relationship; he made love to Michel violently, directly, and without any shame or reservation.

On the few occasions when they did talk – whispering together in bed, or when they were supposedly taking a breathing spell after a tennis match (luckily Matthew had private tennis lessons) – Michel was primarily concerned with the possibility of discovery, the thought that the physical nature of their relationship might be exposed publicly, which was a constant source of worry to him. What if one of the teachers should find out, or worse still, one of the boys? What if Catherine should suspect them? But Matthew rejected all these considerations. In the first place, there was no reason why anyone should discover them; they were very careful. Secondly, it was of no concern to him if they did. "What can they do to us?" he asked. "How can they take away something that belongs to us, not to them?"

Michel was baffled by such answers; it seemed to him that Matthew lived on a plane that had very little connection with the real world, and he went further in what he felt to be his efforts to safeguard Matthew. Did Matthew realize that their relationship was abnormal? That it was unacceptable to society? Did he fully understand that its exposure would mean social ostracism, that Matthew would be expelled, that he, Michel, would at the very least lose his post in the school?

Immovable and unshaken in his own conviction, Matthew dismissed all these things. Social ostracism was of no importance to him, what did he care for the world? The moral guilt which Michel attached to the question of abnormality was even less important. What was the standard of normality and abnormality by which one guided one's life? Was society as a whole normal? From a truly religious or moral standpoint any form of love involving sex that was not specifically – and only – for the purpose of having children, was abnormal. Was a man who visited a brothel more normal than he?

When Michel, sadistically, characterized their relationship as "homosexual, pure and simple," and told Matthew he had to "face the facts," Matthew looked at him strangely, the eternal smile disappearing from his face for a moment. "Well, that's a name for it, if you say so," was what he said finally, but he did not seem in any way alarmed or disturbed, and added: "I love you. That matters." Michel did not look at him and did not reply and Matthew laughed. "You never say that, do you?" he asked. Michel's lips seemed to tighten and Matthew went on: "It's all right. You don't have to say anything. I know how you feel. I know you love me." For all Michel knew, he might be right. Certainly, this was like nothing he had ever experienced.

By December, Michel had begun to feel that perhaps Matthew's attitude was the right one. His fears were alleviated with each day that passed, leaving them safe and undiscovered; but the thing that was most convincing to him was Matthew's certainty, his acute perception of the lessening doubts in Michel's mind. He had never felt so exposed, open and defenceless towards another human being. There was nothing that he could hide from Matthew, nothing that he thought or felt that Matthew did not sense or understand. He knew this from looks that would pass over Matthew's face, the gestures he would make, the way he had of speaking Michel's thoughts and bringing them into the open even before Michel was aware of them himself. He was able to feel continuously more secure in their relationship by sloughing his doubts off onto Matthew where they would immediately vanish.

He came to depend on Matthew as he would never have depended on himself. And with his dependence, he began to believe in Matthew as some people believe in God. It was not that he felt Matthew to be supernaturally gifted, but he was increasingly certain that Matthew had, accidentally, come upon some real secret of life – a secret which is perhaps available to everyone but which only a few people ever recognize or achieve for themselves. What it amounted to, and this seemed especially ironic to Michel, was that Matthew was the only person he had ever known who had complete faith: faith in himself and in what happened to him.

Since a practical, worldly justification of his relationship to Matthew could not be found, Michel looked for it elsewhere. In his own happiness, in the feeling of rightness which Matthew communicated to him, in the consciousness of some superior strength in Matthew, a strength before which he found himself completely unresisting. One week before the Christmas vacation was to begin, one week before they would have to part, one week before their first separation, he collapsed and his capitulation was complete. For him it was the impending separation that was the main cause of his capitulation, and what was, in a sense, his defeat. Goaded and urged by his inner conflicts, he had to come to some understanding, some reconciliation with himself. It was not that Matthew was irresistible, it was not that he could not have denied himself the consummation of their love for each other (at least so he thought), it was an intense desire to be able to believe as Matthew believed, to acquire from him that confidence before which every obstacle seemed to tremble and vanish, and to acquire it before they were separated.

Sitting in his room, he had wanted Matthew with that same blinding desire that had taken him into alleys, with no feeling that Matthew, as Matthew, was the target. The *lust* (he said the word aloud) he felt was unadulterated and shattering. He gritted his teeth and only as it subsided did he think of Matthew. He knew then that he depended on Matthew for everything he did, for the way he felt, for what he thought – and Matthew would be gone in one week! What was about to be taken away from him was the daily bread by which he existed. With a lack of caution that he would never have countenanced in Matthew, he hurried to Matthew's room. After one long moment of staring into his face, he took him blindly in his arms, repeating Matthew's own words of weeks ago. "Don't go!" he cried, "don't go!" And then, stammering through a mixture of shame and shyness, as if a commitment were the unpardonable sin: "I love you and I need you. I can't let you go!"

Matthew held his arms around him and his face seemed to burst with happiness. He had hoped for this moment, for the time when Michel would say this to him; he had even prepared himself for it, but he had not expected it to come with such violence. When they were both quiet again he drew away from Michel a little to look into his face. "Come to Paris," he said simply. "Come to Paris. We can be together there."

Michel's first reaction was of acceptance and relief, as if Matthew had given him the only, and the right, solution; but even as he was about to say "yes" he began to shake his head, almost without knowing why he did so. "No," he said finally, "that would be impossible. Your family is there, you have to be with them."

"My family? What difference does that make?"

Michel's head continued to shake automatically. "No, no," he said. "We can't take a chance like that. I can't meet your mother and Paul. I don't think I could face them. Besides, how would you explain me to them? How could you see me when you're with them?"

"Explain you?" Matthew asked, puzzled. "Why do I have to explain you? I haven't many friends in Paris … none, really. Why shouldn't I see you if you were there? And why can't you meet them? You'll have to meet them some time. Why not now?"

Michel stood his ground firmly. However natural it might seem to Matthew, he was sure that it would not seem natural to Catherine nor to Paul – particularly not to Paul, nor to any man. Why would a young boy be seeing, constantly, a man practically twice his age? As for meeting them … it was hard for him to find the proper words to explain it to Matthew, but for him to have seduced a young boy – for that was what it amounted to – was serious; and it was not only that. He had never talked to Matthew about his past; he could not bring himself, easily, to use words like *seduce* or even *sex* when he talked to him. He felt suddenly that he had been living in a kind of unreal, romantic dream with Matthew – a dream that had to be forced into reality. Matthew was inexperienced, pure, and happy. His lack of guilt or worry was, it seemed to Michel, only a result of his ignorance. In the effort to explain his refusal to go to Paris, he found himself confronted with his past life there and with the necessity of someday having to talk about it, explain it. He was angry with the naïveté and the simplicity of Matthew's suggestion. "Come to Paris and we can be together" – easy enough for him, his life only needed Michel's presence to make it entirely happy, and if he was happy he assumed that everyone else must be happy as well. In part, as Michel had come to know, this was true, but only because of the infectious quality of Matthew's happiness which reached out and encompassed other people. It was not enough to encompass this situation.

"If your mother and Paul see us together, they might perfectly easily suspect what is really going on…"

Matthew shrugged his shoulders stubbornly. "What if they did?"

"Oh my God!" Michel exclaimed. "What do you mean what if they did? We've talked about that before. They won't kill us, no. I don't know what they'd do – it doesn't matter what they do, the thing is that they must never know. I'll meet them sometime when they come up here, when it's perfectly natural for me to meet them."

Matthew sat down on the bed wearily. "Couldn't you come to Paris and not see them, then? You could stay in a hotel and I could come to see you." He looked up at Michel, inquiring, ingenuous, and hurt.

Michel sighed. "You would come to see me. When? How often? And where would you tell them you were going?" He shook his head firmly. "No, Matthew, it's really impossible for both of us. You would be involved in a mountain of lies and I would be sitting in some horrible hotel room waiting for you to come, wondering when I was going to see you again. We can't do it, that's all. And it's my fault, all this. If I hadn't come running up here … you'll have to forget it. It's all we can do."

Matthew did not move from where he was sitting. "I still wish you'd come," he said, "and I still don't see why you're so sure Catherine and Paul would find out anything."

A flame of anger lighted up inside of Michel against what

appeared to be this wall of obstinacy and lack of understanding in Matthew. "You can't have what you want all the time," he said sharply, "without thinking of the risk and the price you have to pay."

Matthew shrank from the harshness of the words. "I didn't mean it that way. I thought you…"

Michel went over to him quickly and sat on the bed beside him. "I'm sorry," he said. "It's all my fault. You don't know what kind of thing you're mixed up in, you don't really know what's happened to you or what it's all about. You only see the happiness between us and nothing else. I suppose there's no reason why you should be able to understand that your happiness is something the world would think of as ugly and horrible and unnatural. But they do and I guess you'll learn soon enough."

Chapter Seventeen

Matthew left one week later and Michel stood in the doorway of the school, watching him as he drove off in the car with several other boys to the station. Because it was cold and the roads were slippery, Catherine had decided not to drive up for him but to let him come by train.

They had managed a final, brief, private farewell a few minutes before the car was to go, and then they had shaken hands at the front door of the school along with all the other boys and teachers. As Michel watched the car disappear, he felt relieved that that last week was finally over. It had been one long farewell with the shadow of their separation hanging over them all the time. From the moment that he had made that impulsive, uncontrollable declaration of love to Matthew, their relationship had undergone a subtle change which neither of them understood completely.

This was the first time that Michel had ever loved anyone in his life. The few girls he had known had been either young schoolgirls with whom he had felt awkward or, later, prostitutes; and the men had never been lovers in any deep sense of the word. With one or two of them he had achieved a semblance of happiness, based on the mutual necessity of sexual satisfaction. But Matthew ... Matthew loved him with a furious directness and with such extraordinary confidence that it was impossible not to respond to it fully. Matthew's assumption that Michel loved him as completely and purely as he was loved had somehow altered him so that he seemed to have achieved, briefly, a new character. He wanted to love him fearlessly and fully and openly, and the desire to do so had split him in two. More and more he was conscious of living a lie, of having someday to expose himself to Matthew for what he really was. He could not love Matthew and leave it at that. His declaration had involved him in a responsibility that he wanted and resented simultaneously. He believed in Matthew implicitly when they were together, but when they were apart his doubts and his fears for the future massed together inside him. Why should he, how could he, assume that Matthew was really different from the other men he had known, or that he, through knowing Matthew, would change? Someday, one of them would get tired of this, one of them would want to leave the other, this idyll he had begun (and with so young a boy!) would come to an end. It was this that he feared more than anything else now. As soon as any semblance of permanence entered a relationship, once the word love had been spoken with any degree of emotion, the eventual breakup (the *inevitable* breakup) was always made more difficult. He was certain, in his heart, that it would not be Matthew who would tire first, and he was already beginning to fear the day when he would hurt Matthew by ceasing to love him. It did not cross his mind that it was possible for them to build anything but a temporary love affair together, and he would bite his lip when he remembered telling Matthew how much he loved him. If only he had restrained himself!

Matthew's problems were quite different. He was hurt and puzzled to find that Michel disagreed with him, that he did not feel the same way about coming to Paris, that he was so full of fears of the future, of people, of the immoral and abnormal aspects of their relationship. He tried to fathom the meaning – a meaning that seemed deep and important to Michel – of such words as immorality and abnormality, but he was always primarily conscious only of his conviction of rightness. He could go so far as to understand that, socially, it was wrong for them to feel and act as they did, but he was unable to concern himself seriously with the consequences, the price. When Michel argued about consequences, he could visualize himself being expelled from school, Michel losing his job – all of it, but his emotions accepted none of these things. Whatever happened, they loved each other, they would manage to be together. The rest of it did not matter to him. The separation of the moment was painful and difficult, but he was certain of his return to the school, he knew that everything would be the same when they were back together again. He was hardly on the train before he began to compose in his mind his first letter to Michel; he would write him at least every day. Over and over he said to himself that it would only be two weeks, and he was not yet absolutely certain that Michel would not come to Paris for at least a few days. Whatever loneliness he felt, however much he resented having to be apart from Michel, he was still predominantly in love and happy. He no longer remembered himself as he had been before, melancholy and lifeless. He was a changed and revitalized human being.

As Michel embraced his mother, who immediately took his coat, his suitcase, his hat – handling them as she would have handled the most precious glass – the smell of cooking and the sight of the trays of cakes and cookies in the kitchen filled his nose and his eyes. He was sickened by the knowledge that his mother had been working for days to prepare for this homecoming and that he would be required to stuff himself and be appreciative. He wondered, pitying her as he did, why women were convinced that a man's happiness depended upon the amount of food one could consume each day. After an appropriate number of sniffs and smells, exclamations over the amount and the variety of her preparations, a taste of this and that, he was able to make his way from the kitchen to his room on the pretext that he was tired and needed a rest. His mother insisted upon carrying his things up to his room for him, showing that she had even lighted the stove, and then embracing him again. Only when she had closed the door and tiptoed away from it and down the stairs as if he were already fast asleep was he able to breathe a sigh of relief and lie back on the bed.

But the room did not permit him to rest. His eyes searched it bit by bit and section by section – his whole life was spread before him. The door to the armoire was closed, but he knew its contents well: his first baby clothes lay on the shelf wrapped in a bundle and his first suit hung from a hanger next to the black apron he had first worn in school. His first pair of sabots, scraped and polished, stood on the floor beside the stove, below the series of pictures of himself which his mother had hung on the wall. Pictures of himself as a baby, a child, a boy, a young man, and finally as a soldier, all grouped in one corner of the room. Near the door, on which his army uniform hung, was a final picture, taken by one of his *friends* in Paris the year before.

From the pictures his eyes strayed to the bookshelves where all his books from childhood were still neatly arranged. There were a few wooden toys on the top of the bookshelf, toys that came from so distant a past that Michel could no longer remember playing with them. And all around the room was the wallpaper that he lived with as a child and a young man. Even now as he looked at it, it seemed to take on life as it had so often done for him when he was a boy. It was a series of hunting scenes in green on a once-white background and, as he looked, the scenes – repeated over and over and over – came to life, the hunters, dogs, pheasants, stags, boars, trees, and rivers seemed to move, pursuing each other across the wall. Their reality was only interrupted at one or two places where the strips came together at the nose of a horse or the wing of a bird and did not meet exactly so that the horse's nose would be enlarged or foreshortened, and the bird would have either an enormous wingspan or have been collapsed into a tiny bird as if by an inner accordion action.

The faint smell of smoke from the wood fire in the stove, the cold afternoon light of the fading sun, made Michel more and more aware of the atmosphere of the room. It carried him back to his childhood with such force that he seemed to become a child again; something inside him wanted to be carried back to the days when this room had seemed huge, when the lighting of a fire had been a great event, when he had lain on the bed and watched the flicker of the fire through the draft of the stove making still further patterns on the wallpaper, so that the hunters joined together in a faltering torchlight procession.

He turned over on the bed and groaned, burying his face in the eiderdown cover. He wished urgently that he was only seven or eight, that the Army, all the women and men he had known and slept with could disappear by some magic, and that he and Matthew could be childhood companions playing at an innocent game. Or, equally impossible, that he could escape from everything in his life into the picture he knew his parents dreamed for him: successful in some respectable business of his own, married to a pretty, young, hardworking girl, father of perhaps three blooming children, two boys and a girl, and coming to visit his parents regularly in his own little car.

After three days at home, three days of eating and sleeping, talking with his parents, seeing a few of their friends in Rouen – people in whom he had no interest and with whom he felt a stranger – Michel decided to go to Paris. He would have to stay through Christmas *reveillon* and Christmas day; his parents would never forgive him if he did not – and Matthew would certainly have to be with his family – and he would have to come back for the *Nouvel An.* Still, it would give him three or four days in Paris.

He had received two letters from Matthew in those three days; outpourings of his love, his hope that Michel might somehow change his mind and manage to come to Paris, cursory résumés of what he was doing, comments on Catherine and Paul. But most of all they were love letters of the most passionate and unbridled nature, remembering the past and conjuring up the happiness of the future, planning for the years to come.

The effect of the letters on Michel was mostly to kindle his desire for Matthew and cumulatively his desire as such. They had possessed each other with sufficient regularity so that his body suffered from the sudden deprivation. In the moment after reading these letters, and he read them over and over, the house and the presence of his parents stifled him. Wild thoughts would run through his mind, suggesting themselves as means for his gratification. At such times, the image of Paris and of his own past there would rise vividly in his mind. Even if he could not see Matthew very much in a few days, there were after all others. He knew where to go … the thought of infidelity to Matthew did not trouble him. It would be a technical infidelity only, Matthew would never have to know. Besides, Matthew did not really understand what it was like for him. Matthew managed to live, somehow, on his love, his romantic fantasy of what their life would be like in the future when they could be together all the time. Matthew was not face to face with reality.

When Michel broke the news of his departure to his parents, they showed their disappointment in everything but words. He had invented excuses about having to help a friend with some work, and they accepted it unhappily but in the same way that they had come to accept everything from him. They no longer made concrete plans about and for him as they had when he was a child, but lived in their hope that things would turn out, if not exactly as they had always foreseen and wished, at least in some way that would be acceptable and would fit in with their dreams. They did not question the need for his going; it was already apparent from the definite manner in which he had spoken; and then there had been the letters from Paris.

Chapter Eighteen

Matthew received Michel's letter on the twenty-sixth of December, the day that he was to arrive in Paris, and as he read it his hands trembled with excitement and anticipation. It was like an extra, wonderful Christmas present. He was weak with happiness and his mind began at once to plot means of spending his time with Michel. When he told Catherine that Monsieur Garnier was coming to Paris he elaborated, adding that one of the boys – a particular friend of his – was coming with him, intimating that he would like to spend as much time with them as possible. Catherine did not object but even encouraged him, offering to have his friends to lunch or dinner or both. She was, in fact, very glad that something had happened that seemed to please her son. Not that she had not enjoyed having him at home. She had been happy to see him again and had found him changed in every way for the better. Even his attitude toward Paul had undergone some mysterious transformation so that he almost seemed to like him. She was unable to explain the difference, but assumed that things were going better for him at school, that he was growing up, that, as Paul had always assured her he would, he was finally learning to stand on his own feet and begin to make his own life.

All the arguments, the unpleasantness, the worry about Paul and Matthew had been wiped away unexpectedly, and Catherine's peace of mind was miraculously restored to her within a few days after Matthew's arrival. Her worries and anxieties, real as they had been, seemed now to have been groundless. Paul, as if he had a gift of foreknowledge, had been right after all. Matthew was a different boy.

His sullenness had changed to a kind of infectious gayety, a genuine desire to please everyone, and his happiness – something that sprang from the center of him – was carried around with him all the time. He was absorbed in his life at school, he wrote letters to his friends daily and talked of little else. They had both noticed that he spoke with particular respect and affection of Michel Garnier, the new teacher that year, and had decided privately that he had a schoolboy crush on the man, which, probably, was all to the good. After a few days, and because of the happy change she sensed in Matthew, Catherine could look back with relief and pleasure on the past few years. The divorce, all the painful decisions she had been forced to make about John, Matthew and Paul seemed to take on a righteous worth in her mind as if she had consciously planned these difficult years in order to reap the rewards of her labor. Matthew, more than ever before, had become (through her wisdom and effort, largely) what she had always wanted in a son: a young person of whom she could be rightfully proud.

When he left the apartment in the afternoon to meet "his friends" at the train, Catherine urged him to bring them back with him, if they cared to come, but also – as she thought, sensibly – suggested that if they had plans of their own they were of course free to do whatever they liked. He had left in a glow of pleasure – partly because of the forthcoming meeting, she knew, but also because she felt certain that he recognized her generosity in allowing him his freedom and at the same time offering her hospitality to his friends. She looked at Paul as they sat together cosily in the living room and, without speaking but by the mere gesture of taking his hand for a moment in hers, managed to convey to him her thanks and her happiness and the sense that her life was, for many reasons, entirely satisfactory. Paul was sufficiently moved by this gesture to hold her hand firmly in his and to assure her with his eyes that the romance and satisfaction which she now felt would continue.

Paul was also pleased because Catherine had learned only a few days before, in a reassuring letter from her lawyers, that the trust fund from which her money stemmed was in no danger – as far as they could determine at present. He recalled the last days of October and shuddered at the memory of the headlines, the frantic cables … when the news that Catherine's fortune was safe had finally come, he had willingly agreed to be cautious for the next year or two. He felt extremely grateful to his wife, her family and her lawyers for not being, as one of the lawyers had written sternly: "involved in specu-lation." It was not that Paul's love for Catherine was not genuine, only that his capacity for love was not very great and was readily influenced by practical questions. He looked at the gold watch on his wrist – Catherine's Christmas gift. For no apparent reason, he remembered his conversation with Françoise and his own final con-clusion. He had absolutely no regrets.

Almost before Michel was off the train, Matthew had handed him the box he had been saving for him. The paper was marked with the prints of his fingers, he had handled it so much, anticipating the moment when he would give it to Michel. He was equally pleased and excited when he received a small package from Michel, and they opened them together in the taxi: Michel's handsome toilet kit, that Matthew had bought secretly and hidden from his family, and the tie for which Michel apologized, it was such a little thing in comparison. But Matthew was delighted and put it on at once, and Michel was enormously relieved that he had remembered to give him *something*, that he had not forgotten that Americans gave each other presents at Christmas, like eternal children.

Matthew thought of Catherine and Paul then, he would have liked to take Michel home with him. He thought of them again at dinner with Michel and more briefly when they lay in each other's arms, his life and happiness filling him to a bursting point so that he was caught in a bittersweet ecstasy somewhere above and between joy and sadness. He had thought of them, but only for a moment, wishing as one does at such times, that everyone could be as happy and as alive as he was. He was in love; and if he could have, he would have created happiness for everyone, with the touch of his finger or the light in his eye.

During the three days he spent in Paris, Michel was rocked and shaken by his emotions. The first evening with Matthew he had been reassured and happy in the presence of Matthew's love and affection. When Matthew had left him, promising to come back the next afternoon, assuring him that he would not have to meet Catherine and Paul – a meeting which Michel very much feared – he had fallen asleep almost immediately. It was only the next morning, when he had awakened in the sombre little hotel room where it was impossible for the light of day to penetrate, that he found himself drained of confidence again. Lying on the bed in the dim light, his love affair seemed sordid and senseless to him, and he had no assurance that Matthew loved him. Even if he did, how could it possibly last, what was to become of them eventually? He was angry with himself for having come to Paris, for chasing after a boy – he could not bring himself to forget Matthew's age. It made him feel old and undignified. He resolved once again to talk things over with Matthew, to convince him that their association was ludicrous, and to leave Paris that evening. But when Matthew came to the hotel that afternoon, when he was once more face to face with his exultation and his pleasure, he could not say anything to him except that he could not stay very long, that he would have to go soon, and to refuse another invitation from Catherine.

The days passed slowly, and Michel was like a sick man in constant pain except for the few brief hours when he was drugged by Matthew's presence. On the last evening, as he waited for Matthew, who was to have dinner with him, he felt exhausted and hollow. The prospect of seeing Matthew did not cause his spirits to rise at all; he had been waiting and waiting it seemed, during all those hours, for the time that Matthew could spare for him, and now he was waiting again. Perhaps it was just the waiting and the emptiness, perhaps it was also the continual sparring with his conscience, the feeling that he was doing something wrong, that his purpose in being here was suspect. Whatever it was, a refreshing sensation of anger began to flow through him. If it had not been so urgently suggested by Matthew he would not have come here in the first place; if he had not been concerned with Matthew – had not wanted not to hurt him – he would not be here now.

With a sudden angry glance at his watch, he got up. Matthew would not be here for at least an hour. He could not stand the waiting any longer, and he had begun to hate the room. He put on his tie, his coat and then his overcoat, looked at his face in the mirror and went hurriedly out of the room. When he reached the desk, he hesitated before hanging up his key and then told the woman at the *caisse* that if the young man came he could wait upstairs in the room.

It was almost nine o'clock when Michel returned. There was something in his appearance that was not quite dishevelled but as if his clothes had ceased to fit him. He opened the door and then let it slam behind him and walked uncertainly into the room. He had been drinking, Matthew knew at once, and from the doorway where he had stood silently he walked and then dropped himself – in one continuous motion – onto the bed. Neither of them said anything, although they looked at each other in the pale light of the solitary lamp over the bed. It was not until Michel had been in the room for several minutes that he noticed the vase on the table: a great, flaming bunch of red roses. "*Très beau,*" he said, "*très beau.*"

Matthew did not reply, but continued to sit silently in the chair.

He had not spoken since Michel had come into the room. Angry with the silence, Michel looked at him again. "Where did you have dinner?" he asked.

"I didn't," Matthew said. "I was waiting for you."

Michel blinked at him. "Why didn't you have any dinner? Have you lost your appetite?"

Matthew shook his head. "Because I said I'd meet you here. I told you that."

"How long have you been here?"

"Since about six o'clock."

Michel looked at his watch. "Three hours," he said. "Well, you know what it's like then."

"I know what what's like?"

"Waiting. I waited today. I waited almost all day, but you didn't come."

Matthew's voice rose against Michel. "But you knew I wouldn't be here until this evening. It was all arranged."

Michel laughed. "It was all arranged! I told you I shouldn't have come to Paris. You have to be with your family almost all the time."

"But you knew that, Michel. I can't help it. If you'd like to meet them...."

Michel looked at him angrily, cutting him short, and then looked at the roses that Matthew had brought him. "You brought flowers, didn't you? What did you bring flowers for?"

Matthew stood up. "You're drunk," he said. "At least you've had too much to drink. There's no sense in talking now."

"I'm drunk!" Michel said, sitting up angrily. "I'm not supposed to do anything except sit here and wait for you, am I?"

"I didn't mean that, Michel. I'm sorry. But what is it? What have I done?"

Matthew hesitated, lost and unhappy. How could he tell him now? What could he say that would get through to him? He felt as if Michel was cut off from him, out of his reach. Still he had to try to tell him, try to let him know what had really made him bring the flowers. "I brought them because I wanted to, that's all. I've always wanted to bring you flowers. They didn't mean anything specially, it was just … well, I'd been away from you for so long."

"*Et bien, et bien, cela va.*"

Matthew went over to him and sat on the floor beside the bed, putting his head on Michel's knees. "I'm sorry," he said, but even as he said it he could feel Michel stiffening against him, and then his head was taken in Michel's hands and Michel looked at him, examining his face angrily. "All you have to do is come over here and put your head down in my lap and then you think that everything is going to be all right, don't you?" He pushed Matthew's head roughly away from him. "Everything's easy for you, isn't it?" he went on as if he was unable to stop talking. "You're young and the world belongs to you. What difference does it make to you if it's different for me, what difference does it make how I feel about anything as long as you think it's all right? If there's any trouble all you have to do is touch me and that will fix everything up, won't it? Well, it's not so easy. I can resist you. I have a mind of my own. You don't own me!"

The tears came to Matthew's eyes and spilled out of them onto his cheeks. He continued to look at Michel silently, there was no sound in his crying. He was hurt in the only way that he could be hurt, by something he could not understand. He shook his head slowly from side to side.

"And don't cry," Michel said sharply. "Do you think that's going to make me feel sorry for you, to have to look at you crying? It's like everything else you do, you can always to the right thing at the right moment: you can laugh, or smile, or cry. You think you know me so well that you know exactly how I'm going to feel when you do something. Well, you don't."

With his face still wet, Matthew stood up. He was not sure of what he was going to do, but he knew that something was happening inside him. Following his instincts, he walked over to the roses that he had placed on the table. Slowly, methodically, he broke the flowers from their stems, dropping them one by one on the floor, and when there were none left, when the decapitated stems stared up at him from the table, he ground his heel carefully into each one of the blossoms, staining the carpet and floor with them, and then he sat down. His hands were in his lap, palms up. He had torn at the roses heedlessly, and now blood was oozing from the ends of some of his fingers, dropping onto his trousers.

Michel had watched him, surprised at first, but it had taken so long that he had felt a gradual sensation of horror coming over him. It was like witnessing an execution, and the sound as each flower was snapped from the stem, and finally as they were ground under Matthew's heel, made him wince.

Matthew stood up again, looking at Michel, withdrawn and cold. He was exhausted by what he had done. He held his arms close to his sides, with the forearms straight ahead of him, looking at the blood on his hands.

At first Michel was unable to move or to take his eyes from the crushed flowers on the floor. Then suddenly he could not bear to look at them any longer, and he jumped up from the bed. There was something angry and wild inside him, some need to attack and destroy, and even what Matthew had done was insufficient to stem the tide in him. "Why did you do that?" he asked.

Why had he done it? He didn't know. He pulled a handkerchief from his pocket and wiped his hands. "I don't know," he said. "I hate flowers. I will always hate flowers – especially roses – from now on."

The bitterness in his voice bit into Michel and, as suddenly as it had come, his anger was dissipated, as if Matthew's voice, like a sure sharp needle, had punctured the balloon of fury inside him. It was not what Matthew had done now, it was what he had done himself. He put his arms around Matthew and rubbed his cheek against him, feeling the wetness on Matthew's face, and blindly, his words muffled in Matthew's shoulder, he said: "Forgive me, Matthew. Forgive me. What have I done?"

When Matthew did not answer, he raised his head and looked at him. "What have I done?" he asked again, but Matthew's eyes only seemed to search his face, unable to understand. First he kissed the boy's cheeks and searched for his hands, only to touch the handkerchief. He took it slowly from between Matthew's fingers and dropped it on the floor, and then he touched the fingers gently. The blood was already drying, but the hands were cold and unresponsive. He covered Matthew's mouth with his own and kissed him again and again. "Forgive me, forgive me," he said, and his arms went around Matthew's body, holding him tightly against his chest. "You have to forgive me, Matthew, or I can never forgive myself, never."

Matthew still did not answer him, did not move. He felt the increase in Michel's breathing, smelled the wine on his lips, tasted it in his mouth; he felt even some automatic response inside himself, but it was inside a self that he did not really inhabit; he was outside of and away from them, looking down at this scene. There was, to him, something not quite natural, something really wrong with what was happening. Perhaps the abnormality, the unnaturalness which Michel had so often assured him was the basis of their relationship – the thing that he had searched for in himself – was being demonstrated to him now. He could sense it in this moment.

When Matthew left, after dressing rapidly in the harsh light from the unprotected bulb over the bed, he was chilled and weak and Michel had not spoken to him again; they had made no appointment for the next day, although it was to be Michel's last day in Paris. He hurried down the stairs of the small hotel, the collar of his coat standing round his neck and accentuating the pallor of his face. He did not feel anything at all until he had run the gauntlet of Catherine and Paul and was safely curled in his own bed in the dark, his knees against his chest and his arms wrapped around them tightly, with the smell of Michel's body still filling his nose. He was very cold.

Chapter Nineteen

Responding to some desperate call of his emotions, Matthew's body had come to his rescue with a moderate degree of fever, inflamed sinuses, a touch of pleurisy and an upset stomach. The illness manifested itself the next morning and reached its peak that afternoon, shortly after Michel's train to Rouen was to leave. Matthew had lain in his bed listening for the sounds of the telephone, the doorbell – any sign from the outside world that touched the apartment – but there had been no word, no messages of any kind. He fell asleep in the early darkness, no longer anticipating and fearing some move on Michel's part; his body was exhausted and his mind was locked in a trap of doubt and bewilderment. He had gone over and over that evening, until the only two facts that he could recognize were the certainty of Michel's determined cruelty – his desire to wound – and the equally certain knowledge that there was no reason for it; he could get no further. The answer would have to come from Michel himself, somehow and sometime, and Matthew looked ahead dully to the time when he would see him again, when he would – he would have to! – say or do something that would explain what he had done. He did not know, and did not even care what had happened to their relationship; he knew only that he would have to understand *why*. Nothing else mattered.

The next morning he had begun to relax into the illness, allowing it to overpower him, accepting the worried looks on Catherine's face, the pills, the medicine, the cups of bouillon. She was worried about him and at the same time she enjoyed having him in bed and taking care of him. She knew the illness was not serious, that it was only a question of days, that in all probability he would be able to go back to school when the time came. Meanwhile, it was like having a little boy in the house again. He responded willingly to her attentions, although he would not eat very much, and she found herself enjoying reading to him or just talking in a peaceful, affectionate, close way. They had not seemed so close in years. She obtained a real sense of satisfaction in taking his temperature, feeling his forehead, rubbing his back and waiting on him efficiently. She had not realized how much she had missed doing things for him, and it was pleasant and warming to be needed and to be able to respond effectively.

The third or fourth day after Michel had left Paris, Scott came to see him. He had been away in the country with Françoise, one of their habitual visits, and he was very glad to see Matthew again. They were embarrassed at first, watching and measuring each other as they talked about what Scott had done, about the school, the weather – not touching on anything more serious. They both sensed that they had grown away from each other and had to allow themselves time to come back to some meeting ground where they would feel easy again. It was Scott who broke the web of banalities by saying suddenly: "Well, how *is* everything, Matthew?"

For a moment, the sound of the words, the insistent accent he had given to the word "is," brought the pain of his predicament to a kind of boil inside Matthew as if his blood was about to bubble over. He wiped his mouth quickly with the back of his hand. "Oh, fine," he said as casually and as flatly as he could, at the same time aware of his need to talk, to try and find an answer from any source. For one hideous, indecisive moment, he stared at Scott's face, considering the possibility of telling him everything, and then he fell back on the bed, exhausted by his efforts at self-control. He looked away from Scott, searching the ceiling to find something to say that would turn the conversation in another direction. "When are you going to get married?" was what finally came to his lips and it was not until he said it that he could look in Scott's direction again. To his surprise, Scott's face colored slightly and he was looking away at the floor. "We've put it off for a while," he said bluntly. "Françoise doesn't want to get married just yet."

"Why not?"

Scott did not reply immediately. Methodically, he measured and checked the feeling that Matthew's question had brought into play inside him: that he wanted to talk about himself and Françoise, that he wanted not to talk about it, and finally that it seemed ridiculous to try to talk honestly about himself to someone so young as Matthew. It was the realization of a similar doubt in Matthew and a feeling that he would understand him, that finally led him to reply.

"She thinks there are a lot of problems we have to solve first," he said, and then eyed Matthew in an attempt to determine whether or not he should go on. Meeting an encouraging and questioning look, intensified by the feverishness of Matthew's face and the intent way in which he held the expression, Scott continued. "I guess it's silly of me to tell you all this," he said apologetically, "but I really don't know what the trouble is. She was all ready to marry me, and then all of a sudden she said that there were a lot of things we had to think about. Where we were going to live – you know, here or America – and whether I was really serious about the responsibilities of getting married and bringing up a family, and had I really thought about marrying a French girl and all that kind of thing."

"What did you say?"

"Well, I said that of course I had and that I wouldn't have asked her to marry me if I hadn't already thought about all that."

"And?"

"Oh, I don't know." Scott knitted his brow and rubbed his cheek with one hand. "That's when things began to get difficult. She said she didn't think I'd really thought about things seriously, and that I was impulsive like all Americans and so on. I told her I wasn't and then we got into a kind of argument and, well, we've put it off for a while."

Matthew looked at him for a moment in silence, and then with an intensity which astonished Scott, said: "If you really love each other everything will be all right. Nothing else matters."

"Yes, I guess you're right." Scott was stirred and touched by the vehemence with which Matthew had spoken and what seemed to him the direct truth of his words. He felt an intimacy and communion with him which startled him. But what he felt most of all was that Matthew did understand him, as if they had been contemporaries and confronted with the same problem. He reminded himself, forcibly, that he had often been surprised by an unexpected maturity in Matthew, and he was glad that he had talked to him. When he left, he felt they had returned to the kind of companionship they had had when Matthew first came to Paris: a friendship that was based on an emotional logic more important than the difference in their ages.

Matthew, in his own way, felt better after seeing Scott. What he had said to him about love seemed to be applicable to his own case as well, and he was less afraid of encountering Michel again. He had, more or less unconsciously, understood that their relationship might have come to an end, even that it might still, but his own words had given him the feeling that it was hopeless, that even if Michel were unable to explain himself and his actions of that night, there was a salvation – a solution – in their love for each other. Perhaps it was up to him to prove to Michel that that love really existed and that it was stronger than anything which attacked it.

In spite of Catherine's protests he got up the next day. His sinuses had cleared up, his temperature was gone, and the only reminders of his illness were his extreme pallor and a faint, recurring pain in his chest. He planned his return to school, his meeting with Michel. He would give him every chance and he would not be angry or even hurt if he could help it. The thought of a noble course of action pleased him in the same way his daydreams had once given him satisfaction, and it gave him a sense of strength and power to realize that he, by his own determined action, could at least affect their future. His hands were not tied, however much it might cost him to use them. He felt a sharp twinge of self-pity when he imagined his course with Michel, but that, too, was not unpleasant.

Catherine, who had been surprised and pleased to find him so happy, so gay, so changed for the better when he had returned from school for his vacation, had been astonished by his sudden illness, and was now further astonished by his rapid recovery (which did not seem quite normal or quite complete to her) and also by his attitude. He was gentle, affectionate and kind – kind in a way that would have been condescending in someone who was not her own son – and he went out of his way to do things for her, to spend his time with her. Unnatural as it had seemed at first, she was flattered and moved by his attentions, and completely unaware that he was trying out his role on her. In a few months, he had come from a daydream of knighthood – in which he had been the generous and courtly rescuer, the central figure in a drama which without his intervention would have become a tragedy – to a living reincarnation of that perfection. He longed to get back to school and to Michel, in much the same way that St. George had undoubtedly strained to reach the dragon. He made excuses for Michel, clothed him in virtue, and tried to disguise the painful doubt which was still centered inside him – plastering them both with good intentions and love … love most of all. But however much he strained to believe in these self-deceptions, from time to time the doubt would push its way through to his consciousness, leaving him weak and in pain and knowing only that he had to see Michel again, that he could not let him go, that he had to understand what had gone wrong.

His stomach continued to quiver uneasily and unexpectedly until the day that he knew he was to leave Paris, until he was certain he would go back on schedule. Only when he was in the car, for Catherine had insisted that she and Paul would drive him back in spite of the weather, did he quiet down again. He was still nervous and impatient beneath the cool exterior which he forced himself to maintain, but like the calm before a storm or the quiet before battle, he knew that there were only hours to wait now. One thing he had not been able to do was to write Michel, and while he regretted not having done so – it would have been proof of his willingness to forgive and forget – it was too late now. The car was already well outside Paris.

Chapter Twenty

What Matthew had not anticipated was the delay that was inevitable before he could see Michel. He had greeted him, and they had looked into each other's eyes with terrible intensity for one instant, and then they had been carried away from each other by the routine of the school, the process of getting back. They saw each other briefly in the dining room, in the library where the boys were assembled in the evening by M. de St. Croix who gave them a short, formal welcoming speech, and then they were separated again by the boys' bedtime and a meeting of the teachers. He could not, he realized, go to Michel's room and he was unable to see him for long enough even to suggest that he come to see him. He began on an agony of waiting which, hour by hour, stripped him of his goodwill, his intentions and his plans. It was hours before he went to sleep, lying instead in the dark with his eyes open wide, hoping that somehow Michel would manage to come to him during the night. It was not until after supper the next evening – more than twenty-four hours after his return to the school – that Michel came to his room. When he had closed the door behind him, they stared at each other in mutual terror, unable to speak or act. After an interminable, unbearable silence, Michel spoke. "I'm glad to see you, Matthew," he said and Matthew, to his own anger and astonishment, burst into tears.

Michel came over to him at once, speaking softly, holding him in his arms, kissing his cheeks until, at last, Matthew turned his tear-stained face to him and echoed the question he had asked him in Paris and had been asking ever since. "Why were you so angry with me? Why?"

As if to still further postpone answering that question, Michel kissed him once again, but this time Matthew withdrew. "No, please," he said. "I have to know."

Michel's shoulders moved and he hung his head. "I'm so glad you're back," he said, and then looking at Matthew's face, still questioning him relentlessly, he asked, in a voice that was barely audible: "Can you forgive me?"

"But I don't know what for! I don't know what I did ... I don't know what's happened!"

Michel was unrelenting. "Please say you'll forgive me first," he pleaded. "Please." And Matthew, confused and unable to hold himself back any longer, threw his arms around him. "Yes, yes, yes. I'll forgive you. Anything! But tell me about it. Tell me what's wrong."

Then, and only then, did Michel begin on a long and garbled, almost incomprehensible explanation. "If you only knew how much I love you, how much better you are than I could ever be. I can never explain this, but..." and he went on and on, reiterating his love for Matthew, his need for him, his apology for what he had done, how much he hated himself, how much more he loved Matthew for being able to forgive him so readily. After a steady stream of words, he became suddenly and morosely silent, and looked Matthew directly in the face. "And ... and," he began hesitantly, "I had to find out something."

"But what?"

"I had to find out if..." and then he broke off, his face contorted with embarrassment and pain.

"If what, Michel?" Matthew insisted.

Michel surged forward, burying his face in Matthew's lap. "No one ever loved me before," he said. "Nobody ever treated me the way you do. I didn't believe it. I couldn't stand it. I almost hated you for a while, as if you'd made me fall in love with you when I didn't want to. I don't know. I don't know *why*. I just know I had to do it."

Matthew did not answer him but held Michel's head in his hands, winding his fingers through his hair. He was puzzled still, he had not been able to extract any logical sense from Michel's words, and yet the pain inside him was eased and he knew that whatever had happened between them, it had come to an end. He knew that he could not forget that night, that the scar inside him would remain, but the sharp digging hurt was gone now, and with his hands he tried to draw the pain out of Michel – even if he could not understand it he could feel it and see it – as if it was something he could take tangibly in his fingers and extract from Michel's heart. He did not want to know any more, he did not want to pretend to nobility or kindness, he wanted to be happy; and his happiness would not be complete until he was assured that Michel was happy, too. When Michel lifted his head and smiled at him, he knew they were both all right, and after kissing him several times, on his hands, his cheeks, his mouth, his forehead, Michel left him, promising to return as soon as he could.

Matthew undressed slowly. He was tired as he had not been for days, but the warmth had returned to his body. He lay in his bed, quiet and secure, and looked out the window. He had not closed the shutters and, as if the weather had contrived to make this particular moment beautiful, the moon cast a brilliant shaft of light into the room and across the landscape outside. There were patches of snow on the ground and they were luminous in the moonlight. He held the covers closely around his body and listened intently for any sound from the hall. The school was going to bed, all the rooms and halls were gradually becoming silent except for here and there the step of someone going to the bathroom, or the creak of a plank in the old house as it settled itself in for the night. When Michel did come, he came so noiselessly that Matthew was not aware of his presence until he had closed the door behind him. Then he looked up to find him standing in the moonlight next to the bed.

☙

Their reconciliation was unlike anything in their previous experience. In place of the straightforward intensity of love and the seizure of happiness which had seemed to be there for the taking, they became intertwined in a kind of love-making which arose more in their hearts and in their consciousness of each other's needs and wishes than from the urgent need to gratify their mutual desire. They spun a protective web about themselves, cherishing their time together, planning for each other, dreaming of the summer and the future, writing each other letters when they were not able to be together, and then reading them over and over. As if they had received some warning, they were more careful than ever before, avoiding every possibility of discovery, even going so far as to sacrifice some of the time they might have spent together in order that it might not seem they were in any way involved. The other teachers and a good many of the boys were conscious of a special relationship, a particular bond between the two of them, but as it was not unusual for certain boys to have heroes among the teachers and for some of the teachers to have their pet students. It did not arouse any comment. Matthew was openly accused of being Monsieur Garnier's pet but the accusations never went beyond teasing and they were not troubled. M. de St. Croix was pleased to find that Matthew, who was such a fine student, should also have made good progress in athletics, and wrote to Catherine praising her son and crediting Michel for having taken such pains with him. When the spring vacation came around, there was no suggestion made by either of them that they should attempt to share it, and after the absence of that one week, they found each other again: ardent, happy and secure in the knowledge that they had several more weeks of time together in school and certain that their plans for the summer would work out.

Matthew was particularly excited because Catherine had decided to spend the summer in Brittany at Requin, a town Paul had known as a boy. When he pointed it out to Michel on the map, he indicated, just to the south of Requin, Pointe Saint-Mathieu. He was sure that it was prophetic, a guarantee of happiness for both of them. Paul had completely forgotten it was there, and Catherine had been very much surprised; she too had thought it was a good omen for the summer, particularly as none of them had known of its existence. Michel smiled; not quite believing in Pointe Saint-Mathieu as an omen, and questioned Matthew further about Requin.

"Mother thinks it's *ideal*," Matthew said, mimicking his mother's voice. "She says it's quiet and out of the way; yet near the little resort of Le Conquet..." he paused, looking significantly at Michel, "where you could stay," he added.

Michel nodded. "Yes," he said slowly. "I don't know, though. Seems to me we're taking an awful chance, Matthew."

"Michel!" Matthew's tone was pained, and he looked at him, crestfallen.

Michel smiled. "Well, all right," he said slowly. "As a matter of fact, I've been there before."

"You have!"

Michel nodded again. "I went there with my parents one summer when I was a boy. I've even been to Pointe Saint-Mathieu, but I'd forgotten it until just now. Of course I was awfully young...."

Matthew was very much impressed with this information. "You see," he pleaded, still uncertain of Michel's acceptance of his plans, "it *is* like fate. You've been there before, Paul's been there before, and it's named after me. Oh, Michel, please don't worry any more, *please*."

So they made their own special plans. Catherine and Paul would be sure to make a great many short trips to Quimper, the Pointe du Raz, along the coastline, and once Michel's accidental presence in Le Conquet was discovered, they'd probably be glad to have Matthew spend at least some of his time with him. Michel agreed, finally, that he would have to meet Catherine and Paul sometime and he seemed to have lost his antipathy to such a meeting. Once they had met, in so isolated a place, it would be only natural for them to see each other, and perhaps – as Matthew had suggested – it would even seem logical for Michel to move to Requin with them rather than spend his time alone at Le Conquet. However it worked out, they would be together a great part of the time, which was all that mattered to them. The elements of subterfuge and secrecy, the faint uncertainty and the anticipation of having these plans work out as they wished, lent a kind of special excitement to their final weeks together, and they could hardly wait for the summer to begin. It beckoned to them as it stretched temptingly ahead of them, warm and bright with the sun, and full of a promise of comparatively undivided time together, something they had never had up to now.

Two days before Catherine and Paul were to drive to the school and pick up Matthew on their way to Brittany, Matthew received a letter from his mother enclosing a letter from his father, and when he said to Michel, "*J'ai reçu une lettre de mon père*," it was the look in his face that made Michel stiffen rather than the announcement itself. He asked him, as calmly as possible, sensing some threat in the way Matthew had spoken, what was in the letter.

"He is coming to visit me this summer. Or at least he wants to. He leaves it pretty much up to me."

If Michel had been the kind of person who could respond without thinking first, his question would have been "What are you going to do?" It was the question he wanted to ask, and it was his need to ask it and his consciousness of that need that prevented him from asking it directly. If you love someone, so much so that there is no corner of their life in which you are not involved, you will yet come to a place which you cannot enter – in them – easily. Matthew's relationship with his father, whatever Michel's place in his life, was his own affair. If there was any decision to be made, Matthew must make it by himself. He rephrased the question in his mind, and then said as mildly as possible: "What exactly does he say?"

Matthew smiled at him: "What you mean is what am I going to do?" He paused, looking away from Michel. "I am going to see him, of course."

All that Michel could manage as a reply was: "Oh."

Once more, Matthew laughed, and there was real happiness in his laughter. He would have liked to take hold of Michel and tell him how happy it made him to know that he minded and feared this intrusion of his father, but he was uncertain of his reaction. Instead, he walked over to him, placing his hand on Michel's shoulder in a gesture that had come to be characteristic of him. "Don't worry, Michel. It won't change anything. My father and his wife are coming to Paris for a month. They will arrive about the end of July. We will stay in Brittany until then and then we'll go to Paris. After that we can do whatever we like. We can go back to Brittany if we want, or not. Whatever you say."

Michel shook his head. "You make it all sound so easy. What is your mother going to think of all this, or your father for that matter? How can you be with me and your father at the same time? I must have been mad! I had a feeling that this summer was impossible – a fantastic dream – a snatching for happiness to which I have no right. And I was not wrong. Already, now, I can see that we are going to begin to pay for this – for what we have already had. You do not get anything in the world without making a payment for it, Matthew. Nothing at all."

Matthew gripped his shoulder, looking at the letter in his other hand. "But you don't have to worry about mother or about dad! You can tell mother right away that you have to go to Paris in August and we can probably go together – she won't have to worry about me going to Paris alone." He read from the letter. "'I want you to do whatever you think is best, Matthew, whatever you really want to do. The apartment will be empty and there is no reason why you cannot stay in it alone, although if you would rather I'll come back with you when your father arrives.'" He looked at Michel again. "When she learns that you're going to be in Paris, she'll probably ask you to stay at the apartment. The only thing is…"

"What?"

"Oh, Michel, she has to like you!" He laughed again. "And she will! I know she will. Think of it, Michel, we'll have our own home in Paris. Can't you see?" The smile disappeared from his face for a moment and he pulled Michel closer to him. "It won't be anything like the last time," he said softly, and they held each other close – it was the first time that either of them had referred directly to that visit of Michel's.

Matthew was still undecided and hesitant. "But what about you, Matthew? How do you feel about your father, about seeing him after all this time?"

"I don't know really. Curious, I guess. I want to see him."

"Yes. But Matthew, seriously. Be serious about all this. Won't he want to see you alone? Won't you want to see him alone, to stay with him? You have to think of these things."

"Why would I want to stay with him when the apartment's there? As for seeing him alone, you don't want to see him every time I see him, do you?"

Michel shook his head. "No, of course not. But I want you to be sure. You must be sure."

"But I *am* sure!"

Matthew's confidence and intensity, his faith that things would always turn out right for him, communicated themselves to Michel. It was difficult to argue with him, it was like challenging an act of faith, but even though he did not argue and let himself be persuaded, Michel was afraid. He had allowed Matthew, because he did not know how to protest effectively, to take the lead in their relationship. It was Matthew who had the ideas, the suggestions, the enthusiasm and the assurance. Michel was forced to admit that however much he tried to believe in Matthew, however much he loved him (which, in itself, was frightening) the thing of which he was fully convinced, the one thing in which he really believed was that Matthew would lead them to certain destruction. His own life had been safe enough up to now, he had taken no unnecessary risks, he had not asked for more than he felt he could pay for; he had forced himself, at least in theory, to accept the possible consequences of his homosexuality, because there was nothing he could do about it. But Matthew was not content with that. He wanted a kind of happiness that was unattainable in any relationship (and yet he seemed to attain it); he paid no real heed to the possible consequences. He was like a person possessed or inhabited by something bigger than himself – it was impossible to think of him as a fifteen-year-old boy. Of course, he was no longer a fifteen-year-old boy. There was something ageless and eternal about him. What he told himself he could do was law, it existed with a logic and reason of its own. Michel was unable either to accept it fully or to combat it. The result of his feelings and his inability to argue was that he agreed, and Matthew wrote to his mother and his father.

Chapter Twenty-one

The last day of school was one that Michel would not forget easily. The boys were packing or waiting around the library or the grounds for their parents or for the bus which was to take them to the train. The halls and the driveway were littered with suitcases, trunks, tennis racquets and all the miscellaneous paraphernalia that passes for luggage in a boy's life. Michel had gone to his room to do his own packing when he received an unexpected visit from M. de St. Croix. He was told that M. and Mme. Dumesnil, the parents of Matthew Cameron, had arrived and had asked to see him. M. de St. Croix added that he himself wished to compliment M. Garnier (he had a way of suddenly addressing you in the third person) for what he had done for Matthew, as he was sure M. and Mme. Dumesnil wished to do, particularly as he, M. de St. Croix, had made it very plain to them that M. Garnier had exerted an excellent influence on their boy. They were waiting in M. de St. Croix's private study, if he would be so kind....

Not only did M. and Mme. Dumesnil wish to thank him for all he had done to stimulate Matthew's interest in athletics, for his kindness to him, but they would like very much to be able to take him to Brittany with them. They had learned, quite by chance, in talking with Matthew that he was going to be at Le Conquet, which was only a few kilometers from Requin. It was Paul who did most of the talking, and his manner seemed to Michel both courteous and sincere. When he recovered from his original surprise, he hesitated, looking quickly at Matthew. There was nothing in Matthew's face except a faint smile of pleasure and achievement. It all seemed safe enough and it was quite possible that it was entirely accidental. He could imagine the conversation: it would have been natural enough for them to ask where he (M. Garnier, in whom Matthew seemed so interested) was going to spend the summer, and equally natural once Matthew had told them, to offer to take him along.

He assured them he was delighted with the offer, but he hesitated to accept as he did not want to interfere with their plans, and then he refused tentatively. He had not finished his packing, he did not want to hold them up, there would not be room for his luggage … but it was Catherine who waved all these considerations aside. Their car was quite large enough, they had sent most of their own luggage from Paris by train and if necessary they could also ship a bag of his that way since they had to pass the railroad, and finally he could take his time about packing as they were in no hurry. "And," she said, smiling at him, "we feel we owe you a great deal after all you've done for Matthew. It would be a pleasure to be able to make it up to you in some small way."

Once again, the decision had been taken out of his hands, and as Michel finished his packing hurriedly he shook his head in wonder. Perhaps Matthew was right. Things had a way of working out almost by themselves if you had sufficient faith to believe in them.

The trip from Normandy to Requin took them several days. To the delight of Catherine and to Paul's surprise and amusement, Matthew helped plan their itinerary – with Catherine's Baedeker and his own Guide Bleu – insisting there were some places in Normandy they must see even though it meant doubling back towards Paris: Tancarville, Château Gaillard; and they must spend one night at Les Andelys. Catherine, after making a perfunctory objection to any change in plans for Paul's sake and because Michel might want to get to his destination, was overruled by Matthew's enthusiasm about the trip, Michel's insistence that he was in no hurry to get to Le Conquet, and Paul's apparent pleasure in satisfying Matthew's whims.

Paul had begun to like Matthew during his winter holiday in Paris and now he saw him not as a truculent and difficult stepson but as a young and attractive stranger, full of life and good humor. He was infected by Matthew's gayety, and it was a relief to have the shadow of Matthew lifted from between himself and Catherine. It was going to be a much better summer than he had considered possible, and he was happy with the addition of Michel Garnier to their party. It occurred to him that he might be willing to occupy some of Matthew's time, and he made a mental note to suggest to Catherine that, since M. Garnier seemed to have no special reason for being at Le Conquet except that it was a place to go for the summer, they might invite him to stay at Requin with them in the little inn. A schoolteacher's pay could not be very large and Requin was bound to be less expensive than Le Conquet.

As he drove the car, listening to Catherine's exclamations of delight over the countryside and the view, he whistled to himself and looked at Michel through the rear-view mirror. A nice enough person, certainly, and Paul was rather glad to have a Frenchman for company. Curious, though, that a man – he must be close to thirty – should have no plan for his summer and that he should be so good a friend to Matthew. What, exactly, was the bond between them? He stopped whistling and his eyes narrowed. This was the man who had come to Paris at Christmas … he remembered Matthew's excitement when he learned that M. Garnier was coming, the amount of time they had spent together, Matthew's sickness. Of course, some other friend of Matthew's had been along, too….

They stopped for their first night at Les Andelys, and over dinner Michel found himself discussing (odd the way Americans could always, and under almost any circumstances, talk about money) the financial arrangements for the trip. Catherine suggested – saying that she and Paul had talked it over and of course did not want to interfere with any of his own plans – that he might prefer to spend the summer with them at Requin. They would be very happy for his company, and the inn was very cheap. She offered, in fact she seemed to expect to have him as her guest for the trip, and it was only his stubborn insistence that made her agree to let him pay his own expenses on the journey. As for Requin, he said that he would have to think it over first, and they agreed to discuss that suggestion later. In the meantime, in order to make his expenses as small as possible, Catherine thought that he and Matthew might share a room on the trip. All of the rooms here, as it happened, were enormous and those they finally took – one for Paul and Catherine, and one for Michel and Matthew – were each provided with three double beds.

Except for her high spirits, Catherine would not have asked the reason for the three beds, or she would perhaps have answered it for herself. As it was, when the old stooped *patronne* led them by candlelight up the stone staircase into a room that was the size of a small ballroom with high stone walls and great windows, the three enormous beds, one of them firmly planted in the center of the room, seemed to leap out at Catherine. She turned to the *patronne* who watched her, her face leering in the candlelight, the soft hair on her upper lip having grown into a heavy mustache, and exclaimed: "*Trois lits? Trois lits dans une chamber?*" The *patronne* smiled at her and then winked comfortably at Paul, wiping her large hand on the apron which hung over her ample dress. Bowing slightly and with an elaborate gesture of the candle, she said, looking firmly at Paul and not at Catherine: *Un pour Monsieur, un pour Madame, et un pour la gymnastique!*" Then she burst into loud laughter and Catherine blushed. She was glad that Matthew was not with them at that moment, and she told herself that there were some things she would never quite understand about the French.

When Michel and Matthew were in their own room, also complete with three beds, Michel began to regain his perspective. Things had been moving too fast for him all day, and he suspected Matthew of connivance with his mother and perhaps with Paul. But when Matthew assured him that he had only volunteered the information that Michel was going to go to Le Conquet and that the rest of it – that he should come with them, that they should share a room, that he should stay at Requin – had all been their own ideas, Michel shook his head and laughed. His anticipatory fears about Catherine and Paul were quieted, he liked them both, and he was allowing himself to feel happy, giving in to his pleasure at being with Matthew. It was a kind of happiness he had never felt in his life before, he told Matthew, that he had never permitted himself to feel. He would have to get used to it.

Matthew laughed at him and tried to reassure him still further. "I told you that things would turn out all right, and they have. Even better than I had hoped. You always ask for trouble, you think everything is going to turn out badly."

Michel looked at him seriously. "Perhaps you're right. I don't know, but I still have the feeling that this is something forbidden, or dangerous." And then he smiled again. "I am very happy, though."

Matthew took his hands in his own. "Think of the time that is stretching before us, Michel. The whole summer belongs to us now. Please continue to be happy."

Michel told himself that Matthew was right, that he had overexaggerated the risks and dangers and was too pessimistic. He remembered Catherine turning to him in Matthew's presence after dinner, and thanking him for what she felt he had done for Matthew. At the time he had had an impulse to flee from all of them. He could not believe his ears. She had looked at him, grave and affectionate, glancing from time to time at her son as she spoke.

"Perhaps I should not say this in front of Matthew," she had said, "but I'm sure he is aware of the change in himself. Whatever the reasons for it, I know you have had something to do with it. M. de St. Croix has spoken so highly of you and Matthew is so fond of you ... I do hope you will seriously consider spending the summer with us. It would make me very happy indeed."

And late that night, reinforced by his mother's liking for Michel, Matthew said: "You see? You have only to see what is happening to know that there is nothing wrong about us. They are happy for us to be together, so it must be good."

It was impossible not to believe him and, in his beginning sleep, Michel saw the days before them as he would have looked upon a garden through some door that had always been closed to him. He could feel his resistance weakening and he prayed that it would disappear altogether, that his conscience would dissolve and vanish, leaving him free to reap the rewards the summer was promising to him. If only he could acquire some of Matthew's strength, feel the same wild and childlike joy that Matthew expressed constantly.

It was not until just before lunch the next day that Michel had a sudden premonition of danger. He had chanced to look up, and his eyes had met Paul's stare in the mirror of the car. Paul had glanced away immediately and then looked back again – a long look, full of curiosity. Michel lowered his eyes uncomfortably and his heart began to beat faster. He remembered that Paul had said practically nothing, he had let Catherine do all the talking … of course, she had said that she had discussed everything with Paul. He squared his shoulders and looked back into the mirror, but Paul was no longer observing him. He cursed himself for having believed that Paul, a man of the world, a Frenchman, obviously shrewd, however easygoing he might seem, would not have suspected their relationship. But it was too late now – he would have to brazen it out. And perhaps it was not really too late … however clever Paul was, he had only his suspicions (Michel was sure of them) and no proof. In any case, he would certainly have to warn Matthew.

Through the conversation at lunch, Michel and Paul continued to observe each other. Michel was careful to seem faintly uninterested in Matthew, smiling at his enthusiastic exclamations, treating him like a child. When Matthew gave him a puzzled, questioning look, he smiled at him affectionately as an older man might smile at some strange child. "I can remember," he said, "when I was as full of life and enthusiasm as Matthew is now. It's wonderful to be young, isn't it?"

Paul smiled at him, agreeing. Yes, it was wonderful to be young. To himself, he said that he did not mean exactly the same thing that Michel meant. He looked at the two of them, still smiling, but remembering deep inside himself what it had felt like to be fifteen, sixteen … he was still not sure about them. His first suspicion was perhaps inaccurate. Garnier was no fool, it didn't seem likely that he would risk his position at the school in order to play around with one of the boys under the eyes of his parents. In the confines of the school, perhaps … boys will be boys and at that age … after all, he had had his share of fun in school, too. But not with any teacher … he hesitated. It was only an accident that he had not been involved with one of the professors – there was an awful lot of that kind of thing going on in schools in his day, no reason why it should have changed since then. He glanced at Catherine, tossing a mental coin – should he or should he not say anything to her? He imagined her reaction: she wouldn't believe him, she'd think he was just being critical of Matthew … no, there was no point in that. But he chuckled to himself. Precious little Matthew, about whom there had been so much conversation, so much worry, so damn much trouble … and what was he doing? He frowned. If he was really right, this wasn't just the usual playing around, the kind of thing he'd done himself. He could be wrong, yes, he *could* be … but if he wasn't. If he wasn't it meant, probably, that Garnier was a pansy. After all, to come on a vacation with a boy! He could imagine them planning the whole thing. "Le Conquet is right near Requin," one of them would have said, "it will be perfectly natural for us to be together," and so on.

He looked at the two of them with renewed interest. Not bad-looking, this man, and not an obvious pansy, of course, but there were things about him: inflections, gestures, smiles ... He shook his head. He was right that Garnier was no fool, and there was no point in arousing his suspicions, he'd have to watch out himself. He remembered the look that they had exchanged in the mirror of the car ... no more of that. As for Catherine ... without looking at her and without changing his expression, he thought of her with a sudden access of sympathy. She was not very bright about a lot of things, but she was – what was the word for Catherine? – she was as *nice*, really, as anyone he'd ever known, and he did not want to hurt her. She wouldn't understand this, she would be terribly hurt and baffled, she would never know what to do about it. She didn't really understand the world at all – at least not the world of men. It was natural enough for this to happen at Matthew's age. He smiled to himself, again. The memory of his own youth had made his blood run a little faster ... it would be an interesting summer. His mind stopped for an instant, thinking of Catherine again. "Perhaps M. Garnier ... Michel," he said, "would like to sit up front for a while?"

"Why of course! I should have suggested it myself."

When they were on the road again, Paul lighted himself a cigarette and settled comfortably behind the wheel. "I haven't said very much, Michel," he said, "...you don't mind if I call you Michel, do you? ... but I thought you might like to know from me that you're really very welcome to stay with us all summer, if the idea appeals to you." He glanced at Catherine and Matthew in the back seat and then continued in a lower voice: "You may know that it hasn't always been easy for Matthew to have a stepfather and I think the summer will be much pleasanter if you do spend it with us. It would be a favor to us."

Michel looked at him, still faintly uneasy. "It's very good of you to say so, M. Dumesnil..." he began, and Paul said quickly: "Paul ...

not M. Dumesnil, please," and Michel continued: "Thank you … Paul. It's just that I don't want to be in the way, you know."

Paul shook his head firmly. "You won't be. And I'm grateful, myself, for what you've done for Matthew. I hope you know that."

Michel blushed. "I think you're both making too much of it," he said, breathing more easily. "He's a good boy … I don't think I've done so much for him."

"Well, we do," Paul said. "And it means a lot to us."

As they progressed further into Brittany itself, through Dol and then north to Saint-Malô and back down to Dinan, they began to feel a change in the atmosphere of the country. The landscape was harsh in comparison with the green fields and orchards of Normandy, and the seacoast was rocky and sharp. The grass and trees were rough and hard from having fought for their existence in this spare land and, like the people themselves, there was an insolence in the way in which they clung firmly to the ground, claiming it as their own. The road wound through the rocky hills, approaching and retreating from the sea, cutting through the small old towns. The people were not quite friendly, seeming to regard the travellers less as potential customers, tourists, spenders-of-money, than as not entirely welcome invaders. Mostly, the Bretons were curious about them, and silently suspicious, and the more they advanced towards Finistère and Requin, the more hostile they became. The sound of the language was different, harsher. It sometimes lapsed into the Breton dialect which they could not understand at all and which bore no relation to French.

Paul told them legends about the country, the superstitious nature of the people who will not, for instance, ever pronounce the word "rabbit." He boasted about the climate, the good, stern qualities of the inhabitants, their intense personal faith which had led them to build innumerable small chapels in place of the great religious monuments of other sections. The Bretons, he insisted, were a private secluded people, they had no desire to impress the world, to show off. This was his France, the country of his forebears. Even the names of the places they passed through were not typical of any part of France that any of them had seen before. Sait-Brieuc, Morlaix, Guingamp; and as they approached Brest, places like Landivisiau, Landerneau, and Guipavas. Near Brest, they turned off the main highway to go through Guoesnou and Saint-Renan and the countless villages with names that Matthew loved: Kervalguen, Kerviniou, and Terbabu, and finally to Le Conquet which was the post office for Requin. Michel had agreed to go on to Requin with them and stopped in Le Conquet only to give his address to the *poste restente*.

From Le Conquet they followed the sea southwards and, at an abrupt turning in the road, Paul stopped the car. The sound and the smell of the sea and the marsh-grass had come closer to them all the time, and now they could taste the salt on their lips and feel the sticky dampness on their faces and in their hair. Paul pointed down a gentle slope ahead of them. The tiny town of Requin lay directly below them like a miniature model, perhaps twenty-five roofs in all, smoke rising gently from most of them, and here and there the sound of a cow bell, a tinkle against the subdued and distant roar of the surf. Behind them, Le Conquet nestled against the seashore, and to the south, jutting up and out into the ocean, Pointe Saint-Mathieu. Beyond it, even from this distance, the very color of the sea seemed changed – darker, almost black, and edged with foam. The swimming there, Paul said, was impossible – the undertow was very treacherous, but it was a beautiful view of the sea. Matthew remembered the phrase in the guide book: *Le littoral y est très découpé, la mer terrible.* Nowhere else on this trip did that particular description seem so apt: here the coastal formations were cut up, chopped, and the sea did seem terrible.

๛

Catherine was delighted. She loved Requin; it was the kind of place and the kind of summer she had always wanted. She was enchanted with the smallness of the town, the cottages, the roads that cut their way between them like dirt trails, and especially the inn. She and Paul had a large room on the second floor and Michel and Matthew small, adjoining single rooms on the ground floor. There were no baths in the hotel. All bathing would be done in the sea or at the hotel at Le Conquet. Even this pleased Catherine, she felt an inner urge to live in what she called a primitive fashion. Nothing could be more primitive, in her mind, than to live in an inn without a bathtub.

From her window she looked out on the small and beautifully ordered garden behind the inn: a bed of flowers at one end and neat rows of vegetables covering the rest of the plot. Just below her window was a bed of onions, the like of which she had never seen before: three or four feet tall with great dandelion-like flowers at their tops. They were as lovely as flowers, and Paul was especially pleased with them; it was right that they should be there, he said, and that they should seem to her like flowers. The onion was the crop of Brittany, the *enseigne* of the province. He told her that the Bretons had tossed onions to the American troops in the World War as a token of admiration and a gesture of welcome.

Beyond the garden stretched the grey-blue salt marshes ending finally in the deeper grey and blue of the sea. No house, no man-made object except the low stone wall marking the land of the inn, stood between her and the ocean. What could have been more perfect? She was in love, quietly, reflectively and deeply, with a man who understood her every mood, a man who made no objection to anything that she loved or wanted. How different it would have been with so many other men – they would have wanted excitement or entertainment – they would have objected to her love of quiet, and they would certainly have objected to Matthew; but not Paul. He had accepted Matthew, at last, almost as if he had been his own son. It was like a miracle, particularly after the bad start they had made together. And the last perfect touch was M. Garnier – Michel, as she now thought of him. He seemed a wonderful companion for Matthew. There were no problems. The summer, like a book with the pages as yet uncut, lay before Catherine like an idyll, a recompense for all the difficulties of the past years.

If you follow the road through Requin towards the sea, about a half-mile from the inn you come to a triple fork – to the north is Le Conquet, straight ahead is the beach, and to the south is Pointe Saint-Mathieu. Matthew and Michel, both of them anxious to see the ocean for themselves, arrived at the signboard and with a smile at the name, took the turning for the point. This way the sea seemed closer, looming up beyond the marshes, wild and untamed as it battered incessantly against the cliffs. The wind from the west, fresh and salty, increased as they proceeded along the road which narrowed into what was no more than a footpath, ending at the top of the cliffs, past the few houses of the settlement, near the ruins of the old abbey for which the point was named and two smaller buildings which, at first glance, seemed also to be ruins. Past these buildings which gave no sign of human life, the path disappeared over the edge of the cliff, below the lighthouse. There they found a small natural track leading down to the crescent-shaped strip of sand between the dark cliffs. It was only there that the water was less rough, the wind not quite so strong. On either side, even in calm weather, the waves hammered against the rocks and the cliffs, aided by the unceasing wind, as if in an effort to break its way into them or drag them into the sea.

They turned back and walked along the path in silence. When they were almost back at the triple fork in the road, they saw a man coming towards them. He was grizzled and weather-beaten, tramping along the road in his sabots, leaning on his stick, a faded blue smock hanging almost to his knees. He looked at them, sharp and suspicious, and did not say anything until he was almost next to them. Then, with no show of kindness, no formality, he said, in the accent to which Matthew could not quite accustom himself – it was so unlike French, he could barely understand it – *"Vous êtes les gens de l'hôtel?"* Michel replied that they were, and the man examined them frankly, still suspicious. *"Vous venez de Saint-Mathieu?"* and he pointed with his stick along the path from which they had just come. Michel nodded to him, and the man started away from them. He turned back, waving his arm at them. *"Faut pas nager la bas, 'y a des courants maudits. Aller à la plage."* And with that he tramped off towards the point himself.

Michel smiled at Matthew. "Evil currents," he said. "We won't go back there."

Matthew put his hand on Michel's arm, returning his smile. "Not to swim," he said.

Chapter Twenty-two

The first two weeks passed quickly, in a daze of happiness for them both. Matthew and Michel were up early, to walk along the muddy roads or to make for the beach where they would lie, stripped and open to the sun (no other people ever came to the beach and Catherine did not swim before lunch), their bodies turning from white to a bright red-brown. Even Michel, as if his wish had been granted at last, no longer held back the feeling of happiness of which he had been so afraid. The days lost their separateness, blending into each other in an unchanging, almost monotonous, round of comfortable pleasure. Their legs and arms grew sleek and hard and strong, and they both began to fill out from the air and the solid country food they ate every day. Matthew's hair became streaked with gold and stiff with salt. Once or twice a week they would drive to Le Conquet for baths, supplies and mail.

Where before Matthew had been excited, ecstatic, and bursting with the power of his feelings, he now became quiet. The slow change in Michel and his assurance that Michel was happy were more than he had hoped for. He talked of the way he felt almost incessantly, but even his conversation was serious and reflective. He was not quite able to believe in his good fortune. As an added proof that the summer was definitely going to go his way, it had come up quite naturally that Michel, since he had to go to Paris in August, would go with Matthew and that he could, if he wished, stay in Catherine's apartment. Another omen, he called it, an additional assurance that their happiness would not be interrupted.

At the end of the second week, as they lay in the morning sun on the beach, Matthew turned to Michel and stared at him for so long a time that Michel felt restless under his gaze. "What is it? What are you looking at?"

"I was thinking," Matthew said, half-playful, half-serious.

"About what?"

His face became serious again. "About what you said about payment. I know that someday we will have to pay for all this ... it's more than we deserve, more than anyone could expect. It can't last. I know it can't last." He rolled over on his back and looked up at the sky. "But I don't care. I want all of it." He took Michel's hand in his. "Tell me that you're as happy as I am, Michel. Tell me it's worth it to you."

Michel looked away from him for a moment, and then for the second time he said, staring down into the white sand, letting it trickle through his fingers: "I love you." He turned to face Matthew and smiled at him. "And I am happy, Matthew. I'm very happy.

Matthew jumped to his feet. "I want to go to the point."

"Now?"

"Yes, now."

"*Mais il fait si bien ici,*" Michel murmured happily as Matthew dragged him to his feet.

"You're just lazy," Matthew said, and they put on their swimming trunks.

When they reached Saint-Mathieu, Matthew insisted on making their way down the cliff to the water's edge and after staring at the water – even today it was black – he closed his eyes, letting the wind batter his face, listening to the pounding of the water.

Michel shivered in the wind and looked at the eddying, restless water and the sharp edge of the cliffs. It was a harsh and brutal point and he was glad when they started up the cliff again.

When they reached the inn, Catherine and Paul were seated outside, waiting for them. Paul waved to them, and Catherine, smiling, told them to hurry – lunch was ready. "When I see you coming up from the beach," she said, "I feel as if I had two sons instead of one."

They dressed hurriedly, the door open between their two rooms and Michel came into Matthew's room, buttoning his shirt. He laughed. "I guess I am a worrier," he said.

"What do you mean?"

"Oh … Paul."

"Paul? What about Paul?" Matthew was lacing his shoes and turned his head to look at Michel.

"Well, I'm glad I didn't say anything to you at the time, but I was awfully worried about Paul that first day on the trip. I was sure he suspected something between us."

Matthew scoffed and stood up. "Paul likes you a lot, anyone can see that. And he's never been as nice as he has this summer. *I* almost like him. Anyway, you're always suspicious of everybody. You don't still think he suspects us, do you?"

Michel shook his head. "No, I guess not. But he certainly gave me a funny look that first day. Gave me the shivers."

"This is the first time Paul hasn't given me the shivers," Matthew said, laughing. "I still remember when I first knew him the way he used to look at me. He looked right through me … brrrr. Makes me cold to think about it."

Michel looked alarmed. "So you've noticed it, too?"

"No, not what you mean. Paul looks at everybody that way. He came into the bathroom one day when I was taking a bath and he looked me over and asked me about girls and stuff like that. But that was the last time. I think he probably does that to everybody when he first meets them. He was just making up his mind about you, that's all. I'm sure he didn't suspect anything. Even if he did, what could he do about it? He hasn't any proof and," he started for the door, "he isn't going to get any either. Come on."

Chapter Twenty-three

Paris-Brest. The names of the towns, the atmosphere of the station with the trains standing in neat long lines, hissing and steaming, the crowds on the platforms; all of these things excited Matthew. He leaned out of the railway carriage, conscious of Michel sitting at his back, smiling at his mother and Paul as they stood on the platform.

Catherine felt a deep bond of affection for her son at that moment. He was so alive, so completely involved in everything that happened to him, she was almost afraid for him. He seemed unable to get enough of the world, as if he wanted it all, wanted to absorb it with all of his senses; he was drunk with living, and it made him beautiful and untamed in her eyes. He had the same reckless charm that had first attracted her to his father and yet with it there was something more, something essential that had been absent in John Cameron. Now, as never before, she was proud that this was her son. He had become, as if he had grown into it instinctively, all that she could ever have hoped for.

It was perhaps the thought of John that made her uneasy in those few minutes before the train left. What was this meeting going to be like, what would the results be? Was there any possibility that Matthew and his father would really like each other, that Matthew might even want to go back to America with him? She could not bring herself to believe that. He would not do that to her. She knew he would remember the promises he had made, promises that had been made without any urging on her part. She was sure he would not fail her.

It was not on the station platform at Brest that these questions had first come into Catherine's mind. She had thought about them ever since she had received John's letter; it was her concern that had made her encourage the visit. It was better, however painful it might turn out to be, to know now, now while the decision was still hers and not yet Matthew's. Whatever happened, Matthew would not be able to make any impulsive decision and act upon it at once. Legally, she could, and would if necessary, keep him here for one more year. At least he would have time to think about it, and it would give her time, too; time for anything.

When the train rounded the curve through the yards and Catherine and Paul had disappeared in the smoke and steam, Matthew fell back on the seat. He and Michel were alone in the compartment, and he turned to look into Michel's face and then embraced him impulsively, drawing away from him almost at once. "Isn't it wonderful," he exclaimed, "one whole month!"

Michel watched him quietly. "With your father," he said.

Matthew's eyes showed concern for a minute, and then he laughed. "You're not going to begin that again, are you? First it was Catherine and Paul and now it's going to be dad. You just want to be consoled, I know you."

Michel sighed. "Well, maybe," he admitted, "but you will be with him a lot."

"Only when it's absolutely necessary, Michel. You know that." He looked away from him down at the plush cushion on which they were sitting. "You think I'm selfish, don't you? I want to see my father, and the prospect of having at least half my time – more, really – with you, makes it all right for me." He looked at Michel. "Maybe I haven't thought of you very much. Will you be lonely in Paris when I'm not with you? Will you be angry with me?" And then the worry deepened inside him. "It won't be like that other time, will it?" he asked.

Michel put his hands to Matthew's lips. "Don't," he said. "Don't. I shouldn't have allowed you to think that I could possibly be unhappy, and I won't be, I promise. I couldn't have done anything else. I could never have stayed away from you. And … nothing will be like that other time."

Matthew knew he meant it, and he was happy again. The fear that had passed through him had disappeared, and he stretched his arms and leaned back against the seat of his carriage. "I'm tired," he said. "I'm tired and I feel wonderful."

Michel smiled at him. One moment he was inexhaustible, drinking in the world around him as if it were so much water placed there for the sole purpose of quenching his thirst, and the next moment he was a child, closing his eyes, the wide smile still on his face, ready to sleep, to sleep and build up energy for the next ecstasy that he was sure was in store for him. His feelings ruled him completely; he was savage and undisciplined. The contrast between Matthew and himself at the same age appalled him. He had been restrained, quiet, and disciplined; compared to him, Matthew was a kind of angel-devil on a perpetual emotional drunk.

The train rocked him gently from side to side, and as Michel listened to the sound of the wheels clicking over the tracks, he looked around the compartment; the cushions wearing thin, the photographs of Nantes, Rennes, Mont Saint-Michel, and below them, facing him, the white material (for all the world like a dresser scarf or an elongated hand-towel) with the word *État* woven into it. By stretching his back and neck he could see himself in the mirror, just the hair, the forehead, the eyes and the bridge of his nose. He looked at this partial face, the eyes staring back at him, and it was as if he were seeing himself through Matthew's eyes rather than his own.

At no time in the past that he could recall had he looked at a train in such detail. He wondered, even, if he had ever ridden in a second-class carriage before. First and third, yes. But second? The very fact of their riding second-class seemed at that moment a form of compromise, a symbol of the agreement they had made with the world. Of course, it was only a result of his inability to meet Catherine on an equal basis ... he, had he been travelling alone, would have been in third class, and Catherine had wanted Matthew to travel first. This was the only place they could meet – somewhere in the middle, a place without character. Not that it mattered.

Even as the impressions of the compartment and his vague thoughts travelled a circuit of their own in his brain, he began to feel, as if it had become a part of him, the movement of the train entering his bones. He was almost frightened. Here he was, hurtling at high speed across the country towards Paris. But it was not the physical movement of the train that alarmed him, rather the impression that he was being fired into some unknown area of experience, rocketing towards a further (a major) development in his relationship with Matthew, without having any conception of what it would be like.

He began to wonder what would happen in Paris. What would Matthew's meeting with his father come to, and how would he, Michel, like that father? The old fear (underneath this new surface fear), the fear that they might be exposed, shot through him briefly and subsided. If they had passed the test of Paul and Catherine, particularly Paul, there was no reason to assume that Matthew's father was going to guess anything about them. Still, he made a promise to himself to be careful, looking ahead with dread to the times when Matthew would not be with him, when he would surely feel his own energy and faith draining away from him without the self-charging battery of Matthew upon which he drew all the time. He wanted to make time stand still, then, to halt this train and force it – and them – back to Brest and then back to Requin and the sea. It was going too fast; the train itself was rushing him, forcing him towards a destination, the nature of which he could not imagine. If only they could have had another month like the last.

It had been a wonderful month for Michel, the happiest time of his entire life. He had come very close to believing everything Matthew believed. He felt self-confident and assured, even bold. In the last few weeks it had not always been Matthew who had decided what they would do, what they would eat, how long they would stay at the beach. It was he who had, from time to time, made a decision, been the first to speak. Matthew, unpredictably, had been delighted. For him it had been a sign that Michel was coming to life in the way that he had come to life at the very beginning of their relationship. He had made decisions for both of them because Michel had seemed to want him to make them; in reality, as long as they were together it was immaterial to Matthew what they did, and to have Michel taking over their direction, gravely and seriously, seemed wonderful. He felt as if the change were taking place in his own heart and not in Michel's, and he responded to it at once.

It had been a wonderful month ... Michel repeated the words to himself, as if searching for some doubt or question in them. *It had been* ... and now it is over? Was that what he was trying to say to himself? Was this something that was over, perhaps for good? Once again, his thoughts began to turn around Paris and the month ahead of them. Even as he thought about it, he was aware that there was some gnawing thing in him that never allowed him to accept anything completely, not even this miraculous happiness. Already he was anticipating and fearing the future. What about Matthew and his father?

In the same manner that he would have peeled the scab from a not-quite-healed wound, he tried to strip himself. How did he really feel? How happy had he been? was he? would he be? He had accepted Catherine and was not afraid of her; the same had been true of Paul – except that he did not entirely like Paul.

But Matthew's father. What would he be like, how would he feel about Matthew? And closer to the center of the wound, as if probing for blood, how would Matthew like him? Whatever else was true of Matthew, however much faith and confidence he had, however strong he was, he was also unpredictable. He seemed to Michel to operate on, to live by, a logic that was peculiar to himself alone. He had never known anyone like him, not even remotely. What had he suppressed in his relationship with his father that might come out in this meeting? That Matthew had put a barrier between his father and himself, Michel knew already. But since that time, Matthew had changed; he had been transformed from a lonely, silent boy into something almost super-human, someone who, in Michel's mind, responded to super-human impulses – he seemed psychic, almost clairvoyant, not quite earthly. Whatever he might have suppressed or forgotten in the past, there would be no barrier between his father and himself now, of that Michel was sure; Matthew had no more barriers in him.

Deeper inside came the real fear, for he had uncovered fear, a fear that had lain inside him waiting for this moment. How much of the suppressed and buried feeling for his father, how much of the love that Matthew should have given to his father during all those years away from him, had been turned into this relationship, like water forced into a wrong channel? And how much of it would be given back to his father – taken away from Michel?

He looked at Matthew sleeping beside him. In that moment, Michel Garnier loved him as he had never loved anything, and in that same moment his heart was penetrated by the knowledge – he had only known it with his mind before – that Matthew could be lost to him. Whether it was because of Matthew's belief that their relationship was, in a sense, infinite, or because Michel had been too preoccupied with either his fears or his happiness, he did not know, but he realized that – whatever he had thought or said about it – he had never before *believed* their relationship might end or that he would ever have cause to be jealous of Matthew. Even now, he was certain, he had at least that much confidence, that he would never lose Matthew to a rival, that Matthew would never desire or even love anyone else in the same way. It was not that kind of competition he feared. But the love that Matthew hurled upon the world, the love with which he overwhelmed everyone around him, was something that still frightened and puzzled Michel. Where did it come from? What frightful need to love and be loved was behind all this? What had produced it?

He realized with a shock that he was almost old enough to be Matthew's father, telling himself that it was impossible, *impossible*, that he was not, in some ways, a substitute for his real father. What would happen, then, when Matthew encountered that father; encountered him openly, ready to envelop him in this whirlpool of feeling?

He had a sudden impulse to take Matthew by the arm, to waken him and ask him all these questions. For whatever confidence and strength he had acquired, he was still dependent on Matthew, he felt that in some magic way Matthew had the key to every secret, that Matthew himself would already know what the outcome would be. But he did not and could not ask him. Something, his new confidence perhaps, mounted inside him, hard and strong. Nothing will take him away from me, he muttered to himself almost aloud, *nothing*. He's mine. It was at that moment that he felt Matthew's eyes on him.

"What's the matter, Michel?"

He did not know what to say, he was torn between telling him everything he had thought and taking him in his arms. He did nothing, only shook his head, waiting for Matthew to say something more.

Matthew watched him, and then put his hand out to him. "You're afraid of my father," he said.

There was no reason to be surprised. Michel was getting used to this, but for a moment the wild question shot through his mind: can it really be true that he reads my mind? "How do you know what I think?" he asked. "What do you do, read my thoughts?"

Matthew laughed. "I always know how you feel, because I feel it. Besides, you said you were worried about my father, and you had that worried look on your face." He made an imitative grimace, adding: "Anyway, I don't read your mind."

"I'm not afraid of him," Michel answered. "I was thinking about him, that's all."

"But you look afraid, Michel. I can see it." Michel did not say anything and Matthew asked him for a cigarette. As he took the package from his pocket and handed it to Matthew, Michel said: "You never smoke, why do you want to smoke now?"

"I used to smoke when I was sorry for myself. I used to steal Paul's cigarettes, it made me think I was getting revenge on him." He took a cigarette from the package and lighted it and then looked at Michel again. There was some half-hidden humor lurking in his eyes; he seemed to be enjoying a secret joke. "Now it makes me feel grown up," he went on, "and besides, cigarettes are supposed to help you think, and I want to think." He coughed and looked angrily at the cigarette. "And cough," he said.

He smoked in silence and then dropped the cigarette to the floor and crushed it with his foot. "Now you smoke," he said.

Obediently, Michel put a cigarette to his lips and lighted it. "Satisfied?" he asked, and Matthew laughed at him. "Do you want to know what I was thinking?" he asked, and his voice was shy, almost timid.

"Yes. What were you thinking?"

Matthew looked away from him out the window and then turned to look into his face. His eyes were shining. "I was thinking about Paris."

In spite of some reluctance – he felt himself being torn away from his thoughts – Michel was pleased that Matthew had not been thinking of his father. "What about it?"

Once more Matthew lapsed into a kind of timidity that Michel neither expected nor understood. "I was thinking, for instance," he began, "that you and I could go to all the places that I used to go with Scott. We can listen to the bells of Nôtre Dame together, and watch the sunset from the roof of the apartment ... I will go away in the morning, oh ... not too early ... to spend the day with my father, and you can meet us for lunch, and then in the evening I'll come home. Just like a businessman going to work every day."

Michel shook his head. "And coming back to his ... housewife?"

Matthew looked at him, laughing. "I'll have to get you an apron," he said. "By the way, can you cook?"

A sudden jerk of the train threw them against each other and they both laughed, looking out of the window. The train was slowing down, shrieking its way into St. Brieuc. Michel was startled to find they had gone so little distance. It was going to be a long journey, now, he knew.

Chapter Twenty-four

Paris, in August is like Paris at no other time of the year. The heat, radiating up from the sidewalks and creating a pale haze over the city, has driven the surface population away to the country, stripping the city of its veneer, closing the expensive shops, depleting the cafés, emptying the taxis. Paris in August is a city that has been reclaimed by an under-population. Shopkeepers, waiters, concierges come out of hiding to stand in groups on the sidewalks, and the streets are no longer filled with tourists, foreigners, and striped-pants. The top level of Paris has gone on vacation, exposing Paris as it really is, and the city herself sleeps on the banks of the Seine, in summer hibernation.

Matthew had left Michel after a late breakfast and walked from the apartment to his father's hotel. Now that the meeting was upon him, he was nervous, walking quickly, his eyes glancing from side to side. He felt peculiarly alone and wished for a moment that Michel was with him. When he reached the Majestic, he hurried up the few broad steps, smiled briefly at the doorman and walked into the lobby. He stopped inside the door and looked around him. The mirrors, the gilt, the palms and marble made him feel suddenly out of place, as if the hotel was emphasizing the gap between himself and his father. He had never been here before; it represented a kind of life about which he knew nothing. The few people sitting in the lobby were not just rich people; his mother had money – he put his hand in his pocket as if to give himself courage, he had money too – but this was more than money. One man, slouched in a chair with a cigar in his mouth, a great blue-vested belly with a heavy gold watch chain strung across it, snapped his fingers and an ornately uniformed bellboy sped across the room to him, to stand respectfully at attention while the man muttered something to him.

Would his father be a man like that? He felt sure that he would recognize him, but would he, too, snap his fingers? Would he be fat and powerful and smoke cigars? The thought of meeting his father frightened him now. He seemed to be leaping back into a past that he had forgotten. Like an intruder, he made his way between the palms and the enormous furniture, to the house telephones near the desk. As he picked up the receiver his throat went dry. What do you say to your father when you haven't seen him for years? What do you call him? He stared at the instrument in his hand and the operator's voice barked at him. He placed it gingerly to his head and said, swallowing hard, "M. John Cameron, *s'il-vous-plaît*."

He waited, listening to the clicks, buzzings and voices, and then the sharp definite sound of the receiver being lifted in some room upstairs. "Hello?"

He swallowed again, working up the saliva in his mouth. "Hello," he said timidly, "uh … Mr." – he could not call him Mr. Cameron! – and then he blurted: "This is Matthew."

There was a sudden intaking of breath and then the voice: "Hello, Matthew. I'll be right down. Wait for me downstairs, will you?"

"Yes." He hung up the phone and walked slowly across the lobby to stand near the elevators. He wished he had never had to come here, that his father had stayed in America, that he and Michel were still in Requin … anything!

He could remember some things clearly, but it was his relationship with him that he had forgotten so completely that no feeling could be re-evoked. He could remember the way his father looked in general, but the image was faceless; search as he might, he could not re-create his father's face, could not remember having looked into his eyes, nor even being addressed by him. He could remember the sound of his voice when he spoke to Catherine, or when he talked on the telephone, but he could not remember himself talking to his father. What had they said to each other, what would they say now?

He was irritated and alarmed at the lack in his own memory and the simultaneous need to have to go back and recall the past. It could not be done, he knew. He would have to meet his father as someone he had never known or seen before in his life. They would have to start all over again, not so much as father and son, but as two unrelated people, two strangers.

The elevator door opened and Matthew saw him. He knew him at once. It was incredible that he should have forgotten his face. It was exactly the same. Well, perhaps the hair was a little greyer and there was a difference, very slight, about the mouth. But most of all, there was something about his father's face that was like his own reflection in the mirror, enough so that it was almost as if the reversed reflection of himself was more a likeness of his father than of his own face which he had, of course, never seen as other people see it. You would have to be in the back of a mirror to see yourself that way, or inside another person.

John knew Matthew also, and moved directly towards him. Although he had been nervous about their meeting, and until the phone had rung his hands had perspired violently, he had felt no shyness, had not expected any barrier between them. Now, when he looked at Matthew, recognizing him beyond any doubt, he felt his self-assurance collapse. In spite of the pictures that Matthew had sent him, he was not prepared for what he saw. It was as if the picture that his mind had retained of his son since the last time he had seen him had diminished in size during the years that he had been away. Matthew not only looked bigger, he looked twice his former size. He was not the same individual John had known, his growth – his extraordinary growth – was not only physical, everything about him was enlarged and altered. He looked more like John, himself, than John had ever realized. Or perhaps, he had not looked like that before. He could not remember. They shook hands automatically, coming together like two mechanical figures, and then they both smiled at once, and the images of each other broke and became distorted as a reflection is shattered when a pebble is thrown into still water.

"Hello," Matthew said. He was overcome by shyness and embarrassment, and the feeling was communicated to John who was only able to say, "Hello, Matthew," in return. They sat down on one of the overstuffed couches of the lobby with a potted palm listening to them, watching them like an immovable sentry. The man Matthew had seen before, blue-vested belly, watch chain and cigar was seated almost directly opposite them and Matthew suppressed an impulse to laugh. "How did you find this place?" he said suddenly. "I'd never even heard of the Majestic before."

"I made the reservations in New York," his father answered. "It's listed as one of the best hotels, a little quieter than the Ritz, they said. I don't know anything about Paris, you know."

"Oh." Matthew looked at his father. "Where's … where's your wife?"

"Edith?" John asked it as if he had several wives, as if he were not at all sure that she was his wife. "Oh, she'll be down in a minute," he said. "She thought we might want to see each other alone first."

Matthew laughed uneasily. "Oh," he said again, and then: "Did you have a good trip over? Did you enjoy it? You were on the *Leviathan*, weren't you?"

"Yes," John answered. "It was fine. Very smooth crossing. We both enjoyed it."

For some reason they both laughed. "Tell me about yourself," his father said. "How are you anyway? Everything all right with you? Do you like it over here? Do you like your school?"

"Oh, I'm fine," Matthew answered. "Everything's fine. I like the school very much. In fact," – he knew he'd have to break the news sometime – "one of my teachers is spending the summer with us. He was in Brittany and he's come down to Paris with me. He's staying at the apartment."

"One of your teachers?" John could not keep the surprise out of his voice, it was almost as if he had not heard correctly. Did Matthew mean one of his fellow-students?

Matthew nodded. "Yes. His name is Michel Garnier. He's … he's an awfully nice guy. He saved my life actually."

"Saved your life?'

"Yes." Matthew looked away from his father and began to give him a rapid description of the near-drowning in the Seine and Michel's concern, the rescue and their friendship. He made it sound as if the rescue was the basis for Michel's presence, the excuse that brought about the invitation for the summer.

When he had finished, John was silent for a moment. "I'd like to meet him," he said simply. "We owe him a lot. How did you happen to swim out so far?"

Matthew shrugged his shoulders. "I guess I didn't realize how far it was," he said.

John's voice changed. "How's your mother?" he asked.

"Oh, she's fine. You know about Paul, don't you?"

"Yes. How do you like him?"

Matthew smiled. "I wasn't so crazy about him at first, but we get along all right now. I just had to get used to him, that's all."

John nodded. "I suppose. I hope you're going to like Edith. She's very anxious to meet you."

"Oh, I'm sure I'll like her," Matthew said quickly, wondering why he said it and what she was going to be like. At the moment of saying it he was dreading her arrival. He clasped his hands and held them tightly together. "It's sort of awful in a way," he said in a small voice. "I'm sitting here telling myself that you're my father, and that I haven't seen you for a long time and…" He looked up, his face reddening. "I suppose it's the same thing with you?"

"Yes, I guess it is, I…" he looked beyond Matthew over his shoulder and then he stood up. "Here's Edith now," he said, and Matthew stood up and turned to face her.

She was tall, taller than he had expected, and she seemed to him to have none of the reserve that he felt in John, and none of his own discomfiture. She was nothing like what he had thought she would be, and he realized that his picture of her had been built on the words that his mother had said to him long ago. He had formed a picture of an anonymous woman that his father was going to marry, that his father preferred to Catherine. The picture had been of some- one unattractive, big-boned, shapeless; it had never occurred to him that it would have been odd for his father to have left Catherine for someone less attractive than herself. And this woman was not only attractive, she was alive, open and friendly. Without waiting for any word or gesture from John, she held her hands out to him. "Well, Matthew," she said simply. "Hello."

Their hands met and she held his two hands firmly, looking di- rectly into his face. Matthew grinned suddenly; the directness of her approach seemed to disentangle him inside. "You're Edith," he said, watching the increase of the smile on her face. He was not surprised, in fact it seemed to him the most natural thing in the world when she moved a little closer to him and put her arms around him, kissing his cheek. As she drew back to look at him again, she took his hands once more and said: "We *are* going to like each other, Matthew, aren't we? Isn't it fine?

And then they all laughed.

Edith turned to John. "What about buying us a drink, darling?" And to Matthew: "You drink, don't you? Don't all boys in France drink?"

"Well ... wine," he said. "Vermouth sometimes ... before lunch or dinner."

"Good." She took their arms, walking between them, and led them into the bar. "I feel as if I'd always known you, Matthew," she said. "You're exactly as I expected you to be. You're terribly like John, you know."

"Am I?" Matthew was very pleased, and he could feel the pleasure spreading through him, and the relief. Everything seemed to be easy now that she was here.

They sat at a small table and John ordered their drinks. "Now what about lunch, Matthew?" he asked. "Where should we eat?"

Matthew looked around the room. "I don't know much about this place," he said, "but I guess it must be good, if you'd like to eat here."

Edith shook her head. "No," she said, "I think this should be a gala lunch. This place is too…" she smiled at Matthew, "too much gold here. Let's go to some famous, expensive place."

"Like Foyot?" Matthew asked.

"Wonderful," she said smiling, and then she put her hand over his. "Tell me, how does it feel to be seeing John after all this time?"

Matthew looked at his father searchingly. "I don't think I know yet," he said. "There are so many things that I think I'm supposed to say or think, but none of that means anything … do you know what I mean? It's easier in a way with you, because I've never seen you before … because…" his voice broke off and he looked at his father again, glad for the pressure of Edith's hand. "You do understand, don't you?"

"Of course," John said. "I know exactly how you feel, I feel the same way myself. Oh, here are the drinks, maybe that will ease things up a bit." They lifted their glasses, and Edith said, looking from one to the other: "Here's to you both."

When they had put their glasses down, Edith began to talk to them again, sensing that they were not yet at the place where they could talk to each other easily. "You don't know, Matthew, how long I've waited for this to happen. There is nothing in the world that I want as much as to have you two really get to know each other as you should. It's been such a shame that you've had to be apart." Coming from her, there was no implication hidden in the words, no criticism of Catherine. She meant, quite literally, what she said, and nothing more, and they were both of them happy to have her saying it for them.

"You're so alike," she continued, "I can't get over it. And I do so want John to have his own son." She looked directly at Matthew then and said, her voice lower: "It's important to me, Matthew. I can't have any children, you know."

Matthew shook his head. He felt as if he should be embarrassed, but he was not. "I didn't know," he said. Then he looked at his father. "Why did you have only one…" He stopped, blushing, and looked at Edith again, and she smiled.

"It's hard to explain about that," John said. "We thought about having another child, but I don't think your mother ever really wanted one after you were born, Matthew. You were always enough for her … I'm not … I mean I don't want to blame…"

"Oh, of course," Matthew put in quickly. "I shouldn't have asked that anyway, but I just wondered. I'd never thought of it before."

Edith lifted her glass, proposing another toast. "Not only to you both, but to the three of us," she said. The way she said it made Matthew very happy.

After lunch, Matthew suggested they drive around in a taxi to see Paris. He directed the driver, telling him where to go, when to stop. He took them past the apartment, then to the Luxembourg Gardens, the Panthéon and the Sorbonne, the Île de la Cité and Nôtre Dame, Les Halles, the Palais Royal, the Louvre and the Tuileries. They left the cab at the Opéra and had an *apértif* at the Café de la Paix, and then returned to the hotel. John and Edith took him up to their suite of rooms, and while Edith changed for dinner, John unlocked his trunk and brought a large package over to Matthew. As he handed it to him, his manner was a little stiff, and he cleared his throat. "I didn't know what to get you," he said, "but I hope you'll like this."

Matthew untied the string and opened the package. In it was a grey flannel suit, almost identical with the one John was wearing. "I got the size from your mother," John said, and Matthew stood up and put his arms around his father. "Gosh, dad," he said, "it's a beauty." When they separated, they were embarrassed again, as if Matthew's sudden gesture was more than they could deal with.

"Want to put it on?" John asked quickly. "If it doesn't fit we can take it to a tailor."

Matthew took off his coat and laid it on the bed and he began to unfasten his belt. His father looked at him for a moment and started away from him. "I'll be right back," he said and walked into the other room, leaving him alone.

Matthew watched the door close behind him, and then he began to unbutton the fly of his trousers. Scott or Paul or Michel would have stayed; the fact that John left him alone was a point of contact between them that he did not share with any other man. He would have left John alone – or even the others. And for that very reason, he half-wished that John would come back and re-establish the feeling of similarity between them that he had felt in the gesture. He stared at the room, looking for anything in it that made it John's room, and not just an overstuffed, overgilded hotel room. Except for the trunk, with its jaws gaping at him, there was no personal touch in the room. No flowers, no object that belonged to either John or Edith. It was a heavy room. The carpet, the draperies at the high windows, the solid heavy furniture and the high ceilings, made it seem hot and oppressive, impersonal and musty. He felt lonely and tired with John gone; his father seemed to have taken something out of the very air when he had left. He lifted the suit out of the box and his own trousers fell to his ankles.

When he had put on the new suit and placed the other one – his old blue one – in the box, he stood in front of the mirror. It looked like a perfect fit. As he continued to look at his reflection, he saw John and Edith coming into the room behind him. He turned to face them, smiling and proud, and Edith came up to him. She was carrying a box in one hand and, as she handed it to him, she ran her other hand down his sleeve. "It looks wonderful, Matthew," she said. "Simply perfect. And this is from me."

He fumbled with the string on the box and then opened the lid. On the top there was a card, reading: "For Matthew, the son I've been waiting to meet for so long," and the box contained a wallet big enough for all sizes of French money – and inside, in the little pocket under which his initials had been stamped in gold, Matthew found five one-thousand franc notes. "Gee," he said, "I don't know how to thank you. It's wonderful and I really need it, too." He looked at her as he transferred his money and papers from his old wallet. "I don't know what to say … it never occurred to me … I mean, I didn't get anything for either of you, I…"

"Oh, Matthew! But of course not. You shouldn't get anything for us, we didn't expect anything from you. Now, stand by John. I want to see you together."

As they stood side by side, Matthew's chest filled up and he looked at his father proudly. He was very little shorter and the two suits were almost identical in cut and color. "We're like twins," he said, and once more they all laughed, and Matthew shook his head back and forth. "They're wonderful," he said, "wonderful."

Matthew got up to leave suddenly. He had wanted to tell them all afternoon, had waited for the time, but no time had come. He did not want to leave them now and there was no way of telling them easily that he had promised Michel to come home for dinner. He had thought of calling Michel, but he was worried about him and could not bring himself to it. He was frightened of the telephone. He did not know how Michel would feel about his father, about anything. He had to *see* him.

Standing near the door, he said, averting his eyes from both Edith and his father: "I have to go now."

They were both startled and for a moment they seemed unable to speak. "But it's our first…" John began and Edith put her hand on his arm quickly. "You're sure you can't stay to dinner, Matthew? Is it very important?"

He nodded slowly. "Yes, I … I made an appointment a long time ago. I didn't…" he looked at them. "I'm awfully sorry. If I'd known…."

She walked over to him and put her hand out to him "Of course, Matthew," she said. "I understand." She looked at John and then went on: "I know it must be important. Besides we *are* both tired, it's been such an exciting day." She kissed his cheek. "You'll come early tomorrow, won't you?"

He nodded. "Can I bring Michel to lunch?" he asked tentatively. "I'm awfully anxious to have him meet you."

John spoke up then. "Of course. We'd both like to have him. Bring him along when you come."

Matthew smiled at them, kissed Edith and then went over to his father and hugged him. "Gee, thanks," he said. "It's been wonderful. I'm awfully sorry I have to leave … if I could get out of it, I…"

"I know, son," John said quietly. "It's all right."

Matthew took the box and after saying goodbye again, they watched him go out the door. When it had closed behind him, John and Edith looked at each other and she walked over to him silently and put her arm through his. They walked, still without speaking, to the window of the room and stood looking down on Paris below them.

"I wonder why he had a date for dinner tonight?" John asked, almost to himself, without looking at her.

"I think it's easy enough to understand, darling," she said. "He was probably very nervous about this. If it had gone badly, it would have been an excuse to get away from us. He might not have liked us, John, and he did want to stay. I think it's natural enough. It's probably very hard on him. We'll have to make it as easy as we can."

John looked at her gratefully and kissed her, circling her waist with his arm. "Thanks, darling," he said, "you were wonderful with him. I couldn't have done it without you."

She smiled. "I love you," she said. "And I love Matthew, too."

Then she laughed. "You've got your hand on my rubber tire," she said and patted her stomach. "I should be reducing, and all this food in Paris…!"

He held her closer to him and kissed her again. "You're the best thing that ever happened to me," he said.

She kissed him back. "Isn't it fun being in Paris, Johnnie? It's like falling in love all over again."

Chapter Twenty-five

Michel stood up when he heard Matthew coming up the stairs and then walked over to the door and opened it quickly. He answered Matthew's greeting without smiling.

"What's the matter, Michel?"

"You're late," Michel said.

Matthew looked at his watch and then closed the door behind him. "I'm sorry," he said, his voice full of apology. "I got here as fast as I could, but I didn't want to seem too anxious to leave them … besides, it's only five minutes."

Michel, with his back to Matthew, put on the coat to his suit. "Five minutes can seem like a long time when you've been waiting all day."

He felt Matthew coming towards him and he held himself stiffly as Matthew put his arms around him from behind. "I know," Matthew said softly. "It's terrible for you, just waiting here, but I really did get home as soon as I could, and I'm here now." Then he turned Michel's body until they faced each other. He backed away from him and spread his arms. "How do you like it?" he asked.

Michel nodded slowly, looking him up and down. "Very nice," he said.

"My father gave me the suit, and Edith gave me this…." He fished in his pocket for the wallet and handed it to Michel. "Isn't it a beauty?"

Michel took it and turned it over in his hand and then gave it back, "*Épatant*," he said and looked steadily at Matthew. "How was it?" His voice was sharper now.

"It was fine," Matthew said slowly.

"You like him?"

"Oh, yes."

"And her, too?"

"Yes."

Michel stared at him for a minute and then said: "I'm hungry. Let's go to dinner and you can tell me all about it."

Although he knew that Matthew would probably want to go to some special place (his allowance was generous and he liked to spend money), Michel perversely steered him into a small, inexpensive restaurant near the apartment. Matthew followed him meekly, afraid to make any objection. Because the place was crowded, they had to squeeze their way to a table where a man and a woman were already seated.

After looking briefly at the menu, Michel looked at Matthew. "So, how was it?" he asked in French.

Matthew shook his head, nodding in the direction of the couple, and did not reply. When they had ordered, they ate quickly and in almost complete silence, Matthew deflated and full of wonder, and Michel hardly noticing him, preoccupied with the conversation of the people around him and the food. When they had finished and paid the check, they made their way out the door where Michel paused for a moment on the sidewalk. He lighted a cigarette, peering at Matthew through the smoke. "Well, anyway it was cheap," he said, "*my* kind of restaurant." He smiled to himself and then added: "Now, tell me all about it."

They started to walk slowly down the street and Matthew sighed. "I don't think there's anything to tell," he said. "We had lunch and then we drove around and then I went back to the hotel with them and they gave me these. Do you like the suit?"

Michel looked at him critically. "Yes," he said. "It's American, isn't it? The pants are too long."

Matthew looked down. "No, they're not," he said. "It's a perfect fit. Dad's pants are…"

Michel gestured at him wearily. "All right. All right. All American suits are like that. They all have pants that are too long. Now, when are you seeing them again?"

"We're supposed to have lunch with them tomorrow. Both of us."

Michel blinked at him. "What for?" he asked suddenly.

Matthew stopped and shook his head. "But you said you wanted to meet them!"

"Yes, so I did." Michel's voice was rough. They were at the corner of the street and he looked up and down. "I'd like a drink," he said.

"Shall we go home?" Matthew asked hesitantly. "There's plenty of…"

Michel smiled, cutting him off. He had suddenly had an idea. "Let's go to a café," he said, more amiably this time. "There's a place near here I used to go when I lived in Paris. It might amuse you."

He was conscious of a sudden quickening of his bloodstream as if he had received an injection of adrenaline; he did not stop to think out exactly what he was doing, or what, if any, were his motives. It was as if his direction had abruptly been taken over by his instincts rather than his mind. When they reached the café, which was also crowded, they had to stand at the bar, and Michel was immediately greeted by the bartender, who took a long and knowing look at Matthew. He ordered cognac for himself and beer for Matthew and then leaned against the bar to look around the room. He lifted his glass to one or two people and then felt a hand on his shoulder from behind. He looked around and was effusively greeted by a man whose face he knew, but whose name he had either never known or had forgotten. "*Et bien, mon cher! Comment vas tu?* Where have you been? We haven't seen you for ages," and Michel replied in the same familiar way. When the man glanced significantly over his shoulder at Matthew, he nodded and smiled. The man moved out from the bar a little to take a better look at Matthew and then whispered something in Michel's ear and they both laughed.

Matthew felt his face going pale and he gripped his fingers around the cold glass of beer. When Michel's friend moved away from the bar and Michel turned to face him with a satisfied smile on his face, he said quickly: "Can't we go now?"

Michel looked at him for a moment, took a sip of his drink, and then said quietly: "But we've only just come."

Matthew's eyes pleaded with him. "Please, Michel," he whispered.

"Don't you like it here?"

Matthew shook his head.

"Why not?"

The direct gaze which Michel aimed at him was too much for Matthew. He lowered his eyes. "I don't know. I want to go. Please."

"All right." Michel turned away from him, laid some money on the bar and they started for the door. Before going out he nodded his head at one or two people, waved at the man who had spoken to him at the bar and then opened the door to let Matthew go out ahead of him. When the door was closed behind them and they stood once more on the sidewalk, he said: "What do you want to do now?"

Matthew looked at him uneasily. "Can't we go home?"

But Michel had still another idea. There was a little place around the corner where he would like to stop for a minute. "After all," he said, and again his voice was kinder, "you've never seen anything of this part of Paris. It's amusing."

Matthew followed him dumbly, unable to understand the impulse that was taking them from place to place. He wanted to ask Michel what was wrong, what he had done, but he was afraid to question him. He seemed so cold and unresponsive.

The little place around the corner turned out to be another café, but this one was empty except for two old men sitting at one of the tables by the wall under a long mirror and a bartender wiping glasses behind the bar. When they entered, Michel greeted the bartender and left Matthew by the door. He walked quickly to the bar, spoke in a low voice to the bartender, handed him some money and then indicated Matthew with a jerk of his head. The bartender looked at Matthew searchingly, his hands holding the glass and towel, and then shrugged and nodded his head. Michel turned, his face flushed and smiling, and gestured to Matthew to follow him as he started for the door at the end of the room, opposite the entrance. He held the door open for Matthew and motioned to him to walk up the dark staircase at the end of the short hall. "Be quiet," he cautioned him, and followed him into the hallway and closed the door behind them. It was very dark, there was only a small bulb in the center of the hall, and Michel guided Matthew with his hand on Matthew's arm. When they reached the top of the stairs, they came to another hall in which there was no light at all, except here and there a faint beam from the wall. He guided Matthew to the first of these lighted spaces and then stood there, his hand still gripping Matthew's arm, looking through the little slit from which the light beamed out. He motioned to Matthew to look with him.

Matthew put his eyes to the slit and his body stiffened. He was conscious only of what he was looking at and the tight grip of Michel's hand around his upper arm. He sucked his breath in sharply and turned away, but Michel was already moving, pulling him relentlessly along with him, until he stopped at the next opening. Matthew held back rigidly until Michel looked at him and said sharply, in a whisper: "*Et bien, regarde!*" And once more he looked. After a moment, he moved his head, and with his free hand and arm unfastened the grip of Michel's fingers and started away from him back towards the staircase.

Michel followed him silently and again took his arm in his hand. "What's the matter?"

"I'm going."

Then the grip relaxed. "All right," Michel said lightly and led him down the stairs and out of the hall into the café.

When they walked into the light, Matthew's face flushed and he walked quickly across the room, not turning his head, avoiding the glances of the bartender and the two men at the table, his hand reaching out for the knob of the outside door. Michel followed him closely, with a wave and a word to the bartender, and when they were once more in the street, he piloted him in the direction of the apartment. They did not speak until they were in the living room. Matthew stood motionless as Michel came up to him and began to unfasten the buttons of his coat. Their eyes met directly for the first time that evening, and as Michel looked at him, Matthew began to shake his head back and forth. "Why did you take me there?" he asked finally. "What are you trying to do?"

For answer, Michel pulled his coat off, threw it on the chair and then pulled Matthew to him roughly. Matthew drew sharply away from him. "No," he said flatly. "No."

"Oh," Michel said casually, "I'm not good enough any more, is that it?"

For the first time since he had known him, Matthew was angry with Michel. He looked at him, staring him down, watching his eyes flicker away from him. "What did you do," he said bitterly, "live there, or just work there?"

Michel looked at him, startled and frightened. "I'm sorry, Matthew," he began slowly, but Matthew interrupted him quickly, shaking his head hard. "Oh, no," he said, "not this time. That isn't enough. I want to know *why*."

Michel smiled. "You think we're so different, then?"

"I *know* I am," Matthew answered briefly.

"I'm not," Michel said. "Actually, neither are you."

Matthew shrugged his shoulders and walked to the door of the living room. "If you feel more at home there," he said furiously, "you can always return. I won't stop you."

"I said I was sorry."

"Yes," Matthew nodded. "You did. You always do. It's never enough, Michel."

"What are you doing to do then?"

"I'm going to go to bed. You can do what you like."

Chapter Twenty-six

Matthew was awakened the next morning when Michel crawled into bed beside him and was immediately flooded with his memory of the night before. He did not look at Michel or say anything to him until he heard Michel's voice in his shoulder, like the voice of a small child. "Can you ever forgive me, Matthew?" he asked.

For answer, Matthew propped himself up on one arm and looked down into Michel's face. "Why do I love you?" he asked. "Why did I have to fall in love with a man? Last night…"

"Last night what?" Michel asked him, apologetic and afraid.

"The whole thing – all of it – was something I don't understand." He looked away from Michel. "Why do you have to do such things? What is there in you that…" and then he stopped, at a loss for words.

Without looking at him, and speaking into the pillow, Michel began to talk slowly. "I wanted to hurt you," he said. "I know that what I did was cruel and horrible … I know you aren't like that at all … but I hated your father yesterday. I hated him for taking you away from me." He tried to explain to him what he had thought about when they had been on the train: "Sometimes I think you love me because your father was taken away from you, and you have to have some man in your life, someone to take his place. I thought you'd made a kind of transference from your father to me, and now that you're together again, now that you've seen him … I still don't know what is going to happen. When I sit here alone in this apartment, waiting for you, I get frightened and jealous. I envy you your whole life … you're young, you have rich parents, you have your life ahead of you, and what place is there in it for me, really?"

"Well, if you…" Matthew started, but Michel silenced him with his hand. "No, wait, Matthew. I had been able to deny everything to myself about your father," he went on. "I had rationalized it and philosophized with myself until I felt that your father was no threat to me, and then yesterday it all came back, and I couldn't even remember what excuses I had made to myself before. I only felt that he was a threat, that he was taking you away." Even as he spoke he was caught in a wave of self-pity. "You have to forgive me, Matthew, I couldn't stand it if you didn't, but I think all of this is because I'm not used to love, I don't believe in it the way you do. Before I met you, I thought it really didn't exit, or that … well, that I had no right to it."

"What do you mean, you had no *right* to it?"

"Just that. After last night you know what kind of life…." He bit his lip. "Anyway, you changed all that, and now it's as if there's something inside me, something stronger than I am that wants to destroy us. There are times when I can't stand your happiness. I feel that I have no part in it, that everything wonderful about us comes from you. You make all the happiness for us both and I feel unworthy. I want to bring you down to my level. I envy you and I'm jealous of you because of what you are, the way you feel things, the way you know what you want. You make me feel inferior."

"If you really feel that way," Matthew said, "then you will destroy us." He got out of bed slowly. "We'd better get up," he said.

Chapter Twenty-seven

Matthew had been nervous without Michel the morning he first met his father, now he was nervous about their meeting. After what had happened the night before, however much their conversation of the morning had affected it, he felt that Michel was no longer predictable. What reckless gesture – and after last night, he thought of Michel as capable of anything – might he make that would complicate this situation even more? In addition he felt drained by the things that had been happening to him; he was less confident and certain of his own strength and ability to carry the weight of his conflicting emotions.

He had listened to what Michel had said about his father and their own relationship without comprehending the words; they puzzled and confused him. He had always had enough affection for everyone he loved; but envy, jealousy, transference had no real meaning for him – and the idea that his love for his father could mean a decrease in his love for Michel was incomprehensible. Further, that his love for Michel was something he should have given to his father (which was the way he understood it) did not make any sense at all. Was love something that was apportioned, allotted to different people without your participation or choice? He could understand the possibility that his love for Michel was greater than it would have been had he, himself, needed love less – it was more important to him because he had been lonely and withdrawn – but he sensed some further meaning in Michel's words. It was as if Michel had said that under other circumstances they might never have loved each other at all, and it was this that confused him. He did not feel that he and Michel had been *destined* to meet and love each other, but he did feel that it was an accident which had given his life meaning. If he had loved his father more, if he had been allowed to be with his father, did that mean that he would love Michel less? He did not understand it. It was hard to think about clearly, for he was approaching the meeting between Michel and John and Edith, and he had begun to dread it.

There was nothing to do but face it, and he was happy at the thought of Edith, who seemed to him safe and secure. It was unjust and illogical that a meeting between two of the people he loved most in the world should be something to fear. It had not been true of Michel's meeting with Catherine. He had had, then, moments of considering the possibility that they might not like each other, but here was the possibility that Michel and John might not only dislike each other, but that Michel might even be active in his dislike, his jealousy of John. Matthew's mind leaped to the word *jealousy* as if he had given himself, unconsciously, a clue to the entire difficulty. It was an emotion he had never experienced and one that he had no means of understanding. It was savage and cruel; it had made Michel turn on him in a successful effort to wound him. Yet it did not mean that Michel did not care for him, which only puzzled him that much more.

In Matthew's heart, whatever the reconciliation of this morning, he carried the pain of the night before. He had been betrayed and lacerated. He was afraid, and his fear was limiting the spread of his happiness. He loved Michel. How is it possible to be afraid of the person you love most in the world?

Before they were halfway through lunch, Matthew felt that his worries were groundless. His father had, with only a slight reddening of his face, put his arms around him and embraced him when they met, and so had Edith. They had welcomed Michel with the same warmth that they had created between themselves and had extended to Matthew, and he drew upon their obvious joy of the moment, their pleasure in being with him. What he liked most about them was that they had accepted him, not singly and individually as two different people, but together. They made room for him in their home.

Once more a word glowed like a light in his mind. *Home.* He had never thought much about it – it was a word that did not exist in French. You were *chez vous*, you were *à la maison*, but you were not home. He had had a home in America, with Catherine and John, but it had not been like this. The love he felt now from his father and his stepmother was something that had never existed for him before. The feeling they carried around with them was the feeling, the sensation, the atmosphere of a place, not only of two people. As if they took their home with them everywhere they went. Matthew suddenly felt that he could not stand any more affection, any more love. It was too much for him, and even the strength of his own feelings, the things that originated inside him, could not stand up to the burden of love that was showered on him.

Adding to the weight that was already insupportable, Michel, far from creating any scene that would have alarmed Matthew, was at his best. He had established an immediate rapport with both John and Edith, and with them he was a different human being. He was older, he even looked older, he had turned into Matthew's uncle or a very much older brother. It was the way Scott had felt about him. First, Michel had suggested that Matthew was perhaps lavishing some kind of filial love on him, something that should have been given to his father, and now – for all Matthew could tell – he was seeing the reverse of that in action. Michel was almost as much his father as John. Was it possible that it was not he, Matthew, who had misdirected his love, but that what Michel felt for him should have been reserved for a son?

As if he had thrown his hands in the air in confusion, he felt a kind of explosion inside him. It was much too complicated. He would have liked to stop thinking forever. What he thought only dissipated the clarity that had always been in his heart. His mind seemed to him to be nothing more than a trap. Reason, pure reason, was something Matthew did not understand. It had no logic or sense for him. He believed and acted on something that he felt in the center of his body. It was as much present in him as his hands or his ribs. He knew exactly where it was, even. But this … this turning and twisting with words and ideas and possibilities; there "transferred" or "repressed" emotions had no reality for him, and created nothing but more questions, more doubts.

After lunch, John suggested that they all go back to the hotel for a while. When they started to go, while Michel was hailing a taxi for them, Matthew remembered that it had been discussed over the coffee, but the surprise he felt when he realized that they were going there now disturbed him. He had not, in a way, even been with them at lunch, and his participation in the conversation had been mechanical. Was this what thinking could do to you? Lock you up in yourself so that you could not share yourself with the people around you, so that you did things half-heartedly and automatically? A vista of tormented and unending thinking presented itself, stretching out before him. Was it always going to be like this? Where was his certainty and sureness, what had happened to them?

Shaking himself out of his self-absorption after they had arrived at the hotel, Matthew followed Michel and his father down the hall, with Edith's arm in his.

"You look a little tired today, Matthew," she said, and then she squeezed his hand in hers. "I suppose it's the excitement of yesterday. It was the same with John; he couldn't stop talking about you last night."

Matthew was pleased, much more pleased than he expected to be.

"Yes," she said. "Oh, Matthew, I'm so happy for you two. It seems too good to be true, as if you were making up right now for all the time you've been apart."

She was, and Matthew was touched to see it, very moved as she said this. He had thought of her as substantial, thicker in a way than Catherine, for instance, but now what he had called substantial seemed more than that – real strength and perception. It occurred to him that she must love his father very much to feel all of this so strongly. He had never seen a woman express just that kind of love before. His own relation with his mother seemed flimsy in comparison with what this woman, his stepmother, was giving him. He pressed her hand in his and would have kissed her if he had had the courage. "We *are* making up for all of it, Edith."

The word, her name, rang out in the hall. Where yesterday it had been natural and easy to call her by her first name immediately, today it seemed almost disrespectful. Whatever ease he felt for her, he also felt gratitude and respect; he felt that he owed her a great deal, as if it was she who had kept the bond between himself and his father alive. He loved her and he wanted to tell her so, but for once it did not come easily to his lips. The idea embarrassed him. The word, which he had used so much and with such facility, was not quite good enough – did not exactly express what he felt about her. It was unrelated to what he felt for Michel, or his father, or what he had felt for Scott; it was not even the same love he felt for his mother. He would have been overjoyed if she had, at that moment, put her arms around him and held him close to her. He wished she would.

When they were in the suite, John took them over to the open window, arranging chairs for all of them. "I'll send for something to drink," he said, and when he had ordered, he came back to stand behind Matthew, putting his hand on his shoulder. "Well, Matt, how goes it?"

He was grinning at him, pleased to have him here, but the question – even though it was not really a question and did not require anything but a perfunctory answer – stopped Matthew short. If he could only tell him! If he could tell his father of the confusion and wildness in his heart, if he could ask him all the questions he was asking himself. He was sure that this man, solid, strong as a brick wall, would be able to answer all of them. This man who had called him Matt.

No one else had called him that, ever, and it had taken him back in one instant to years before. The gap in his memory of his father no longer existed, their past relationship was not out of reach any more. That was what he had called him, this was the way he had looked at him, this was the way they had both felt. Only, Matthew could not tell him anything now. How could he ever tell him of his love for Michel, and what it had done to him? But in those moments with his father's hand on his shoulder, his eyes looking into him with kindness, age, strength ... something had to come out.

"What is it, Matt? What's the matter?"

Perhaps it was the concern in his father's voice, the shift in his eyes from happiness to pain. Whatever it was, Matthew felt then as lonely as it was possible to feel. He could not stop the tears from rushing to his eyes, and he stood up and threw himself on his father, burying his head against his shoulder.

Through the mist of tears that had come into Edith's eyes, she looked at them and exclaimed: "Oh, my God!" For the first time in her life she saw tears in John's eyes, too.

Chapter Twenty-eight

Feeling the dampness on her arms and hands, Edith took a handkerchief from her bag, wiped her hands, her forehead and her cheeks and then took out her compact and mirror. Without looking in the direction of the girl sitting next to her, she said, "I had no idea it got so hot in Paris. This is almost as bad as New York."

Françoise Lauret turned her head to look at her. She liked this comfortable, ample woman. "It's unusually hot this year," she said, watching Edith fix her face and replace the compact in her bag, and then suddenly, as if they were resuming rather than beginning a conversation, she asked: "What do you think of Matthew? How do you really like him?"

"He's a perfect darling," Edith replied emphatically. "He's very like John, I think; at least John must have been like that when he was young." She looked at the four figures – John, Matthew, Scott, and Michel – on the tennis court. "A little oversensitive, perhaps," she went on reflectively.

Françoise nodded. "How do you like his friend?"

"Michel? Oh, very much. Matthew really seems to adore him." She looked at them once more, critically this time. "I think it's too bad he's so much older than Matthew; Matthew doesn't really seem to have any friends his own age," and then she smiled at the girl sitting next to her. "I can't help think that it is important for young people to be with young people. It can't be good for them to be with older people all the time. Don't you agree?"

Françoise shrugged her shoulders, but she was not dismissing the question. "Different people have different ways," she said. "Before it was Scott; Matthew was crazy about Scott. I was almost jealous of him!" She laughed. "But you know he seems to have to adore someone."

"Yes," Edith agreed, "I think he does, too. I suppose it may be because of the divorce. I'm so glad he and John are getting along so well."

"Yes," Françoise said, "and I'm glad you're here. You're good for Matthew. He loves you."

"Yes, he does," Edith said. "And I certainly love him." She examined Françoise affectionately. Of course, she had known at once that this girl was living with Scott; it would have taken someone subtler than Scott to hide it from her, and she wondered if they were planning to get married. It would be a pity if they weren't – she was very right for him. "When," she asked, "if I'm not butting in, are you and Scott going to be married?"

Françoise's eyes widened. "I don't know," she said immediately, and then added: "I'm not sure that we are, even."

"Oh, well perhaps I…" Edith was interrupted by a shout from the tennis court and looked up in time to see Matthew leap the net and shake Scott's hand hard. Scott, admiring and happy, exclaimed: "Boy! Who's been teaching you this game? You can play!"

Matthew, hot and smiling, looked in the direction of Michel, his eyes full of affection: "He has. He's a wonderful player. Better than any of us. He's been holding back today."

The four of them walked over to the bench, and Scott put his head to the water fountain, letting the water run over his face and then wiping it off with his hands. "Wow, it's hot," he said and sat down on the bench. His hand reached over to Françoise and squeezed hers. "Hi," he said, absently affectionate, and Françoise smiled at him. John, still standing, looked down at them. In all the years he had known him, Scott had never looked so happy, so full of life, and he was very pleased to see it.

᪣

Matthew had been conscious of the way the game was going. Most of the play had been between himself and Scott, almost a singles match, for both of them were playing up to their limit. In the last set, with only one point against him and only one point needed to win, Matthew had missed a high shot from Scott. But it was his serve, and he had put everything into it, firing the ball across the court so that it just missed the net and hammered into the court just inside the line. The game was his. This was the third time that they had played here – the four of them – and for some reason, as if they had avoided it purposely, Matthew and Scott had never played a game of singles, yet when they were not playing together, when they played doubles, it was against each other and not against a team that they played. John and Michel, sensing some undercurrent of rivalry that needed to be thrashed out between them, had let them go; it was as if they understood that it was something that could not be fought openly, but only in this way. Matthew did not understand it himself, but now he knew that it was over and he had won, which had been important to him. And Scott had not let him win easily, he had played hard against him. It was an honest victory. Matthew, now, felt a wave of friendship for Scott, some shadow that had been between them for a long time had been destroyed by this victory.

It was not only towards Scott that he felt friendly. Everyone was wonderful to him these days. After that overemotional scene in the hotel with his father and Edith, something had settled inside all three of them. The embarrassment, the strain of overfeeling no longer existed and Matthew felt comfortable and easy with them. Most of all, Michel seemed to approve his relationship with his father and stepmother, seemed to enjoy them himself, and there had been no more anger, no quarrels. Michel had gone out of his way to make up to Matthew for that night, so that even that had been banished from

Matthew's memory as if he had only dreamed it. The whole summer was what he had hoped it would be, and much as he really loved his father and Edith, he was looking forward to the time when he and Michel would once again be in Brittany, when most of their time could be theirs alone.

He looked up at the sound of Michel's voice: "How about some singles, Mr. Cameron, or are you too hot?"

"Fine, Michel, fine!" his father said, adding: "But remember, I'm an old man now, you'll have to take it easy."

Matthew thought it was strange, but he also liked Michel's calling his father Mr. Cameron. It was a gesture of respect, and in some way it seemed to be for Matthew's benefit. He watched them now, going out onto the court together. It was so nice, he thought, when the people you loved got along well together and liked each other. Françoise and Scott liked Michel, too. Matthew sighed to himself. He wouldn't have been so worried about it alone, but Michel's incessant references to the possibilities of discovery and exposure had troubled him, he realized, more than he had known, and it was a great relief that all of these people: John and Edith and Scott and Françoise, suspected nothing and accepted Michel perfectly naturally. They did not seem to notice or worry about the difference in Michel's age and his own. Thank God!

Michel and John were, or so it seemed, fairly evenly matched. They were restraining themselves, watching each other's game as if they had never had a chance to observe it before, and there was something at once serious and playful in their manner which compelled silence and attention on the part of the spectators. They expected something to happen; the atmosphere between the two players was mounting slowly towards a real test. Neither of them betrayed this in their faces; it was more in their bodies that the tensions had begun to show. The first two sets went quickly enough, Michel winning the first one 6-4 and John the second 6-3. It was only at the beginning of the third and last set (two out of three was enough in this heat) that their balance and reserve loosened. Their faces had deepened in seriousness and they were playing more intensely. There was still no feeling of recklessness, no really brilliant shots were made, but Matthew was sure that something was going to happen. He was certain Michel would win; he was, unquestioningly, the better player, and a good deal younger than John. It surprised Matthew that he seemed to hold himself back all the time, as if he didn't want to win. He was also surprised at his father, because John was playing better than he had ever seen him play, his shots were more accurate and his judgment and timing were good, better than Matthew expected. He felt that he was watching a real struggle, it might actually be close, unless Michel should decide he wanted to win.

Suddenly, and it was as obvious as if the ball had been fired in their direction, the whole feeling of the game changed. With the score at 5-4 in his father's favor, Matthew felt John relaxing into his play, it was coming more easily to him, as if he was certain to win, and he did win the first shot. His face was concentrated but not serious, the way in which he glanced at Michel was friendly; for him it was still a game.

Matthew looked at Michel and drew in his breath, almost in horror, for what he saw was a person transformed. Had he looked a second later, he might not have seen it at all, for the look that had come into Michel's face was fleeting and he at once resumed an ironic and competent-looking mask, but in that moment Matthew had seen cruelty, anger, near-hatred in Michel's eyes. He hesitated before serving, looking at John, examining his ground and his aim, and then as if he had been roused from some inner torpor, he began to play. It was all over with very quickly – 5-5, 5-6, 5-7. John didn't have a chance. Michel's playing had been more than brilliant; it was a calculated victory, devoid of sportsmanship, stemming from some deep urge not only to win, but to defeat mercilessly. He had struck the ball as he would have fired a gun, aiming only at John's weaknesses. When he had won, he threw his racquet in the air and walked off the court.

He made no gesture then even to speak to his opponent, but let John follow him from the court, winded and streaming with sweat.

No one said anything at first, and Matthew knew by the prickling of his skin that they had all seen what he had seen. It was Scott who said, finally, and lamely: "I thought you had him there for a while, John," and attempted to laugh. He turned to Michel, and his voice was quite cold: "You can really play, Mister," he said evenly. "You've been holding out on us."

Michel smiled. "Thanks. It wasn't anything." And then he stepped unexpectedly in front of Matthew to where John was sitting on the bench next to Edith. "Thank you, sir," he said. "That was a fine game."

John shook his head, wiping the sweat from his forehead with his handkerchief. "It was a pushover," he said, looking up at him. "You took that game in a walk. I didn't have a chance."

As if they were waiting for what might be said next, there was complete silence in the group, and they all looked at Michel, who said quietly and distinctly: "I felt like winning. I don't often feel that way, but I felt I had to win."

Matthew and Scott were the first to break away from the group to change their clothes in the clubhouse, and as they changed, Scott watched Matthew stripping off his clothes and getting under the shower. He wondered what had happened to Matthew. He had changed, it was something more than just growing up. He also felt relief at the result of their game; he was glad that Matthew had won, knowing that it was necessary and at the same time an impulse that Matthew could not bring into the open; he seemed to have felt that he had to beat Scott without anyone knowing it. Scott knew that it had been a hidden, personal victory for Matthew. He was glad for himself if only because something had cleared between them now, some vague and indefinite hostility had been wiped away in that tennis match.

As he undressed, he continued to stare at Matthew. What did the boy see in this Michel Garnier, for example? A nice enough guy in his way, but something funny about him: the thing that had happened when he and John were playing together. He'd made John look like an old man. It had not been any ordinary sporting victory, Michel had trounced him and Scott didn't like it. He made a mental note to ask Françoise what was going on; there was a girl who saw things. She never missed a trick. She'd know what was up with this Garnier.

But his mind kept coming back to Matthew. There was a real change in him; he was older, he had acquired a mysterious maturity that didn't make complete sense; in the ordinary way he was still a wildly enthusiastic and emotional kid, but, at the same time, he seemed really old. More than that, he knew a lot, a lot more than anyone saw at first glance. It wasn't in anything he said or did, it was more in the sound of his voice, the movements of his body, the quick appraisals he would make of people. In a way it was as if he had … Scott looked at Matthew's face as he came out of the shower. Why hadn't he thought of that before? The kid had gone and got himself a girl someplace, that was it!

Scott felt a wave of tenderness, concern, and responsibility towards Matthew at that moment. Whatever had happened between them, for a while he had felt like a father to Matthew, and what he felt now was what he would have felt if he had just learned that his own son was having his first experience with love, or was in the middle of his first affair. He wanted to say something, to let Matthew know that he knew about it and that he was glad because it seemed to be going so well, but something stopped him. Since he had thought of it, recognizing that what had happened to Matthew could not possibly be anything but a sexual coming-of-age, he had acquired one doubt. It stood out all over Matthew that he had arrived into manhood, but there was one thing wrong. Where was the girl?

Scott remembered himself when he'd first found out what it was all about, when he'd first been in love. The very first experience was something he had hated, he had felt degraded and unhappy, but later when he'd been in love seriously for the first time, it had been the most wonderful time in his life, the way it seemed to be with Matthew now. But where was the girl? He was sure that he was not mistaken, and while it was conceivable that the girl, whoever she was, could not be in Paris and Matthew had to be, then Matthew would surely have been morose, unhappy, miserable. Something was wrong. Something didn't add up. Maybe Garnier would know, they were awfully good friends; if anyone would know, he would.

Matthew came up to him and they looked at each other. In both of them there was a frank examination of each other's physical selves, as if they were estimating each other's manliness. Matthew's young smooth healthy body … he was just sixteen. Sixteen in July. That was another thing that seemed odd to Scott. Matthew was so self-possessed for his age; Scott's first affair hadn't been until he was almost twenty, he could never have had an affair at sixteen! There had been a lot of fooling around, but that wasn't what was happening to Matthew, he was through all that, Scott knew. You could tell it from the way he looked at you, the exultation he had in his body.

Scott shook his head, puzzled, and stepped under the water, letting out a shout. Matthew had left it full on and ice cold.

Matthew laughed loudly and Scott turned to look at him through the water dripping over his face. There was nothing unhappy about that boy, and it wasn't the laughter of any boy, either. Whatever Matthew had, whoever it was, she was right here in Paris. Dammit, if he wasn't the sly one … and only sixteen, too. It was incredible.

Chapter Twenty-nine

"Oh you men!" Françoise said with an expression of disgust.

"What do you mean, 'oh you men'?"

She laughed at him. "Oh, Scott, how can you ask such a question? Do you mean, really, that you only thought of that today? Of course he's in love, anyone could see that at once." And then her face was serious. "But I think it's too bad that it had to be like that. He's such a nice boy."

Scott looked at her, puzzled. What was she talking about? Had Matthew confided in her? "What do you man? What are you talking about?"

She examined Scott's face and then went over to him and kissed him. "Do we always have to talk about Matthew? Is that going to start all over again?"

He kissed her back. "No, but..."

"No buts," Françoise said quickly. "I have something much more important to talk about than Matthew. Mrs. Cameron, Edith, wants to know when you are going to marry me. She knows we're living together."

"How do you mean she knows? What did she say to you?"

Françoise laughed at him. "Not everyone is so stupid as you, Scott. She knows. She didn't say anything, she just said, 'When are you and Scott going to get married?' She wants to make an honest man out of you."

Scott looked at her gravely. "Well, when are we going to get married, Françoise?"

"Yes. When are we … or, perhaps, just are we?" She turned away from him. "I like living with you, Scott…" and then she turned back suddenly. "Maybe I'd like being married to you, too. We'll see."

Scott kissed her again. "I wish I could understand you better, darling. We're happy together, we love each other. Surely we've been together long enough now…."

She shook her head. "Don't, Scott. I've tried to explain how I feel about it, but you're like a little boy. You can't understand the difference between an affair and marriage. You think it's enough that we love each other, that we like to sleep together. You're not practical enough for me."

"Practical! If I marry you I'll never have to worry about that. You're practical enough for both of us. As is it now, we live better and less expensively than when I lived alone."

Françoise laughed at him. "When you lived alone, you used to go out. Now you want to spend all your time in bed. That's why you save money."

Scott sat down on the bed and pulled her down beside him. "What's wrong with that?"

"It's indecent. We aren't married."

He lay back on the bed and looked out of the window at the tree tops. "I can't get over Matthew," he said, glancing quickly at Françoise. "Can you imagine a kid his age having an affair – like us, for instance?"

She looked away from him. "Matthew again."

"Oh, don't be angry, Françoise. You know how I feel about him. I'm happy for him, he's almost like my own son, you know that."

She stood up. "Yes, I know."

He got up from the bed and stood beside her. "What is it, Françoise? What's the matter?"

"Nothing."

"But I know there's something…" he paused, recollecting her words. "Why did you say that about being sorry it was like this. Like what?"

"I don't know."

"You do too know. What is it? You wouldn't have said it if you hadn't meant something. Has Matthew talked about it to you? I know you know something you aren't telling me. What is it?"

She turned to face him and put her hands on his shoulders. "Do you really want to know?"

"Of course I do!"

"Will you promise me something then? If I tell you?"

"Of course I will. What?"

"Promise me you won't be angry with Matthew. That you won't do anything without thinking."

He looked at her, more and more puzzled. "Of course I won't do anything to Matthew. What on earth are you talking about?"

"About Matthew being in love, naturally." She shook her head sadly, looking into his eyes. "Are you really honest with me, Scott? Don't you know? It is so obvious to me, I can't believe that you don't understand Matthew better than that."

Scott spread his hands hopelessly. "Françoise, please. What are you talking about?"

She looked at him again. "It's..." and then she turned back to him suddenly. "Matthew's in love with Michel," she said.

"With Michel?" He looked at her, troubled, and then his face cleared. "Oh, *that!*" he exclaimed with relief. "For a minute I thought you meant..." he stopped and looked at her face. "Françoise, I thought you ... you don't mean...?"

She nodded. "What else, darling?"

Scott dropped his hands to his side and then, with an abrupt gesture, he took Françoise's shoulders in his hands gripping them tightly with his fingers. "Do you know what you're saying?"

"Let me go, Scott. Of course I know what I'm saying. It was bound to happen."

"What do you mean, 'bound to happen'?" His voice was really angry now.

She pulled herself away from him. "You hurt my shoulders," she said. "Besides, I wish you would stop asking me what I mean. It's perfectly clear what I mean. It should have been obvious to you long ago." Her voice rose, equalling the anger that had been in his. "*Tu es vraiment aveugle,*" she went on. "He was in love with you, and you never even saw that!"

"He never wanted to sleep with me!"

"*Voyons, Scott! Ne cries pas, veux-tu?* How do you know he didn't want to sleep with you? If he didn't it was because he didn't know enough to want to, that's all. Anyway, now he knows. Even you knew it, and you don't see everything!"

He stood up, looking down at her. "Françoise, if you..."

"Oh, Scott! *Laisses-moi tranquille!* Is it my fault what happens to your Matthew?"

"Why didn't you tell me this before? How long have you known it?"

"Was I supposed to assume that you did not know it?" She paused. "I knew it as soon as I saw them. I can understand that John and Edith would not know, they don't think that way ... but you, Scott, after all..."

He sank into a chair, burying his head in his hands. "Are you sure, Françoise?" he groaned. "Are you positive? I can't believe it."

"Of course I'm sure! Do we have to go on talking about it? What concern is it of ours? What do we have to do with it?"

He raised his head. "How can you say that? I've known John Cameron all my life practically, and Matthew ... my God, Matthew's like ... how would you feel if someone in your own family ... oh, you wouldn't understand. Jesus!"

She shook her head and then took his hand in hers, rising to stand next to him. "Scott," she said firmly. "You must not get so excited. Things like this happen all the time. There is nothing you can *do*." Her voice hardened. "You can't blame it on Matthew. If John Cameron and Catherine had thought more about Matthew and not so much about themselves, it might never have happened. That Catherine!"

"What's the matter with Catherine? What do you mean, if they'd thought more about him? Do you think they should have gone on living together no matter how they felt about each other, just because of Matthew? Don't you think he would have known that, don't you think he would have sensed how they felt, why they were staying together?"

"You Americans!" Françoise exclaimed. "You don't know what marriage is. When the honeymoon is finished right away you think about divorce. Don't you know that marriage is dull? Yes, it is boring, but it is also comfortable. But do you want comfort? No, you must have love, ecstasy, excitement, romance! You want the impossible. You talk about how Matthew would feel if John and Catherine had not divorced. Maybe he would have liked it if they had stayed together on his account! How did he feel when they did get divorced, or doesn't that matter? And why did they get divorced?"

He shook his head again. "You know all about that. John was living with Edith."

"John was living with Edith!" Françoise repeated, sneering at him. "And do you think that has never happened before? Maybe he couldn't help it, maybe Catherine was a bore – in fact she must have been. But no, right away there has to be a divorce, and what for? To save her injured pride. Because she has been betrayed. Is that all there is to marriage, then? If we got married and had children and you slept with somebody else would you expect me to divorce you?"

Scott looked at her, puzzled. "But I wouldn't … well, if I did, I suppose I would expect you to."

"You wouldn't! You know that now? You know what you're going to do in fifteen or twenty years from now? When I'm ugly and fat and you're used to me? And you're sure I'd divorce you? Give up my home, my children, break up my life and theirs? Well, I'm not so sure. I am not so sure that I am so proud. Maybe I would reduce, put on some lipstick and find a lover!" She was becoming angrier as she talked. "But no, I suppose that is horrible to you. Dishonest, or not pure enough for your conscience. You have the morals of a little boy. Well, life is not like that, Scott."

Scott's voice was flat. "I don't know about all that," he said sighing. "I'm thinking about Matthew. I know this kind of thing goes on … but to have it happen to someone you know! I don't care about the rest of the people. But this … it's horrible! It's … well, I can't believe it."

"Someone you know!" She turned away from him quickly. "When you talk like that, Scott, you make me sick. What kind of people do you know? Are they all pure and righteous? Do they all have your morals? Do you pick your friends because of who they sleep with? And Matthew! After all, he's in love, he's happy. Is that so terrible? He can't help it. Has he done something so much worse than the rest of you men?" She nodded her head angrily at him. "I know about men, Scott, what they want, what they like. You think Matthew has done something awful. It's no worse than what all men do."

Was she determined not to understand him? "You don't see at all," he said. "That kind of thing … well, everyone knows about that, we're used to it. But this … why, it's abnormal, unnatural. It's all wrong."

"Why?"

"Well, it is, that's all. If you don't see it, I can't explain it to you. Everyone knows it's wrong."

Françoise shrugged her shoulders and sat down. "Whatever it is, Scott, there is nothing you can do except to forget it. And for your own sake, for my sake, don't say anything to Matthew about it when you see him tomorrow."

"Forget it? Have you gone mad? You want me to forget it and let it go on? It has to be stopped, can't you see that?"

She raised her eyebrows. "It does? And just how do you propose to stop…"

He did not let her finish. "I'll have to talk to John about it. After all, Matthew's only sixteen, he's not responsible, he..."

"Only sixteen! Not responsible! Why? Does he have to be twenty-one before he is responsible? And how are you going to stop it by telling John? What is he going to do? It will break his heart!"

"He'll have to know someday," Scott said bitterly. "He'll have to find out that his only son is ... a fairy."

"*Why?* Because you have to tell him? So you can say to yourself 'I did everything I could for Matthew. I did my duty. I tried to keep him from the path of sin'? Oh, Scott, you know Matthew. He's not a fool – he's young – but he's not a fool. Maybe he does not know how responsible he is, or what is really happening to him, but if you tell John, or if you talk to him about it, anything might happen. Let him have whatever happiness he can get out of this. He's had a bad enough time already. Don't make it worse."

"But I must..."

"You must nothing!" she exclaimed. "What business of yours is this? Would you like it if John came and told you that you had to stop living with me?" She hesitated and then smiled scornfully. "If he's anything like you, he probably will now. Now that Edith has guessed about us."

"Oh, don't be silly, Françoise. John would never do any such thing, he..."

"*Voilà!* You said it yourself. John would have too much sense to interfere in what is not his business."

Scott walked over to the window. "You don't understand. It isn't the same kind of thing at all. There's nothing abnormal about us, we..."

"We live in sin," Françoise said, mocking his tone. "We violate the law and the commandments. How can you stand it?"

"Oh, Françoise, please! I wish I knew what to do. I can't face Matthew tomorrow and just do nothing."

"Oh, Scott, *oublie tout cela, donc!* What can you do? There is nothing."

He thought for a moment, scratching his head. "Yes, there is," he said.

"What, Scott. What are you going to do?"

"I'm going to write to Matthew."

"Write to Matthew! What can you say to him?"

"I'll tell him that I can't see him, that I know about the whole thing."

"Scott, you must be mad!"

He sat down at the table in the window and took paper from the drawer and then looked around for his fountain pen.

"Do you know where my pen is?"

"If I did I wouldn't give it to you."

He did not answer her, but walked across the room to the closet and opened the door, reaching in to get his pen from his coat.

"I have to do this," he said, returning to the table. "I can't let Matthew think that I know about this and accept it."

"But what makes you think that Matthew thinks any such thing? He is probably certain that you know nothing about it. Scott, you must not write to him; let him know that you love him, that you want to help him – that way perhaps would be possible. But to write him a letter!"

"I couldn't talk to him now," he said slowly. "I don't want to see him."

He unscrewed the top of the pen and began to write. She reached across him and took the package of cigarettes form the table. When she had lighted one, she threw the package back on the desk and sat down behind Scott, looking angrily at his back. "And you wonder why I hesitate to marry you," she said, her voice tired and bitter. "You love Matthew, you say, but rather than try to understand what has happened to him, rather than make any effort to help him, you only make the gesture that will satisfy your conscience. You react like a nasty little schoolboy, and you write him a letter with no thought of the consequences for him. You don't care how he is going to feel when he gets it, you don't even give him a chance. That's how much you love him…" she hesitated, and then added: "that's how much you love anyone."

Scott's back stiffened, he hesitated for a moment, and then he began to write again.

Chapter Thirty

Matthew:

I have just learned, quite by accident, something that I should have seen myself, but that I did not see, I think, because of my affection for you. You can guess what it is without any more explanation from me. I am writing to tell you that I feel it would be better for us not to see each other, and I will not see you tomorrow. I am calling John to explain that I cannot make it.

The only thing I want to say to you is that I hope you realize how John and Catherine would feel if they knew about this (I will not tell them, of course) and how unfair it is to put them in the position of being able to see it. If they have not, you can be sure it is their love and trust in you that has made them, as it did me, blind. If only for the sake of your parents, if you cannot consider yourself, you should break off this friendship with M. Garnier before they suspect the nature of your relationship to him.

I am sorry to have to write you this way, but I could not see you under the circumstances. You know that you will always be able to count on me as a friend.

Scott

Matthew folded the letter and looked out of the window. Then, feeling Michel's eyes on him, he handed him the letter, watching him as he unfolded and read it.

There was no change of expression on Michel's face as he read, but when he had finished, he stood up and laid the letter on the table. Looking away from Matthew, he said: "Well, it had to happen some time. I warned you."

"Yes." Matthew nodded dumbly. "It must have been Françoise who told him." He shifted his shoulders uncomfortably in the chair. "I guess you can't blame her for telling him. Still, I wonder how she knew?"

"Ha! I know her type all right. And it's just like a woman. She knew that Scott was fond of you, but she would have to tell him, she wouldn't be able to keep her mouth shut." He walked over to Matthew and put his hands on his head. "Don't take it too hard, Matthew. It's happened, there's nothing you can do."

"I know."

Michel walked away from him and then looked at the letter again. "'You know that you will always be able to count on me as a friend,'" he mimicked Scott's voice savagely as he quoted. "Oh, sure. When would you need a friend more than right now? What does that mean, that he will lend you a hundred francs? A fine friend he is to you!"

"Oh don't, Michel, please! You don't know Scott the way I do, you don't like him."

Michel looked at him, astonished. "You mean you still like him – after this?"

Matthew nodded. "Of course I do."

"Why the…"

"Don't, Michel, please!" Matthew's voice was not angry, but urgent. "Leave me alone."

Michel looked at him and then sat down. He could not understand this. In Matthew's place, he would have hated Scott, whatever kind of friendship they might have had before. The smugness of the letter, the pompous moral tone! The man was an ass and Matthew was well rid of him. Friend!

The telephone rang and Matthew answered it quickly.

"Yes. Yes," he said into the mouthpiece. "Now?" He looked at Michel, lifted his shoulders as if there was something he did not understand and then said: "Well, all right. Yes, I will. Yes, I'll be here." And then he hung up.

"Who was that?" Michel asked.

"Françoise."

"Françoise Lauret? You mean Scott's girl?"

"Yes."

"What did she want?"

"She wants to see me. She's coming over. She's just down the street."

Michel laughed. "I want to see this!" he explained.

Matthew shook his head. "No, Michel. She wants to see me alone. She said so. She said she wouldn't come if you were here."

Michel stood up. "Who does she think…"

Matthew's voice was tired. "Please, Michel," he interrupted. "Don't begin on Françoise now. I said she could come and I said she could see me alone. Now please…"

"Well, what do you want me to do?"

"Go out for a while. She won't be here very long."

"Go out?" His tone was full of amazement.

"Only for a little while, Michel, maybe half an hour, that's all. Please?"

"Oh, all right." He looked at Matthew, concerned. "What do you think she wants, Matthew? Why is she coming here?"

"Oh, Michel, I don't know. I'll tell you later. She said it was important and I said all right. Now please go, and don't be angry with me. It's difficult enough without that."

With unexpected understanding, Michel took Matthew's head between his hands and looked into his face. "I won't be angry," he said. "I'm sorry. I'll go." He walked out of the room and opened the door into the hall. "I hope everything is all right, Matthew. And I won't come back until I know she has gone."

"I'll meet you at the *Deux Magots*," Matthew said. "Dad and Edith are going to meet us there at six anyway. Then you won't have to stand around wondering whether she's still here. I'll get there as soon as I can."

"All right. Goodbye, then." Michel smiled at him and closed the door behind him.

☙

Françoise had waited, certain that Michel was with Matthew, until she saw him leave the building. She watched him walking away and then came out of the dark arched tunnel-like entrance of the building up the street from Catherine's apartment. Luckily, Michel had gone in the opposite direction. She wondered if it had not been a mistake to call Matthew; in any case it was too late now. She started resolutely up the stairs and then stopped as she heard the door open behind her. She turned and found herself face to face with Michel, coming up the stairs after her.

"What are you coming here for?" he asked bluntly.

She looked at him thoughtfully, although her heart was beating a little faster. "I'm not sure," she said slowly. "It was just an impulse … I … I'm sorry for Matthew. I tried to keep Scott from writing that letter."

"How did Scott find out about us?"

"I told him."

He laughed quietly. "What for?"

She looked at him very seriously. "I don't really know that either. Scott is … well, you do tell such things to some people, don't you?"

"You should have known he would…"

She held up her hand. "Don't let us get angry," she said, her eyes boring into him. "Matthew is a boy and you are a man, if you follow me. Scott has done what he thought he had to do, and," she paused, "I assume that you have done what you thought you had to do, too."

Michel lowered his eyes. "I think that's our business." He said lamely.

"Yes, you would say that, wouldn't you? Everyone seems to have their business very much on their mind. I suppose I'm just trying to flatter my own ego that I'm not as bad as the rest of you by coming here ... but I don't think it can hurt Matthew to know that he has *one* friend."

"I think if people let Matthew alone..."

"I quite agree with that," Françoise said. "But they haven't let him alone, have they? And now, if you'll pardon me..."

Michel looked up at her quickly. "Don't tell Matthew you..."

She shook her head and her lips curled. "No, I won't."

She watched him out the door and then continued up the steps. It opened just as she knocked, and Matthew stood before her. "Come in," he said.

She sat down in the living room and lighted a cigarette, looking meanwhile at Scott's letter lying on the table. Matthew had left it there purposely. She could not be coming about anything else.

She offered him a cigarette and he shook his head. "Well, Françoise, what is it?"

She indicated the letter. "It's about that, Matthew."

"What about it?"

"If it hadn't been for me, Scott would never have written it."

He shook his head. "It doesn't matter," he said.

She leaned over in her chair towards him, and he scrutinized her with undisguised interest. He had known her for quite a long time now, but for the first time he was looking at her as a person, something other than an obstacle between Scott and himself. He was trying to see what it was that Scott felt about her, how she felt about Scott. She was, although Matthew told himself inwardly that he was no judge, almost beautiful. He didn't like the looks of most French women, he didn't think they could compare to the American girls he had seen in Paris. Her hair looked as if it had been dyed, she wore too much make-up, her fingernails were too long, in fact she was too carefully put together. In spite of that, she was attractive, she was a complete, real person. He was certain that her impulse to come here, her interest was a friendly one – more than that, sympathetic. Not that he wanted sympathy! It was the last thing he wanted.

"I don't know why," she said, "I thought I had to get myself into this, Matthew … it may only make it worse for you. But I told Scott. He had said something that made me think he knew … about you and Michel. That was why I told him. Of course, after it was too late, I realized he did not know; he would not understand. I want to apologize."

"That isn't necessary, Françoise."

She smoked her cigarette. "Perhaps, but I hate what he wrote to you, Matthew. I tried, but I couldn't stop him."

"It doesn't matter," Matthew said.

"Oh, but it does matter, Matthew, believe me it does. I think his letter was wrong because you … because what you do is not his business." She stopped again and sat back in her chair. "That isn't what I meant to say, Matthew. What I want to ask you is not to take this too seriously. Not everyone will feel as Scott does, and certainly they will not write to you – not such a letter. He is such a *moraliste!* I do not feel that way, for example. I do not understand this entirely, but it does not make me feel differently towards you."

"Why are you telling me all this?"

She sighed and thought of her conversation with Michel on the stairs. "I don't know…. Perhaps all human motives are vile; perhaps I am only trying to show you that I am more understanding than Scott. But I like you, Matthew. I know that you have not always liked me, but that is over now and I do like you; I want to go on liking you. But mostly I want you to know that whatever Scott has written to you, he wrote the letter impulsively – he will regret it. He really is a friend of yours, Matthew. He loves you."

She stood up suddenly, walked over to Matthew and kissed him swiftly on the cheek. "Don't feel too badly about this. I know that no one can do anything now, that Scott has hurt you. But please do not think of it as too serious. He did not mean it, really."

He stood up also, and looked at her, uncertain as to what he should say. "It was nice of you to come," he said at last. "Thanks."

She picked up her bag from the table and looked at the letter again. "I'll go now," she said, "but throw away that letter, Matthew. Throw it away without looking at it again."

He smiled but did not reply and then he walked with her to the door. She paused in the doorway, with her hand on his arm. "For myself, Matthew, I hope you will be happy. Not everyone is the same … be happy while you can. And if there is anything, *anything*…."

"Thanks again, Françoise."

They looked at each other silently and then he closed the door behind her and listened to her footsteps going down the stairs. He walked back into the living room, picked up the letter and reread it. He folded it over, took his wallet from his back pocket and stuck the letter into it.

Chapter Thirty-one

It was over and they were going to go. In less than four hours they would be out of this restaurant, at the Gare Saint Lazare, leaning from a train window and trying to say all the things that they should be saying now because there would be no time then. As if they all knew that what they would say to each other would not matter, because already they were caught in the beginning intensity of farewell, they ate, they smiled, they talked about something or anything. Matthew wondered if it had not been a mistake for him to come alone; it would have been easier with Michel there.

He tried not to look up from his plate because, when he did, one or both of them would be looking at him in the way that you look at someone who is not looking at you and, when his eyes met theirs, the look would change. What is it, he asked himself, that we are all trying to convey to each other now? All the things – at some time during this month – all the things that needed to be said, had been said.

"The beef is awfully good," Edith said, and then she laid her fork too hard upon the plate. "Matthew," she went on, "will you come to visit us, really?" Before Matthew could answer, John put a restraining hand on her wrist. "We'll have to write to Catherine about it, darling," he said, but she paid no attention to him. "What I wanted to say, Matthew," she continued, "is that we want you to come. You do know that, don't you?"

"Yes," he said. "Of course I do. I'll come." She sighed and looked away from him, and John, his hand still on her wrist, smiled at his son.

Matthew heard the people coming in behind him, watched them being seated at the table next to them: two young men. And one of them, catching Matthew's eyes, did something. Matthew was not sure just what it was: a gesture of his hand, an extra look that pierced him, or perhaps just that he looked too long or sat down not quite quickly enough, so that Matthew turned away and stared at his plate again. He wished he could shake himself out of the fatigue that enveloped him. He was not tired or sleepy, but exhausted. Time had slowed down with him so that his own movements and the movements of others were slow and deliberate. He glanced back at the two men, and immediately that one – the one who had looked at him before – looked again. They were the kind of young men, Matthew knew, that he had seen in the café with Michel.

Matthew gave a start, half of recognition, half of fear. That man, and he, himself, *knew*. This was the way one knew things – it was the way Françoise had known about himself and Michel. He knew it as if they had told it to him. He stopped looking at them, not allowing his eyes to stray away from the table, but he could not stop up his ears, their voices kept hammering at the side of his head.

He looked at Edith. She had come suddenly into his life; she was so different from what he had expected, instead of creating a new picture in his mind, she had destroyed an old one. Now, as he watched her, she fascinated him. She made him feel safe with himself. She was, he knew, very happy with John; but it was a different happiness from his happiness with Michel, or John's happiness with her, or Catherine's and Paul's. No one thing seemed to predominate in Edith's pleasure in her marriage or her relation with John – or with anyone. She was, in Matthew's eyes, the most satisfied woman he had ever known. She was something other than happy, because the very word *happiness* suggested to Matthew a temporary state. Edith lived on no peak, what she had inside her seemed to be hers permanently. His love for his father was more desperate, something that caught his heart from time to time, but what he felt for Edith made him quiet, gave him assurance and confidence. And it did the same thing for John. They belonged together absolutely. He could not imagine them apart. She was like one half of John.

The sounds and the conversation from the table next to them kept intruding on his thoughts, and he made, in his mind, the inevitable comparison between those two men, himself and Michel, Edith and John. What he felt from his father and stepmother had a rightness, an ease, a belonging quality that everything else lacked. The very sound of the relationship of the two strange men was artificial and inadequate in comparison. The feeling that they engendered and which emanated from their table was distasteful. And what of himself and Michel? Thrown against this projection of Edith and John, Matthew could only feel a lack in his love for Michel. With Michel, he did not have the same solid foundation of certainty that he had with Edith, let alone what she shared with John. His own relationship with Michel seemed to him precarious compared to this, as if they lived on the edge of a precipice which threatened them continually. He was not thinking of the moral or social problems of their relationship; he did not think about Françoise, or Scott's letter, it was the inner core of the relation, the basis, that concerned him. However much Michel might talk about normality, abnormality, right or wrong, the essential wrong was their inability to achieve what he felt from these two people. His instincts told him that such a balance was impossible for himself and Michel. Was it essentially because of the unnaturalness? Male and female, positive and negative ... is the very emotion which two positives, two males, create, something that produces inadequate emotions? Is the projection of such a relationship bound to be sterile? In the same way that such a union cannot produce children – the natural result, as Matthew had told himself and Michel, of sex – is it also impossible for them to produce a solidarity of feeling which is, in its own way, creative? Edith could not have children ... she had said so.

Matthew knew that through his feeling he had stumbled onto

something that was logical. It was not important whether or not social or so-called moral considerations were observed or disregarded, it was the defiance of – more than that – the inability to produce natural results, tangible or intangible, that was the root of their abnormality. He was interrupted by his father's voice:

"Well, Matt," it said, "this is the last time for a while."

"Yes, dad."

John reached across the table. "Son," he said, "we'll work it out. In a year it will be up to you, you know, and Edith and I want you to do what you really want to do."

"I know," Matthew nodded hastily as he said it.

"But there are things you have to think about," John went on. "You're growing up now, you've got to begin thinking about the future. After all, someday not too far away, you're going to be earning your own living, you're going to get married. It's not too early for you to think about those things. You're not a boy any more."

What could it possibly be like to be a father? Or to be married? Would he have a son someday? Would he be saying something like this to a boy twenty-five or thirty years younger than himself? Would he be trying to tell him that he loved him? Of one thing he was certain: he'd never get a divorce once he got married. Married! He thought of Michel waiting at the apartment, and once more he heard the voices of the young men at the table beside them. To be married, to be a father... Could you go from this into a marriage? Would he leave Michel and marry a woman someday? Marry a woman and live with her the way he and Michel had lived together – were living together now? "Why did I have to fall in love with a man?" he had asked Michel, and now he would have wanted to ask his father that same question, to tell him everything. "You'll be earning your own living ... you'll be married...." He assumed it naturally, that was what people did, that was what sons always did, that is the way the world is ... only it isn't. Why did he have to be wrong?

He looked at the two men again, and although once more the

man's eyes met his, Matthew looked harshly into them, forcing the man's eyes down. He was not like that! He looked, blazing defiance from his eyes, at his father's face, and John was looking at the two men. Matthew glanced at them and then looked back at his father and their eyes met. John's fingers drummed the table impatiently and Edith looked at them both.

From what he saw in his father's face, he knew that John knew, and how he felt. He remembered, with relief, that John did not know about himself and Michel – he would have betrayed it if he had – and it was proof that they were not like these men. Or was it only proof that love is really blind? That people see in the people they love only what they want to see, that their minds refuse to recognize anything that does not fit in with what they must see in those they love? Beyond whatever his father had not seen, outside of what his father would or would not feel about Michel and himself if he did know, there was the fact of similarity between themselves and these two men. The relationship, however he might try to justify or excuse it to himself, existed. It was only the manifestation that was in any way different. *Au fond*, it was identical. They were, both he and Michel, *homosexual*. He whipped himself silently with the word. There was no getting away from it.

Oh, Christ! Why had he been selected for this? What had he done?

It came out of himself, from deep inside him. "I wish I were going with you." And he meant it. He could not bear to have them looking down on him from the window of the train, he could not believe they were really going. Each of them held one of his hands. "I will come to America," he said, "I promise I will," and they bent down to kiss him, as if his words had hurt them. "It won't be long, son," his father said gently. "I'll write to your mother."

And then Edith: "Write to us, Matthew. Write to us often." She took his head in both her hands, and her face – for the first time – seemed to Matthew disarranged. "I wish you belonged to me," she said.

But he didn't quite belong to them. Not enough to get on the train with them, only enough to have to make this hideous farewell, to have to watch the train pulling out of the station, until finally even their heads were no longer visible. "*Défense de se pencher…*" or something like that was in all the trains. "Don't lean out of the window, or you'll get hurt."

❧

He walked down the long platform and through the station. He did not want to go back yet, he could not face Michel. He had wanted to go with them so much that even the thought of Michel had been erased by that wish. What was he? Unfaithful, in a way, to everyone? His mother would be disappointed in him because he liked his father and Edith so much; if Michel ever knew how much he had wanted to go with them, he would only say that he didn't love him; and his father – if his father knew about himself and Michel – he would never be able to accept it; he would never understand. He would look at him with the same hostility, the same incomprehension with which he had looked at those two men in the restaurant.

The real meaning of John and Edith leaving – the core of this farewell – was something that Matthew knew instinctively. He did not realize it with his reason, but he knew it physically, with his hands, with his whole body. A prop, a support, had been removed, taken away from him. He was thrown back on his own, to fight his way through his problems by himself. It did not matter, he knew, that Edith and John did not know anything about his situation; they supported him, they believed in him, they loved him unquestioningly and in a way that no one else loved him. His mother, even, did not love him in this way. She had to have something from him; he was, in her mind, *hers*. It was not the same thing at all. With the presence of Edith and John, with the force of their support, their backing, he would have worked all of this out somehow. He had been able to draw on them for strength and energy, and now even that was lost to him, and something of himself had gone away with them.

It was not very far from the Gare Saint Lazare; he decided to walk home. He hoped, guiltily, that Michel would not be waiting for him. He hated waiting, perhaps he would have gone out. Matthew wanted to be alone, and he felt cut off from everyone now. First it had been Scott who had cut himself off – if it had not been for that he would have telephoned Scott right now – he would have talked to him about it, he would have asked for his help. But now there was no one. The very strength he had lost with Edith's and John's departure made him need to talk about it. In a way, he had lost all of them because he could not be honest with any of them; if he were really honest with them, they would all reject him as completely as Scott had done. He could not be honest with Michel about his father, he couldn't tell his father about Michel, he couldn't really tell his mother even about his father, let alone Michel, and Scott – well, Scott had shown him. He was separated and alone now, and all because of what? Because of his own happiness. "You pay for everything." Those were Michel's words and this was the way he was beginning to pay. He was shutting himself off from the people he loved most, because it is impossible to love them and hide things from them at the same time.

Why did they all want so much from him? Michel wanted him to love him more than anything in the world, he had to be first. His father wanted him to be, expected him to be, a businessman, a father, like everyone else. His mother expected him to love her best, to be loyal to her – "I'll always take care of you, mother," he had said once. Did that mean, had he thought then that it meant, to the exclusion of everyone else? Had he cut himself off from his father when he had said that? As for Scott, Scott had taken himself away and in spite of what Françoise had done, coming to see him, trying to comfort him, it was Scott she loved. He could not even see her or talk to her about it.

Michel was home. Matthew saw the light from down the street and, with another start of guilt, he wondered if it was possible that Michel had left a light on and gone out. But when he came up the stairs, the door was open, and Michel was standing in the doorway waiting for him.

"Hello," he said and walked past him to sit in a chair in the living room.

Michel followed him into the room and sat down opposite him. "It's bad, isn't it?"

Maybe it was all right, maybe by some miracle Michel would really understand. He looked into his face. Was this the same face that he had seen playing tennis with his father? Was that really true, did he have any good reason to believe that Michel hated his father?

"Yes," Matthew said. "Oh, Michel, you know how it is. I hated to see them go. I wanted to go with them. I don't know when I'll see them again."

Anyway it was out. He looked at Michel, wondering what he was going to say.

"I know," Michel said. "I understand." And then he smiled. "But think, Matthew. We have a whole month ahead of us now, and you'll get over this; it's only natural, but you'll get over it."

Would he? Perhaps. It was possible to forget everything in time, but right now he was not over it. A month together ... he tried to think about it, to imagine it in his mind, to project himself into it happily, but his words at the station were still in the front of his head; he had wanted to go, he had given up that month with those words.

"It's all so complicated," he said.

"What is?"

"Everything. You and me. Catherine. Dad and Edith. Scott. Why does it have to be like this? Is there something wrong with people – what makes us the way we are, for instance, so that we are wrong to be happy together? You have to pay for everything, you said once, but why? Why?"

"It isn't as bad as all that, Matthew. You'll feel differently tomorrow. Besides, are you really so unhappy?"

Matthew shrugged his shoulders. "I guess not. I'm just mixed up, that's all. I can't understand why we have to be different, why we can't be like the rest of the world. Why we can't get married and have children..." he looked at Michel and blushed. "Well, of course *we* can't, but I mean..."

"What, Matthew?"

"Oh, you know. I've said it before. Why did we have to fall in love? Why can't we be ordinary, normal people and fall in love with women? What's the matter? What's really wrong with us?"

Michel looked away from him. "I knew it. I've seen it coming. Now you are asking yourself all the questions I once asked myself. You cannot answer them, Matthew. Possibly it's fate. I thought I had answered all those things for myself – until you came along and changed everything."

"But how did you answer them? How did you answer for what you were – what you are? What we both are?"

"I've told you, Matthew. Fate – or destiny ... God's will, if you prefer."

"God's will!" Matthew looked up sharply. "I don't believe in any of that. I think it's up to us. If we're wrong it's our fault. If we're right then we have ourselves to thank."

Michel was still serious. "But you have to believe in some authority, Matthew. You are not omnipotent, you can't do everything. You are like all the rest of us."

"Oh, all right, Michel. But why can't we at least be happy then? I was so happy with you, it was like living in a dream, it was the most wonderful thing in the world and now ... what's happened? I feel as if I could never be happy that way again, as if I'd lost the most important thing I ever had."

"It's just as well, Matthew. It's time you did."

"What do you mean?"

"You have been living in a dream. You loved everything and everyone. You thought life was wonderful. You couldn't go on like that. You had to see the way things really are, sometime. Life is not a dream, and people are not wonderful. They are selfish, ruthless, cruel, egocentric. You had to know that, to see it for yourself."

"I don't think they are," Matthew said. "You aren't, Scott isn't, my father and Edith aren't…"

"Oh, Matthew!" Michel interrupted him. "How can you say that? Did your father think about you when he got a divorce and then married Edith? Did your mother think about you then? Or when she married Paul? Don't you think they were thinking about themselves? Was Scott so loving and forgiving? Have I always been so wonderful to you? Everyone thinks of themselves first, Matthew. Always. Look at your own dream, your own happiness. Was it so unselfish? You created an imaginary world in which you could live happily. It was not real, it had to come to an end. It was just as selfish as anything else. We can still be happy, but in a different way, even in a better way."

"But it was not a dream, Michel! You believed in it yourself!"

Michel shook his head. "No, Matthew. I loved it. I loved seeing you so happy, but I never shared that dream – to me it was nothing more than a dream. Wonderful, but unreal. It did not really exist for me, ever."

"You mean for you it was only…"

"Don't, Matthew. The fact that it was not the kind of dream … the same world to me as to you … does not make it bad. I have always tried to warn you, to tell you, but you have never been able to understand me. It was this moment for which I was trying to prepare you, that I wanted you to see. It is not my fault that I could not see it all as you did, it does not mean that it was *only* whatever you were about to say. It was wonderful. Being in love is a wonderful thing, always."

"What was it, though? What did it really mean to you?"

"It was the happiest time of my life … it is the happiest time of my life, Matthew. But it wasn't new and incredible the way it was for you. I am older than you are. I live on the ground and you live in the clouds. My love for you is very real, very much on the earth."

"How?"

"*Mais mon Dieu!* Surely you know. You didn't fall in love with my mind, did you?"

"No, I fell in love with you – all of you – but when you call it 'on the earth' it sounds … oh, I don't know."

"Oh, Matthew, Matthew, wake up. Forget that dream. You want to be like everyone else, well be like them! Live in the world and not up in the air somewhere. Perhaps it is true that your sex life is different, that you love and want men and not women, but you are like everyone else in every other way – at least you could be, if you'd stop thinking the way you do. You have a wonderful mind, you understand things that few people understand, I don't know how you do it. But you have to face life as it is. You must accept things and not try to change them. Be yourself and you will be like everyone else."

Matthew heard only part of that. "What do you mean, maybe my sex life is different?"

"Just what I said. It is. You want men and not women. I don't know why; that is the way it happens to be. There is nothing you can do about it."

"No," Matthew said quickly. "It's not like that, you know it's not like that and it has never been. I don't want men. I love you, that's all."

Michel stood up, rubbing the back of his neck with his hand, and then stopped suddenly before Matthew's chair. "Matthew," he asked him, "what does loving me mean?"

"Not what you said," Matthew answered. "It hasn't got anything to do with men or women; it isn't what you say it is. I can't help loving you. I'll always love you."

"What do you think love is, Matthew?"

"I don't know. I just know that it isn't what you think it is."

"Then why...?" He stopped as if he could not go on, looking back at Matthew with troubled eyes. "Matthew, think back. Back to the first time. It wasn't just ... Oh, Matthew ... you wanted me and I wanted you. Admit it to yourself, be honest with yourself. Nobody can help these things. I am not trying to say that what you feel does not exist, but admit that you love me with your body."

Matthew looked at him. "That just makes me feel closer to you," he said slowly. "You talk as if it was everything."

"No. No I do not, but it is not nothing. If it was not for that we would not be here together. Don't you see that?"

Matthew looked away from him without replying and Michel went on: "You said yourself that it was in your blood. Don't you re-member saying that?"

Matthew nodded. "Yes. Yes, I remember, but I didn't mean it that way, I can't explain it. Oh, sometimes I wish you'd never..."

"I'd never what?"

"Why didn't you leave me alone that day? Why didn't you just let me drown in the river?"

"Matthew!"

"I hate myself," Matthew said firmly.

"But *why*?"

Matthew shook his head from side to side. "I don't know, I don't know, but it's all wrong. I just know that it's all wrong."

"It's that Scott!" Michel exclaimed.

"Scott has nothing to do with it. Leave Scott out of this."

"Why?"

"Because he has nothing to do with it, that's all."

Michel laughed. "Oh, Matthew! Leave Scott out of it. After what he wrote to you? I suppose you would like to be like Scott."

"Yes, I would. I wish I was like Scott and not the way I am."

Michel sat down again and stared at him. "Sometimes you make me sick," he said flatly.

"I make myself sick. I'm not surprised that I make you sick."

"Matthew … people are the way they *are*. You can't change them."

"I don't believe it," Matthew said suddenly. "I don't believe that. I'm not a special way. It is not true that I cannot change. I will change. I won't go on being like this. I know it's not right. I have to change it."

Michel stared at him silently and finally he leaned out of the chair to look more closely at Matthew. "*Tu veux dire, alors, que tout est fini?*"

Matthew looked back into his eyes. "Finished? Why?"

Michel stood up. "Matthew, Matthew," he said. "Forget it, forget it. Let's not talk any more tonight. Let's go to bed and forget this."

Chapter Thirty-two

Those last two days, the two days after John's and Edith's departure that they had planned to spend in Paris before returning to Requin, had sputtered and died. That night, after Matthew had seen his father leave, he had lain rigid and untouchable next to Michel and although he had, as Michel had told him he would, felt differently the next morning, there was a space between them across which they were unable to reach. It had all begun that night. During those two days they had treated each other with overconsideration and courtesy, straining against each other's atmospheres. They avoided looking directly into each other's eyes as if to avoid seeing the inner recognition of truth, of their own awareness of the falsity between them. When they moved, walking around the apartment, passing each other, there was exaggerated care in their movements as if they were trying to avoid breaking an object, or as if it was important for them not to touch.

During that time, Matthew had wanted to be back in Brittany, back on the sand and in the sun; at Requin, whoever you were with, in a way you could be alone. But Requin was no help, the place itself, the presence of Catherine and Paul brought no *rapprochement*; they were still separated by something that Matthew was sure was in himself and for which he was to blame. There was a weight in him that he felt constantly and through which he saw everything as if through a lens or a filter. His own words, and Michel's possible interpretation of them, were magnified and distorted in his mind. "I know it is not right. I have to change it." Those were the words he had said to Michel that night and he knew that he could not expect Michel to make any gesture towards him, that it was up to him to heal the breach.

Yet even at Requin, even with the sea and the sun around them, he could not bring himself to make any gesture or speak any words. He was obsessed by his effort to determine exactly how Michel felt about him, about everything, feeling that until he was sure of that he would not be able to do anything except continue to exist in what seemed to be a complete vacuum. The thing he feared most, the thing that held him back, stopping movement completely, was the possibility of rejection. If he had made a gesture, and it had been refused (he could imagine the sarcasm in Michel's voice under such circumstances) he could never have stood it, so he did nothing.

Their second morning on the beach, they lay together on the sand and he looked at Michel lying beside him, his eyes closed. He was not asleep, Matthew knew, it was just easier not to open your eyes when you could not look directly at the person with you. The way the hair grew on the back of Michel's neck was something Matthew had never really noticed before; but now, with the sand below his head and the great wide blue of the Brittany sky behind it, it was as if he had seen it for the first time. He experienced a violent wave of nostalgia as he looked at Michel now, he wanted terribly to go back, to shatter this wall that had been built up between them, and his hand moved involuntarily to touch Michel's neck, until he drew it back, still afraid.

They swam and lay on the beach until it was time for lunch and then they walked back to the inn. They had hardly spoken to each other all morning, occasionally exchanging a formalized smile, something they would ordinarily have reserved for strangers or enemies.

It was Catherine who, inadvertently, helped to bring them back together again. In the middle of lunch, when the usual banalities of the weather, the food, what she had been reading and the temperature of the water had been discussed and put aside, she said: "Is there anything troubling you, Matthew?" He looked up quickly and shook his head. "No, mother, why?" and she dismissed her question, saying only: "You seem so quiet, I just wondered."

However meaningless this exchange of words had seemed, and however little she pursued them, she had opened something by asking a direct question. She had talked to Matthew as soon as he had returned and he had given her all the news of his father and Edith and Scott and Françoise. He had been insistent about describing what they had done in elaborate detail, but he had spoken from the surface of himself only, and Catherine had known that there was something he was keeping from her, something that he was afraid to reveal and that she was, perhaps, afraid to see. She had not asked him what it was directly; thanking God that there was still almost a year left, a year during which time whatever it was (she was certain only that it was in some way connected with John) would be sure to come out. She had time. She could afford to wait, and she had made no comment on the change she had felt at once in Matthew. The ecstasy was gone from him, the brightness which had startled her when they had first come here was no longer in his eyes; she was sure that something was wrong. Direct questioning might only enlarge it, hide it more deeply inside him, and she could not afford that risk.

The simplicity of the question and then the dismissal of the subject had served a purpose, however, and it was, for the time being, enough for her. He had exchanged a quick, involuntary look with Michel and then looked away again. Michel, then, knew. He would have talked to Michel about it, which she could also do, if necessary. It served the additional purpose of voicing, for the first time, something that had been in all their minds; it was not only Catherine who had felt the change, Paul had remarked upon it, Michel felt it obviously, but no one up to now had mentioned it openly to Matthew. In a way it cleared the air, having been voiced when they were together. His denial meant nothing; she had expected it.

The look that he had given Michel, without having time to think or to hold it back, was like the entering wedge in the solid wall between them. It was the first time that they had looked at each other honestly in several days.

Michel went to his room after lunch and Matthew came in through the door between their rooms and sat down. It cost him some effort to come in without knocking, but it went further towards lessening the gap and Michel looked directly at him, smiling. "Hello," he said, and Matthew, embarrassed, said "Hello," in reply and sat on the edge of the bed on which Michel was stretched out. He put his hand out tentatively in Michel's direction and the smiles grew on both of their faces. Michel reached for his hand and covered it with his own. "A month is a short time," he said, "and we are wasting it."

"I know," Matthew said quickly, "and it's all my fault. I'm sorry."

Michel sat up quickly and put his hand on Matthew's cheek. "Don't be sorry," he said into Matthew's ear. "Don't be sorry," and he put his arms around him. They did not speak then for a long time and when Michel did speak again it was only to say, "You see, Matthew, in the long run it all comes to this. Don't fight it."

He had barely finished speaking when there was a knock at the door. They exchanged a glance of alarm and Michel tightened his hand around Matthew's arm. "Who is it?" he called out.

"It's me." It was Paul's voice. "Is Matthew in there, too?"

"Yes."

"We're going down to the beach. Are you coming?"

"We'll be right with you," Michel answered and tightened his grip on Matthew's arm still more. It was only when Paul's footsteps faded down the hallway that his fingers relaxed. He kissed Matthew quickly and stood up. "Come on," he said, laughing. "Let's go with them."

Walking towards the beach with Catherine, following Michel and Matthew, Paul glanced at her from under his eyelids. There was a question in his eyes about the woman he had married. How much did she know about anything? She was not insensitive but, like everyone else, she saw those things that she wanted to see probably. He considered his own position briefly. It was not actually any of his business, but whatever doubts, whatever suspicions he had had up to now needed no further confirmation. Matthew and Michel had been together in Michel's room. Not that that proved anything ... but, still, if one was not blind! From what he could see in her face and from what he knew of his wife, she did not even suspect anything about her son and Michel.

"You're worried about Matthew, aren't you?" he asked her.

"Yes, a little."

"Why?"

She looked at him in surprise. "He's changed so. He's so different from when he went to Paris. But we've talked about that, Paul."

He nodded. "Of course, but what do you think it is? His father?"

"What else? He probably doesn't want me to know how much he liked John, he probably feels disloyal to me. I'm not quite sure what I should say to him. Of course, I want him to love his father. I'm happy that he does."

Paul laughed. "Are you really?"

"Naturally I am. What do you mean?"

"You don't want him to go to America? I don't think he wants to at all ... and if he does, he'll get over that. It must have been a shock to him, seeing John for the first time in so many years." She looked at Paul then and sighed. "It was what I was afraid of when John suggested this visit. It isn't that I don't want Matthew to know his father, but you can see for yourself what has happened. He's torn between the two of us now; instead of feeling whatever is natural to him, he's trying to feel what he thinks we would both want him to feel. It must be very difficult for him at the moment."

"He hasn't really talked to you at all, has he?"

She shook her head. "No, but I think he's talked to Michel about it. I think I'll have to have a talk with Michel myself." She looked up at the two figures ahead of them. "It was really providential that Michel came to spend the summer with Matthew. It would be so awful if he had no one to talk to."

"You like Michel, don't you?"

"Of course, you know I do. Don't you?"

Paul took a package of cigarettes from his pocket and lighted one of them, cupping his hands against the wind. "Yes," he said slowly. "I like him all right. Not as much as you do perhaps."

"Why, darling?"

"I don't know. Probably it's not important."

"I like him," she said, "but more important than that is that I think he's done wonders for Matthew."

Paul looked at her. "Yes," he said. "He's certainly done wonders for him."

It was something sardonic in his voice that made her stop and turn to him. "What do you mean, Paul?"

He laughed and looked at her, blankly innocent. "Just what I said. I agree with you."

She shook her head. "Sometimes you have a way of saying things … I…"

He did not give her time to finish. "Look," he exclaimed, pointing at the sea. "I've never seen it so beautiful!"

She gave him another sidelong glance and then looked towards the sea. It was very beautiful today.

They lay on the beach, and Matthew looked at his mother from time to time. He was almost happy again, things had – in a way, thanks to her – straightened themselves out; he was close to Michel once more, the troubles were draining from his mind. He wanted to do something that would make up for his inability to talk to her, make some gesture that she would understand as he meant it; he did not want her to worry about him.

"Let's go in swimming, mother," he said suddenly, excluding both Michel and Paul by the tone of his voice.

Catherine was surprised and she did not particularly want to go into the water at that moment, she had almost fallen asleep. But when she saw the appeal in Matthew's eyes, she understood his gesture and responded to it. "I'd love it," she said, and sat up to put on her bathing cap. They walked to the water's edge leaving Paul and Michel alone together on the beach.

The two men looked at each other. They had not been alone before, and the look they exchanged now was very like that first meeting of their eyes in the mirror of the car. As they examined each other, it was partly (in both of them) with surprise at finding themselves unexpectedly with no third person between them. Whatever he had thought about it during the summer, Michel was certain now that Paul *knew*. He was not alarmed, he was not even surprised, but he was immobilized. If he knew now, he had known all summer, and he had done nothing – he had not told Catherine, which was the only thing he could have done. Why not?

As they continued to stare into each other's faces, Michel was surprised at his own lack of fear. His mind seemed to him very steady, very clear, and he felt curiously sure of himself. Paul, as a type, was not unknown to him – he would have had a good reason for silence, and Michel deduced that the reason must lie in his relationship with Catherine…. But that was not enough, there was some other reason as well. What was it? And why had he chosen this moment (there was no attempt to disguise the knowledge in his eyes) to let Michel know he knew?

Paul dropped his eyes and smiled as he looked away from Michel. "It's been a fine summer, hasn't it?" he asked casually.

Michel nodded. "It certainly has. How was it during August?"

"Fine," Paul said. "Fine."

"Did your wife … did Catherine miss Matthew much? Was she worried about him?"

Paul looked at him again, not answering his question. "How did John Cameron like you?" he asked.

Michel returned his look steadily. "All right. He is very nice."

"That's good. Everything worked out then?"

Michel nodded. "Of course."

"Catherine didn't miss Matthew too much," Paul said then. "Did he miss her?"

"I don't think so, after all...."

"After all," Paul's voice cut in quickly, "his father was there, and you were there."

"Well, yes. But I don't think Matthew..." he hesitated, trapped in his own sentence. He didn't think Matthew *what?*

Paul's lip curled. "You didn't think Matthew what, Michel?" It was just as if he had read Michel's own question in his mind.

"I don't think he had time to miss her," he said. "We weren't gone so long."

"No," Paul said quietly, "and you were happy together, weren't you?"

Michel caught his breath – there was certainly no room for doubt any more. He was saved from having to search for some reply by Catherine and Matthew coming up to them. Although their arrival gave him a momentary breathing spell, it also frightened him. If they had come a minute later he might have known just what was in Paul's mind, what he was going to do. Not only did he know – but he was going to do something about it, now. He looked up at Matthew drying himself with a towel. He would have to warn him. If he could invent some excuse to get him alone....

He was startled by Catherine's voice. She was still standing above them, next to Matthew, and she smiled down at them both. "I think I'd like to go on back, darling," she said to Paul, and both Paul and Michel came to their feet.

"Already, darling?" Paul asked in surprise. "We haven't been here more than half an hour. I'd like to stay a little longer." He glanced at Michel and exchanged a look with his wife. Catherine remembered their conversation on the way down to the beach and extended her hand to Michel. "Then you'll take me back," she said gaily. "You spend entirely too much time here on the beach anyway, and besides there's something I want to ask you."

"Why yes, of course," Michel said quickly. He looked at them both and then at Matthew. What was going on? Did they both know about it? Of course, that was impossible, but the look they had exchanged ... he couldn't refuse now. What about Matthew? His eyes met Paul's again and once more it had been that same steady stare.

He had taken Catherine's hand when she offered it to him and now he felt her pulling him faintly, and he turned to smile at her. It was too late to do anything about it now. If only Paul would leave Matthew alone. Matthew would never know how to cope with him. As he walked away from them, Matthew flopped down on the sand beside Paul, and Michel tried to catch his eye, to warn him with a look, but Matthew was not even looking in his direction. "Don't you think Matthew should come in?" he said to Catherine. "It's not so terribly warm this afternoon."

She looked at him astonished. "Why, it's a lovely day! Are you cold?"

"A little," he said.

"Well then it's time you went in," she said, "but Matthew's perfectly all right. Besides, I do want to talk to you."

"You do?"

"Yes, about Matthew," she said.

He waited for her to continue, and after a brief pause she went on. "I can understand that it is probably hard for him to talk to me about his father, but he is so fond of you, so close to you, that I thought perhaps he had talked to you about him, or that you knew how he really felt. After all, you were in Paris with them."

"Yes," Michel said, "he has talked to me, and I can understand the delicacy of your position. I can see why you would not want to question Matthew directly about John."

"Well, what do you think, Michel? How does he feel about his father … in relation to me, for example?"

Michel hesitated. "I think there is some real conflict in Matthew about both of you," he said carefully, "but I don't think it is anything to worry about. John is very nice, very attractive, and Matthew is very fond of him. I think perhaps he expected not to like him … I think, if you don't mind my saying this, that he thought perhaps he was not supposed to like him."

She looked at him sharply. "But…"

"I didn't mean," he went on hastily, "that you had done anything to make him feel that way. I think it is quite natural under the circumstances that he would feel that. With John he must feel the same, that he is not supposed to like you. The divorce, the break between you and John must have made him feel, unconsciously perhaps, that he had to split himself between you. If he did not feel it at the time, he must surely feel it now. It is very difficult to like two people who are … not hostile, perhaps … but who are, at least, opposed. Catherine," he paused and looked at her, "may I suggest something to you?"

"Certainly. What?"

"I think you should talk to Matthew. I think you should let him know in your own way and in your own words that you understand the difficulty in his position; tell him that his choice next spring is an absolutely free one. I am sure that if he knows that you are able to be open with each other … then there will be no more difficulty. You might even suggest that he visit John in America next year. If you do that, it will be real proof of your concern for him."

"Do you think he wants to do that?"

Michel nodded seriously. "I don't want to alter any of the facts, Catherine. I think he does – now. And I think if he has any feeling that you oppose that wish, it will only strengthen it. If necessary, when the time comes, let him go for a visit. If you do it that way, I am sure he will want to come back, that when any real choice comes up he will decide to stay with you. At the moment, he is not himself, he has been under an emotional strain. What he wants most, loving both of you as he does, is to bring you together – not literally, it is the natural response – and since that is impossible, then you must both help him and be generous with him. I think if you talk to him directly and honestly, from your heart, it will give him greater confidence and trust in you."

She looked at Michel with surprise and admiration. "I think there is a great deal in what you say, Michel, and I am glad you've been so honest with me." She took his hand in hers. "And one more thing. I want to thank you again for everything you have done for him. It has been wonderful of you to give up your summer this way; you must have had many other things you wanted to do. Matthew is barely sixteen, after all, and you're a man. I can't tell you how I've appreciated your interest and affection. I had no right to expect it."

Michel smiled at her. "I have had a wonderful summer," he said, "and Matthew is a fine boy, Catherine. It has been no sacrifice on my part, I assure you."

"Well," she patted his hand maternally, "it is very sweet of you to say that, although I am sure it is untrue."

And they smiled, conspiratorially, at each other.

Chapter Thirty-three

They watched Catherine and Michel until their figures disappeared beyond the bluff and then Matthew looked at Paul, curious and embarrassed to be alone with him. He had been alone with him before, but there was something intimate in this aloneness that had been thrust upon them by the abrupt departure of Catherine and Michel. He hoped he would talk about him to her, explain things that he could not explain himself. He was sure Michel would have no difficulty.

He felt he should say something to Paul, the silence between them was growing heavy. "Did you swim a lot while we were gone?" he asked.

"Not so much. We didn't do a great deal of anything. We drove around some, Brest, Quimper, Morlaix … you know … your mother read a lot, we walked. Tell me, how was Paris?"

"Oh, it was fine. We had a good time."

"You liked your father and his wife?"

Matthew nodded. "Very much." There had been times when he had not quite trusted Paul, but now he felt some warmth from him. He had realized suddenly that Paul was very close to his mother, closer than he was himself; that he was in a sense a door to his mother. "Was Catherine … was mother worried about that?" he asked.

Paul dug his hands into the sand and then let it flow out through his fingers. "No, I don't think so," he said. "She wanted you to love your father."

"Are you sure of that, Paul? Does she really?"

"Yes, of course she does. Did you think she didn't?"

"I didn't know," Matthew said. "I certainly hope you're right."

"Of course I'm right."

Matthew looked at him gratefully. It was the first time he had been able to smile at Paul unreservedly, without holding something back, without feeling suspicious of him. Maybe he wasn't such a bad stepfather after all.

To Paul Dumesnil there was a certain excitement in being able to fit into a situation which was not exactly what he would have chosen for himself. It gave him a feeling of superiority, a consciousness of an ability in himself that other people did not always have, a feeling that he was getting away with something. He had made, with almost no effort, an impression on Matthew. For the first time, he knew that Matthew trusted him. It was of no personal importance to him, one way or the other, but he liked to be in the center of things, close to the core. He did not like being left out of anything. He did not necessarily want to bring anything out into the open, get himself actively involved, but he liked the feeling of knowing that people knew what he knew, that they sensed that he was not fooled by anything. In fact, he needed to have them know that about him; it substantiated his ego. He was amused at Matthew's gullibility and naiveté. Matthew, to him, was someone standing perilously close to the edge of the precipice, it would amuse him to be able to give Matthew the slight shove necessary to push him over.

"What else did you do while you were in Paris?"

"What do you mean, what else?"

"Well, you weren't with your father all the time, were you?"

"Every day. Why?"

Paul laughed. "How old are you, Matthew?"

"Sixteen. You know that." Once again he eyed Paul with distrust. There was something about him he could not fathom. He always seemed to be enjoying some private joke.

"That's right," Paul said. "Of course I knew that." He turned on his side, leaning on one arm and looked at Matthew. "Do you mind if I ask you a question?"

"No."

Paul looked away from him for a moment, playing with the sand. "I have a certain responsibility towards you, I'm your stepfather," he said.

Matthew felt himself withdrawing, the suspicion was growing inside him. "Well?" he asked.

"Oh," Paul said deprecatingly, "don't be stiff with me, Matthew. You're growing up. You know what I'm talking about. You..." he paused, considering. "I just wondered if Michel had taken you anywhere in Paris that I might have taken you, for instance." He looked at him suddenly and intently. "How much do you know about girls?"

Matthew looked away from him, feeling the color rising to his face. "Oh, *that*," he said.

"Have you ever had a girl?"

"What do you mean?" was all Matthew could say.

Paul laughed again. "There's no need to be embarrassed," he said. "Everyone has to have a first time. You're not so young as all that. Haven't you thought about it?"

Matthew did not know what to say. He stared at the sand, wishing Paul would stop.

"Don't you like girls?" Paul asked.

"They're all right," Matthew said. He was blushing furiously now.

Paul hesitated, and then said in French: "*Est-ce-que tu t'abuses?*"

Matthew looked firmly at the sand and did not reply.

Paul put his hand on Matthew's shoulder. This was the kind of a moment he liked, he felt himself in complete control of the situation. Whatever he did, whatever he said, with the knowledge he had of Matthew – which had been confirmed in all they had said – he was absolutely invulnerable. The only person Matthew could go to, for any sort of help, would be Michel, and what would Michel do to him? "Maybe you really don't like girls, is that it? Is that why you don't want to talk about it?"

Matthew's face was livid now. Even by looking away he couldn't hide it from Paul. "I don't know what you mean," he said.

Paul laughed again, harder this time, and his hand moved gently, slowly, on Matthew's bare back. When he spoke the laughter had faded entirely from his voice. "I think you know what I mean," he said. Matthew moved back, trying to escape the feel of Paul's hand, but he could not bring himself to shake it off. He was afraid of Paul. He did not want to precipitate anything.

"You're awfully fond of Michel, aren't you?" Paul's voice went on, digging deeper and deeper into him.

"What if I am?" He turned to look angrily at Paul.

Paul raised his eyebrows, making a wide gesture with his hand, and let it fall back on Matthew. "I'm not objecting," he said. "You sound almost angry with me. Are you angry with me?"

Matthew shook his head. "No. Why should I be?"

"No reason at all." His fingers continued to trace an outline on Matthew's spine, and then he said slowly, "How do you happen to like Michel so well?"

Matthew laughed nervously. "That's a silly question. Why does anybody like anyone else? I don't know."

"Isn't there a special reason?"

"What do you mean?" He felt the fear constricting his chest. Paul must know.

Paul's hand strayed down from Matthew's back, over his swimming trunks, down to his bare leg below them and then back up again. "Oh, nothing," he said idly.

Something burst inside of Matthew, he couldn't stand this any longer. "Take your hand off me," he said.

Paul looked at him, removing his hand, and his eyes were cold and amused. "It's off," he said.

"Good," Matthew replied.

And then Paul leaned close to him, putting his hand under Matthew's body, between his stomach and the sand. "Do you think you can fool me?" he asked, and Matthew's face went slowly from red to white. "Do you think I don't know about you two?" Paul's voice went on like a knife in his ear. "Do you think I'm blind? Maybe you can fool your mother, but you can't fool me."

Matthew, keeping his head sternly away from Paul, said: "What are you going to do?" There was no sense in denying it now.

Paul smiled at him. "Nothing," he said, wide-eyed and surprised. "What would I do? It's nothing to me I don't mind." And then his hand moved against Matthew's stomach, and he whispered: "Why do you hate me, Matthew? I understand you."

Matthew turned to face him, withdrawing his body from the touch of Paul's hand. He did not see Paul, really. What he saw was the look in Paul's eyes, the hair on his chest, the movement in his throat. And he could smell Paul, but it was not the sweat he smelled, it was not an odor that was peculiar to Paul … it was … he remembered Michel in Paris that night…. "*I want you.*" This, then, was what Michel had told him about, this was the alley, the soldier … the room above the café.

Paul moved suddenly, turning Matthew on his back and holding him hard against the sand. He pressed his body against Matthew and stared down into his face. "I was young once," he said, "I know what it's like. I don't blame Michel."

Matthew's body moved of its own accord, shrinking away from him. "You…" he began and then stopped, he didn't know what to say.

"Now just take it easy, Matthew," Paul's voice went on. "You don't want me to tell your mother, do you?" He smiled. "It's different with me. I don't mind. I like a little fun myself once in a while." Without any warning, his body pressed more heavily, his chest was hard against Matthew's, his eyes black and intent, staring into Matthew's. "I know how it is," he said.

Matthew stared back into his face. He could not move. It didn't matter about the face, or the pressure of that body on his own. The real pressure was in himself, in his remembrance of the way he had (not wanting to) kissed Michel back. He had *wanted*...

With a sudden, blind force, Matthew threw Paul from him and jumped to his feet. He looked at Paul on the sand and then ran from the beach, hearing Paul's laughter ringing in his ears.

Chapter Thirty-four

He ran as if pursued until he reached the fork in the road. He hesitated there and then broke into a quick walk down the road to the south, away from the inn and the beach where he had left Paul. He had to be alone now, he could not face Michel or Catherine, or even the people who ran the inn. He had to be alone.

He walked along the road and when he came to the top of the bluff, he skirted the buildings of Pointe Saint-Mathieu, staying close to the edge of the bluff, overlooking the water. He barely looked at the ruined church or the houses near it, he did not want to see anyone.

When he was at the end of the point, where the land trailed down into the ocean, he did not stop, but continued down the path until he was on the narrow strip of sand. He did not go near the water but sat down, his back against the rising cliff, the afternoon sun shining down on him, and beyond the sand, the sea stretched black and angry into the western sky. The tide was low now and he could see the rocks projecting here and there. How strange it was that the sea could change in so short a distance from a bright welcoming blue to this dark, restless, foaming water.

Mechanically, watching the land disappear into the sea, the word *Finestère* came to his mind. *Finis-terre*. Land's End. From here it really looked it ... it was the end of Britanny, the end of France. The end of the earth....

❧

As long as his body had been in motion, running or walking, the pain, humiliation and disgust inside him had been kept in check, but now there was nothing to hold it back, nothing to keep it from rolling over him so that he was almost drowned with the feel of it, the bitter taste in his mouth. He had been as shocked and startled by Paul as if a snake had struck at him unexpectedly. Paul was his stepfather, *his stepfather!* He repeated the words over and over to himself dumbly and righteously, knowing at the same time that they were not the real core of what he felt. There was something more behind all this, something insidious, the closest thing to evil that he had ever known. The conflicts that had been generated inside him by Scott's letter, his inability to reach out honestly to his father, the gap between himself and his mother; all these things were magnified beyond all reason. There was no one to whom he could talk, he felt unprotected, alarmed and alone. Only gradually did the real impulse behind Paul's gesture come into focus so that he could see it. The thing about it that bit deeply into his consciousness, filling him again and again with intolerable shame and anger was that it was he, himself, who had brought it on. If the situation had been different, if the fact of himself and Michel had not existed and communicated itself to Paul, this could not have happened. That Paul himself was horrible was beside the point; the real point was that he had touched something in Matthew that Matthew could not deny. It was as if Paul had reached into him and laid a sure hand on a point of similarity between them. He was obsessed with the idea that he was, in his way, as bad, as miserable a creature as Paul.

Matthew loved the space around him, the countryside, the ocean, the sunlight, all of it. But when he looked around now, he longed for some demonstration from nature to equal the bitter violence he felt in himself. Even the wind had died down today. He got to his feet and took one last angry look at the water, then started up the cliff. His bare feet (he remembered suddenly that he had left his shoes at the beach with Paul) dug into the rocky surface of the cliff, he would have liked to draw his own blood.

Even as he came close to the top of the bluff, he did not know where he was going, only that it was necessary for him to keep in motion. Better go back to the inn, to face whatever was to be faced – there was no guarantee that Paul would not tell his mother – than to stare at it in himself. His body quivered; it was impossible to keep it quiet. No matter where he was going, he had to keep moving.

He was startled to see the two people standing at the very end of the point. They heard him coming up – they must have, for they turned to look at him – and they both smiled in his direction before turning back to look out over the sea. A young man and a young woman, the man's arm seeming to hang loosely around her waist. Even as Matthew watched them, looking at their backs, the movement of their hair in the breeze off the sea, he blushed. He was not like them, he was different. He could never bring his lover down here, openly, to look at the Point. He could never let the world know what he felt. He walked away from them slowly, back past the houses, the ruins, toward the marshes and the fork.

There was nothing to do but go back. He could not risk keeping them waiting, having them wonder about him. As for Paul, it was not fear of what Paul night do or say that drove him back as if to prevent some action. Paul would, of course, do nothing; nothing, that is, except hold the knowledge over his head, dangling it above him with a smile, a glance, a gesture of betrayal. He could see him now, happy to threaten, to play with him as a cat would play with a mouse.

Chapter Thirty-five

Finally back in his own room, the flat non-committal bed, smooth and hard, waiting for him; Matthew flung himself upon it, and his body oozed sweat from every pore, as if the tide of feeling inside him had found physical expression and would no longer be denied. He felt and smelled this wet oiliness on his body as if he were smelling his own emotions. He rocked his head against the pillow, recalling dinner and wondering how he had lasted until now. Even the food that he had managed to eat had turned into something poisonous in his mouth, and he knew that he had not disguised anything, really, that his exit, however much he had tried to make it easy and natural, had been a plea to them all to leave him alone.

It had only been the imperative look in his eyes that had prevented Michel or his mother from questioning him, but even that was not enough, he knew, to keep them from doing something. One or both of them would surely follow him here, peer into his face, place a hand on his forehead, ask him what was wrong. And Paul! Paul, confident, easy and good-humored, had explained everything. He had brought Matthew's shoes back with him, had paved the way for his return as if he had oiled the doors of the inn to receive him silently. He did not know what Paul had said to them, but it had been enough so that he had not been questioned; their curiosity and their concern had been deferred temporarily.

Unceasingly, his mind circled and circled inside him, like a prisoner searching for some improbable, non-existent exit from his dungeon, and even through this mental clatter, he could hear the footsteps in the hall: more than one person was advancing on him, approaching like the jailer with the evening meal, or the executioner and the priest. If only they would leave him alone!

The knock on the door, the cautious opening, finally his own half-stifled response: "Come in" and then Michel and Catherine both came to the bed.

"Are you all right, darling?" It was his mother, and she sat on the edge of the bed, looking into his face, her hand touching his head. "Are you sick? Is something wrong?" and finally: "What is it, Matthew, what is it?"

He shook his head at her slowly, blinking his eyes, and then leaped into the refuge of physical illness. "I don't feel very well," he said. "I don't know what it is. I'll be all right if I lie down for a while, I think."

"Was it something you ate?"

He could almost have laughed at this question, but he shook his head again.

"Did anything happen this afternoon? Paul said you seemed distressed, but he didn't know what was wrong. He said you told him you wanted to be alone."

He did not say anything at once, watching them instead, and his mother turned to Michel, a mute appeal on her face. Michel nodded and started out of the room. "I'll come in and see you later, Matthew," he said, and then added: "If you want."

Matthew looked at him. "All right. I'll feel better in a little while, I guess."

When Michel had left them, Catherine leaned over him and put her arms around him. "You darling boy," she said softly, "tell me what it is. Can't you tell your mother?" and then she drew her head away to look into his eyes and search his face.

He wanted to tell her then. It came over him in force, reaching out to her, almost as if something inside him was begging him to tell her; surely, if anyone could listen to him and understand him, it would be his mother? But he couldn't. The image of Paul, having to tell her that ... he could see the look in her eyes, the gradual coldness that would enter them as surely as if he had told her – as if it was happening at that very moment.

"I can't talk about it, mother," he said, "I can't." And as soon as he had said it, he knew that he had committed himself, he had let her in. Sooner or later he would have to tell her after saying that ... well, all right, perhaps it was natural and right that she should be the one; who could be more understanding...? But not yet, not now.

"Oh, darling," she said. "I've never seen you like this. We were all so happy here, it was so wonderful to see you so gay, so ... I can't bear to have you..."

"Don't, mother, please. *Please*."

"All right, darling. All right. Not now, then."

She stood up, her hand still on him. Perhaps he was right, perhaps there was some reason why he could not talk to her easily about whatever it was that was causing him such anguish, but he must talk to someone. She stiffened her body and looked out the window. She reminded herself that even if she was his mother, even if she was the closest thing to him in the world ... the important thing now was that he should have the help he needed. If he could not get it through her then perhaps through someone else. If only he would talk to someone. Michel perhaps.

"Do you want to see Michel?" she asked.

"Not right now, mother. Later maybe."

It seemed to her to be an admission; she felt some hope in those words. Perhaps Michel would be able to get it out of him, in some way that she could not.

She bent over the bed and kissed him. "Whatever it is, Matthew," she said, "*whatever* it is, it's all right. I love you darling, and I can't bear to have you suffer ... I..."

"I know, mother," he said. "I know. But not now. Not now."

"All right, darling. I'll go. But do try and get some rest."

When the door had closed behind her, he breathed fully again; the space of the room seemed to enlarge and spread itself around him in impersonal coldness. He was relieved, as if his tensions could fill the room, releasing the pressure on himself. He could not sleep, he could not even think, but he lay there dull and flat, inanimate, as if he were only able to watch time passing relentlessly over him.

He turned his eyes faintly in the darkness at the sound of the door opening again. It was Michel, coming over to him, coming to his bed, reaching out for him, covering his hand gently. "They've gone upstairs, Matthew," he said, "but your mother asked me to let her know if there was anything you wanted, or if you wanted to see her. She asked me to talk to you." He looked at Matthew, who had only stared at him, seeming not even to hear his words. "What is it, Matthew?" he asked urgently. "What is it?"

Receiving no reply, Michel put his arms around him and held Matthew close to him. "I hate to see you like this, it makes me hurt inside," he said. "What has happened to you?"

Something broke in Matthew at that moment, and he tightened his arms around Michel's body, feeling the weight inside him rising and rising until it began to overflow and the tears streamed out of his eyes and his body shuddered with his crying. He did not speak, but the pain flowered out of him in a torrent, pouring onto Michel's shoulder. It did not last very long, but when it was over, Matthew drew back from him and looked at Michel, the faint outline of a smile on his lips. As if to thank him, he put his hand out to Michel's cheek and held it there for a moment, and then he lay back on the bed. From what he saw in Michel's face, he was sure that Michel understood something of what was going on inside him, and because of it the great need to be alone altered. He wanted to have Michel next to him, to feel the safety of another pair of arms, another body.

"Let's go to bed," Michel said quietly. "I'll sleep in here. I don't want to leave you alone. You don't have to talk."

Matthew smiled at him gratefully, finding a glimmer of hope in the words, and Michel began to unbutton the buttons of his shirt, undressing him as he would have undressed a child; gravely and quietly, with infinite tenderness. When Matthew was in bed, feeling cleansed by his tears and by the gentleness in Michel, he watched Michel undress himself with the same seriousness, the same importance. When he was in bed next to him, he put his head on Michel's shoulder and his arms around his chest. He was cold and the warmth of Michel next to him communicated itself to Matthew, reaching into him and comforting the raw edges of his fear. He felt quiet and momentarily safe. Tomorrow was tomorrow, but tonight it was all right, even with the threat of the next day hanging over him, tonight was all right.

It was with a sense of panic that he felt the movement next to him, the passing of Michel's hand over his back. His body stiffened faintly, and he listened for the response – a response he hated and feared now – inside himself. There was nothing in him that went out to meet this, nothing there except blankness and terror. His back arched and he lifted his head to look at Michel and then to drop back on the pillow. But the movement did not cease and Michel's head pursued his until finally it was over him, and Michel's lips were on his cheek.

"Don't," he said sharply, "don't do that!"

But the voice, cajoling and sympathetic, said: "Matthew," in faint surprise, and then persistently: "What's the matter?"

"I said don't!" He heard his own voice lashing out at Michel, and this time it made Michel withdraw from him until he had risen on his elbow to stare down at him, repulsed. "*Mais qu'est-ce que tu as, quand-même?* What *is* the matter with you?"

"Nothing," Matthew answered, his voice hard and cold. "Nothing. Just leave me alone. Go away and leave me alone!"

Michel considered him silently, uncertain. The rejection, the coldness – the hatred, even – in Matthew's voice hung over him, as if waiting to descend upon him and strike him. The force of his feeling, his need, soured and changed inside him, building itself into equal hardness. He moved away from Matthew, increasing the space between them in the bed until their bodies no longer touched, and then he said, quietly: "You might at least explain this to me, Matthew."

Matthew shook his head violently. "Leave me alone, that's all. Leave me alone!"

Michel held back his anger. After all, there was something wrong. He suspected Paul, but he was sure Matthew would have told him that ... it would be dangerous to bring it up and perhaps add to whatever this was. "Why, Matthew?" he asked as gently as he could. "What is the trouble?"

Matthew flared up at him again: "Stop asking that! Why do you always have to..." he hesitated. "That's all you ever want!"

Michel felt the blood filling in his cheeks, tapping against his forehead, making his hair stand on end. He could not hold down his anger. He laughed a hard, rude laugh. "What a fool I am! You are nothing but a little baby! When will you learn that you cannot throw people around at will ... walk out on them without some explanation. I will leave you alone, even if this finishes us for always, but I want to know why. You are going to tell me why!"

Matthew glared back at him, breathing strength into himself, collecting it from the force of Michel's anger. "All right," he said bitterly. "I will. It's because of what you've done to me; you've destroyed me, you've helped me to destroy myself. You're a man, you know about these things, but you have to have what you want, you don't care what happens to me. You knew what this was like, you knew what would happen – you've always said so – but nothing would stop you. You *wanted* me – that's all it ever was with you, you said it, you said you wanted me, and now you've had me and you can't get enough. You're like all the rest of them ... you should have stayed in that place in Paris ... you're perverted!"

Michel stopped him with his hand, clamping his fingers on Matthew's wrist like a vise. "*Perverted*!" he echoed savagely. "And what are you, you and your holy innocence? You're perfect, aren't you?

You never wanted me, did you? You can forget yourself, can't you? You don't remember as far back as I do, do you Matthew? You don't remember the first time you kissed me! The things you've done! No, you're unsullied, unspoiled, pure, wonderful! You and your high and mighty morals! We're all scum, the rest of us, no one is good enough for you! Well, I will tell you something, *mon petit*; you are like everyone else, and you might as well admit it. If it had not happened with me, it would have been someone else, some other pervert – since you like that word so much! No, you say to yourself, it is all your fault – *I* have ruined your precious little life, haven't I? Well, take it back! Take it back and dream about it!" He paused, breathing hard, and stared down at Matthew. "The only thing you've ever loved," he went on, "is Matthew Cameron. *Tu t'en fous de moi, de tout le monde!* When you spit on me, Matthew, you spit on yourself."

He stopped, spent and exhausted by the fury of his words; words that had poured out of him so that he hardly knew what words he had said. And Matthew, as if the weight had been increased a hundredfold as this torrent ripped its way into him, stared back at Michel, listening to the pounding of his own violent heart.

"Paul," he said, and his voice was almost normal now, the fury and anger were gone from it, he spoke apologetically. "Paul tried to…" he hesitated, and then said, clipping the words off sharply. "He told me he knew about us and that he understood, that he liked a little fun himself once in a while…" The words were bitter on his tongue and he turned to Michel: "Oh, Michel, he…"

But Michel did not let him go on. "So that's it! So that's what this is all about. I thought so." But his voice was still cold, Matthew searched vainly for the sound of warmth or friendship in it. "And what if he did?" he went on angrily. "Don't you know anything at all? Don't you know anything about Paul? Couldn't you tell he was a son-of-a-bitch by the look on his face? Why do you think he married your mother? Do you think he would have married her if she hadn't been an American, if she hadn't had money?"

Matthew stared at him: "What?"

"You heard me!"

Matthew reached out with his hand, but Michel pulled away from it. "No," he said, "it's no use. It won't work. It's too late."

"But Michel," Matthew said, "if you knew what it was like, the way he…"

"Oh, Matthew! The world is full of people like Paul. What did you expect? It had to happen someday, it was just as well that it was Paul. What is all the fuss about? When are you going to start growing up? When are you going to get over the idea that the world is doing something awful to you. You asked for it, or Paul would never have done it. You expose what you are and you ask for that kind of thing, and then you begin to cry when anything happens. You are what you are, Matthew, and if you want to use the word 'pervert,' then go ahead. You're nothing more or less than a fairy … yes, a *fairy* … so accept it. If you weren't, it wouldn't have happened. What would you do if a woman wanted to go to bed with you? Are you too good for the human race? You think nothing ever happened to anyone else…."

"Oh, Michel, I…"

"Oh, stop whining! Why don't you go and see your *maman* and tell her all about this? Tell her I have ruined you and then you will be cleansed of your great sin, so that you can face the world, pure and righteous. I've had enough of this! What a fool I was, falling in love with a boy! A little mama's boy!"

He got out of the bed, angry and embarrassed with his nakedness, and picked up his clothes and shoes from the floor. He stalked across the room, walked through the door leading to his own room. When he had closed it behind him, Matthew heard the key turn in the lock.

Chapter Thirty-six

Could it be? Catherine was sure she had heard Matthew's voice, almost as if he had shouted. She listened hard again but she could only hear the sound of the wind now. She turned to look at Paul, sitting next to her in the bed, a book open on his lap. "Did you hear anything, Paul?"

He shook his head. "No, what?"

"I thought I heard Matthew's voice. I was almost sure of it. As if he were shouting." And then she looked away, saying, almost to herself: "I'm awfully worried about him, Paul."

Paul shrugged his shoulders. "I didn't hear anything." He put his hand on Catherine's arm. "You baby him too much, *chérie*. He is all right. He's probably sound asleep now. You know how boys are at his age, there's nothing unusual for a young boy to be moody or troubled. It happens to everyone."

She shook her head. "No, Paul. I know. I'm his mother. I know this is serious." She got out of bed and slipped her arms into her negligee, her feet into her slippers. "I won't be gone long, darling, but I must go down and see. I am sure I heard his voice."

Paul smiled. "All right, all right. But I tell you, you are making too much out of this. He will get over it."

"Over what?"

He looked at her blandly. "Over whatever it is," he said.

"I'm going to see anyway." She walked firmly out of the room.

She did not knock on Matthew's door, but opened it quietly and walked over to his bed. When she was next to it, she put out her hand and whispered: "Are you asleep, Matthew?"

"No," he said. "What is it?"

"I thought I heard your voice, darling. Did something happen, did you have a quarrel with Michel?" As she said the words – the question sprang quite naturally to her lips – she realized that this was the first time she had considered the possibility that he might be having trouble with Michel. It was Paul who had said to her once that Matthew was "in love" with Michel, the way young boys are so often in love with their teacher or with some older friend. And, of course, he had been right. That love, she understood now, was an imitation of what came later in life, an initiation into the love of man and woman. How thoughtless, how stupid of her not to have thought of this before! The torments, the violence, of adolescent love are important and terrible … if she could let him know that she understood, that she knew, that she herself had experienced this … she was such an idiot! Turning him back on Michel, making him talk to Michel, talking to Michel herself … how could she have been so stupid?

"Darling," she went on, "don't be afraid to tell me about it, whatever it is. If it's something between you and Michel, I'll understand. It was so silly of me not to have seen that before, to realize that perhaps you were in some sort of trouble with him. Things like that happen to all of us, Matthew, it is nothing to be ashamed of, nothing you can't tell me about. But you must not hold it inside yourself, you can't do that."

He reached for her hand and held it, and she could feel him relaxing slowly under her words.

"It is something about Michel, isn't it?" she continued. "I know it is, darling. I know it."

He nodded his head slowly. "Yes, it is."

"Then what is it? Tell me. Tell your mother."

Could he tell her? In a way she seemed almost to know already.

The things she said: "things like that happen," "it's nothing to be shamed of" … she couldn't have said that if she hadn't guessed, if she didn't understand. He felt a great wave of longing and affection for her. He could remember criticizing her privately, finding her artificial and imitative, comparing her unfavorably to his father, thinking that she never really understood anything. And yet now, in the moment when he needed someone most of all, she had come to him, knowing, guessing in some sure way … sensing the core of the trouble, offering him support and help.

"Mother … I…" He could not bring himself to say it outright.

"Mother … you do know, don't you?" He waited and searched for any resistance that might come from her, as if he had already told her, but he felt nothing except warmth and sympathy flowing out to him. "Mother," he went on, "I love Michel."

She leaned over and kissed his cheek. "Of course you do, darling. I knew that. But what's happened? Have you had a quarrel with him? Did something go wrong in Paris?"

Was it possible? He had said it and she had not reacted against him, she had heard his words and she had not said anything? She understood? It was all right?

"I don't know when it started, mother," he continued, "but it's been getting worse and worse all the time. And then tonight…" he hesitated, it was impossible that she really understood, he could not go on without some confirmation, the doubt in his mind was still too great. "Mother," he began again, "do you really know what I mean? Can you forgive me?"

"What you mean about what, baby?" she asked.

"About loving Michel. You aren't angry with me?"

"Angry with you?" She laughed. "Of course not, darling. It's perfectly natural! Why when I was your age, I had a teacher in school and I worshipped the ground she walked on. Angry with you! Of course I'm not angry with you!"

He shook his head. He could not stop now. "No," he said, "I

don't mean that. It's not natural, it couldn't have happened to you."

She smiled at him and put her head close to his. "Darling," she whispered, "I do know what you mean. You mean because he's a man and you're a man, don't you? I felt the same way, I think. I thought there was something wrong with me. That happens to almost everyone, Matthew. It isn't wrong."

She did know! It was incredible! He had misjudged her completely, from the very beginning! "Oh, you aren't angry," he said. "You don't mind!"

"Of course not. Now tell me, what happened?"

He looked up at her. "There's such a lot to tell, mother. It all began at school last fall." He paused. "There's so much I have to tell you about him, about us both."

She smiled at him. How providential that she had come down! And who could have been putting ideas into the child's head … "unnatural!" "Wrong!" Had he been talking to his father? Was that it?

She walked around the bed and sat on it next to him, dropping her slippers from her feet to the floor. She was, Matthew realized, in exactly the same place where Michel had lain only a short time ago. She leaned back against the headboard and put her arm around him. "Now, darling, go on," she said affectionately.

The warmth of her next to him, the security of her arm on his shoulder … it was true, she did understand and she would help him, she would make everything all right.

"I never told you," he said, "that I almost drowned in the Seine, did I?"

She drew back suddenly and then increased her grip on his shoulder. "Darling, no! What do you mean?" He felt her shivering against him.

"It's all right," he said quickly, "I didn't drown. Michel saw me out in the river and he saved me. If it wasn't for him … he's a wonderful swimmer."

"Yes, I know, Matthew, but what had happened?"

"I don't know," he said. "I swam out too far, it was almost as if I wanted to drown, in a way."

"Matthew! Were you so unhappy, did you hate the school? Oh, Matthew, why didn't you write to me? Why didn't you tell me about it before? This is terrible!"

"No, mother, no," his voice tried to soothe her. "I don't know what it was, but it wasn't your fault. I wasn't unhappy. I just ... I don't know. It wasn't that I wanted to die. It was just that when I thought I was going to drown, I didn't mind. It was funny."

She shivered again, hugging him. "It's a terrible story, Matthew. Terrible."

Then he laughed. "It's all right, mother. I'm alive now. I didn't drown. Anyway I only told you because that's the way it began."

"What began?"

"Michel and me," he said. "That's when I fell in love with him."

"Because he rescued you?"

"Not exactly," he said, looking at her tentatively. "It was after that. He came up to my room to see how I was, and he sat next to my bed and talked to me for a while – he was awfully nice to all the boys, mother – and when he was going to leave, he leaned over and kissed me. He didn't mean anything more than that, I guess."

"Of course he didn't, darling! Have you been thinking he did? Is that what the trouble was?"

Matthew shook his head. "What do you mean? I don't understand." Had he heard her wrong before? Didn't she know what he meant?

"It's perfectly natural that he kissed you, Matthew. He must have sensed how lonely you were, how much you needed affection."

"Yes," Matthew said. "I guess he did. I was lonely then."

"Of course you were, my darling. And I think it was my fault. I should have known. I shouldn't have sent you away to that school."

"No, mother," he protested, "it wasn't your fault. Really it wasn't."

"Sweet," she murmured to him. "But go on."

"Well," he said slowly, "that's when it started. He didn't go. He stayed there with me. That's how it started."

And then he felt it. Her arm stiffened slightly, her body moved – only a fraction of an inch – but it moved … away from him.

"What are you trying to say, Matthew?"

"Don't you understand?"

"No. No, I don't." Her voice was blank, incredulous, unbelieving.

Matthew did not say anything at all. He held himself rigidly beside her and waited for whatever she might say next. Nothing would have induced him to go on talking.

"Matthew," she said at last, laughing slightly, "it almost sounds as if … you must explain yourself more clearly … I…"

They were both silent, and then Matthew said: "I don't know how to make it any clearer, mother, it's … what else can I say?"

"Matthew. Are you trying to tell me that you…" her voice was absolutely cold now, "…that you and Michel have been…" she did not know how to complete the sentence and she fumbled for words. "That you and Michel have been," she began again, "…that you've had sexual…" and then her voice stopped finally as if it had struck a stone wall.

"What else?"

She removed her arm from him and she seemed to tower over him then. "I don't believe it," she said. "I would have known. Paul would have known. It's impossible!"

"Paul does know," Matthew said, suddenly hot and angry. "Paul knows all about it. He told me so on the beach, he … he went further than that. He said he understood perfectly … that he liked to have fun himself was what he said."

"Leave Paul out of this," she said, cutting in on him. "Don't try to drag Paul into this, Matthew. I know Paul too well. But that you and Michel … it's unthinkable, it's horrible!" She turned her eyes directly into his. "I'd rather you were dead!" she exclaimed, her voice like a hammer striking a nail.

She got up from the bed woodenly, found her slippers and put them on. Not until she reached the door did she say anything, and then she turned to him with her hand on the knob. "We'll talk about this in the morning, Matthew," she said, and opened the door and walked out.

Chapter Thirty-seven

Michel had heard Catherine's voice, but he could not hear anything that she said, or any of Matthew's words. He was unable to sleep and he had been alarmed when he had heard her coming into Matthew's room. The way Matthew was feeling, the little idiot, he might do anything, might even tell her everything. And that would lead to God knew what disaster! He saw his job, his future, his reputation, sliding relentlessly away from him. He should never have left Matthew that way. Whatever it cost he should not have lost his temper. He cursed himself for it now.

He waited for her to leave; he would have to talk to Matthew. He would have to pound some sense into that boy; as things were, anything could happen, they might get involved in something that would be the ruin of all of them. It was incredible, stupid, ridiculous. How had he ever been such a fool as to get himself mixed up in an affair with *a boy*! And when he did, to have chosen this wild, unpredictable American boy!

Was that the door? He could not be sure. He listened again. No sound. He lay on the bed, and the minutes hung over him as he stifled his breathing in order to hear better. Damn the wind! Time dragged relentlessly and slowly on … and then, yes, he was sure of it, he heard the door into the hall closing. He leaped from his bed and walked quietly over to the door into Matthew's room, leaning over and listening at the keyhole. No sound of any kind came from the room. His eyes were accustomed to the darkness now, he had been staring at it for what seemed hours, and he looked across the room to the bed. Not only was Catherine not there, no one was there.

"Matthew," he whispered urgently, but there was no answer. With a last quick look around the room, he walked silently, catlike, across the room to the bed. There was no one there at all! Now what had happened? It was crazy. Where had they both gone in the middle of the night? Had Matthew told her and had she moved him away, taken him upstairs, freeing him from the evil influence of himself next door to her son? No, that was idiotic. Catherine would never have understood. She would have been furious with him, she would not have forgiven him or protected him. She would have been out of her mind! Even Matthew, surely, would not have told her. He would not have been that much of a fool.

Whatever had happened, wherever they were, there was no point in his staying here. What if they should come back? He went quickly to his own room, closed the door and turned the key in the lock, grimacing again at the sound it made. There was nothing for him to do but go to bed and wait.

Two or three times during the night, he walked to the door and listened, turned the horrible key, peered into the room. No one. No one at all! What could have happened? Where had Matthew gone?

He lay back on the bed, smoking cigarette after cigarette, waiting for the daylight. He was sure of one thing, with the daylight he would know for certain what had happened. Whatever it was, it would be better to know. Anything would be better than this intolerable, impossible waiting!

As soon as the first faint light of the sun appeared on the eastern horizon, Michel got up. He dressed quickly and vaulted out of the window onto the soft earth, wet with dew. If he took a walk in this early windy sunrise, maybe that would be better. Anything to get out of that room, away from that vigil.

Automatically, he started between the little thatched houses, in the direction of the beach. The wind was from the west, fresh and strong in his face and hair. He looked over the roofs of the houses, beginning to glow in the advance rays of the early sun. The tip of the sun itself was just under the edge of the horizon behind him. It was, whatever happened, a perfectly beautiful morning. He turned his head back to face the wind, to smell the damp fresh air, the smarting tang of salt, almost as if spray from the sea....

From the sea....

He quickened his pace and then broke suddenly into a run. Even as he ran he knew that his running was senseless, that what he was thinking was impossible, and yet he could not stop running. His body was reacting to something stronger than his mind, pushing him forward. When he reached the triple fork, he did not hesitate, even for a second; his feet carried him naturally to the south, to the place from which they had first looked at the sea, he and Matthew, to the point.

Although he ran quickly, his breathing coming hard and fast, he felt that he was running a useless race against time. The few houses of the town of Saint-Mathieu, silent and unawakened, mocked at the slowness of his pace. It was only when he was past them, approaching the lighthouse and the cliff, that he slowed to a walk. The impulse that had carried him forward had died within him, replaced by a dreadful anticipation. He forced himself forward, walking now, his hands clenched, his ears filled with the roar of the sea battering against the point. Over the ruins of the church, the morning edge of the sun burst into the sky. At the edge of the cliff he stopped, staring into the blinding sunlight, and then his eyes blinked and looked down ... down to the strip of sand, the distinct footprints leading in one single trail into the black water.

Appendices

Editor's note:

This edition of *Finistère* has been thoroughly enriched by contributions from the poet Edward Field. Not only did Field assist with contacting the author's estate, but he has generously provided notes and excerpts from his own exhaustive attempts at forging a biography of Fritz Peters. Also included in this appendix is an expanded version of Fields' essay, "Son of Gurdjieff," which first appeared in *The Harvard Gay & Lesbian Review*, Winter 1996, Volume III, Number 1.

In early correspondence with Field, when we had initially secured the rights to reprint this edition, he said, "I'm absolutely over the moon that you're re-issuing *Finistère*!" With the poet's wind in our sails, Little Sister's Classics is thrilled to offer these important documents.

Photographs of Fritz Peters
Documentation by Edward Field

Fritz in 1932 – On the back he wrote "Quelle sourire!!" Then tore off his companion of that happy time – when the love affair had gone sour?…

Second Lieutenant Fritz in uniform circa 1952 (he received a "battlefield" commission during World War II). Called back into service during the Korean War, his papers list him discharged as "physically disqualified." Perhaps the military authorities discovered his stay in a VA hospital mental ward when he cracked up after WWII, which he wrote about vividly in his first novel *The World Next Door*. Or, more likely, his alcoholism and homosexuality got him into trouble.

Fritz in 1965 – A down-to-earth
author portrait about the time
Boyhood With Gurdjieff was published and when he was living
with Lloyd Lozes Goff.

Fritz in 1970 – Written on the back are the
words "Talking as usual."

Son of Gurdjieff: In Search of Fritz Peters
by Edward Field

Boyhood with Gurdjieff, a memoir featuring the famous teacher and mystic, has remained in print ever since it was first published in 1964, and *Finistère*, published in 1951 and one of the first gay novels I ever read, has continued to be available in various editions until about a decade ago, but I had never come across anyone who knew their elusive author. As far as I could tell, Fritz Peters had lived his life apart from the literary world, or at lease the parts of the literary world I've been involved with.

I was naturally curious about someone who had written so brilliantly about both his spirituality and his sexuality. His two famous books simply do not fit comfortably together in the mind. They appeal to two different constituencies, which nevertheless are not incompatible, for in history notable figures shared Peters' spiritual development and same sex attraction. I should think that this would make him a subject of particular interest, but Peters himself has remained invisible, both before and since his death in 1979. This is partly due to the continuing hostility of the Gurdjieffian world over his homosexuality. But at the same time it is difficult to understand the indifference of the gay community toward the author of a gay literary classic like *Finistère*.

My involvement with this elusive author came about largely through an extraordinary pair of women who were involved in spiritual studies. I met them in Greenwich Village, to which I gravitated as a student after World War II. The Village had always been receptive not only to political radicalism, but to what might seem as an alien opposite – seances and Ouija board-playing, cult figures like Madame Blavatsky and Edgar Cayce, and mystical poetry of the Kahlil Gibran sort. Even if religious terminology – words like "God" or "spiritual" or (God forbid) "my soul" – were frowned on in the world of Modern Poetry I was part of, many poets followed T.S. Eliot and W.H. Auden into one church or another after the war. But none of this was for me. Raised a dogmatic atheist, I never saw the "spiritual" dimensions or origins of my Marxist and Freudian beliefs, both of which pretended to supersede religion. But I read about the flamboyant Gurdjieff and his thin-lipped disciple Ouspensky, for they were very much part of European intellectual life in the period *entre deux guerres* that otherwise seemed so romantic to me.

It was difficult not to be dazzled by a colorful rogue like Gurdjieff with his ideas that challenged conventional thought. And much like Gurdjieff, who had groups of lesbian disciples, I have always had an affinity for lesbians, so perhaps it was inevitable that my rigidity on spiritual matters was eventually loosened in the sixties, not only by taking the Native American religious drug peyote, but by meeting, at poet May Swenson's apartment in the Village, the couple Betty Deran and Alma Routsong, comfortably large-bottomed and bosomy ladies who would become very much part of my search for Fritz Peters. They were involved in the typical occult pursuits of Ouija board sessions, astrology, and even attempts at magic, following alchemical formulae. This was all very dubious, if not laughable, to an atheist like me, but once I let myself relax and participate, I found these two highly intelligent women quite astute in their contrapuntal reading of astrological charts.

Betty was a true medium, and we had a number of entertaining sessions at the Ouija board, once contacting my supposed literary "helper," Jack London, who seemed too impatient with me in his peppery, Irish way to offer much help with my writing problems. A more electrifying session followed the assassination of John F. Kennedy, who announced to us from "beyond" that he was not at peace because KILLER ROAMS FREE. Betty, in her job as an economist at a Rockefeller Center think tank, successfully presented unorthodox solutions to economics problems, given to her by the ghost of Maynard Keynes via the Ouija board. The two women even used the Ouija board to work out plot details in a novel that Alma was writing. They communicated with the real-life subject, an early American primitive painter named Mary Ann Wilson, who told them her story, resulting in the by-now-classic lesbian novel, *A Place for Us*, later retitled *Patience and Sarah*, written under Alma's pseudonym, Alma Routsong.

Both women had uncanny powers, though it was Betty who was the pioneer in their occult researches. She was the shorter of the two, with snapping black eyes, dark hair, and a toothy grin on her round face. She had started out as a Christian Science nurse, and followed the usual path of popular metaphysics – theosophy, astrology, palmistry, and alchemy – but eventually came upon the teachings of the Greek-Armenian Gurdjieff, for whom as an Armenian-American she felt a particular affinity and who, as we soon learned, had been so influential on Fritz Peters' early life.

After Gurdjieff's death in 1949, the movement that continued, purporting to teach his "system," developed a decidedly anti-homosexual bias, like most spiritual groups. Paradoxically, books about Gurdjieff have been written by a number of the controversial teacher's often-prominent lesbian disciples, demonstrating that there was no conflict in Gurdjieff, at least, over their sexual orientation. One can only infer that homosexuality, though not to be proclaimed, was no bar to participation in "The Work," at least for women. Gurdjieff, himself from a Middle-Eastern culture that was not hypocritical about or bothered by such things, gave top marks to young Fritz Peters' boyishly rosy behind in the community bathhouse (as Peters related in his book), where the Master of Eastern Mysticism liked to line up all his naked male disciples in order to compare, with ribald comments, their bodies and particularly their genitals. On this last point at least Gurdjieff had no reason to be shy, since he was said to have the biggest schwantz of all.

After locating a study group led by the main Gurdjieff teacher in New York – a forbidding personage named Lord Pentland – Betty was soon accepted, and quickly gained notice for her aptitude and ingenuity in "The Work." I followed her course of self-development with growing respect. Under her influence, after years of Freudian therapy – with its limited, if theoretically correct, blaming for our messed-up lives on parents and childhood traumas – it was a relief to consider other ways of looking at things, such as the Buddhist idea that one must take responsibility for one's own life, and most shocking to me as a Freudian, of seeing one's parents as chosen, in order to further one's development. The game of astrology was even fun, and the character readings according to astrological signs seemed no more arbitrary than any other theory in which I had believed. And ignoring the Christian part of it (which as a Jew was repugnant to me), the Christian Science idea of invoking the self-healing powers of the body began to make sense. Most useful of all in the long run, I began doing yoga exercises.

The Gurdjieffian idea that we are all asleep – though not too different from the Christian "Sleepers, awake!" – now struck me as an important principle, and a formulation much akin to Marx's "Workers of the world unite! You have nothing to lose but your chains." But unlike Betty, though I read Gurdjieff's books as well as the ones about him I could find (including Peters'), I was not much tempted to join a Gurdjieff group nor any other organized study. Poetry remained my "way," and along with daily yoga exercises, I would have to take care of myself, whatever the perils of life.

It was after Betty Deran broke up with Alma Routsong that I first heard about Annie Lou Stavely, a teacher of Gurdjieff who was living in Portland, Oregon. Williams had been a student of the openly lesbian Jane Heap in London, and after returning to the US had attracted a circle of disciples of her own in Portland, where she held an administrative job at the state university. On a visit to Lord Pentland at the Gurdjieff center in New York, she was introduced to Betty who, on the rebound from Alma, immediately fell in love with her.

In spite of the refusal of the Gurdjieffian teacher to entertain the possibility of a love affair with a woman, Betty precipitously gave up her well-paying job in New York to follow Mrs. Stavely back to Oregon, where Betty hoped, over time, to persuade her that she needed a woman in her life. Meanwhile, the canny Mrs. Stavely seemed quite willing to have a born problem-solver like Betty in her midst.

It was in Oregon that Betty received my letter announcing that I had finally met Fritz Peters, the author of *Boyhood With Gurdjieff* and *Finistère*. Astoundingly, I learned in her reply that her Mrs. Stavely had once had an affair with him.

When I met him in New York in the early seventies, Fritz Peters was a tall, buoyant man of about sixty, possessed of the kind of aging-boy looks of a Christopher Isherwood, or perhaps it was the similar barbershop haircut – closely clipped on the sides with a lock over the forehead – and the drinker's nose. In an age of longish hair and relaxed dress, Fritz persisted in wearing the kind of conventional, slightly seedy suits I associate with alcoholics trying to maintain a look of respectability: he even wore a bowtie, a dapper holdover from the fifties. And I could tell that he drank. He had what I can only call a boozy manner, though I never saw him drunk.

Not knowing much about him then, there was nothing surprising that I found the author of *Finistère* – one of the early landmarks in gay fiction – to be completely homosexual in orientation, even if, during our dinners out, he indicated that he had once been married. I learned later, though, that he had two marital strikes out, and possibly three! But it was not unusual in that era for homosexuals to try to go straight and get married. I myself spent years with a psychoanalyst, who immediately decided that my homosexuality was at the root of all my miseries, and set out to change me. But even if Fritz had once been in conflict over his sexuality, like I was, perhaps the new open atmosphere of gay liberation had also had its effect on him, though he expressed scorn for gay groups and, as I was to learn, for the Gurdjieff study groups as well. Looking back, I continue to be puzzled at myself for not asking him, on our occasional dinners out in the Village, anything at all about *Finistère*'s genesis, much less the story of his life. But I sensed something wounded in him, and I respected the depths of pain and the scars of humiliation that his buoyant manner seemed to deny. I would never have brought up the past unless he brought it up first. I myself in those years was struggling with my own lifelong feelings of worthlessness, so he probably sensed a fellow sufferer in me. But I will never stop kicking myself that when I had the chance to quiz him about his life, I let it pass.

Fritz was living at the Arlington, one of those small hotels in midtown New York City left over from a grander era, on West 25th Street off Fifth Avenue. Once elegant, it had fallen into seediness. The ornate façade was marred by greying curtains and yellowed window shades, and on the sills outside the rooms stood milk cartons and food containers. Called SROs, for Single Room Occupancy, these old hotels were mostly used as permanent dwellings by the elderly, often on pensions or welfare. I later saw snapshots of Fritz's room, which looked quite respectable if minimal, but at that time I imagined a sagging bedstead and stained sheets, threadbare carpets, the various smells in the hallways, and an old bellhop in uniform who ran errands for the aging tenants, perhaps fetching pints of booze for desperate old souls. It had that stale atmosphere about it.

Fritz had a job as a legal secretary, and he seemed satisfied with it, especially by the irregular hours demanded by the exigencies of the firm's court cases. His employers must have been delighted with such a crackerjack worker, for whatever Fritz did, he believed in doing well.

I suspected that mental troubles and possibly breakdowns, exacerbated by drink, were recurrent over the years, and by the time I met him he had accepted the shabby level of life he could maintain. But to me he was a famous author, and I asked him why he wasn't writing any more books. His answer was that he wasn't interested in being a professional writer, committed to turning out one book after another. He preferred to write only when he felt he had a book in him to write.

Nor did he seem at all interested in exploiting his reputation in the Gurdjieff world. In my respect for Betty and her absorption in the training, it was astonishing to me now to learn that this man – who, from the evidence of his *Boyhood With Gurdjieff*, was as much an authority on the master as anyone alive – had contempt for anyone claiming to teach the so-called "Work." He sneered at what this teaching had become, and denied it had anything to do with what Gurdjieff had taught. So if Fritz Peters considered all the various Gurdjieff groups in existence as inauthentic, they should have been paying attention to him, if they were interested in studying the real Gurdjieff system. But this did not seem to be the case.

Though Fritz's two famous works were available at the time, I knew nothing of his other books, which by then were all out of print. It was not until much later that I found a copy of his first novel *The World Next Door*, published in 1949, dealing with a character's breakdown and subsequent stay in a mental hospital, in which Fritz reveals his earlier thinking about his homosexuality, for the protagonist talks about it in an open way that must have been startling at the time. Perhaps Fritz got away with this because his character was in an institution. Ditto descriptions of patients masturbating in the wards, and sadistic guards forcing them to give blowjobs. This was raw stuff for 1949. The "hero" admits to a doctor having had a homosexual experience, even that he was in love with the man, but denies that he is a homosexual because the sex "just wasn't any good." Besides, "it didn't last.... It wasn't right, somehow." But then it turns out that on his military record is still another homosexual experience involving a general that the army tried to hush up. He even admits that "in the beginning, I was willing to be a fairy ... but it didn't turn out that way." The implication is that he had decided not to be, one that was his thinking then, at any rate.

Finistère, published two years later, is for me the quintessential homosexual novel of the postwar decade, even though it ends, as the period demanded, with the suicide of the young protagonist. In Fritz Peters' obituary in the *New York Times* in 1979, the subject of the novel was described as "a destructive homosexual relationship," although the book was clearly about the destruction of a youth by his family after they discover his in-no-way-destructive, even healthy, love affair with his tutor, a very different cup of tea indeed, but in keeping with the *Times'* editorial policy of that era. All the major media had the same bias. I remember, when *Finistère* appeared, discussing it with a friend who, in hopes of becoming a reviewer for *Time* magazine, was assigned by the book editor to write a sample review of the novel. A professional reporter, my friend asked the editor whether he should take a viewpoint that would conform to *Time*'s homophobic policy of the period, or to review it honestly. The editor demanded honesty, but then of course failed to hire my friend when he treated the book with the seriousness it deserved.

A third novel, *The Descent*, came out in 1952, this one set in Santa Fe, where Fritz was living during his second marriage. It seems much less revealing than the previous novels, though its nine characters do represent different aspects of Fritz's nature, perhaps carrying out the Gurdjieffian principle of the "enneagram," one of the basic diagrams of existence. This clumsy esoteric structure does not add much to the novel, and it disappeared with barely a ripple. Depressing as that must have been for him, along with the conflict between married life and his homosexual needs, his writing seems to have lost its momentum, and he was not to have another success until the mid-sixties, when the circumstances of his life were very different.

၅

Boyhood with Gurdjieff, published in 1964, tells of Peters' teenage years spent at the Château du Prieuré, Gurdjieff's Institute for the Harmonious Development of Man outside Paris. His residence there, during the mid- to late twenties, came about at the insistence of *Little Review* editors Margaret Anderson, who was his aunt, and Jane Heap, lesbian lovers who had moved their magazine to France and become followers of Gurdjieff. Apparently, Fritz's mother Lois, the sister of Margaret Anderson, was making a mess of her life by falling into a series of destructive relationships with men, even doing time in a mental institution herself. Margaret and Jane, believing that living with her was unhealthy for Fritz and his brother Tom, persuaded the unhappy mother to relinquish her sons and allow the two women to raise them. As a passionate disciple and, later, teacher of Gurdjieff's ideas, Jane thought that the Institute for the Harmonious Development of Man would be an ideal place for the boys to grow up, offering them a unique opportunity to sit at the feet of the master and develop into "harmonious" men themselves. The more sensible Gertrude Stein, who was a friend of the two women but no worshipper of Gurdjieff, did not approve of the rarefied atmosphere of the Prieuré, and considered it unsuitable for American boys. At their only meeting, the powerful doyenne of the American avant garde and the mystic Gurdjieff were reported to have circled around each other warily. Jane must have agreed to some extent with Stein's opinion, for she asked Gertrude and her friend Alice Toklas to look in on the boys, to give them books, and see to their darning and mending, the latter being Toklas's province, of course. Stein and Toklas also took the boys out on motoring excursions and celebrated American holidays with them, such as traditional Thanksgiving dinners.

Those motherless, albeit instructive, years with Gurdjieff were indeed important to Fritz Peters' development, and perhaps living in the undeniably magnetic presence of the great man may have succeeded in rescuing him, to some extent, from the crippling effects of his mother's behavior. He reports in *Boyhood with Gurdjieff* that he fell in love with Gurdjieff from the start, and for a while at least, was something of a fanatical disciple. Once, when Gurdjieff was convalescing from an automobile accident, he was asked to stop mowing the extensive lawns at the center to give the injured man the quiet he needed. But Fritz had been told by the mystic just before the accident to continue mowing "no matter what happened." So Fritz thought his mowing might be necessary for the Master's recovery, and refused to stop. Oddly, he told my friend Betty later that the incident had involved not him but his brother Tom. But he did not feel there was any requirement for an author to tell the truth. This also conformed to Gurdjieffian teaching.

I have only been able to construct a spotty chronology of Peters' life. Much is shrouded in the reluctance of survivors, especially the Gurdjieffians, to speak with me, as well as by Fritz's own reserve in writing about himself directly, though the first two novels have clear autobiographical elements. The *New York Times*, in its obituary, reveals that he was born Arthur Anderson Peters in 1913 in Madison, Wisconsin. And from the published memoirs of his aunt Margaret Anderson, I gleaned some facts about his mother's family background and his early years. Fritz was a nickname he got from his forbidding resemblance as an infant to the German General Von Hindenburg. His childhood coincided with the height of Chicago bohemia, when Margaret Anderson founded her celebrated journal *The Little Review*. Fritz's mother soon dumped her unacceptably conventional husband to join sister Margaret's artsy entourage in a makeshift encampment on the shores of Lake Michigan with her two sons. But she did not stay there long before she took another fling at romance, a pattern she would often repeat, with or without the boys in tow. It was after a decade of their flapper mother's shifting household that in 1924 the eleven-year-old Fritz and his older brother Tom were enrolled at the Prieuré, the years so vividly recounted in *Boyhood with Gurdjieff*.

Responding to a questionnaire about his future in the final issue of *The Little Review*, dated May 1929, Fritz reports that he hoped to stay at the Prieuré until the age of twenty and always wanted to "work with Mr. G's method." But before the magazine appeared he had already left, willingly, in 1928, when his mother asked him to return to Chicago to live with her and her current husband. To get away from the Prieuré, he had to stand up to the formidable Jane Heap, with whom he always had a difficult relationship, and to the more formidable, but more reasonable, Gurdjieff.

The traumatic events recounted in *Finistère* are most likely to have occurred shortly after Fritz's four years at Le Prieuré, during a summer abroad with his mother and stepfather. Although there must be fictional elements in the novel, I do not for a minute believe that the basic plot was a mere fantasy. An adolescent American boy joins his mother, who is spending a period in the French provinces with her new husband. She hires a French tutor for her son, and the master/pupil relationship blossoms into a love affair. But when this is discovered and broken up, his stepfather compounds the boy's shock and grief by attempting to seduce him. In the context of the era's negative attitudes toward homosexual behavior, and the humiliation the boy suffers, it is quite believable that he becomes suicidal, though his walking into the sea follows the requisite literary formula of that time: i.e., if you are homosexual, the only thing you can do is to kill yourself. But the novel, beautifully written, has an authenticity and intelligence that gives it a stubborn life.

Whatever the truth in this story, about this same period in his adolescence, there is also evidence of a sex episode with his brother Tom, which he dealt with in a later unpublished novel. Clearly, homosexuality was already problematical for Fritz.

With the spotty education he had received at the Prieuré, he says that he found it impossible to graduate from high school or qualify for college. This is unconvincing, for surely someone as intelligent as him could have managed to get the educational requirements if he wanted to. But perhaps he saw a college education as unnecessary for a "creative" writer, though there is no evidence that he did any writing during his twenties. In fact, whatever he was doing with his life, he was not exhibiting any direction or purpose.

By the age of twenty, in 1933, Fritz was working at the World's Fair in Chicago. A year later, he was in New York, studying typing and shorthand at a business school. But he returned to Chicago from time to time, probably because his family was centered there. It was in Chicago, in the late thirties, that he commented on the problems that the black novelist Jean Toomer, author of *Cane*, was having in setting up a Gurdjieff study group, especially with the newspapers hounding Toomer for marrying a white woman.

Fritz never lost touch with Gurdjieff throughout these years, and met up with him or accompanied him on his frequent fundraising visits to America "to shear the sheep," as Gurdjieff outrageously put it. (Elsewhere, in the same comic if heartless style, Gurdjieff referred to his disciples as rats he experimented on, when he wasn't assigning them animal correlatives to illustrate their faults.) Though many of his most prominent disciples were banished or became disillusioned over the master's at-times incomprehensible behavior, often calculated to shake disciples from their rigid outlook, Fritz Peters and Gurdjieff seem never to have wavered in their mutual affection. It was this deep bond and intimate familiarity with Gurdjieff's teaching that led Fritz into his lifelong contempt for the presumptuous claims by the followers to teach "The Work."

By 1942, with the war on, Fritz became an enlisted man, serving in the 29th Infantry Division. It was while he was stationed near London that he had the affair with Betty Deran's beloved Annie Lou Stavely, who was in one of Jane Heap's study groups there. After the

Prieuré closed down for good and was sold in 1933, Heap had conducted her own Gurdjieff groups in Paris, but had shifted them to
London in 1936, after which Williams became her student. Williams
was curiously not a lesbian, though reportedly was married to a gay
man. In a letter to Fritz, she reveals her feelings about the marriage,
calling the period of her affair with Fritz "an oasis in the desert"
for her. The poetry that Fritz wrote for her, though of little literary
interest, reveals already his charming, sophisticated, if cynical self.
Their heterosexual affair continued during Fritz's various leaves and
furloughs from the American army during combat duty in the later
stages of the war.

During the army's march across Europe, Fritz received a battlefield commission, and after the Battle of the Bulge – a bloody, desperate, and hopeless attempt by the Germans to reverse the course
of the war and a horrifying experience for the infantryman – Fritz
managed to secure leave from the front and visit Gurdjieff in Paris.
He was clearly in a state of battle fatigue, but Gurdjieff, using his esoteric healing powers, had a temporary restorative effect on the young
soldier's nerves. But nothing could repair the underlying instability
from childhood dislocation, and Fritz suffered the postwar collapse
and hospitalization described in his first novel, *The World Next Door*.
It seems to have been a brief postwar marriage to Mary Louise Aswell, the distinguished literary editor of *Harper's Bazaar*, who had
welcomed to its pages the likes of Truman Capote and Tennessee
Williams, that got Fritz writing at last.

Committed by his family to a Veterans Administration mental
ward, the hero of *The World Next Door* is subjected to brutal pro-
cedures, including shock treatment. The portrait of the protagonist
is clearly that of Fritz, with the characteristic arrogance and feisty,
almost quarrelsome nature I remember so well. The novel confirms,
not surprisingly, that his mother too had spent considerable time in
mental institutions, though by the time of the novel, she had settled
down in a fairly stable marriage.

Unlike the Freudian novels that were coming into vogue, *The World Next Door* never reveals the deeper causes of the protagonist's breakdown beyond vague mentions of his serving in the recent war and conflict with his mother. Fritz, like most Gurdjieffians, was anti-Freudian. But the book brilliantly analyzes the politics of hospitalization, and is unsparing in describing the outer manifestations of insanity, as well as the strategies the hero uses to gain his release. For this, it was warmly received, encouraging Fritz to take the next step and write *Finistère*, a further confrontation of his homosexual feelings. Whatever the situation of his marriage, Mary Louise Aswell was celebrated for introducing a number of homosexual writers into the pages of *Harper's Bazaar*, and she would certainly not have exhibited the typical homophobia of the era.

In this postwar period, up to Gurdjieff's death in 1949, Fritz managed to attend some of the master's famous dinner parties in Paris, which Gurdjieff used as an opportunity for various teaching exercises, often involving humiliating his stuffier guests, supposedly for their own good. But Gurdjieff's technique of getting his disciples drunk, again for their own good, could not have had a positive influence on the young veteran, for whom drinking would remain a life-long problem. Moreover, Gurdjieff's axiom, "Whatever you do, do a lot of it," though good advice for his cautious followers, would have been dangerous justification for an incipient alcoholic, especially one who would spend most of his life trying to drown his homosexual guilt and live straight.

While I doubt that Gurdjieff himself would have cared about Fritz's homosexuality, the movement somehow became dominated by Ouspensky, Gurdjieff's famous rock-jawed puritanical disciple, who was adamantly opposed to homosexuality, considering it to be a wrong use of energy. The attitude of the "higher ups" in the movement, as one follower described it to me, was that Fritz was just an-other "homosexual living in Greenwich Village, as if his place was 'under the rug'." Even without other reasons to, was it any wonder then that Fritz drank? And it was these same "higher ups" who de-rided him for taking seriously what they considered a comic turn on the part of the master, in which Gurdjieff anointed Fritz as his heir.

This happened at one of those dinner parties in Paris after the war, when someone asked the great teacher who would carry on after his death. With his luminous eyes, Gurdjieff looked around the table at the disciples who had come from far and wide, their hearts were probably beating like Cinderella's sisters in hopes of being the chosen one, and suddenly announced, "Fritz!" pointing to the astonished young man. "Fritz is my heir!"

For the rest of his life, Fritz Peters could never escape his identi-fication with Gurdjieff, as if he had inherited part of the mantle, along with the awe, and considerable resentment, of the followers, and he was uncomfortable with it, especially with the cult that emerged after Gurdjieff's death. Writing *Boyhood with Gurdjieff* must have been an attempt to deal with this burden, but since the book instantly became a classic in the enormous and growing Gurdjieffian library, it put the unfortunate Peters back in the center of the maelstrom. Still, even while shying away from it, he had to be struggling on a deeper level to lay claim to his Gurdjieffian inheritance, for by writing the book, he established himself as one of the unimpeachable authorities on the subject.

Ever since Fritz's death, I have persisted in trying to find out more about him, sending out letters on the slimmest chance of acquain-tance. Close-mouthed like all the surviving Gurdjieffians, Annie Lou Stavely answered my queries by first saying that he was better forgot-ten. Later relenting, she sent me a mess of photos and manuscripts

he had left in her care, family snapshots with his children in Albuquerque, and others which he appears to have taken to show his
children his room at the Arlington Hotel, the law office where he
worked, and one of his lawyer bosses, a good-looking young family
man named MacCarthy, whom he obviously had special feelings for,
and with whom he socialized during his irregular hours on the job.
Also among them were pages from an older family album featuring
pictures of the infant Fritz and his brother Tom; a girlish-looking
Fritz at age nineteen; Fritz the guide at the Chicago World's Fair of
1933; and Fritz the war-time GI, some of which appear here (more
can be found on the Fritz Peters website *www.fritzpeters.info*).

With my attempts to contact Fritz Peters' family proving fruit-
less, and Annie Lou Stavely and even his publishers stonewalling me,
it was in the gay community where I struck gold. My complaints to
a correspondent, the writer Samuel Steward, about my frustrations
produced a remarkable account of a meeting with Fritz, while the
renowned painter Paul Cadmus, going through his diary, found nota-
tions of dinner parties with Fritz in the sixties. So for a brief time, at
least, there was evidence Fritz had mixed in gay and artistic circles.
It was through Samuel and Paul that I located Fritz's papers at Boston University, where his daughter had deposited them, and which
revealed more details of his life and work.

Samuel Steward, best known under his pseudonym Phil Andros
as a writer of gay porn, and an adviser to the famous Dr. Kinsey on
homosexual matters, wrote me before his death in 1994 that he had
kept notes on all his sexual partners – his Stud File, as he called it
– and could give me details of an escapade with Fritz, whom he had
pursued in Chicago in 1952 because of his admiration for the novel
Finistère. Fritz was living in Rogers Park then: "I remember him as
being blond and really drunk...." Even so, "Fritz was reluctant when
I finally did get him in bed because his underwear wasn't the clean-
est.... [Later] he burst into tears and began to drink even more ...
ranting about how he really wasn't gay...."

Which not only explains Fritz's marriage, as well as its breakup, but makes the writing and publication of *Finistère* – so sympathetic to homosexuality, so daring for its time – a mystery. One can only wonder at the complexities of the human heart, and Fritz's was one of the more complex. Steward's letter concludes, "I'm sorry, but he seemed so difficult to know, so withdrawn and afraid of being near or around someone gay or being afraid of being thought gay himself that I just couldn't spend the time with him that I should have...."

Paul Cadmus informed me that in 1963 Fritz was living in New York with Lloyd Lozes Goff, one of Cadmus' models from the thirties and by then a painter in his own right, that Cadmus had gone to their Manhattan apartment for dinner parties, as noted in his diary. "Yes, indeed, Lloyd and Fritz were 'lovers,'" Cadmus wrote. "I seem to remember it was to be 'forever' but ... I gather Fritz was quite 'unstable.'"

Goff was a decade older than the fifty-year-old Fritz, and must have offered security to a man who had fled his feelings for so long. If so, it is to Goff that we owe that marvelous book *Boyhood with Gurdjieff*, written during their affair. Significantly, the photo on the book jacket was taken by Goff and he is among the four dedicatees. In a burst of energy, Fritz turned out two more novels, *Night Flight*, published in England though mysteriously not in the US, and another as-yet-unpublished novel, the manuscript also dedicated to Goff, attesting to the seriousness of the relationship and his gratitude to the man who helped him accept himself at last. They were still together four years later, by the evidence of Cadmus' social calendar of 1967.

This latter unpublished novel, found among his papers, has several chapters about Fritz's relationship with his brother, focusing on their sexual experience during adolescence, which turned out to be significant for Fritz though not for Tom, who turned out to be conventionally straight.

But the literary creative streak eventually ended along with the love affair, and Fritz, probably following his Gurdjieffian-inspired unruly temperament, was soon on the loose. Working irregular hours as a legal secretary and living at the Arlington, he again retreated from a literary life with the excuse that he would only write when he had a book to write. He did manage to complete a second memoir, *Gurdjieff Remembered*, published in 1971 by Samuel Weiser, founder of the leading bookstore for spiritual literature in New York City, and years later in Albuquerque, he began another novel and completed a somewhat-fragmentary third book on Gurdjieff, *A Balanced Man*, that circulated in manuscript surreptitiously among Gurdjieffians.

~

I was in Portland, Oregon, giving poetry readings in the Northwest and staying in the house of the woman who arranged such events for the same university that Annie Lou Stavely worked for when I spoke to my hostess about the Gurdjieffian guru in Portland. My hostess recognized the name at once, exclaiming, "You don't mean little old Berta Williams, secretary of the Theater Arts department? She can hardly answer the phone properly!" This, in a tone that dismissed Mrs. Stavely as anyone ever to be taken seriously. I trusted my friend's opinion, but Gurdjieffians are supposed to blend in with the population, I thought to myself, and reserved judgment.

On a later tour in the Northwest, I visited my friend Betty in the old-fashioned wooden house where she was then living with Mrs. Stavely, still not as the lover she would have wished to be, but as assistant/companion. Betty had quickly become invaluable, taking over many of the tasks of everyday life, and especially, helping with Mrs. Stavely's ever-growing number of followers.

Mrs. Stavely, who was probably used to lesbians coming on to her from her Jane Heap days, was unfortunately still adamant against trying it out for herself. But if Betty never succeeded in winning her over, Mrs. Stavely managed to make Betty try heterosexuality, which she acceded to, briefly, in hopes of getting Mrs. Stavely to loosen up by example. Cunning Mrs. Stavely, though, did not have a yielding nature and never gave in.

Though the affair with Fritz during and possibly after the war had probably broken up Mrs. Stavely's marriage, it must have been this affair that had given the sexually uncertain Fritz the confidence to get married. Turning gay men straight is a curious ambition of some heterosexual women. In the case of Fritz it temporarily succeeded, much as her attempt to convert Betty was briefly successful.

When Mrs. Stavely retired from her job at the university, she bought a farm nearby, where Betty and her other disciples followed her. As Gurdjieff had done, she kept them all busy building new wings and porches onto the house, and launching into various erratic projects. Visiting there, and seeing her living in a torn-up house in mid-construction, I asked her when the work would be finished. "Never, if I can help it," she replied firmly. On consideration, I said to myself that this was one smart old lady to have set herself up so well for old age. I could see that she would be taken care of devotedly until her death by her "students."

In 1975, Fritz told me that he and Mrs. Stavely had made contact with each other again, almost certainly through the sly intervention of Betty, who was not above such things, which led to Fritz's old lover inviting him to visit her center. Curiously, Fritz came back from this initial foray highly elated, announcing to me over dinner at the Gran Ticino, one of his habitual restaurants in Greenwich Village, that she had invited him to live on the farm and teach the Gurdjieff system. He described for me his bouts of drinking with male disciples who were wowed by meeting someone who had been so close to the legendary master, and under the influence of alcohol, the steamy embraces they had shared in the rural darkness. And he clearly reveled in being treated as an important personage, the heir of Gurdjieff. Perhaps too he saw the Oregon colony as a good place to slip into a peaceful old age, surrounded and looked after by adoring young people, as Mrs. Stavely had done, something which a third-rate New

York hotel room did not offer.

Scandals and defections were nothing unusual among Gurdjieffian groups, which from the beginning were rife with betrayals, suspicions, accusations, and frequent disillusionment and departures, even expulsions. Mrs. Stavely might have initially seen Fritz Peters as a useful agent in "awakening" her followers in Oregon, radiating the Gurdjieffian spirit he had imbibed directly from the master, or even – with his outspoken, abrasive manner – as an irritant. Though she could not have foreseen the extent of his drinking and openly homosexual behavior, all the more shocking against the conservative backdrop of rural Oregon, Fritz's great prestige as the author of *Boyhood with Gurdjieff* could not be denied. And he was, presumably, a dear old friend, whatever the stormy events of the past had been. Perhaps he was ready to settle down and be a suitable male companion for her, someone in her own age group who shared her past associations.

In *The World Next Door*, Fritz talked about his Christ complex. Now, his emotional instability was only increased by the adulation he received from Mrs. Stavely's followers, and Fritz was clearly in a manic phase when he returned from the initial visit and regaled me over pasta at the Gran Ticino with his adventures. After he closed up his affairs in New York and was ready to fly back to Oregon to settle on the farm, he announced grandly to me, "You may accompany me to the airport," as if he were God's Anointed. This meant that I was being honored by being chosen to drive him there in my battered VW bus. It was not quite the vehicle he merited, but he was oblivious. At last, he was being enthroned as Gurdjieff's heir. I got the distinct impression that he was going to be the farm's resident guru, with Mrs. Stavely his handmaiden.

But it turned out that Annie Lou Stavely was not about to accept second billing. It was no time at all, perhaps a week or two after Fritz left, before I got a telephone call from him, not in Oregon but, astonishingly, New Mexico, informing me that the whole thing had blown up. I learned later from Betty that from the minute Fritz arrived, he started turning the place upside down, trying to run it as Gurdjieff would have, while drinking everything in sight. Betty had enjoyed having a gay man on the premises with whom she could speak frankly. But his behavior had been so impossible, so disruptive to the orderly routine of classes and "teaching" projects, Berta Williams had him shipped out on a plane for Albuquerque where, he told me, he had moved in with an old friend of eighty-three who lived in a big adobe house and needed someone to cook and deal with household matters that were getting to be too much for her.

(It was after Fritz's death, when I informed Mrs. Stavely that I wished to write a book about him, that she relented and sent me the sheaf of photographs that he must have inadvertently left behind when she reasserted her authority and hustled him off to the airport, and order on the farm was restored.)

Soon after this, Betty herself caused a ruckus at the farm, where by now, with her problem-solving nature, she had made herself indispensable, one would think, as Mrs. Stavely's "right-hand man." Gurdjieffian philosophy was not anti-sexuality, and Gurdjieff himself had had a well-known, even scandalous, neo-pagan love life with his numerous female disciples, spreading his biological progeny far and wide. But under the aegis of Mrs. Stavely, "The Work" took on the more puritan cast of the London-based Ouspensky school, and when Betty and the wife of one of the young disciples fell in love, it was not looked on kindly by the straight-laced Mrs. Stavely, resulting in their expulsion.

But Betty was unabashed, and without a backward look, she and her friend went off to India to join the entourage of Baghwan Shri Rajneesh, the latest guru on the scene and one who was, unlike Mrs. Stavely, a great promoter of free sexuality in all forms. This new devotion to Baghwan may even have been encouraged by Mrs. Stavely as a way of getting rid of the disobedient, troublesome couple. As a Gurdjieffian, such manipulative behavior would be entirely acceptable.

~

I heard from Fritz in Albuquerque from time to time – long rambling phone calls that often interrupted me at my typewriter, and only ended when I told him I had to go back to work, which he always respected. Fritz also sent letters occasionally. He was eighty pages into a new novel, he told me, played the piano for recreation, and I learned for the first time about his children. His son, also called Fritz but nicknamed Peto, was at the University of Arizona, and his daughter Katherine was a teacher at a school for the deaf in Santa Fe, though it didn't sound like he saw them much. It would be perfectly understandable if they were leery of this unconventional parent, who had caused so much disruption in their lives.

For his part, Fritz was avoiding what I suspect were many old acquaintances in the area. There had been a drift of Gurdjieffians to the Southwest over the years, attracted by the spiritual centers of Taos and Frank Lloyd Wright's Taliesin West, which may have been what drew Fritz to the place after the war. But in his letters to me during the seventies, Fritz expressed contempt for these people who were so eager to worship him.

There were to be no more manic phases; his brief fling at wearing the crown that he had inherited from Gurdjieff was over, and he was back to cynical normalcy. But if Fritz had landed on his feet again after his expulsion from Oregon – becoming *The Balanced Man* of the title of his final book – it was not to last. His elderly housemate Julia was rapidly going senile. Soon, Julia no longer recognized Fritz, asked him what he was doing there, and ordered him to get the hell out. Her family took over her affairs, and seeing Fritz as an outsider trying to get his hands on the estate, got a court order and evicted him. His lawyer told him he had no choice but to comply, so he found an apartment in downtown Albuquerque that he shared with an immigrant from India, not a lover but someone whom he said he found tolerable. He was thinking of returning to New York, perhaps for the publication of the new Gurdjieff book. Another publisher was interested in reprinting *Finistère* and his other books as well.

There was a brief, hurried letter dated April 16, 1979, describing various ailments – blood pressure, heart, dentures – medical treatments. Then I got a call from him in the hospital. He promised to write fully.

He died, according to the brief *New York Times* obituary, on December 1979, in Los Cruces, New Mexico.

Perhaps his was an author's ideal fate: the man forgotten, but the works remembered. Nevertheless, I believe that his was a life that deserves to be rescued from oblivion. I see his two classic books as representing two sides of a nature that could never quite be reconciled, resulting in a strangely unfocused and – despite the considerable achievement of these books – unachieved life. I hope this new edition of *Finistère* arouses enough to bring *The World Next Door* back into print, and perhaps the unpublished novel as well.

Out west on one of my reading tours in the seventies, the period when so many different spiritual disciplines were in the air, I was sitting around with a group of students and mentioned Gurdjieff. A young woman in a granny dress broke in with, "Oh, he's peaked," implying that she and her friends had absorbed Gurdjieff's teachings and moved on to the next big thing, perhaps Carlos Castaneda, Maharishi Mahesh Yogi, and beyond. The young grasp things more by instinct, and don't have the time or patience for lengthy studies. But perhaps she was also saying that the excitement of discovery was over. These days, I, too have lost the thrill of discovering new possibilities that once lurked in the books of Gurdjieff and other teachers, and the hope that my life would somehow be suddenly transformed. Yet it was changed by those years of my friendship with Betty Deran and Alma Routsong and then Fritz Peters, and I live differently today because of them.

NOTE: With such large gaps, this must remain a first, provisional study of Fritz Peters. But until survivors who knew him are willing to testify, or documents turn up, much of his life necessarily remains shrouded in mystery. I would like to thank Matthew Weseley for his invaluable help in my research.

7442 Edith Boulevard, N.E.
Albuquerque, N. Mex. 87113

January 22, 1976

Dear Edward:

It was also a relief to hear from you! I was afraid that due to
the delays in your letter getting to me that you had taken off on some further travels.

I am particularly interested in knowing that your tour may take you
as far as Albuquerque because I shall most certainly be here. I am officially
"retired" here and plan to make it my permanent home (as permanent as anything
ever seems to be in my life). I no longer have any problems about typing, and
have a good new Selectric typewriter (that's how spoiled one gets working in a
law office) which is fairly easy on my left wrist. I wrote my Grudjieff book
(short) with my right hand on a standard portable and the best I could do was
to depress the shift key with my left hand once in a while. It wasn't a
very pretty looking manuscript when I sent it off to Weiser, but at least they
seem to want to publish it although they are now talking about adding a little
more material.

I am glad to hear that Betty Deran is back in New York and is being--
as I am sure she would always be--helpful. I don't know what you will get
from Mrs. Staveley about my stay in Oregon--not much, I would think. I imagine
she would be, as all the Gurdjieff people seem to be, rather close-mouthed
about the whole thing. I still think of that whole thing with horror, and
I've even had an occasional nightmare about it.

I'm sorry to hear that Neil had so much bad luck, what with being
burgled and then the novel not being snapped up, but very glad to know that
Betty has given him some direction. So give him my best, please.

I'm about eighty pages into my novel and fairly happy with it,
although I imagine that I will do my usual and rewrite the whole thing
from scratch when it is finished. I usually do that as a form of editing
if nothing else. The form of the book is complex and I sometimes get mixed
up in figuring out what the hell I'm doing.

Good luck with the anthology (it might be a bore assembling it,
but I should think it would be fun as well) and I really hope you will make
it out here. We've had an extraordinary winter: one snowfall and perhaps
two cloudy days since I've been here. Otherwise nothing but brilliant sun-
shine and today all the doors are open and it's in the high fifties.

I hope everything goes well for you, and look forward to seeing
you before too long.

All the best, Edward.

Affectionately,

Here Fritz claims I wouldn't get from Mrs. Annie Lou Stavely the story of his ejection
from her Gurdjieffian farm in Oregon, but he doesn't tell me the lurid details either,
another "closed-mouth" Gurdjieffian himself. But luckily I got the story in all its colorful details from my pal, Betty Deran. – *Edward Field*

423 Sixth Street, N.W.
Albuquerque, N. M. 87102

November 16, 1977

Dear Edward:

I was happy to get your letter of October 22 (only very recently) and glad to have all your news. It's been a long time since I wrote you and a good deal has happened. Julia went completely berserk and wanted to know "who that man was who was around the house" and asked me to get the Hell out. I talked to her family (who were under the somewhat dubious impression that I was "living" with her and "what I was I trying to get from her" (she has property worth about $200,000), so I also talked to her lawyer who told me that I was in a very dubious position (I never used that word twice in a letter before) and to get out, so I did. I found a wonderful old-fashioned apartment in the middle of downtown Albuquerque for a reasonable rent, furnished,and am now working part-time in a law office (three blocks away) to supplement my Social Security income. I have a roommate, one Frank Sundram, who was born in Bombay and has been in this country for about 11 or 12 years, and who is <u>bearable</u>, which is more than I can say for most people--and we have two bedrooms with DOORS on them.

Never heard of Zenna Henderson, and Sci-Fi has never been a bag of mine anyway. Don't know anything about Bagwan Shree Rajneesh; in fact I am sick UP TO HERE of almost all the occult bullshit that is flying around. There are any number of "groups" out here and they are really up shit creek for my money. I get treated as. if I were some sort of high muckity-muck, and they are "impressed" because I knew the great man. They also <u>teach</u> his work, knowing absolutely nothing about it. But I guess if you can't be a good mechanic, cook, waiter or some other sort of useful human being, you can always be a Gurdjieff leader and fill the empty with the empty.

I hope to get back to New York before Katherine Voor Zanger's prediction comes true, but Albuquerque is on the target for Russia's or China's first bomb, so if I stay out here I may go with it before you do. Who knows (or cares, in the long run)?

My kids are fine. My daughter works for the School for the Deaf in Santa Fe (60 miles north) and my son is in Albuquerque in his second year at the University and doing great guns: Straight A's and stuff like that, which makes him slightly boring.

I have a new publisher in California, my third Gurdjieff book is in the works, and he is reprinting FINISTERE and hopes to reprint in paperback, everything I have ever written one of these days. Contracts coming up next week. The news about Mme. Deranian was interesting, but what the Hell does she want to go back to Oregon for, and why did she think the literary world would be easy?

I have a feeling that there's some sort of overtone of hostility in this letter, but I assure you, my friend, that none of it is directed towards you. I am just bored with the cannon-fodder to whom I exposed all the time, so please do not take it personally. I am glad that Neil is with you and that you are working on his book. Give him my love, and much to you, as always,

Fritz

Fritz's cranky tone was always refreshing, including his slamming all the spiritual "seekers" and especially Gurdjieffian groups. Gurdjieff believed in the usefulness of people like Fritz as the "irritant" that would jolt his disciples out of their set, unthinking ways. – *Edward Field*

April 11, 1990

Dear Mr. Field:

Thank you for your letter but I'm afraid I won't be any
help to you with your projected biography of Fritz Peters. So
far as I know, no one has written anything about his life except
himself, and perhaps that is enough. I never met his children,
and spoke to his wife on the telephone only once. Nor do I know
the addresses of any of them today. I don't have any journals
or letters as I never see the point of keeping such things once
the person who gave them meaning is gone. Actually, I don't
think there are many people today who would be interested in
Fritz, though he was a vivid personality in his own time and is
remembered as such by those who knew him. I imagine there are
not too many of them left.

I wish you success with your future writings and that you
find a subject of more general interest than Fritz Peters.
With best wishes,

Sincerely,

Annie Lou Staveley

Aug 31 1994

Dear Mr Field

Sorry, I don't remember anything
about the questions you ask regarding
Fritz Peters' possible Memories. It is all
so long ago it is hard to believe anyone
could still be interested any more. I
must confess I am not.
Kind Regards
Sincerely
A. E. Staveley

When I started searching for Fritz Peters' life, I was frustrated time and
again, as in these two notes from his old friend, fellow Gurdjieffian, and
former lover. Then, miraculously, before she died, she sent me an envelope
of photos and manuscripts that Fritz had left behind when she kicked him off
her farm. – *Edward Field*

2016-x 9th st, brk, ca, 94710. 1-II-XCIII

Dear Edward,

Your letter called up all kinds of old fragile ghosty things and lots of
"joinings" whereby one thing led to and mebbe clarified another, or at least
set about my being as accurate as I could about things that happened a long
long time ago. The Stud File that I kept for Kinsey [and myself--O sweet
book of memories!] wasn't a whole heluva lot of help, just indicating the
date and the place (Chicago--), size of dingdong (average, parlor), and what
happened (childishly encoded--I blew him), but then memory began to enlarge
and help recall some things... I remember him as being blond (was he?) and
really drunk--which at that shaky moment in my own life was VERY annoying,
since I had gone into AA on August 10, 1947 and was still not on completely
firm ground. But I was certainly a lot more stabilized than he was, because
he burst into tears about five minutes after he shot his wad, and began to
drink even more (it was in my place, and to prove my AA strength I had from
the beginning kept whiskey & gin around, not for myself but for my tricks
who wanted it--and with every drink they took I felt even more smug &
superior, so it was a kind of testing for me.) But Fritz was really beset
by the "agenbite of inwit" as from my teaching of Anglo-Saxon just then had
led me to refer to "remorse of conscience," and he burst into tears and some
ranting about how he really wasn't gay, and I became more and more impatient
and he finally left, still teary, and me--I was also being shaken and irritated
and I <u>think</u> that was the last time we ever saw each other. I was then not
quite tattoodling yet (dint begin it until about 1954) but I was a real tough
cookie even so, and running around with a literary crowd from the U of
Chicago--the Wendell Wilcoxes, James Purdy, Gertrude Abercrombie et al--
and gradually becoming so pissed off at teaching that I was already casting
around for something to do as far removed from Ivied Ivory Towers as I could
git. So when it is all boiled down and reduced ad absurdum, it wasn't the
greatest sexual experience I ever had in my life, and resulted in my abandon-
ment of further quest for Mr. Peters's handsome (as I remember it) body.

Yes, I do regret our not seeing each other--and you're so right about the
incompetence of those dimwits at A Different Light--the last time I read
there, Mister Labonte had gone to LALA land, and I was left to the scrawny
be-zitsed mercies of a crew who quite possibly had never got beyond "See
Dick run" in the realm of litrachoor. I have not yet bought your book, and
I thank you for your generous offer; and if there is anything of mine (of
which I have any copies) that you would like to have, just lemme know.

I am currently aching from some dental work. When I was 30 I tried to find
a dentist who would pull all my teeth (having been raised on Mellin's Food
instead of leafy veggies), and of course no one would do it, having their
cold & calculating eyes on future profit$, so I have had to suffer under
their tyranny right up to the present day. And now at my age the trauma of
having them all yanked seems like too much, so it's the Way of the Root Canal
for me. And since there are no more cocks to gum one's way around, there
seems small point to all that greater bother.

Take care,

∽ Sam

I hit pay dirt in my quest when I wrote to the porn writer Samuel Steward, with his
graphic report of a sexual episode. – *Edward Field*

P.O-Box 1255
weston.ct.06883
16 June 93

Dear E. F.

Here are a few tid bits of information about Lloyd Goff
that may, but mostly may not, lead somewhere.

My friend, Jared French met him at the Tiffany Foundation
in Oyster Bay (both on scholarships there) and through him
I came to know him. Small, well-proportioned, good figure,
posed for me (1934 - 37 ish). I did quite a few drawings
of him. He posed for my painting Venus and Adonis.
Adonis is a good likeness at the time. We had a brief
affair. He worked for the WPA projects. I think he was
my assistant for a while. Also for Reginald Marsh and
for Edward Laning. He did two government murals, mentioned
in Democratic Vistas. Post office and Public Art in the New Deal
by Park and Markowitz (Temple University Press)
We saw each other seldom after the 40's but remained
friends.

The last address I had for him was 136 West 75, I think
this was where he lived with Fritz but I'm not sure.
After his death a relative who inherited, I guess, sold some
of drawings I had done of him, to help him with one of his
mural projects. The gallery he sold to was Ann or
Anne Ryan now on 57th St. She might be able to connect
you to the inheritor who might know something or other
about Fritz.

I doubt that Lincoln K would help you. I don't offer
my help or name in that connection. I don't think he
knew Fritz, just liked the books.

This is about all I can think up at present I'm
sorry to say.
Lots of good wishes for your "quest"

Paul Cadmus

Paul Cadmus filled in more of the blanks, especially about Fritz's love affair
with painter Lloyd Lozes Goff. – *Edward Field*

30 MacIntosh Drive
Poughkeepsie, NY 12603
June 25, 1994

Dear Edward,

Just a brief note to round out our phone conversation from Alma's house. The conversation strayed away from your manuscript and so I didn't get a chance to make a couple of observations I had in mind.

Point one, a little bit of what you report is not quite accurate, but since you are using pseudonyms it probably doesn't matter. Let me know if you want that kind of nit-picking detail.

Second point, I think a highly relevant aspect of Fritz is the fact that he never felt bound by facts, either in his writing or in his conversation. I remember his telling me that he considered it an author's prerogative to embellish a story in whatever way was needed to improve the tale. He explained this to me when I questioned him about the difference in something he had told me in private and later told with much embroidering to a group. Your readers might be particularly interested to know that the famous "lawnmowing" story in <u>Childhood with Gurdjieff</u> was his brother's experience, not his own. But, as Fritz said, it made a better story to tell it as if it happened to himself.

You might want to know that Alma in fact is contending with very serious illness. She has had to undergo several surgeries and chemotherapy treatments over the past year, for a combination of diverticulitis and cancer of the ovary. So far she's holding her own, but because she still has one of those awful "bags" refuses to socialize (supposedly in time that part of her trauma will be reversed, but healing has been impeded by the chemo). I have just brought back from Oregon some wonderful stuff called kombucha, a fungus that is grown in sweet tea. Drinking the tea supposedly builds up the immune system and prevents cancer and lots of other ailments. We are starting to use it ourselves, on a preventive basis since it is impractical for Julie to stop smoking because she is assailed by horrible symptoms every time she quits. By the time you come back home we will know more about kombucha's effects; you may be interested in some too. Let me know.

Best to Neil - hope your summer is wonderful.

Love,
Betty/Elizabeth

Betty Deran, who got to know Fritz on Mrs. Staveley's farm in Oregon, also filled in some blanks, especially Fritz's delusion that now that he was in residence, he and not Mrs. Stavely was the leader of the Gurdjieffian colony. – *Edward Field*

Bibliography

Compiled by Michael Bronski

The World Next Door
New York : Farrar, Straus, 1949
London : Victor Gollancz, 1950

The Book of the Year
New York : Harper & Bros, 1950

Finistère
New York : Farrar, Straus, 1951
London : Victor Gollancz 1951

The Descent
New York : Farrar, Straus and Young, 1952

The Brothers
unpublished, 1953

The General/ Spring in Brittany
unpublished, 1963

Boyhood with Gurdjieff
New York : Dutton, 1964
London : Victor Gollancz, 1964

Gurdjieff Remembered
London : Victor Gollancz, 1965
New York : Samual Weiser, 1971

Blind Flight
London : Victor Gollancz, 1966

The Record of a Journey
unpublished, 1971

A Certain Melancholy
unpublished, 1974

Balanced Man: a Look at Gurdjieff Fifty Years Later
London : Wildwood House, 1978

FRITZ PETERS was a novelist and writer of books on philosophy; his novels included *The World Next Door* (1949), *The Descent* (1952), and *Blind Flight* (1966). He lived mostly in New York City, but eventually moved to New Mexico, where he died in 1979.

MICHAEL BRONSKI made several contributions to the gay liberation movement of the 60s, including writing for a variety of gay and lesbian publications. In 1984 he published the pioneering book *Culture Clash: The Making of Gay Sensibility*. His writing reflected the changing face of the gay male subculture in writings he published in the anthology *Flashpoint: Gay Male Sexual Writing* in 1996.

photograph of Fritz Peters courtesy of Kate Peters

LITTLE SISTER'S CLASSICS is a series of books from Arsenal Pulp Press, reviving lost and out-of-print classics of gay and lesbian literature. The books in the series are produced in conjunction with Little Sister's, the Vancouver bookstore well-known for its anti-censorship efforts.

www.littlesistersbookstore.com